MW00774090

Death
at an
Irish Wedding

Also available by Ellie Brannigan

The Irish Castle Mysteries
Murder at an Irish Castle

Writing as Traci Hall
The Appletree Cove Romance Series
Just One Kiss
In the Dog House

The Scottish Shire Mysteries
Murder at a Scottish Shire
Murder at a Scottish Social
Murder in a Scottish Garden
Murder at a Scottish Wedding
Murder at a Scottish Castle
Murder at a Scottish Christmas
Murder at the Scottish Games

Writing as Traci Wilton
Salem B and B cozy mystery series
Mrs. Morris and the Ghost
Mrs. Morris and the Witch
Mrs. Morris and the Ghost of Christmas Past
Mrs. Morris and the Sorceress
Mrs. Morris and the Vampire
Mrs. Morris and the Pot of Gold
Mrs. Morris and the Wolfman
Mrs. Morris and the Mermaid
Mrs. Morris and the Venomous Valentine

Traci Hall writing with Patrice Wilton
The Riley Harper Mysteries
Danger at Sandpiper Bay
Death in Sandpiper Bay
Deception at Sandpiper Bay

Death
at an
Irish Wedding

AN IRISH CASTLE
MYSTERY

Ellie Brannigan

CROOKED
LANE

NEW YORK

Copyright © 2024 by Traci Hall

Published in the United States by Crooked Lane Books, an imprint of The Quick Brown Fox & Company LLC.

Crooked Lane Books and its logo are trademarks of The Quick Brown Fox & Company LLC.

Library of Congress Catalog-in-Publication data available upon request.

ISBN (hardcover): 978-1-63910-921-0
ISBN (ebook): 978-1-63910-922-7

Cover design by Olivia Holmes

Printed in the United States.

www.crookedlanebooks.com

Crooked Lane Books
34 West 27th St., 10th Floor
New York, NY 10001

First Edition: December 2024

10 9 8 7 6 5 4 3 2 1

This book is dedicated to my hubby Christopher—though murderous weddings are fun to write, I count my blessings that ours was simply perfect. I love you! To Mom, and Sheryl, and my family of readers—thank you for your encouragement that there will always be a need for stories, and human authors to write them.

Chapter One

McGrath Castle, Grathton Village, Ireland
September

Rayne McGrath and Ciara Smith stood shoulder to shoulder on the landing of the family castle, waiting for their guests to arrive. Rayne had inherited the castle in June, around the same time as her bridalwear storefront on Rodeo Drive was involved in a crime. Born in the US of A, she'd never dreamed she'd be living in Ireland, and certainly not *here* without her beloved dad, Conor, or her Uncle Nevin—both men dead too soon.

"They're late." Ciara glanced at her watch. A breeze from the fifty-five-degree weather lifted a cropped bleached-blond curl. "It's after seven. What if something went wrong?"

Another summer shocker was the secret cousin, a year older than Rayne, she'd acquired at the reading of her uncle's will. The legal document decreed they had one year to bring the failing castle out of the red, together, or some serious end-of-the-world repercussions would ensue, triggering the death knell for Grathton Village. The McGraths had been caretakers since the seventeen hundreds.

"They'll be here any minute," Rayne said in a soothing voice.

Rayne and Ciara shared gray eyes but were otherwise complete opposites. Rayne liked luxury and modern amenities, while her cousin was happy in jeans and rarely remembered her cell phone. Ciara embodied unbridled passion; Rayne channeled her Celtic energy into design.

Eight months remained until Uncle Nevin's deadline. Rayne juggled online orders for her custom bridal gowns with overhauling the tower attached to the manor for a wedding venue, in hopes of fast cash. The cousins worked closely with the castle staff to preserve the manor for the McGraths no longer with them as well as future generations.

Heavy stuff.

Rayne heard tires as a vehicle drove slowly toward them, but it remained out of sight.

Her gaze sharpened on the stone, timber, and thatch barn in the distance, the pole and satellite dish behind it painted to blend with the landscape. Internet had been a sore spot between the cousins though necessary to drag the property into the modern age. Rayne had learned that the younger generation had moved away from Grathton for jobs and the current population whittled down to less than five hundred people. If she and Ciara didn't succeed, the entire village risked being absorbed into neighboring Cotter Village.

The silver grill of a black town car appeared beneath an arch of trees like a movie set from *Gone with the Wind*. Tori Montgomery, the bride-to-be, had texted that they were all beat from their day of travel, so the new castle chef, Frances Coplan, had prepared a light buffet in the dining room rather than a big sit-down dinner.

"This is it," Rayne whispered, her fingers crossed behind her back for luck that everything would go smoothly. July's effort to bring in a profit had been an epic fail and she'd had to sell her designer purses to keep them afloat. "It's do or die."

Ciara tucked her thumb into the pocket of her blazer, fighting a nervous smile. "Aye. Yer about out of handbags."

Rayne was down to her last two favorite purses—a Hermes bubblegum pink bag worth $30,000—she'd had no idea its value as she'd bought it at an estate sale from an aged Hollywood actress for a pittance, and the Dolce and Gabbana café design worth $10,000—that had been a gift from her mom for college graduation, and she refused to part with it.

The tower with the turret hadn't been as simple a project as Rayne had hoped. She'd sold three days of "rustic" for a romantic getaway to an adventurous young couple which had generated 7,500 euros.

They'd promptly refunded the money when the fireplace backed up and smoked the newlyweds out. Flames erupted, but Rayne and Ciara had stopped the fire from spreading with a fire extinguisher in the landing. Instead of an influx into the bank, Rayne had paid for a doctor's checkup and a honeymoon suite in Dublin for two days, grateful not to have been sued.

It was now mid-September. The tower's interior walls had been scrubbed and painted; the fireplaces all cleaned. There were four large chambers with en suite bathrooms, one per floor. Each level had three thin windows once used as arrow slits back when it had been built for fortification and they'd installed specialty glass panes. The inside steps were also new as was the railing. The best place for cell reception in the tower was still the rooftop because the rock was so blasted thick.

"Nothing can go wrong this time," Rayne murmured. Everyone, from the Lloyd family to the new staff, had practiced their roles.

"Ye almost burned the castle down." Ciara shifted her body toward the car as the driver parked to the right, followed by the second car. "Just don't feck it up."

Rayne swallowed her retort about the castle being made of stone and focused on their guests.

The eight-person Montgomery-Anderson bridal wedding party consisted of bride-to-be Tori Montgomery, her parents and hotel magnates, Joan and Dylan Montgomery, and her maid of honor, starlet Amy Flores. The groom was up-and-coming heartthrob actor Jake Anderson, with his best man and brother, Josh Anderson.

Traveling with them was Jake's righthand man, Ethan Cruz. Amy also had an assistant, Tiffany Quick. Tori had designated the rooms, choosing Josh on the main floor of the tower, then Amy, and the third and fourth levels were for the bride and groom.

Her parents would be in the largest cottage, while Ethan and Tiffany would share the second bungalow. Both had been furnished in an antique Irish style, but with modern amenities like upgraded bathrooms, televisions, and cable. New mattresses and comfy couches. Each cottage had two bedrooms and a sleeper-sofa.

Most meals would be in the manor, and there were always the village pubs and the Coco Bean Café if folks wanted something different. Tonight was Thursday, the wedding was Saturday, and the guests flew home Monday morning. Piece of cake, Rayne thought.

Jake Anderson exited the first car, followed by Tori. Jake had to be the most beautiful human being she'd ever set eyes on, and that magnetism conveyed itself on the silver screen. Tori was a lucky woman, but then he was also very fortunate to be marrying an heiress. This wedding would rake in $25,000, not including the other half of the bride's dress, $7,500, for a total of $32,500. That would make up for some of the losses incurred in the ongoing process of getting the manor and the property ready for guests.

Tori was five foot five and thin, her beauty enhanced by cosmetic surgery. Her hair was golden, her skin tan; a walking-talking Barbie. Jake was tall and buff with dark-brown styled hair, and perfectly calculated scruff at his chiseled jaw. Dark denim jeans, silk shirt.

In August, Rayne had called Tori about a final fitting for a bridal gown the heiress had ordered in February, when Tori had a mini meltdown over the too-big Christmas wedding and the guest list already at four hundred. Leaping on the chance to help, Rayne offered the Irish castle property as an alternate venue if Tori wanted a rustic getaway instead. Tori, a self-proclaimed control freak, had kept her designer dress with her so it hadn't been part of Landon Short's gown-heist in June.

Rayne's ex Landon had done serious damage on her thirtieth birthday that she was still reeling from. A shout-out from Tori Montgomery could boost her bridalwear business reputation despite not having a storefront on Rodeo Drive. Her positive review of this unique destination might launch them in the Hollywood set, full of people with disposable income. The only hitch was that Rayne had promised to keep the wedding participants a secret, with no social media, until after they went home on Monday.

Dylan Montgomery climbed out from behind the wheel and slammed the door. He was tall and had silver tips on his dark brown hair. His wife, Joan, got out the other side. She was as blonde as Tori, their faces also plastic—but done well.

Chin up, Rayne descended the steps in her country-lady sage plaid pants with brown leather boots and a cream cashmere sweater. She'd never met the Montgomerys other than Tori, but they'd had three fittings in person to make sure that the design for the gown, one of the more expensive she had this year at $15,000, had molded to Tori's slim frame. The last fitting had been in May before Rayne's world had turned upside down, when her boyfriend had stolen her couture dresses and emptied their joint bank account.

The heiress hadn't mentioned Landon or seemed alarmed that Rayne had inherited a castle. Maybe in her cosmos, that was no big deal.

"Tori! So good to see you again!" Rayne gave the heiress a half-hug and smiled warmly at everyone as they gathered around. "This is my cousin and business partner, Ciara Smith." Ciara was at her side, and they all exchanged hellos.

"What a gorgeous place," Joan said. Dylan nodded, his astute gaze cataloging the property as his eye paused on each mossy stone casing. The stone lions, the twenty-foot-wide landing, the fragrant flowers planted in boxes on the steps made a statement. Rayne often did that same assessment. Could be a Hollywood thing.

"Thank you," Ciara said demurely. "It's home."

Cormac Lloyd, the McGrath butler, joined them, very official in his black coat, white shirt, and black pants. "Welcome to McGrath Castle."

The Montgomerys hummed in approval.

"Are we staying inside?" Joan asked.

"No. You'll be in a private cottage just a short walk away," Rayne said. The cottages were a half mile down the grassy path, which wasn't far. In the country one walked all the time, unlike LA.

"Oh!" Joan conveyed disappointment in that single word.

"The rooms in the tower are the only rental spaces attached to the manor," Rayne quickly explained. It was a solution that allowed them all privacy while earning money. "The wedding party has four suites, and the rooftop is accessible from the outer staircase, with terrific views of the lake and gazebo."

"We get to tour the whole thing, yes?" Dylan's tone was that of a man used to getting his way or else.

"Cormac will escort you around the public rooms if you set a time when he's available," Ciara said. She nudged Rayne.

Amos Lowell appeared with a wave striding down the gravel path toward them. The grounds manager was ruggedly handsome with his dark-blond waves and broad shoulders. Blarney, Rayne's Irish Setter, trotted at Amos's heels. They'd discussed keeping the pup contained in the barn while the guests arrived, but Blarney had a mind of his own.

Aine Lloyd, Rayne's bridalwear protégé as well as maid for the castle, stood at the top step of the landing, pristine in a crisp black shirt and pants. She was joined by her mother, Maeve, in a similar uniform. "I'll take those folks to the blue parlor who'd like a refreshment before dinner," Aine said.

Tori raised a perfect brow at Rayne. They knew each other but weren't friends, per se. It was awkward to find footing between stranger and guest. Rayne hoped it would get easier with time. It had to be even more odd for Ciara and the others who had lived in the manor longer. "I'd prefer to see my room first," the heiress said.

The second car had emptied of its occupants. Jake's brother, Josh, couldn't compare in sheer gorgeousness and didn't try, his hair dyed black and gelled into a mohawk. Ripped jeans, Converse. Josh had a guitar slung over his shoulder as he slowly exited the vehicle.

"Liquid refreshment sounds good to me. I'm Amy Flores, Tori's BFF." The petite redhead held out her hand, flashing silver and gold rings on her fingers. Her fitted thigh-length floral-patterned dress was paired with purple stilettos—beautiful without Botox. Then again, she probably wasn't even twenty-five and didn't need fillers.

"Hello!" Rayne clasped her hand and shook lightly.

"Tori's bragged about this dress since February when she approved your design," Amy said with a sweet nose scrunch. Rayne had seen the actress in several recent films as well as TV sitcoms. "That gown is stunning but weighs a ton. I know because it's packed in the trunk. We were low riding, right Tiff?" Amy had been shotgun in the second car, driven by Ethan. Tiffany shut the door of the back seat with her hip as her hands juggled a notebook and her cellphone.

"Right," Tiffany agreed.

Ethan and Tiffany were bookends in the looks department—dark hair and eyes, with a competent demeanor that assured anyone that they could handle anything—an important skill when dealing with rich people and movie stars.

"Tiff and I were going over the notes for the ceremony Saturday. Tori had a few last-minute tweaks to the vows—along with the last-minute wedding. Did you have a cancellation or something?" Amy gestured to the castle. "This place must be booked solid."

Rayne prayed that someday it would be so, but if she knew one thing about appearing successful it was to never show desperation. "We're just happy to help Tori out."

"Nice to meet you all." Tiffany's hair was pulled back in a bun, and she wore a nude palette of makeup. Stylish black glasses perched on her nose.

"Hey." Ethan pocketed the keys with a mock-shudder. "Haven't driven on that side of the road since I was at university." His accent hinted at English.

"I'm not used to it yet. Welcome." Rayne, slightly overwhelmed, took in a discreet calming breath, glancing at Ciara. Her cousin strode toward the back of the second car, speaking softly with Joan. A natural.

Rayne exhaled. "All right . . . who's ready to join Aine and Maeve for that drink?" She'd bring Tori's gown to the studio. Nothing could happen to that dress—it had over one thousand Swarovski heart-shaped crystals.

Jake and Josh exchanged a look and answered in unison, "Drinks!"

"I'll show the Montgomerys their cottage," her cousin offered. Joan had hooked her arm through Ciara's.

"I'll take the first car. There's limited room to park by the cabins. If you drive, please be careful," Cormac said. "We have dogs on the property. Ducks. Sheep."

"This place rocks." Josh slung the strap of his guitar bag over his shoulder. His fauxhawk didn't budge.

"I'll carry the luggage to the tower," Amos suggested.

What a well-oiled machine, Rayne thought with appreciation. As if this wasn't their first rodeo.

"Jake, I'd like it if you'd help with the bags." Tori pouted. "Before you run off drinking with your brother. This isn't a hotel."

Tori had said she'd wanted to see her room. Maybe Amos could escort the heiress and Jake when he brought the bags. Josh stacked his guitar on top of his black suitcase, and Amy rolled her pink bags next to Josh's.

"Fine, fine," Jake said. He didn't lose his boyish charm at Tori's high-pitched complaint, no doubt used to it. He hefted three large suitcases from the trunk. Coach, of course, in light gold. The black suede was probably Jake's.

"Rayne, didn't you mention a buffet?" Tori asked, fingers to her temple. "I'd sooner skip the drinks, get something to eat, and deal with life in the morning. I'm exhausted."

Rayne looked around at the group—everyone agreed with the bride. Smart. "Sure. Aine and Maeve, please escort our guests to the dining room instead. We'll join you as soon as the luggage is sorted."

Tori's mouth pinched. "Rayne, you'll take the dress?"

"Of course." The problem with heiresses was that sometimes they acted like heiresses.

Tori, Amy, and Dylan walked up the stone steps to meet Aine and go inside the foyer. Tori's father appeared more interested in refreshments than unpacking. Rayne knew Cormac and Ciara would help Joan.

Amos and the Anderson brothers grabbed the luggage for all four guests, then trudged around the property to the left and the brand-new exterior entrance to the tower. The inside could also be locked, making it private.

Amy paused at the top near the front door where Maeve waited and snapped her fingers. "Tiffany!"

Tiffany, next to Ethan at the second town car, looked up, then at Ethan who murmured, "You've been summoned. I'll unload your bags and then find you."

"Thanks," Tiffany said. She was the most demurely dressed of them all in a soft black pantsuit. "I owe you one."

Ethan tugged his trim goatee. "Noted."

Tiffany crossed the gravel and hurried up the stairs without a smile; she reached Maeve as the rest had moved on ahead and stepped inside.

What caused the tension between the starlet and her assistant? Blarney nuzzled Rayne's fingers to get her attention, so she patted his silky head.

Ethan opened the trunk of the town car. "The gown is really heavy," the assistant warned. "Let me help you."

"I've got it. You be sure to join everyone for a bite to eat." Rayne balanced the garment bag protecting the dress in her arms.

"I will, after I park. Thanks!" Ethan closed the trunk and got behind the wheel.

Rayne carefully walked to the steps, calculating that the dress weighed about thirty pounds due to the crystals. Ethan drove slowly down the path that showed fresh tracks from the previous car. By the time she reached the landing, he was out of sight.

It felt surreal to have paying guests at last. Rayne hurried from the foyer up the stairs to the sewing studio and hung the garment bag in the closet. She'd wait to steam the gown until after a fitting with Tori tomorrow morning.

She returned to the dining room. A sideboard along the wall held porcelain plates, cloth napkins, crystal glasses, and sterling silver utensils as well as a variety of food.

Frances had provided tarts, both savory and sweet. Homemade bread to make sandwiches filled with ham or thinly sliced beef. Dylan palmed a tumbler of amber whiskey. Tori nibbled at a plate of raw vegetables fresh from the garden and stuck to water. Amy drank a fragrant lemongrass tea and scowled with disapproval when Tiffany chose whiskey. "Hidden calories in alcohol," Amy said primly. Tiffany sipped in defiance. Her long almond-shaped manicure was in perfect yin- yang swirls, hinting at subdued personality.

Ciara and Joan walked into the dining room, laughing over something. Jake and Josh arrived, followed by Ethan. Amos stayed clear, and Rayne didn't blame him. He was probably commiserating at the barn with Dafydd Norman, Ciara's fiancé. Dafydd's part in this weekend's festivities was to lead horse rides or guide trail hikes. As the manor shepherd, he knew every last rolling hill.

Rayne remained on the fringes of what was going on, in case she was needed, but to her relief most of the Montgomery-Anderson wedding party was ready for their beds by nine-ish.

"Any bars open?" Josh asked.

Amy tilted her head, red hair spilling over her shoulder. "Aren't you tired?"

Jake's brother and best man shrugged. "Just askin'."

"Our bodies don't adjust just because the clock is different," Tiffany said, sounding like she was in agreement with Josh. It would be six hours earlier, so three in the afternoon.

"We have two pubs on the main street you turned off of to come here," Rayne said. "And a third that is farther to the left, past the gas station, and a little behind it. About a mile tops."

"We have a car," Ethan reminded them. "But that seems walkable."

"I want to go to bed," Tori said again, raising her brow at her fiancé, Jake. "I've been up since four."

"Guess that means that I also want to go to bed." Jake stroked his finger sensually down Tori's arm.

"Get a room!" Amy laughed. "That's right, you have one. I suppose I'll catch up on my script. What's up for tomorrow?"

"Horseback riding or hiking," Ciara said. "We have gorgeous hills. Churches. Ruins galore."

Tiffany and Ethan exchanged a smile. Were they friends? More than friends? "Ruins sound awesome," Tiff said.

"The path around the lake is two miles," Rayne said. "You can see the beginnings of a maze my uncle planned to uncover, but we're leaving that project for later."

"I didn't bring running shoes," Joan said.

"I saw your boots, Mom, those will be fine," Tori said.

"The level of activity is up to you, but I suggest working on your appetite for our chef's unique takes on a traditional Irish meal tomorrow night. Afterward, we can do a bonfire by the gazebo."

"I'd like to see the local stores," Joan said. Dylan groaned good-naturedly.

"We have some quaint shops," Ciara assured her.

"I could listen to your accent forever," Joan told Ciara. "My mother was from Cork. I am very interested in the special Irish features you've added to the wedding."

Tori had asked for a light touch, no shamrocks or leprechauns, and it had been fun to research Irish customs that ran the gamut from handfasting to a wishing ring.

By nine-thirty, the Montgomerys, Tiffany, and Ethan had gone to their cottages. Rayne escorted Tori, Jake, Amy, and Josh past the downstairs rooms to the interior tower entrance she'd created and slid back the pocket door.

Jake kept his hand on Tori's hip, as if he couldn't not touch his love. So sweet. It was often a thing where the bridesmaid and the best man hooked up at a wedding, but Rayne didn't sense any flirty vibes between Amy and Josh. Josh was cute, but no Jake.

Rayne wished them all a good night.

"Night," Tori replied in an exhausted tone. "Bet I won't need any melatonin to crash."

"Three glasses of that amazing whiskey will knock me out too." Jake followed Tori up the stone steps. "Sleep tight!"

Amy waved as she hurried toward the staircase to the second level. Rayne and Ciara had found an old suit of armor in the attic, bigger than the one on the second floor, and placed it in the corner. "This tower better not be haunted," the starlet murmured as she glared at the metal figure. "I'm queen of the rom-coms, not cheesy horror flicks."

Josh whirled on his heel and grinned. "I'd pay extra to see a ghost, Rayne. Can you hook me up?"

Rayne figured the castle just might be populated with all kinds of spirits, including her cousin Padraig, who'd died here as a teen, and now her Uncle Nevin, killed on the property while mowing the lawn. Her Aunt Amalie, who'd died of a broken heart.

"No promises. See you all in the morning." Laughing, Rayne walked from the interior entrance to a set of backstairs that enabled them to traverse the manor without returning to the central staircase. She'd had battery operated sconces installed for motion-activated LED lights.

Blarney met her at her bedroom door, tail wagging, and she patted his russet head, then led the way inside. The wall where she'd kept her collectible purses was almost bare, down to two. "This could be the success we need, pup."

Rayne kissed the picture of her and her dad on the fireplace mantel, and another of her, her mom, and her dad, taken in LA before his death. Her mom, Lauren, and best friend, Jenn, had pushed their visit to December because her mother was filming a special Christmas holiday for her sitcom, *Family Forever*, which wasn't going to be renewed after twenty years.

Things were tight financially, so a part of her was glad to wait. Lauren had sent the wedding dresses recovered from Landon's theft for her brides—but oh, she deserved a big win.

Rayne snuggled beneath the covers, Blarney's warmth at the foot of the bed better than a heating pad. The creaking sounds the old manor made were soothing to her as she drifted toward sleep. *It's our time.*

* * *

The next morning, Frances created a traditional Irish breakfast buffetstyle, consisting of fried eggs, white pudding (flat pork sausage patties that Rayne much preferred to black pudding—ew) beans, mushrooms, and roasted tomatoes. Fresh soda bread. A selection of toast. Orange juice with or without champagne, coffee, or tea. Though the recently widowed woman was surly, Frances could cook and that mattered more to the residents of McGrath Castle than her absent sunny nature.

Rayne filled a plate and made herself a sweetened coffee with cream. Jake, on the left end of the table next to Josh, ate and conversed with Tiffany, who had fruit, eggs, and coffee. Was that on the Amy-approved diet?

Amy had chosen an outfit straight from an Irish country catalogue: thick mocha sweater, plaid scarf, jeans, and boots. Her alabaster skin showed zero freckles beneath a fine powder, her red brows arched perfectly, her mouth created a crimson bow. Rayne was tempted to ask the brand as the lipstick didn't smudge during breakfast.

By contrast, the starlet's assistant had a naked face and her hair back in a bun, which only emphasized Tiffany's natural beauty. Rayne noticed a golden hue in her brown eyes. Her Moleskine notebook was under the woman's cellphone. Old-school notetaking in case the phone didn't work?

Rayne neared the table looking for a place to sit. Ethan, Dylan, Joan, and Amy but no sign of Tori. Maeve brought in a silver carafe of hot water and put it down by the basket of tea bags.

"And where is the bride-to-be?" Rayne asked with a broad smile.

"In bed. Tori didn't sleep well after all." Jake rested his elbow on the arm of his chair, moss-green eyes warm with concern. "Claimed she heard noises all night. I don't think she's going to do the horse-riding thing. It's not required, is it?"

"No." Rayne sat down opposite the brothers, next to Amy. "I have a small confession—I'm scared of horses, so I won't be with you either, but Ciara and Dafydd are both avid riders. It'll be fun."

"Was Dafydd the hunky Viking who helped with the luggage?" Amy batted her long lashes, silky enough to be mink extensions.

"No. That's Amos Lowell, grounds manager." Rayne couldn't be mad as the description fit the man to a tee.

Amy sipped coffee, her keen eye connecting with the guys; the women in the room were not on the starlet's radar. "Too bad for Tori. I slept great."

"No ghosts?" Josh teased. He bit into a sausage patty. Rayne noted the brothers had similar chins and foreheads, though Josh was clean-shaven. Josh draped a black leather jacket the same color as his faux-hawk over his chair; Jake had a sage cardigan sweater that made his eyes look even more sultry.

Rayne had warned Tori of the cooler weather despite the label of summer, and she was glad to see she'd shared the memo.

"If there were, I didn't hear them." Amy stared hard at her assistant as if calculating how close she was to Josh and Jake. "Tiffany, make sure to bring the camera. I'll want video of me riding around the countryside. I had to take lessons as a kid for a part in a movie."

"This is a *secret* getaway, Ames." Jake gave the starlet a half-smile so charming it guaranteed complicity. "Please keep your millions of fans waiting until after we get home, okay?"

After a swallow of coffee, Amy nodded. "Right. Operation Elopement of Hollywood's hottest couple has commenced."

Jake's cheeks tinged with rose, and Josh snorted.

Tiffany patted her lips with the cloth napkin and dropped it over her plate. What did the woman have against smiling? Unlike the others in the party, her tone was professional rather than friendly. "You want the camera as well as the phone?"

Amy frowned at Tiffany. "Didn't I just say so?"

Jake lifted his mug, but it was empty.

Ethan, in khakis and a snug sweater, brought around the coffee carafe and topped off Jake's mug, then Tiffany's, then Josh's before coming to Rayne and Amy's side of the table. He must be accustomed to keeping the peace. He didn't pour until Amy nodded slightly. What a diva, Rayne thought to herself as Ethan filled her mug. "Thanks." Beauty would fade with time and then what would this young lady have?

Rayne wouldn't blame Tiffany for quitting.

Ethan returned the carafe to the buffet table and sat down again. Rayne smiled at Dylan and Joan. "How did you sleep?"

They'd just gotten everything on the grounds completed with days to spare. Paint, fixtures, bedding. She'd been very proud of how they'd come together as a team. Gillian Clark, their full-time hire from Grathton Village was a competent electrician, along with handyman Bran Wilson, who had a knack for plumbing that had saved the castle a lot of money with their skills. Aine had created patterned gray-and-white curtains with matching tablecloths and napkins for the bigger bungalow, and Rayne had done the other one in sky blue.

Dylan buttered a slice of whole grain toast. "Great. The mattress was surprisingly up to par, Rayne."

Rayne hid a smile by ducking her head and allowing her hair to fall forward, a curtain of black. She'd worn it loose to her shoulders this morning. "I'm glad you were comfortable."

Joan smacked her husband's arm. "He's a mattress snob. It's not personal . . . but they were comfy. I'll be delighted to tell people about this rustic gem once we're home again."

That's what Rayne wanted to hear. "Thank you."

Ciara and Dafydd, having eaten in the kitchen already, entered the dining room. Dafydd wore his customary cap, and was growing a beard rather than sport his usual clean-shaven jawline. "It's about time to head to the barn," Ciara announced. She glanced around the room with approval at the boots and pants. "I've planned a stop at the pub after our morning ride."

"Now we're talking," Josh said. "We went to one of the pubs last night!" He elbowed Tiffany, and the young woman rolled her eyes. Rayne was pleased to see a smile play around her mouth. Josh and Amy might not have vibed, but Josh and Tiff apparently did.

"Wonderful!" Rayne said. She didn't want anyone to be bored here, and Americans were notorious for their need to be entertained.

"You did?" Amy stared from Josh to Tiff. "I didn't hear you go out, Josh."

Josh knocked on the wood of the table. "Stone walls, Ames. You shoulda come with us."

"Nobody told me about it," Amy said with a sniff.

"It was last minute," Tiff explained. "We weren't out late."

"Yeah. The pub closed at midnight," Ethan said.

"You went too?" Amy sounded hurt. She turned her shoulder to give Jake a flirty smile. "Well, I wanted to get my beauty sleep. I'm reading for a new movie on Tuesday. I got the script before we left LA."

"What movie?" Jake asked. Of course, he'd be interested, as he was in the industry.

Amy whispered, "It's top secret. If I told you, I'd have to kill you."

Chapter Two

Amy placed her fingers on Jake's arm and laughed becomingly. Jake joined her merriment, rich brown locks bowed to red, close enough to intermingle. Rayne noticed the starlet still didn't share the title of the possible movie.

"I need to stop at the cottage for my camera," Tiffany said. "I'll meet up with you guys at the barn."

"It's OK, Tiff." Amy smiled up at Jake. "We'll keep Jakey's secrets."

Their guests filed out of the dining room after Ciara and Dafydd.

"Well!" Maeve clasped her hands when they were gone. "That was exciting."

Aine smoothed her apron over her clothes and started to stack plates. "That Jake is sure handsome. Josh and Ethan too, but Jake . . ." The young maid sighed. "A hush-hush wedding, and Amy with a secret movie. I feel like I'm dreaming."

"You can't share anything you hear at the castle," Rayne cautioned.

"I won't!" Aine said, her palm to her heart.

"I think they enjoyed their breakfast." Maeve gestured to the remaining food. "But they aren't big eaters."

"They remind me of you, Rayne, when you first came, counting calories." Aine snickered.

"I'm converted!" Rayne said. "Should I help clean up?" There were a lot of dishes.

"No—we've got this," Maeve said.

"In that case, I'll be in my studio." She had two November dresses to work on as well as steaming any wrinkles from the bride's gown. She was nervous that she hadn't had a chance to remove it from the garment bag yet. "Will you message me when Tori wakes up? I need to do a last fitting for her."

Maeve smiled wide. Aine was her mother's mini, from their bright red hair, to the charming gap in their white teeth. "That I will, lass. Things are going splendidly."

Rayne hugged the woman who'd been a champion organizer behind the scenes. "I don't want to jinx anything but so far so good."

Hustling upstairs, Rayne unlocked the studio that had once been Aunt Amalie's pink parlor. She'd toned down the pink walls with calendars, schedules, and white boards so they were hardly noticeable. There was plenty of space for her three sewing tables, shelves of supplies, and multiple dress forms. She'd covered the antique mauve furniture with neutral throws and patterned pillows. The gem of the room was her fashionista aunt's large walk-in closet stuffed with classic designer clothes.

Rayne retrieved the gown from the garment bag and hung it over a dress form. The bespoke design exuded luxury with silk, Swarovski crystals, and ostrich feathers. She hoped Tori would be happy in it.

As she waited for her client, Rayne began cutting out a pattern in a challenging gossamer fabric when a knock sounded.

"Come in!"

Rayne eyed the door, expecting Maeve or Aine, but Tori stood in the shadows. Soft floral perfume, her signature scent, preceded her.

"Hey! How are you feeling?" Rayne checked her watch in surprise. Almost two? She often lost track of time when she was busy creating. "I bet you're hungry."

"Not really." Tori slid into the sewing studio on graceful feet. She'd trained to be a ballet dancer, but it had never gone anywhere. "Where's the dress?"

Curt. To the point.

"Hanging up to be steamed," Rayne assured her. "I thought we'd do a final fitting, so I'm glad you're here."

Tori placed her palm to her flat stomach, stick thin in black jeans and a cowl-neck sweater. Her golden hair was up in a messy bun.

"We have our work cut out for us." Tori's attitude was one of expectation. "I won't have any scrimping on quality because of the slight change in plans."

Slight change? Christmas ceremony to a rushed September Irish wedding without a hiccup? Rayne and the others at the castle were doing their best. "When would you like to try on the dress?"

Rayne got up from her table, gesturing to the headless dress form where she'd hung the silk confection. The mermaid silhouette had a daring bodice bracketed with sheer panels to allow a glimpse of Tori's skin and meant to be snug. A thousand crystals twinkled. Downy ostrich feathers danced from the hem.

"Now."

Rayne bit her cheek to keep from reprimanding her client for being rude. "Certainly."

Tori immediately slipped out of her jeans and top without a care for modesty. Since Rayne had already taken her measurements, it wasn't a shock, but still. She walked to the door and locked it.

Tori sighed dramatically. And yet, in all the conversations they'd had, Tori's dream had never been to be on stage or before a camera. Did marrying an actor bring her close enough to the action? And her best friend was also an actress. Could be the drama was infectious.

"Careful now," Rayne said softly as she helped Tori into the confection, Tori standing on tiptoes as if she was wearing heels. They faced the long mirror that Rayne had installed on the wall.

"I love it," Tori said.

"You're beautiful." Rayne slowly zipped the back so as not to pull or accidentally tear the fabric around the zipper. Her stomach clenched and what should have been a smooth tug upward jammed.

Oh no.

Had Tori gained weight? Impossible! The dress was so form fitting that five pounds would make a difference.

Tori froze. "Is there a problem?"

"Uh." Rayne released her hold on the zipper and flexed her fingers.

"Rayne?"

She swallowed and blew on her fingers to dry them. Nerves had made her sweat.

Tori sucked in her breath and Rayne inched the zipper upward. "Breathe out slow."

"Something is the matter with this gown," Tori said snidely. "I suggest you fix it by tomorrow."

Fix it? It wasn't like she could just add a panel to the sheer bodice! Rayne lowered the zipper. "Let's get new measurements."

"Nothing has changed." Tori stepped out of the gown and Rayne draped it on the dress form. "You must be mistaken."

"Tori, the last three fittings, that gown fit like a glove, and you know it." Rayne wasn't accusing but kept her gentle voice firm.

She scanned the heiress's figure, pausing at Tori's waist. Was it just slightly thicker? Rayne brought her gaze up to Tori's wan face. *No.*

Though Rayne hadn't said a word, her expression caused Tori to collapse to her knees. "I'm preggers. You have to help me." She blinked up at Rayne with an angst-filled gaze, tears streaming down her cheeks. "Jake will kill me for ruining his career."

Rayne inwardly panicked but eventually calmed the bride down enough to stop her from crying. "We need new measurements," she said.

"I've been starving myself, but it hasn't helped." Tori dabbed at her blue eyes, the honey-blond lashes thick with tears.

"That can't be good for you or the baby," Rayne said, double and triple checking her measurements before offering Tori a soft blanket and a chair by her worktable.

Tori wrapped it around her shoulders like a shawl and tucked her feet beneath the chair. "You have to make that dress fit. I'll pay you extra."

Rayne raised her palm. "It was meant to be skintight. Give me a minute." She smoothed the gown, studying the zipper. The bodice with sheer plackets. Luckily, she only needed to find an inch.

"Well?" The question warbled, making Tori sound frightened rather than demanding.

"I will figure it out." Rayne studied the heiress. Was she really scared? "If Jake would actually hurt you, then you shouldn't marry him."

Tori blushed. "It's just a figure of speech, Rayne."

"So, will you tell him?"

"Not yet." Tori's eyes narrowed. "And you can't either—or, or, I won't pay you the other half of the money for my dress deposit."

"You don't have to bribe or threaten me, Tori." Rayne didn't like it but thought she understood. In Tori's world, wealth was a bargaining tool. "I'll do it because you're my client. I don't gossip."

Tori rose from the chair and let the blanket fall. "Thank you. I think I'm going to skip dinner."

"Why?"

"My bestie's got a nose like a bloodhound—between her and her assistant, I'm surprised they haven't figured something out already because of the change in venue. Amy adores gossip—especially if it's something she can use for her advantage."

Rayne's brow furrowed. "In that case, you shouldn't miss it. The dinner tonight will be an Irish meal with modern takes—tomorrow is the medieval feast to celebrate your wedding. Your friends, and your parents, are going to expect you to happily be part of the festivities."

"You make a good point." Tori slipped her jeans and sweater on again. "Friends. I see the way Amy flirts with Jake. Am I a fool for getting married to the sexiest man alive?"

Rayne had witnessed the flirting this morning at breakfast and put it down to Amy rather than Jake, though he had responded in an easy manner. "Do you love him?"

"Sure." Tori sighed and placed her hand over her stomach. "I mean, Jake doesn't want kids *yet*, but he does eventually. I'm Catholic, and I can't not carry this baby. I'll tell him later. What will it matter after we tie the knot?"

Rayne had so many questions, but Tori shook her head and strode to the door. "I'm going to rest. What time will the command performance be at?"

"Dinner is at six."

"See you there. Don't say anything," Tori reminded her as she left. The door closed quietly.

With a groan, Rayne reached for her tiny scissors and sat on the window seat for the best natural light to begin taking out her handiwork. If she could move each placket of the bodice a sixteenth of an inch, it would equal an inch. The needlework would need to be by hand, but by the next day, and the four-thirty ceremony at the church, the gown would be steamed and fitted to the new measurements, allowing Tori room to breathe.

It wasn't the first time she'd had to burn the midnight oil.

Ciara knocked on the door, then walked in. Panicked, Rayne checked her phone for the time and realized it was already half-past five. "Hey." Ciara nodded at the gown. "How's it going?"

"I have a few adjustments is all," Rayne said. She wished she could share the why of the adjustments, but a client needed to trust her to keep her freaking secrets. Especially the epic ones.

"Sorry to bother you, then, but Tori and her parents are asking about you." Ciara looked at the bodice in pieces. "Can you come down to dinner?"

Rayne wanted to say no but then that would give the game away for Tori that something was wrong with the dress. "On my way, cuz."

They left the studio, Rayne locking the door behind her. There was nothing she enjoyed more than the satisfaction of a happy bride and that's what she focused on, rather than Tori's meltdown.

"How'd it go today?" Rayne asked. They'd discussed their individual roles while guests were at the manor. Ciara wanted to stay behind the scenes as Amos and Dafydd were rather than sit at the table for most meals, but Rayne needed her cousin's help to entertain people. As they were co-owners in this venture with equal stakes in the outcome, Ciara had eventually agreed.

They'd found adoption papers for Ciara in Uncle Nevin's sporran as they'd readied him for his funeral. Ciara was her uncle's natural daughter, and they'd only discovered one another after Ciara's mother had died when Ciara was twenty-two. Every time Rayne brought up the idea of going forward with the adoption to make Ciara a "legitimate" McGrath, her cousin balked and refused to discuss it. With emergency after emergency at the castle, it had taken a back seat though it was far from forgotten.

"That Josh is a flirt," Ciara said. "Any female was fair game—he even flirted with his mare. Loved the Sheep's Head pub and really hit things off with Beetle."

The tattooed bartender no doubt was a kindred spirit to Josh. Rayne chuckled. "I can see that. Did everyone have fun?"

"Yep. Joan had a pale draft. I like that lady a lot but there's no forgetting that they're loaded and not just regular folks."

"How so?"

"Well, Dylan just paid for everybody's tab in the pub. That got him a lot of cheers." Ciara glanced at Rayne as they walked. "And Joan's wearing enough gold and diamonds to be a menace if she was left by herself."

Rayne bowed her head. "She better not lose anything. I trust everyone in the castle but still . . ."

"It's insured," Ciara laughed. "I asked her about it. She had a fair argument of why own it if ye can't wear it?"

"I agree with her."

"I knew you would," Ciara said.

They reached the main staircase and headed down to the foyer.

"We stopped in at the church because the Montgomerys wanted to meet Father Patrick in person as they've only been in contact online." Ciara paused.

"What is it?" Rayne asked. She hoped there wouldn't be a problem with the mass. Joan and Dylan had been working directly with the priest for their daughter's ceremony.

"Father Patrick's heard some grumbles from the villagers about the wedding venue here at the castle, and he thinks we need to be prepared. I didn't want to tell you, but Father Patrick disagreed, so . . ."

Rayne put her hand to her racing heart. "What grumbles?"

"Relax," Ciara said. "This is why I didn't want to mention it." She touched the pulse at the base of her throat. "I can see your vein jumping from here."

Passing the table with the bog oak statue of an ancient warrior on the main floor, Rayne asked, "Do the Montgomerys know about the unhappy villagers?"

"No. Father Patrick was discreet. He *is* a priest."

The dining room door opened and Aine smiled at them, unaware that she'd interrupted a conversation Rayne wasn't finished with yet. Oh well. "I was just coming to get you both," Aine said.

"We're here now." Rayne waved at everyone as they entered the chamber. "Hi!"

Ciara took her seat near Joan and Dylan at one end, leaving the other for Rayne. The table, set for ten, looked magnificent. Silver cloches covered savory dishes on the sideboard. Everyone had drinks, from water to whiskey. She nodded with thanks at Maeve, Sorcha Ketchum—the doctor's granddaughter who filled in when needed at the castle—and Aine. Cormac would serve the food from the heavier platters.

Frances planned on staying in the kitchen. In her opinion a chef didn't need to be seen or heard like a rockstar, though it worked for Gordon Ramsey.

"And what kept you?" Amy asked. She flipped an auburn lock from her forehead, every molecule a star.

Her guests had all changed from jeans to slacks or dresses. Rayne had been so lost in the last-minute alterations that she hadn't had time. "Unlike the movies," she joked, "this place keeps us all very busy—add in the sheep and the gardens, the upkeep of the buildings . . . well." Rayne sent a serene smile around the table. "I also have two bridal gowns for November that I'm working on."

Tori relaxed at Rayne's believable explanation for being unavailable. "I feel very lucky to have a Modern Lace original."

"How did you and Tori meet?" Ethan asked. "Not here in Ireland . . ."

"I discovered Rayne," Amy said. "On the set of *Family Forever* when I had a cameo, sheesh, I think it was mid-January? Lauren mentioned she had a daughter with a bridalwear shop on Rodeo Drive. Jakey, you'd just popped the question."

Joan grinned. "New Year's Eve."

"I've never heard this." Tiffany tapped the notebook on top of her cellphone but didn't pick it up. "What's the connection with Rayne again?"

"My mother is Lauren McGrath—she stars as Susan Carter in the *Family Forever* sitcom." Rayne folded her napkin across her lap.

Exclamations rounded the table. "You come from Hollywood royalty," Jake said, sounding impressed. "No wonder you didn't bat an eye when you met us all. You'd be surprised at how people can react to movie stars."

"Gorgeous. Famous. Talented." Josh winked over his tumbler of whiskey. "You single, Rayne?"

Amy tossed her napkin at him.

"Definitely," Rayne said. "I have no time for a relationship."

Tiffany opened her notebook, flipped to a page about midpoint, then smirked at Rayne. Rayne got the feeling she knew about Landon Short and was no doubt going to share the story in her own time. If not now, later. Hadn't Tori mentioned that Amy loved gossip? Who better to fuel those desires than Tiffany, her assistant?

Cormac served each person lamb from the platter. Sorcha followed with roasted potatoes, then Aine with sauteed greens, then Maeve with soft rolls. Rayne skipped a whiskey with her dinner though she wanted one, opting for a clear head.

"What's the plan for later tonight?" Ethan asked.

"We should go back to the pub," Josh said as they were midway through their meal. "Beetle said he'd give us a discount."

"I don't want everyone wasted," Tori said. "Tomorrow is our wedding day." The heiress peered imploringly at Jake, her parents, then Rayne and Ciara.

"It's lashing rain," Maeve said. "So, no bonfire, alas. It should pass soon enough, and tomorrow blue skies are predicted. Good luck for your wedding day."

"We have a billiards room," Cormac suggested. "If you'd like to stay here."

Aine said, "It has a dartboard as well as music. A stocked bar."

"You got me there, doll," Josh said as he lifted his tumbler to the maid. "I'll bring my guitar."

Aine blushed.

Tiffany smacked him and shook her head. "Will you cut it out?"

"I'm just joking! You got no sense of humor, Tiffany," Josh protested.

"It's true, Tiff," Amy agreed. "None. Like God forgot to grant you a funny bone."

Tiffany bristled.

"I think that sounds perf," Tori decided. "Josh, you suck at guitar, so Amy'll be in charge of music, and we can do pub things on Sunday as a group before we go home."

"Ouch." Josh winced. "What's billiards?"

"It's like pool," Rayne explained.

Josh pushed aside his dinner. "I'm in. I'll partner with Tiff, since I have no talent and she has no sense of humor."

Tiffany touched his wrist and gave him a shy smile. "I like the way you play guitar."

Josh waggled his brow and scooted closer to Tiff. Yep, they had chemistry.

Jake reached for Tori's hand. "I don't care what we do, babes. Whatever makes you happy. If you'd prefer for us to stay here, then that's fine by me. I'm just glad you're feeling better."

Tori kissed his knuckles. "My Romeo."

"Where did you learn such nice manners, Jake?" Joan asked.

"Josh and I were born in South Carolina, Hilton Head," Jake said. "Being polite was drummed into us from birth."

"Southerners are known for their manners," Dylan said.

"That's right," Josh concurred with a raise of his glass. "And the nuns at Catholic school polished them up."

Rayne laughed along with the rest of the guests around the table. The brothers were very charming and the Montgomerys seemed pleased by their daughter's choice of a husband. Did they know of her condition?

"If only our parents were still alive . . ." Jake let the sentence trail off.

"They would certainly be proud," Joan said. "We are your family now."

After dessert of apple spice cake or Guinness chocolate layer cake with Baileys Irish cream frosting from the Coco Bean Café (Tori had neither and Ethan had both), Dylan and Joan opted for their bed and the downy mattress.

"You young people have fun," Joan said. "But not too much. We want a radiant bride tomorrow."

Dylan chuckled and pressed a kiss to the top of his daughter's golden hair. "You can't help but shine, darling." He took Joan's hand,

and they left. Cormac followed, offering to drive them to the cottage because of the rainy weather.

"What would you all like to do next?" Rayne asked. "If you don't want to play billiards, there's a large round table in the library where you could play cards. We have pinochle or Uno."

"I'm not ready to hit the sack," Josh said, winking at Tiffany. "I vote for the, what did you call it?"

"Billiards," Rayne said. "Ciara is an ace player, but I am no good. I wasn't at pool either, to be fair."

"Let's go!" Jake said, getting to his feet. He smiled at Rayne, then Ciara, charm seeping from his tones that tempted her to say to heck with the dress. "Will you ladies join us?"

"Not tonight. I've got some things to catch up on." Rayne read her watch, nine already, and rose as well. She had the bride's gown to alter.

"I'm going to check the horses before I turn in." Ciara stood, her chair scooting backward. "Country hours."

"Bed seems great to me too," Tiffany said with an exaggerated yawn.

Amy shook her head. "I don't think so, Tiff. We need you and Ethan."

Tiffany firmed her mouth but didn't argue. Josh snickered. Jake looked at Ethan. "That okay with you, dude?"

"Brilliant," Ethan said. He forced a smile. Amy clapped and rushed to his side, tucking her hand into the crook of his elbow.

"Come with me." Rayne placed her napkin on her empty plate. "What I love about the layout of the manor is that if you think you're lost just find the center staircase and go left or right from there."

"Is that a real shield on the wall?" Ethan asked.

"Aye, it's from a McGrath ancestor," Ciara assured him. "Night!" She chose an umbrella from the bin and skipped out the front door, the sound of rain pitter-pattering on the porch steps.

Tori, Jake, Josh, Ethan, Amy, and Tiffany all followed Rayne to the billiards room. While going through the attic several months back

Rayne had discovered the billiards table, with all the accoutrement, and a dart board. What had been an unused parlor was turned into a games room with speakers and Spotify.

"Is it easy?" Tiffany asked.

Ethan shrugged. "The main difference is that a pool table has pockets, and a billiards table does not."

"I want the bar before the games," Josh said. "I'll make us wicked drinks."

"Tomorrow is a big day," Rayne said, hoping they wouldn't stay up too late. "After the wedding, we'll host a medieval feast here, complete with local ales and a smoked whole hog."

Tori turned slightly green, and Amy—for the first time since they'd arrived—appeared to notice that her best friend wasn't a hundred percent.

"Are you still tired, Tor?" Amy asked. "I hope you don't have the flu."

"No! No. I'm fine." Tori chose a cue stick. "Pick something danceable for tunes, okay? Jake, you and I are a team. Let's bet a grand that we win."

Amy laughed. "Tiff, you do the music. Me and Josh will kick butt!"

"But I want to play with Tiff." Josh tickled the assistant's waist. Tiffany started to giggle but stopped when Amy gave her a death glare.

"Amy," Ethan said in a cajoling tone, "I was almost pro during college. We should team up and take their money."

Amy's grin had faltered at not being chosen but now returned, full wattage. "Deal."

With her guests settled, Rayne left them to party and found Aine in the kitchen with Maeve, Sorcha, and Frances as they finished the dishes. "The meal was wonderful—great job! I'll be upstairs if you need me. I've got some alterations to do for the bride's gown."

Aine was Rayne's apprentice and understood this was not an easy task. The dress was snug, with individual crystals hand-sewn to gossamer fabric. "Good luck."

It wasn't quite midnight when Rayne finished moving the bodice seams and unfolding them for the extra inch required. She prayed that Tori didn't eat so much as an apple slice between now and the ceremony.

A firm knock reverberated through the door and Ciara, followed by Aine, rushed in.

Ciara admired the dress that any Disney princess would be proud to wear. "That's gorgeous."

Aine asked the crucial question. "Were you able to alter it?"

"Almost done," Rayne said, her eyes scratchy. "I just need an hour in the morning but I'm ready to call it a night. What's up?"

"Aine heard a loud argument going on," Ciara said. "She was worried and woke me to see if there was something to be done. Will you come with us, since you actually know Tori?"

"Sure. Who was it?" Rayne asked.

"It sounded like Jake," Aine said. "But it wasn't Tori—her voice is higher pitched."

The three left the studio and walked down the hall to the central staircase where they paused. "I don't hear anything," Rayne said. "Let's go downstairs."

They reached the stone foyer. Nothing.

"Maybe people were just excited," Rayne said.

"It didn't seem like that," Aine said. Her chin jutted. "I wouldn't have interrupted you unless I thought it was important."

Ciara nodded. "We all understand that the survival of our home is at stake."

Rayne stepped down the hall toward the billiards room. "Tori was adamant that she wanted everyone rested. You're sure it wasn't her? Couples argue especially in times of stress."

Aine kept in sync with Rayne and Ciara. "Positive. That leaves Amy or Tiffany. They kind of sound alike."

"You think Josh and Tiffany are dating?" Ciara asked. "She sure blushed when he teased her."

"I don't know. Usually, it's the groomsman and the bridesmaid that hook up over the wedding festivities."

Ciara rolled her eyes. "That's an actual thing?"

"Yeah," Rayne said.

Aine opened the door to the billiards room. "Nobody's here."

They were gone but the lights were on. Rayne shivered as a tickle of apprehension raced up her spine. Used glasses were on the bar, a whiskey bottle almost empty. Josh, probably, had found the stash of snacks as well and had dished out bowls of pretzels and peanuts.

Aine stepped toward the mess, but Rayne called her back, exhausted as they all must be from such a long day. "Let's take care of it in the morning."

"You're sure?" Aine joined Ciara and Rayne in the threshold, flipped the lights off, and the room went dark. Electric sconces flickered in the hall.

Just then, Blarney howled an alarm, barking up a storm.

The three women looked at one another, and then ran for the front door. Once outside in the brisk night air, Rayne hurried down the stone steps, turning right at the grass toward the tower. The lawn was damp but at least it was no longer raining.

Blarney rushed to her, head down, but his fur was on end. He howled again.

A figure sprawled stomach-down on the ground below the turret. Rayne sprinted closer and saw Tiffany Quick, her neck at an odd angle. The woman's eyes were open, her glasses missing. It was only because Rayne had admired her yin-yang manicure that she noticed both hands had broken fingernails.

Chapter Three

"What's wrong with her?" Aine asked, her voice trembling. "What's the matter with Tiffany?"

Rayne straightened as Aine neared, her mind spinning. Aine, eyes wide, was only nineteen and even though Rayne had never seen a dead person before, she instinctively stepped between Tiffany and Aine to shelter her, steering her back toward the stone stairs. "We need to call the ambulance."

Ciara murmured a shocked curse and patted her denim pockets. "Nine-nine-nine. I don't have my mobile."

Rayne pulled her phone free, her fingers shaking. Blarney leaned against her calves, his body quivering. "I'll call." She kept her back to where Tiffany lay.

"What if she's still alive?" Aine wailed. "We can't just leave her there."

Rayne didn't see how that was possible. "Let me check again if she's breathing, all right?" She handed her phone to Ciara. "You call the Gardaí. Tell them to hurry!" Her thoughts scrambled as she neared Tiffany's body, hoping she'd get up and brush the grass from her clothes, but there was no way the young woman was moving again with her neck bent like that.

Ciara murmured into the phone that there was an emergency at McGrath Castle. "One of our guests is . . . dead." A pause, then, "We had an event for a wedding this weekend, and it seems like one of the guests must have fallen from the tower." Ciara arched her brow at Rayne and fluttered her fingers in a signal to hurry. "We're checking her pulse right now."

Aine sobbed on the step.

Rayne kneeled by Tiffany and placed her fingers on her wrist, the grass making her knees wet. Tiff's skin was cold to the touch, and there was no beating of her pulse. The assistant had changed clothes from dinner—she'd been in linen slacks but now wore jeans, black boots with a loose sole, and a T-shirt. No jacket. "Nothing," she said. Her stomach clenched. This wasn't like the dead people on TV. The emptiness couldn't be portrayed properly on a screen, the lack of a soul. Her dad had been cremated and when she remembered him, it was his smile, not his illness.

"No pulse," Ciara relayed to the operator.

Aine wrapped her arm around Blarney. The dog was snuggled next to the maid, offering comfort in his special way.

"Ta." Ciara pressed the end button and gave the phone back to Rayne, who remained on her knees as she tried to make sense of this tragedy. Had Tiffany accidentally fallen from the rooftop?

Rayne stood and put her phone in her pocket, shivering with cold and shock. "What did they say?" She studied Tiffany, searching for answers. The black frames of her glasses poked from under her body. She didn't see a phone or purse, or the notebook she'd carried everywhere. She gulped down a wave of nausea. Could be they were beneath her too.

"The operator said help is on the way." Ciara rubbed her arms. "An ambulance and the police."

Aine sniffed and scrubbed her cheeks with her palms. "This is terrible. I don't understand what happened to her."

Ciara paced the grass between the steps and Rayne. "Was Tiffany the one you heard arguing with Jake?"

Aine shrugged. "I don't know."

Rayne turned to Aine and Ciara. "Should we wake up the guests? Amy, at least?" It was after midnight now, and very cold—none of them had grabbed a jacket as they'd dashed out in response to Blarney's howl.

"Probably not," Ciara said. "They better hurry or I'm going inside for a coat."

Rayne's teeth chattered, and she gestured to Tiffany in her lightweight shirt. "She isn't wearing a jacket either."

Ciara tucked her hands into her jean pockets. "So?"

"Tiffany was staying in the bungalow. That's a good half mile away—she'd need a sweater or something."

"You're right. She wasn't sleeping in the tower." Ciara joined Rayne and looked down at Tiffany. Why had she been near the manor at this hour?

Rayne peered up at the turret on the tower. There were no lights on from the sliver of the arrow windows. The rooftop was dark as well. She couldn't imagine Tiff and Jake in a loud argument less than forty minutes ago. "I can't fathom her arguing with anybody, but especially not Jake."

"She was quiet and kept to herself," Ciara said.

"Except with Josh. They flirted." Aine leaned into Blarney and crossed her ankles, the black uniform pants not holding up against the cool stone under her bum.

"And maybe Jake didn't like it," Rayne suggested, thinking aloud. "It didn't set a good impression for the Montgomerys or something."

"If something happened during billiards, Joan and Dylan weren't there," Ciara said.

"You're right." Rayne tossed the idea aside. "Jake probably would have talked to Josh about it rather than Tiffany anyway."

"If there was a problem," Aine agreed. "Jake is so wonderful."

Rayne gave the teen a partial smile. Crushes like the one Aine had on Jake were harmless and sweet. And, brought in money at the box office. She turned to Ciara. "How did Tiffany and Jake seem while on the horse trails today or at the pub?"

Ciara ruffled her curls. "I was mostly with Joan; she says I remind her of her mam when she was young. I'll ask Dafydd if he noticed anything unusual."

"Okay. Jake hadn't seemed to pay Tiffany any special attention that I had noticed," Rayne said, her skin rising in goose bumps from the cold damp air. The fact that there was a dead person next to her had nothing to do with her chills. *Uh huh.*

"Which leaves Amy that he'd argued with," Ciara said.

"And we definitely saw Amy and Jake flirting in the dining room at breakfast," Aine said. Her tears slowed. "It's possible that could have turned heated. I wish I'd stayed to listen!"

"You did the right thing, Aine." Rayne could easily imagine the theatrical starlet causing a scene. Perhaps what Aine heard was Jake telling (shouting at?) Amy to behave.

Which didn't explain Tiffany falling from the top of the tower.

Blarney alerted them to a car coming down the drive. Ciara and Rayne stood by Aine, who remained seated on the stairs.

Headlights from a town car brushed them on the porch, and Rayne realized that it wasn't the EMTs or police but one of their guests. Ethan waved when he saw them and then rather than drive to the bungalow he'd shared with Tiffany, he pulled over and rolled the window down. "What are you ladies doing?"

Rayne's teeth clicked together from the cold, and she was tempted to slide into the car to get warm. Her inclination was to be quiet about what had happened to Tiffany until they knew more. A death at the manor wasn't *good*, no matter how one looked at it. She couldn't think of a single reasonable explanation for them to be freezing their behinds off. Rayne knew as well that there wasn't a way for Tiffany to have just *fallen* from the roof. The walls were over four feet high, and the crenellations of the turret were even taller.

"Stargazing." Aine jumped up from her seat and eyed the night sky. Not a single star was visible behind the gray clouds.

"It's cloudy," Ethan said.

"You know the UK, being from London." Ciara rocked backwards to peer at the moon. "The clouds will blow over."

"That's fair enough." Ethan didn't sound convinced. "Is everything okay?"

"Yes," Ciara said. "And where were you off to?"

"The petrol station for smokes." His English accent deepened. "I'd given tobacco up in the states, but here, I'm compelled by my old ways."

Rayne forced a chuckle. So long as he didn't get out to have a cigarette here . . . blasted sugar cookies snickle fritz. She'd been raised not to swear because her mother played a Christian character on her sitcom though after twenty years, the show was ending. No way would Lauren McGrath suddenly let loose with profanity, and Rayne's go-to curses proved Ethan's point that old habits die hard. Ethan turned off the engine and climbed out, unwrapping a pack of smokes. "Want one?"

"No, thank you." Rayne shook her head. Aine and Ciara also declined.

Ethan, awkwardly realizing that he might be intruding, shoved the cigarettes into his pocket. "All right. Well, I'll see you in the morning. D-day, as they say."

But it was too late, and the ambulance arrived with sirens blaring, followed by a police vehicle. The Garda parked behind Ethan as if to block him in. Rayne recognized the officer once he climbed out; Garda Dominic Williams had a fair complexion and freckles and despite the misunderstanding over her uncle's demise where he'd originally thought Nevin's death an accident, he seemed proficient at his job. His partner, a woman Rayne hadn't met before, exited as well, adjusting her hat over dark hair.

Aine waved the ambulance between the police car and the stone stairs. The driver turned the sirens off and put the vehicle in park.

Both medics hurried out. The driver asked, "Where is the patient?"

"There," Aine said, pointing toward Tiffany's body.

Garda Williams turned to Ciara. "You called this in, Ciara?"

"Aye," Ciara said curtly. The pair had a complicated history. He hadn't initially believed Ciara's insistence that her dad had been murdered. Add that they used to date a million years ago, and, well . . .

"I'm Garda Kaitlin Lee." The female officer nodded familiarly at Ciara and Aine before she turned to Rayne. "You must be Lady McGrath."

"Lady?" Ethan smirked. "You didn't mention that over dinner, Rayne. Snazzy."

Rayne would bet that Ethan was tipsy—hence the desire for cigarettes and company. When she'd shockingly inherited the castle in her uncle's will, with Ciara to be kept on as manager, the title of Lady came with it but wasn't a moniker American-born Rayne wanted. She hadn't wanted the crushing debt either, or the year deadline, yet here she was, with Ciara at her side, working their fingers to the bone to save the castle and village anyway. "I'm Rayne McGrath," she said. "And this is Ethan Cruz."

"So, what happened here?" Garda Lee asked.

The taller medic was older than his rounder comrade who had knelt to get Tiffany's vitals before shaking his head. "DOA. She's gone . . . I'm sorry, but we can't transport the poor lass."

"Body?" Ethan repeated in a dumfounded tone.

"Tiffany is . . . dead." Rayne glanced from the Gardaí to Ethan, unsure what to say.

Ethan paled. "Come again?"

Garda Williams stepped between Rayne and Ethan. "I'm Garda Dominic Williams. You knew . . . the deceased?"

"Yes," Ethan said with a stammer. "We're sharing a bungalow."

"Lovers?" Garda Lee asked.

"God, no. Associates. Professional." Ethan reached for his cigarettes again but didn't bring them out.

"Coroner is five minutes away, Williams," Garda Lee said after reading a message on her phone.

"All right." Garda Williams pulled his attention from Garda Lee to Ethan. "Stay here, sir."

Rayne rubbed the goose bumps on her arms, and Aine's teeth clicked together. Though freezing, a part of her wanted to stay and listen to the Gardaí. To share what she knew. To help.

"Can we go in? I'll make everyone tea," Aine offered in a small voice.

Garda Williams studied the earnest young woman. "Only to the kitchen and stay there, quiet. Your folks are sleeping?"

"For now." Aine's pale lips were blue. "Da is a light sleeper, and I'm surprised he's not up yet. The sirens and all."

"We're heading out since the Gardaí are here, and we can't do more," the tall driver said. "The coroner will make the official call. Sorry about your friend." Both medics got in the ambulance, and the driver carefully reversed before turning around and driving away.

Garda Lee jotted something into her tablet.

"Just the kitchen, then, and we'll be in shortly." Garda Williams spoke in a soft yet firm tone.

"Ta." Aine scooted up the steps to the front door without a backward glance.

"Poor lamb. I don't think she's ever seen anything like this before," Ciara said. "I was with my mam when she passed, and Da . . ."

Rayne shuffled her feet, her arms wrapped around her middle. She'd never been grateful before that she hadn't been with her dad at the end.

The front door opened, and Aine skipped down the steps with extra coats for Rayne and Ciara from the kitchen.

"Thank you," Rayne said, putting it on. Warmth countered the shivers of her body.

Ciara quickly shrugged hers on too. "Bless you, lass."

Aine dipped her head and scurried back inside.

"Cozy enough now?" Garda Lee remarked. "I'd like to see the body."

Easy for her to say, as the Garda was wearing a thick navy-blue-and-yellow jacket and hadn't been outside for the last fifteen minutes.

"Tiffany is over here," Ciara said. Rayne followed Ciara.

"What happened?" Garda Lee asked.

"We don't know. We came outside when we heard Blarney howl, and found Tiffany here." Rayne placed her fingers to the hollow of her throat. "She, well, wasn't moving or breathing, and we called the ambulance." There was a little bit of crumbled crenellation from the rooftop on the grass.

Ethan had followed behind the Gardaí, despite Garda Williams telling him to stay put. He saw his associate and cried out in amazement. "Tiffany! I . . . I can't believe it."

"I told you to stay back," Garda Williams said. "Go! Sit in your car." He frowned. "Did you just get here? Where were you? I'll need a statement."

"The petrol station for smokes." Ethan stumbled backward. "We were going to have drinks."

"You had plans to have drinks with Tiffany tonight?" Garda Williams asked.

"Yes. At the bungalow." Ethan looked back over his shoulder. "I was going to meet her there, and we were going to talk about the wedding."

"Whose wedding?" Garda Lee asked, confused.

"Our guests, Tori Montgomery and Jake Anderson," Rayne explained. "Tomorrow at the church. Father Patrick is officiating."

"And where are they?" Garda Williams asked.

"In the tower," Rayne pointed to the five-story structure. "Josh—the best man—was on the first floor, then Amy–the maid of honor, then Jake and Tori—the bride and groom."

"We'll have to interview everyone." Garda Williams sank to his haunches next to Tiffany and examined her body. "Secure this immediate area."

"Okay," Rayne said, her teeth chattering. "Tori's parents are in the largest cottage. Ethan and Tiffany were to share the smaller cabin."

The Garda brought out his phone, making a note. His pale fingers had a dusting of blond hair.

"Williams," Garda Lee said, reading a notification on her tablet. "The coroner's here."

"Thanks. Mr. Cruz, move your car to the side. Come to the porch when you are done. Rayne, Ciara." Garda Williams stared up at Rayne. "I want you to gather everyone together. No talking about what happened, all right?"

Rayne raised her brow, not seeing how that would fly. "I'll try."

"Where?" Ciara asked. "The blue parlor?"

"That would be fine." After a searching gaze at Ciara, Garda Williams returned his attention to Tiffany.

The coroner pulled up in a white van, and Garda Lee greeted a man with thick gray hair in a trench coat and boots. His assistant balanced a large flashlight on a stretcher they'd use to collect Tiffany's body.

"Dr. Rhodes," the gray-haired man said by way of introduction, bobbing his head at Rayne and Ciara before asking Garda Williams, "What have we got?"

"You were fast, sir," Garda Williams said. "We haven't had a chance to examine the scene."

"I hadn't gone to bed yet," the coroner said. "I'm just ten minutes away. What happened?"

"Could Tiffany have jumped?" Ciara asked.

Jumped! Rather than fall . . . that sadly made more sense from the layout of the rooftop.

"No," Ethan declared. "No way. Tiffany would never jump. She was afraid of heights."

"We are investigating, sir," Garda Williams said to the upset man. He rose to his full height, knees creaking from his kneeling position.

Garda Lee brought out a roll of white crime scene tape rather than the yellow Rayne was used to in the states that read in blue lettering: Garda No Entry.

"Come on, Ethan," Rayne said. Jake's assistant listened about as well as Blarney. "Let's go inside."

"This isn't real. Can't be." Ethan craned his neck as Rayne hooked her arm through his and climbed the stairs. He smelled like whiskey and tobacco.

"It'll be all right now," Ciara said gently to Ethan. "We'll warm up over a cuppa."

Rayne opened the door and came nose-to-nose with Cormac in a hastily donned jacket and slacks, shoes loosely tied, as he straightened. Aine must've woken him.

"Beg pardon!" Cormac said. He stepped back and rubbed his nose. "Are you all right, milady?"

She'd been more surprised than hurt. "Yes, sorry."

"What's going on?" The butler patted his flyaway silvering hair and smoothed the bushy eyebrows over his brown eyes.

"There's a wee incident with one of our guests outside," Ciara said to Cormac. "Rayne, I'll take Ethan with me to the kitchen, if you want to wake the folks in the tower. We'll meet in the blue parlor as soon as you're done."

"Jake will be devastated," Ethan said. The assistant patted his jacket pocket as if to assure himself that the cigarettes were still there.

"Why devastated?" Cormac asked.

"Tiffany is dead," Ethan said loudly.

"What?" Cormac responded sharply.

Rayne left Ciara to handle the fallout of the tragic news and went to the interior tower door. It was locked, but she had a key and opened it.

Deciding to start at the top with Tori and Jake and work her way down to Amy, then Josh, Rayne couldn't shake her state of disbelief. How could this have happened? She knew for a fact that the stone wall on the roof was sturdy and not a safety hazard. Accidental fall? Impossible, which meant Ciara might be right, and it had been a deliberate choice.

Tiffany had seemed unhappy, yes, constantly working in her notebook for Amy, but she had Josh to tease her and Ethan's friendship as well. They'd had plans to meet over drinks at their shared cottage.

Up to the third floor, then the fourth, where Tori had requested the bridal bower. Rayne knocked on the door, then knocked louder. "Tori? Jake?"

She heard movement, then tousle-haired, bare-chested Jake Montgomery answered the door.

No wonder Tori wanted this man all to herself. His abs were as chiseled as his jaw, his features fine yet so masculine. She pulled her gaze to his face rather than the direction of his navel.

"What's up?" Jake blinked. "Everything all right?"

Not such an odd question considering his hostess was waking him up at, she checked her phone, quarter to one in the morning.

"Hi—listen, can you and Tori meet us downstairs?" Rayne did her best not to stammer as she tripped over plausible excuses. "There's a . . . there's . . . we just have some questions we need to go over."

"For the wedding?"

Dear God, the wedding. "It's important."

"What is it?" a high-pitched feminine voice asked. Tori, wrapped in a white silk robe and wearing her sleep mask on her forehead, entered the living area from the bed chamber.

Rayne had kept the medieval aesthetic but had the ultimate in luxury with carpets, tapestries, and lighting. The furniture, found in the attic, was original to the manor.

"Rayne has questions . . . about the wedding."

"That's ridiculous," Tori announced. "This time of night?" Her mouth pursed in anger.

"It does seem that way," Jake agreed as he woke up a bit more. "Bizarre. Are you sure?"

"It's a . . ." Rayne shrugged. She didn't have the golden gift of gab her cousin did to come up with quips on the fly. "All I can say is that it's very important."

Tori stared at her as did Jake.

"Please," Rayne said.

"I'll give you five minutes, then I'm going back to bed." Tori whirled, the silk robe flying behind her.

"Blue parlor." Rayne exhaled. Hopefully Aine and Ciara would make enough tea for everyone. "See you there."

Next was Amy's door. The woman was awake and dressed, manuscript pages in her hand. "Boo!"

Rayne's eyes widened. "Oh, hey."

"I heard you knock and figured it's got to be a summons for some strange Irish starlight ceremony. You realize we didn't have a bachelorette party, this wedding was so rushed?"

Rayne didn't answer. Of course, the ever-curious starlet would want to know what was happening. "Blue parlor. There will be tea."

Amy slammed the door in Rayne's face.

Yikes. Divas!

And last was Josh on the main floor of the tower. She knocked and knocked but there was no answer.

Amy joined Rayne on the landing as she swept down the stairs from the second floor. "He's probably passed out."

Tori and Jake came down the stairs. "It's a party in the stairwell." Tori sighed. "Should you call your brother and see if he's okay? He was drinking pretty hard."

"Maybe he's already in the parlor." Jake scowled but then seemed to remember himself and grinned at Rayne. "Is this a surprise bachelor–bachelorette party?"

"That's what I think!" Amy agreed.

Rayne hurried ahead. It was no party and there was no freaking way they could be married now. What would Tori do, since she was pregnant?

Rayne opened the door to the large chamber, painted accurately as well as decorated in blue, with a fireplace, a sofa, two love seats, and several armchairs. Easy seating for twelve or more. So far it was the Gardaí, Ethan, Ciara, and the Lloyds. No Josh.

"What is going on?" Tori's tone lifted with confusion. Not sure if there were cameras and she was supposed to be happy, because she certainly was *not*, or if she could let her temper fly for being woken up and dragged from bed the night before her wedding.

"Have a seat," Garda Lee said. She and Garda Williams stood before the empty fireplace.

"Who are you?" Tori asked in her heiress tone.

"I'm Garda Kaitlin Lee, and my partner is Garda Dominic Williams. Now, have a seat." Her serious expression got the message across. This was no time for fun and games or to play the diva card.

Tori and Jake sat on the edge of a couch with Ethan on the other side. Amy chose an armchair. Ciara, Aine, and Cormac squeezed in together on a love seat. Maeve poured tea into cups from a trolley.

"No Josh, and no Tiffany," Amy said in a snide voice. "We can guess what they're doing."

Ethan glared at Amy.

"Where are they?" Tori scanned the room. "Where's my parents? Should they be here too?"

"Your parents are at their cottage. They're fine," Garda Williams said.

Garda Lee folded her hands before her. Her weatherproof coat was open to reveal her vest with all the gadgets on it, from a baton to a flashlight. "When was the last time you saw Tiffany Quick?"

"At the billiards room," Tori said suspiciously. "Amy's right. She and Josh were behaving ridiculously. He was making her drinks extra strong to get her wasted so he could hook up with her, you know?" She leaned toward Jake. "If your brother is in trouble with the cops, that won't go over well with me or my parents."

"Josh is probably asleep!" Jake said. "I told him to sleep alone. Tiffany was off-limits."

They all looked at the Gardaí.

Garda Williams stared back at them, then gave Garda Lee a quick nod. "I regret to inform you that Tiffany Quick is dead," Garda Lee announced.

Even though Rayne already knew this, it hit her like a punch in the gut.

The chattering in the room fell silent.

Rayne watched Amy, Jake, Tori, and Ethan. It did seem odd that Josh wasn't there. Had Aine heard Josh and Jake, and not Jake arguing with a woman?

That didn't make sense, as the brothers had similar deep voices.

"How?" Tori asked.

"Did Tiffany suffer from depression?" Garda Williams swapped her question with his without an answer.

"She suffered from being overworked," Ethan told Amy in a snide tone.

"What are you talking about?" the starlet demanded.

Tori wrapped her silk robe around her body, kitten heels on her feet. "You gave her a lot to do—just kinda piled it on."

Amy appealed to Jake with large doe eyes and the mega hunk gave a mini shrug. "It seems that way, at least to us."

"For the record, I pay her very, very well." Amy turned to the Gardaí, stricken by the criticism. "What happened to her?"

"We are investigating her death. The coroner has taken her body to Kilkenny. We will need to notify her next of kin," Garda Lee said.

"Tiff told me she didn't have any family," Ethan said.

"I think you're right, Ethan. I can check her résumé when I get home." Amy shifted as if uncomfortable, her silk loungewear slippery on the leather armchair.

"Why did you ask if Tiffany was depressed?" Jake asked.

Neither Gardaí answered.

"Did she hurt herself?" Amy's lower lip quivered. "Well, Tiff was a spiteful woman. It's possible she overreacted to being fired when we return to LA."

Tori's jaw dropped. "You told her she was going to be fired, and yet you expected her to work through my wedding? That poor girl. I can't believe you!"

"That is over the line," Jake agreed. "You could have waited until Monday to let her go."

"Little you know," Amy said, fighting back. "Tiff did the bare minimum."

"Tiff was always working for you, writing notes in her notebook," Jake said.

"You have it all wrong." Amy scooped soft red hair over her ear. "That black Moleskine? That was her diary. Guess what, peeps. She wanted to write an exposé about this weekend and sell it to the highest bidder."

Rayne gasped and exchanged a glance with Ciara, whose mouth was agape.

"No!" Jake said. "She wouldn't."

Amy raised a hand. "Don't worry, Jakey. I told her it went against the contract she signed, and I'd sue her so fast her head would spin."

"When did you find this out?" Tori demanded.

"Yesterday on the plane from LA. I happened to read her little diary, thinking it was notes for me about the wedding vows." Amy huffed a breath. "Wrong."

"And you didn't mention it?" Tori turned her attention from Amy to Jake. "You should call Josh. Make sure he's okay. Wait—how did Tiffany die?"

"I was trying to be thoughtful," Amy said, tilting her nose. "*Bestie.*"

"They think Tiff jumped from the tower," Ethan interjected since the Gardaí weren't answering.

Jake stood in alarm. "Tiffany jumped from the tower? The same tower we are staying in right now?"

Tori glared at Rayne, her chin trembling.

It wasn't Rayne's fault, but this could be the end of the wedding venue.

Just then, Josh was escorted in by one of the other Gardas. His body was loose, relaxed. He smelled like weed and beer. "Hey. What's with the cops everywhere? I'm out past curfew?" He laughed at his own joke but no one else did.

"Where have you been, Josh?" Tori demanded. "I told you I wanted a lowkey night."

"I'm not marrying you," Josh stated. "I was at the pub playing darts with my new friends. Bran gave me a lift on his moped when Ethan here texted that there was a five-alarm fire at the castle." Josh raised his phone to Ethan. "Thanks. Didn't think you were serious."

"Tiffany is dead," Jake said coldly.

Josh straightened, or tried to, but it took him three times.

"You, as they say in Ireland, are acting the maggot," Ethan drawled.

Chapter Four

"You're Irish?" Garda Lee asked Ethan with interest.

"No—grew up near London and had an Irish roomie at uni. Never at a loss for colorful sayings." Ethan's mouth pursed. He wasn't taking Tiffany's death lightly, as Josh seemed to be, but in the man's defense, he was blitzed and would have a sore head tomorrow.

"We do have some right fair sayings," Garda Williams agreed. "So, are you and Josh here mates?"

"Not so much," Ethan said. "I'm Jake Anderson's assistant. Josh and I spend a lot of time together by default."

Josh winced. "Ouch. I might have said we were friends." He shook his head. "So. Tiff's dead. Jumped from the tower? Amy planned to fire her when we all got back home."

"How did you know that?" Amy demanded. "You just got here."

"Tiff told us over pints the other night." Josh gawked toward his almost sister-in-law. "Tori's got to be pissed because now her wedding is ruined."

"You missed the part about Tiffany writing an exposé," Jake said. "Or did you know that too?"

"Bro! Chill out!" Josh clasped his hands to his heart.

48

"She's got that Moleskine notebook, all the time," Tori said with a shiver. "I thought she was working for you, Amy. I had no idea. I let down my guard around her."

"It's not about you right now, Tori," Amy said. "My employee is dead."

Tori glared at Amy and tucked her hand through the crook in Jake's arm. He'd tossed a loose tee over his sculpted chest and had slippers on his feet.

"We'll look for a notebook in her possessions," Garda Lee said. "She didn't have that on her person, or her mobile. Do any of you know where those things might be?"

Amy looked speculative but didn't reply. Josh jutted his chin at Ethan. "Maybe it's at your cottage?"

"Possible. She's got her laptop and luggage in her room." Ethan patted his jacket pocket. "I ran out to get smokes. We were going to chat. I could have listened to her . . ." His voice grew thick with emotion. "Talked her out of any rash decision."

"I'll need everyone's timelines," Garda Williams said. "Ethan, when did you see Tiffany last?"

"The party in the billiards room broke up around ten-thirty. Tiff and I made arrangements to meet up and have a drink at the bungalow as soon as Amy excused her for the night."

Garda Williams glanced at Amy. "That's late, eh?"

"She was paid a very good salary," Amy said, hefting her chin.

"Were you giving her a nice severance too?" Tori asked. The temperature in the room might have frozen, her demeanor was so cold.

Amy batted her eyes, the mink lashes like butterflies. "It was up for discussion depending on how well she did over the weekend."

"Did what exactly?" Garda Lee asked.

"Tiffany manages my social media accounts as well as coordinating with my talent agent." Amy curled her legs beneath her as if just chatting with her friends.

"How long did she work for you?" Garda Williams asked.

Amy scrunched her nose. "Tiffany's been with me for about a year and her contract was almost up. I hadn't planned on renewing her services, even before the exposé I found. She was just using me for my connections in the biz."

"What are you talking about?" Tori asked incredulously.

"She wanted to be a movie star." Amy shrugged.

"So, you think she jumped because she was gonna get fired?" Josh asked in disbelief. "From what I saw of Amy's treatment of her, she was probably glad to take the severance pay and start over fresh."

"Shut up, Josh." Amy shook her finger at him. "As usual, you've no idea what you're talking about."

"Don't I?" Josh smirked. "Tiffany wasn't allowed to wear makeup because then she'd be prettier than you. She wasn't allowed to flirt, either. You were jealous plain and simple."

Amy stood in anger.

"Sit down," Garda Lee ordered in a curt tone.

Amy was going to argue but thought better of it. She slowly perched on the edge of the seat. "I was not jealous. Tiffany didn't have that star quality. Jake has it, Tori has it, I have it. You, Josh, don't." She turned to Ethan. "You don't either."

"Not anything I care about, Amy, so put your claws away." Ethan smoothed his goatee.

"You don't want to be in the spotlight, Ethan?" Tori asked. Rayne wondered if the heiress was mollified at being included in the starlet's list.

"No. I have my business and marketing degree. I started off as a model in LA but quickly realized that I don't like the camera. My choice." Ethan shrugged. "I had offers."

"Sure, you did," Amy said. "It hardly matters now. You're what, forty?"

At that, Ethan's face turned red.

"I'll go back to the cottage with you to collect Tiffany's things," Garda Lee said, stepping between Amy and Ethan. "When we wrap up here." She shifted to Garda Williams.

"This was supposed to be a quiet getaway for the weekend so that we could elope," Tori said softly. "Share our vows among family."

"Wedding is tomorrow?" Garda Williams asked.

"Yes." Tori dabbed a knuckle beneath her damp lashes.

"You can't go through with it," Josh said in disbelief.

"You can't," Ethan seconded.

Rayne, spellbound, wondered what would happen.

"Tiffany Quick wasn't *my* assistant," Tori said coolly. "I am here to marry Jake. Our schedules are so busy that it is now or never, and I refuse for it to be never. Right, Jake?"

Jake buried his head in his hands, pulling at his hair. He raised his face, angst clear to read. "Damn, Tori, I'm not sure it's a good idea. The public might tear my reputation apart like wolves over a bone."

Amy half stood, then sat back after a glance at the Garda. "I don't know, Tori. What if someone finds out? It's tacky."

"Let me repeat—this is a *secret* weekend getaway. My parents are very wealthy. I barely know Tiffany, and if she planned on doing an exposé, then I really don't want to give her the power of ruining my wedding. It's not fair." Tori rested her hand, the one with the huge diamond engagement ring, on Jake's upper thigh.

Rayne thought that sounded reasonable.

Ethan exhaled loudly.

Josh snapped his jaw closed. "Bro. You can't be serious?"

Jake didn't answer but kept his focus on the floor.

"Your brother loves me," Tori said. "You are not part of our decision-making process, Josh, so don't think you can sway him."

Jake's heartfelt sigh showed his torn emotions, drawing Rayne in.

"I've seen you in the movies," Garda Lee said shyly to Jake. "I love them all."

"Thank you, darlin'," Jake drawled. "I'd be happy to catch up with you later about it, if you'd like an autograph."

"Now isn't the right time," Garda Williams chided his partner.

Garda Lee blushed. "Sorry."

Tori scoffed at the officer. "Ridiculous."

"Now what?" Ciara asked.

Rayne's question was more specific. "Can our guests go back to their rooms in the tower?"

"No. Not tonight," Garda Williams said. "I want to see things in the morning light."

Just then the officer who'd brought Josh in earlier entered with Joan and Dylan at his heels. "I'm sorry, but they were very determined. Saw the coroner's van and demanded to know . . ."

"Sweetheart!" Joan pushed through everyone to gather Tori in her arms. "Are you all right? I've never been so worried in my life. I knew this place was too rustic. Too quaint."

"Mom!" Tori chided. "We are all fine. Can I stay with you and Daddy? The tower is off limits until tomorrow."

"Maybe the next day too," Garda Lee interjected.

The Montgomerys turned on the Garda. "What happened?" Dylan asked.

"We will work as fast as possible." Garda Williams didn't answer the question despite the evident concern in Dylan's voice. "We'll be back in the morning with further questions." He scanned his notes. "To clarify, did any of you see Tiffany after ten-thirty?"

"No," Josh said, and affirmations circled the group.

"I need to get my clothes," Amy said. She turned to Ethan and Josh. "Can I bunk at your cottage?"

Jake looked from Tori to Tori's parents who didn't offer for him to sleep over, so he stepped next to Amy. "Me too."

"Fine," Ethan said. His shoulders drooped. "What a bleedin' disaster."

"I'll go with you all to collect clothes," Garda Lee said.

Josh, Amy, and Jake joined her while Tori looked at Rayne. "The wedding dress is done?"

"A final fitting in the morning." Rayne knew her client had to be upset over what to do, though she didn't show it.

"Perfect." Tori hiked her chin and followed Garda Lee.

Jake was staring hard at Amy—was that blame in his gaze?

"I didn't do anything wrong, Jakey," Amy said. "If Tiffany was weak, that's on her. Get therapy and drugs like everyone else—me included."

"You do drugs?" Garda Williams asked, overhearing the conversation.

"Back off, Officer. Prescription for anxiety." Amy filed past him to hurry after Tori so she could get a change of clothes.

"You better go, too," Garda Williams suggested to Josh. "We don't know how long it will be before you can get inside your room."

"Fine. But I sure wish I'd stayed at the pub. Met a cool guy, Bran Wilson, in addition to Beetle, the raddest bartender ever. And Richard, he's hysterical. Said he works here at the castle?"

"He runs the mill," Rayne confirmed.

"Bran's done some contract plumbing on the property," Ciara told Josh. "Richard is a standup guy too."

Josh patted the spikes on his fauxhawk. "I'm not looking for new best friends. Got my brother, and I thought Ethan," he addressed his brother's assistant, "but you're a cold dude."

"Knock it off," Ethan said. "Any chance we can talk your brother out of a colossal mistake tomorrow? It's in poor taste to go through with the wedding. His box office appeal is as a sexy young man available to every woman. Married dings the fantasy."

Josh raised his hands. "Tori's driving that train."

Rayne knew why. Oh well. How could someone as organized and seemingly put together as Tiffany decide to end things so permanently?

Not to mention, Amy firing Tiffany on Monday and yet expecting the woman to work through the weekend despite it. Perhaps not the whole point, but how much would an exposé on a secret wedding (and secret baby) bring?

Joan gave a delicate cough, reminding them that she was in the room. "Tori wants the wedding to continue—and we want our daughter to be happy. Jake will be very, very wealthy and that will take the sting away from any box office issues, I'm sure, Ethan."

Dylan rocked back on his heels. "We can talk about this over breakfast, but I don't think our girl will change her mind."

"Josh!" Amy called from the doorway. "Hurry up or wear those same jeans for days. The police are waiting."

"Coming," Josh said.

"I'm going out front to smoke," Ethan said, pulling the pack from his pocket at last. Cormac exited and Maeve finished her tea, hanging at the edges of the gathering to observe in the event she was needed. She'd confessed to a healthy curiosity when she'd first met Rayne.

Rayne stood next to Ciara, Aine, and Garda Williams. She remembered Tiffany's manicure. She stepped closer to the officer. "Do you have a moment?"

"What is it?"

"Tiffany's nails had a perfect manicure at dinner—and they were broken tonight." Rayne imagined the assistant overwhelmed by Amy and possibly ashamed over being caught for the exposé and deciding to end it, but then changing her mind at the last minute, gripping the stone for all of her worth.

Garda Williams said, "I'll make a note about her nails."

"Before the billiards game," Ciara mused. "I noticed them as well."

"Where did they play billiards?" Garda Williams asked. "I was under the impression that you'd stayed in tonight."

"Here. We'd planned on a bonfire, but it was too wet because of the rain. Tori wanted a quiet evening, and they didn't have bachelor or bachelorette plans," Rayne explained. "Everyone was hanging around in the billiards room."

"I wasn't aware you had one," Garda Williams said, glancing at Ciara.

"It's new," Ciara admitted. "Rayne and I found it when we were rummaging through the attic."

"They left quite a mess," Aine said. "Dirty glasses and dishes. Cues on the table."

Garda Williams held up a hand with interest. "I'll need for you to leave everything as it is."

To Rayne, that sounded like an investigation rather than acceptance of the jumping from depression theory. Of course, her mother's show, *Family Forever*, came to mind. What would Susan Carter do? "Was there a suicide note?"

Garda Williams touched the brim of his cap. "We will let you know what we can."

Rayne remembered from Uncle Nevin's demise how little communication that meant from the police.

"We've heard that before," Ciara griped.

"It's important for our business to know what happened to Tiffany." Rayne kept her tone even and reasonable.

"We helped you last time," her cousin said.

Garda Williams tightened his jaw, not pleased by the reminder. "Don't clean the billiards room or the tower rooms, including the roof. I've cordoned off the outer staircase with caution tape as well as the lawn outside. I'll do my best to be here by eight. When is the wedding ceremony?"

"Four-thirty," Rayne told him.

"All right." Williams shrugged. "I'll try to get answers as soon as possible."

"Thank you," Rayne said. Dominic Williams had to be aware of the pressure Rayne and Ciara were under to save the village. Rayne hadn't been invited to call him Dominic. Ciara, having had a relationship with him, sometimes did.

"Just find out what happened to Tiffany and clear the tower so we can get our guests back in," Ciara said in a crisp tone.

Aine's brows rose in surprise. It had been a while since they'd heard this snippy version of Ciara. Sometimes a person behaved defensively to hide their true feelings. It wasn't the first time Rayne had wondered if there were residual emotions between them.

Joan and Dylan Montgomery were whispering together as they scanned the blue parlor. "This chamber is magnificent," Joan said.

55

"Thank you." Rayne and Ciara spoke in unison.

"I am so sorry about Tiffany," Rayne said.

"Tori didn't know this Tiffany person—we'd all just met her," Joan said. "It's sad, yes, but not enough to stop our daughter's wedding to the man of her dreams."

Ciara made a sympathetic humming noise. Rayne feared the Montgomerys would refuse to pay the venue fee if the wedding was canceled. It would be a financial disaster for McGrath Castle.

Goodbye Hermes bag.

"However we can be of help," Rayne said, outwardly calm, inwardly screaming.

"It's been a nightmare to reschedule everything," Joan confessed. "From the Christmas venue of four hundred guests, to now. And to keep it under wraps too? You've both been champs about it."

"We are certainly doing our best," Ciara said. "Are you concerned about tomorrow?"

Joan waved her hand. "One doesn't reach this level of success without learning a few tricks to keep the paparazzi away."

"Tori texted us while you all were being questioned that Tiffany planned to write a tell-all." Dylan snorted with disapproval. "Not the kind of woman you can trust."

"Amy should have known better than to hire someone so, well, unworthy. I don't know what our Tori sees in the vamp, but they've been friends since they met on a yacht party in France." Joan sighed and shook her head. "Opposites attract, maybe?"

Joan and Dylan exchanged a glance.

"Amy can be amusing," Dylan conceded. "Makes Tori laugh and not be so serious all of the time."

Cormac returned and announced that Tori, Amy, Jake, Josh, and Garda Lee were waiting for the others in the foyer.

"That's my cue," Garda Williams said. "Mr. and Mrs. Montgomery? I'll walk with you to the cottage if you don't mind. I have a few questions."

It was now after one in the morning.

"Will there be breakfast in the dining room?" Dylan asked.

Maeve nodded. "A buffet, again. Also, at nine—considering the late hour. Sleep well."

Joan and Dylan followed Garda Williams from the blue parlor, leaving Aine, Maeve, Ciara, and Rayne.

"I'm shocked over what happened tonight." Maeve's green eyes shimmered

"Mam, did you hear anything out of the ordinary?" Aine asked. The Lloyds had a suite on the first floor; the billiards room was also on the first floor, but at the opposite end of the manor.

"No. I was out like a light—it's a lot to feed an additional eight folks. Good though!" Maeve said before Rayne or Ciara could ask.

"You'll tell us if it's too much?" Rayne pressed.

"I will but it isn't, so don't worry about it, all right? Gillian is a huge help and can work indoors or out. Sorcha prefers inside duties. But, that is all to say, I didn't hear a thing—not even when Cormac woke up when he heard Aine in the kitchen. He is a light sleeper, bless him."

Aine nodded. "I don't know how I'm going to sleep tonight. I'm too jazzed up."

"Did you see Tiffany yourself, dear?" Maeve asked her daughter. She murmured a little prayer. "How awful."

"It was. Blarney alerted us to, er, the problem." Aine shook her head. "It's a tragedy to be sure."

"Life is precious," Maeve said. "Did you get to know her?"

"A little." Aine hugged her mother. "When I'm in uniform, I try not to be seen unless the person wants to chat, then I can be open though usually, it's a quiet chore. Change the linens and towels. Empty the trash. But Tiffany seemed lonely."

"Let me guess," Rayne said, "Tori doesn't chat?"

"Nor Amy either." Aine smirked.

"I've trained you well." Maeve smoothed her hand over Aine's hair.

"Hate to break up the party, but we should go to bed," Ciara said. "It will be dawn soon and the animals need feeding, no matter what else happens."

"Maybe Dafydd can do it for you?" Maeve placed her teacup on the trolley. "And Amos will pitch in. You should sleep, *a mhuirnin.*"

Normally Rayne would vote for sleeping in as well, but she had a gown to finish, and if the Gardaí would be tramping all over the property, she had to be prepared to be available when they arrived, which meant early.

"I've got my alarm set for six-thirty," Rayne confessed. "How present do I need to be for tomorrow's activities?"

"Uh, all of it, Rayne!" Ciara said, gray eyes touched with panic. "The Garda here at eight. Breakfast buffet, champagne brunch at the Coco Bean Café. Back here to prep for the wedding at four-thirty. Gillian promised the horses and carriage will be ready at four."

"Drinks and then the medieval feast; the Irish band at the gazebo afterward. Bonfire." Maeve collected the empty cups and placed them on the trolley.

"For those guests who have free time, Amos and Dafydd have offered to take them horseback riding again," Aine reminded them.

"Perfect. We gotta keep them happy," Rayne said. "No pressure." She turned to her cousin. "It was nice of Bran to give Josh a ride from the pub." She'd met Bran Wilson a few times. He was in his thirties with brown hair and glasses.

Ciara snorted. "We've hired him to do some plumbing, paid in cash, so you'd think he'd be appreciative of our business venture, but he's been snide about it to some of the other shops in the village."

Rayne's shoulders slumped. Would their efforts ever be enough?

"I'm knackered." Maeve grabbed the handle on the tea cart. "I'll just give these a wash and hit the hay."

"I'll help, Mam. Let's go. I'm happy to leave the dishes in the billiards room for now. What do you think the Gardaí are looking for?" Aine strode toward the door.

"Tiffany's phone and Moleskine," Rayne said. "Maybe a note? It will be easier to see in the light of day."

Rayne's phone dinged a text from Tori, saying that the Gardaí had just left her parents' cottage.

She texted to ask if the items had been found.

Tori answered right away. No.

"The Gardaí are gone, and no, they didn't find Tiffany's phone or the notebook." Rayne sighed. "I wonder . . ."

"What?" Ciara asked.

"Well, if they might be up on the turret, where Tiffany jumped from."

"You don't think she fell?" Aine asked.

"There's no way to accidentally fall over," Rayne said.

"That's what I was thinking too," Ciara said. "She must have jumped."

Maeve sucked in a breath. "It's awful. A fire, a death . . . what if the tower is cursed?"

"Mam!" Aine said. "This is the twenty-first century. The chimney fire was caused by a blocked flue, and Tiffany had been caught doing a bad thing, with the exposé, and fired. Maybe she decided she couldn't live with it."

"Things are always better in the morning," Maeve said in a sage tone.

"Good thing, because it will be here in a few hours," Ciara quipped.

"I don't believe in curses," Rayne declared. "Now, a ghost or two maybe, but why would one of our own ancestors be against us saving the manor?"

"You're right," Maeve conceded. "I've been listening to Gillian too much. The woman is a hard worker, but she's got a very dour disposition."

"That she does," Aine agreed. "I've noticed that she and Frances get along very well though. Two peas in a briny pod."

Maybe it was the gray weather that had them so down. They were natives though, so probably didn't even notice. Rayne missed her California blues skies.

Rayne sighed and looked around, realizing that Blarney wasn't with them. "On that note, I'm going to find my dog and my bed."

"Blarney was a hero," Aine said. "Howling to let us know something was wrong."

"He was, wasn't he?" Rayne blessed the day Blarney had come into her life.

The women broke off in different directions with a last goodnight called. Rayne whistled for Blarney and when he didn't come, she went out the front door to the porch.

Cormac was striding toward the steps with a flashlight, Blarney at his side. The scent of rain remained in the air, though it had stopped pouring.

She waited for them to reach the top stairs, the white caution tape to her right. "There you guys are!"

Cormac dipped his head at her, and they went inside to the foyer.

"How'd it go with the Gardaí and our guests?" Rayne asked.

"Fine, fine. The Montgomery family was happy to share space with their daughter, but I think it's been some time, perhaps never, that Tori Montgomery slept on a foldout couch," Cormac murmured. "Posh hotel money."

Rayne winced. "Too rustic? Why didn't she sleep in the other bedroom?"

"Joan's got it made up for a dressing room, with makeup and clothes everywhere. The lads and Amy were fine. The Gardaí didn't find Tiffany's phone or her notebook, but they took her laptop, luggage, and handbag."

Rayne nodded. "I can't believe Tiffany was alone in the world."

"Garda Williams will get to the bottom of what happened. We should get to bed," Cormac advised.

"You're right." Rayne checked the phone. "One-thirty already? I'll be up soon." Six-thirty loomed. "Thank you, Cormac, for everything. It feels so overwhelming right now."

"It will pass," the kindly man said. "We will succeed. You were smart to think of offering the manor for a wedding venue. I was right surprised at the amount of money folks are willing to pay, but you've got them here. And another in November."

"Now to keep them," Rayne said. "If the Montgomerys don't give us a good review, we could be back at the starting line."

"It's all right, milady." Cormac squeezed her shoulder. "Don't smack your shin on a stool that isn't in your way."

"What?" Rayne shook her head in confusion.

"Don't borrow trouble." The butler winked. "I'll see you in the morning."

"Night, Cormac."

She and Blarney went up the main staircase and walked to the left. She listened for spooky sounds but there was nothing out of place.

The tower couldn't be cursed, and she appreciated Aine's coming to the manor's defense. The truth was that Gillian Clark didn't care for Rayne. She was stubborn and prickly, and if Rayne wanted something done from the new hire, she had Maeve ask.

Gillian had incredible strength. She'd taken over the job of mowing the castle grounds with the smaller tractor mower. Amos had suggested her employment, and Rayne hadn't questioned it.

He'd been behind Frances's hire as well. Maybe Amos had a thing for crabby women?

What did that say about herself? Rayne smiled. She and Amos had flirted but no more. Landon had rocked her world with his duplicity, and she wasn't sure she could trust her own judgment. She hated that.

Rayne reached her bedroom and she and Blarney went inside. She got ready for bed in an instant. Her last thoughts as she drifted off, her gaze on the pink Hermes bag, were that she could maybe get them through the end of the year if she sold it.

She didn't want to sell it. It was no surprise that she dreamed of pink bubble gum.

Chapter Five

Rayne's alarm went off at six-thirty, and, with a groan, she rolled out of bed. Blarney, bright-eyed, wagged his tail ready for the day.

"Must you be so cheerful, boy?" Rayne groused.

Blarney sat on his haunches and lolled his tongue as if to say, yes, he really did.

She jumped into the shower and after a dose of cool water to rinse, she was wide awake if not chipper.

Rayne thought of wearing yoga pants to slip to her sewing studio, but with her luck, she wouldn't have time to change before nine o'clock breakfast, and she didn't want to make that mistake again.

She jammed her legs into black skinny pants with pockets, UGGs, and a hip-length sweater with big black and white squares that she'd bought at the only clothing shop in town that carried a mix of used and new. This gem was hand-knit by a parishioner at church, and she loved it.

After towel-drying her long dark hair, she twisted it in a special clip that would not only keep it out of the way but create waves when she removed it. Black-and-white square earrings, black braided bangles, and she was good to go even if she didn't get a chance to change before brunch at the Coco Bean Café.

Rayne left her room and went downstairs, entering the kitchen where Frances stood at the stove. Ciara sat at the kitchen table, as did the Lloyds. She let Blarney out the side door in the kitchen, near the cellar and Frances' very cozy room. Cozy in this instance meant shoebox-small.

"Morning," Rayne said.

"It is," Ciara stated.

Without a word, Frances gave Rayne her coffee just how she liked it—with cream and sugar.

"I need an extra caffeine boost," Aine said. "I've had tea, and now I'm having coffee."

"Let me know if that works," Rayne said with a laugh. "Doubling down like that."

Cormac and Maeve drank a dark Irish breakfast tea, as did Ciara, who added honey. Black seemed to be the color of the day, as that's what they were all wearing in some fashion, right down to Ciara's stylish black denim jacket over a mock turtleneck.

Rayne reached for an apple. "This should get me through until breakfast."

"What will you be doing?" Cormac asked.

"Working on the bride's wedding dress," Aine said.

Frances clucked her tongue to her teeth and stirred what smelled like a savory sausage hash. The chef had worked in Cotter Village but had lost her husband in a traffic accident months ago and needed a change. "This will be done in an instant and a wee bit heartier than an apple."

Rayne had accepted the fact that castle life, with the outdoor activities as well as the steps she logged just by walking inside the manor, required more calories than what she'd consumed in LA.

"It smells wonderful, but I'm on a time crunch. Thank you, though, Frances." Rayne bit into the juicy apple, which had been grown on the property. "The guests have loved the meals."

"It's not a bother," Frances said. "Will we be having the medieval feast as planned? Cormac mentioned the lass's death last night. I use earplugs to sleep, so I didn't hear a thing."

Rayne dabbed her lips with a napkin. "I haven't heard differently. The Montgomerys seemed certain that the show will go on."

"Unbelievable," Maeve said with disapproval. "I hope that today clearer-headed decisions will be made. How can one start a life on the wrong foot?"

"Should you worry about the dress, Rayne?" Ciara asked.

Would the bride continue, or not? Rayne might save herself some work by waiting. Then again, she knew what the others didn't: Tori was pregnant, and Catholic, and needed a husband.

"I'll get it finished, just in case."

Ciara sipped her tea with a head shake. "Suit yourself. I'm not rushing this morning—Dafydd is taking care of the animals with Amos's assistance."

"I've already fed the men," Frances said. She tossed a look at Rayne. Her hair was shorter than Ciara's, and dark brown, like her eyes. "There's plenty."

Before she changed her mind and stayed in the warm kitchen, Rayne topped off her coffee and rinsed her hands in the kitchen sink.

"I'll see you guys at nine for breakfast, oh, unless Garda Williams needs me earlier," Rayne said. "I hope he has answers."

"Don't hold your breath," Ciara warned. "He's slow."

"I like Garda Lee," Aine said. "She's pretty."

"An important aspect for being a Garda," Cormac teased his only child.

Aine blushed and looked at Rayne. "Do you need help?"

"Not this morning but I'll let you know." Rayne was impressed with the quality of work Aine showed, which was why she was happy to mentor her in the seamstress biz.

"There are rooms to tidy, pet," Maeve told her daughter.

Rayne stepped around Cormac, seated at the table. "But not the billiards room or tower suites until we get the go ahead from the Gardai."

"That's right." Maeve rose and gathered plates from the cupboard. "Let's have a leisurely breakfast then."

"I say we enjoy this interlude, because it's going to be a full day—wedding or no. Medieval feast or no. Cleaning or no." Ciara shook her head.

"I can always use help with peeling veg," Frances said. She gave them all a wicked grin before she turned back to the stove.

"Shouldn't have spoken up, a *leanbh*," Cormac kidded.

Aine sighed as she brought salt and pepper from the pantry to the table. "I don't mind helping, Frances."

"You're a good lass." Frances placed the cast iron skillet of goodness on a trivet in the center. Rayne's mouth watered but if she stayed for even a bite, she would lose all her willpower and delay the work on Tori's dress—and $32,500 for the castle coffers was a hefty incentive.

Mug in hand, Rayne carefully went upstairs and turned to the right, past the suit of armor that her cousin Padraig had scared her to tears with by making her believe it was possessed by an angry spirit, and the paintings on the walls. Halfway down the hall, she detected the fragrant dried lavender and roses from bouquets she'd made for the studio.

Rayne loved fashion, design, and beauty. The creating of beautiful things made her happy. If it brought joy, then it was a skill worth honing, to her mind. Her parents had both agreed and encouraged her imagination. Her mother was an actress, her father, a poet who dabbled in paints. When she'd showed a talent for art, they'd gotten her private lessons. Her sketches were a part of her process for making gowns and her sketchbook was never far from hand.

Dafydd, Amos, Richard, and Cormac had taken her sketch for the gazebo by the lake and made it a reality. The covered space provided shelter from the rain, built-in seating, and a hardwood floor for dancing. Manifesting 101 through pencil and now they had barn kittens and swans. Ducks. Geese. Sheep. So many sheep. Opening the private home to the public would bring in revenue and get the castle out of the red. Step one in the long-term plan to protect the village.

The couple coming in November planned on getting married in the sixteen-by-sixteen gazebo and would stay in the bungalow the

Montgomerys were in right now. Their wedding party consisted of a best friend each, who'd sleep in the smaller cottage. They'd hired a local photographer from Kilkenny for professional photos and had already promised that Rayne could put them on the castle website.

She'd agreed to no social media for Tori and Jake's wedding, not seeing any other choice to receive the windfall of money, but Tori had promised that afterward they could share as much as they wanted.

Almost to the door.

"Rayne? Wait up!"

Rayne turned, a drop of hot coffee spilling on her thumb, and exuded neutrality as Tori hustled toward her.

The heiress was a wreck. Shadows under her eyes, no makeup, heck, not even a comb for her tangled blond hair.

"Tori?" Her watch said it was only half past seven.

"I've been calling and calling," Tori said.

Ah, that's what Rayne had been missing. Her cell phone.

"Sorry." She'd need to run to her room—down the hall but on the opposite side of the castle—hence the reason that Rayne was able to log in 10,000 steps a day, no problem.

Tori reached her and clasped cold fingers around Rayne's wrist. "I think there might be a problem."

There were many problems, and the death of Tiffany Quick wasn't even the beginning. "Can you give me a hint?" Rayne gestured toward the door to her studio.

"Yeah."

"We can talk inside—it's private."

"Good idea." Tori glanced over her shoulder as if she was frightened. "Hurry! I am dodging Amy."

"Oh!" Rayne pulled a ring of keys from her pocket. Front door, tower doors, studio. Car. Office. Her room. This one was pink, in Aunt Amalie's memory.

Rayne slipped the key into the studio door, to find that it was already unlocked. "Huh?"

"What is it?" Tori asked.

"Well, as you can see, I lock the door." She'd done it last night when they'd left, right? She'd been called away because of the argument Aine had overheard with Jake and another woman.

"And now it is not locked? My dress!" Tori hurried in before Rayne, spilling coffee onto Rayne's hand.

"Ouch!"

"Sorry." Tori didn't sound sorry. "Where is my gown?"

"Hang on a sec." Rayne placed her mug on a coaster at her work desk and blew on the red mark spreading over her skin.

Tori hovered next to the gown Rayne had draped on a dress form yesterday.

"Hmm." Tori peered closely at the brackets Rayne had sewn so delicately by hand. "This is lovely. But, it's obvious it needed to be bigger. I'm so fat!" She started to cry.

"You are not even a little bit, listen to me on that," Rayne said. This might be pregnancy hormones talking. "Nobody will know about the alteration, I promise."

"Well, I'm not so sure." Tori crossed her arms. "The door not being locked doesn't bolster my faith in you at all."

"What do you mean?" Rayne blew on the burn. Lack of sleep, a surge of hormones—what else could go wrong?

"Can you tell if somebody has been in this room who shouldn't have been?" Tori sounded panicked.

Rayne exhaled slowly, calmly, and thought about last night.

Ciara had come in with Aine to tell her that Aine had overheard an argument. Rayne had hung up the gown, her eyes admittedly tired. Perhaps she'd forgotten to lock the door to the studio, but nobody had a reason to snoop in here.

If this was a problem with future brides, then Rayne would consider adding more security to the door lock, like a thumbprint or keypad.

"Aine and Maeve. Ciara. Me. Can you be more specific with your concerns?"

"I wish I didn't have to." Tori's lower lip trembled, and she wrapped an arm around her thin waist.

"Well, I would appreciate it." Rayne cautiously sipped her coffee to keep from making a biting remark.

Tori spread her arms to the side, her face pale. "Amy texted this morning that Tiffany had asked her about my wedding dress, and if it needed to be altered. If there was a *reason* for a rushed wedding."

Rayne stilled and studied her client. "You've mentioned that Amy is . . ."

"She's damn nosy," Tori said. "What if . . . she found out . . . Tiffany, or Amy, they can't know what's going on right now."

Rayne raised her gaze to Tori, who was riding the edge of another breakdown.

"There is nothing to find out. Because you had a dress altered doesn't mean that you're . . . pregnant." Rayne whispered the last word.

"What if her suspicions are written down in that stupid notebook?" Tori asked. "Where is it? I'd love to get my hands on that." She gasped. "What if Amy stole it from Tiffany, and that's why it's missing?"

Rayne shook her head even as she wondered if it was possible.

"What if they argued so much that Amy took it from Tiffany and Tiffany, well, she just decided to . . . jump." Tori cried softly.

"As revenge? That doesn't make sense." Rayne circled the dress form. She'd created a shrug out of soft white ostrich feathers that matched the feathered hem of the gown. The ensemble would be stunning and rival the big names in bridal fashion. "Tori, hon, you've got to calm down. It's not good for you to be so upset."

Had it been moved at all? The zipper.

Her stomach clenched tight.

The zipper was up, when Rayne had left it down. She hadn't bothered to zip it up because her stiches were loose in the event she needed more room somehow. She hadn't wanted to pull them and risk damaging the silk.

"What is it?" Tori was so close that her expensive perfume overpowered the pleasant scents of lavender and rose.

"Maybe," Rayne conceded. "The zipper might have moved, but I'm not a hundred percent on that." Though she was, it wouldn't help her emotional bride.

Tori covered her face with her hands. "This could be terrible."

Rayne left the dress form and returned to the threshold of the studio, surveying her space. Her scissors had been knocked from the worktable. She would never leave them on the floor—they were expensive.

Not handbag expensive but still . . .

Someone had been in her studio.

*　*　*

"Before we jump to conclusions, let me ask Aine and Maeve if they've been in to clean or straighten this morning," Rayne said.

Tori nodded. "Is the dress . . . ruined somehow?"

"Of course not, but let's try it on to be sure." With a last look for anything obviously out of place, Rayne went to Tori's side.

"I can't believe this." Tori's cheeks were flushed.

Though they should be talking about Tiffany and her death, Rayne knew Tori meant the dress. "It's not a big deal to have last-minute alterations," Rayne said again. "A lot of times women will change their heels not realizing that it affects the hem." Though the ostrich feathers allowed a more fluid hemline in this dress, the point was valid.

Tori blinked. "Really?"

"Really." Rayne removed the gown from the dress form as Tori stripped to her thong.

Because it was such a tight fit, it wasn't intended to slip down over the shoulders but up the calves and hips. Rayne and Tori both breathed a sigh of relief when she was able to get the zipper closed all the way.

"Amy can kiss my ass," Tori declared. "With her vague hints. She'd be the last person I'd tell a secret to."

Rayne feared she was missing something about the dress. The zipper. But everything seemed to fit just right. The tiny-diamond-bright crystals winked becomingly. The Swarovski crystals had been in various sizes of hearts.

"You look lovely, Tori. The dress is perfect, and you are perfection in it. Jake will be tongue-tied when he sees you."

Rayne smoothed her hand down the sides and swallowed a gasp that she hoped Tori didn't hear.

It was miniscule but one of the heart-shaped crystals was missing. It couldn't be! She trusted her stitches. Oh so casually, she scrutinized the floor around the gown but didn't see it anywhere.

Had whoever broken in to her studio taken one? For what purpose?

Rayne must have a crystal close enough to this one that Tori wouldn't notice it missing. The rest of the bulk crystals had been taken in the Modern Lace dress heist.

For herself, she was in sheer panic mode. She checked her watch. Eight in the morning. First order of business—get rid of Tori so that Rayne could search the floor at eye level for the crystal. Second, if she couldn't find it, it sure seemed like sabotage. She'd need to ask Nolan Rourke, manager of Oasis Fabric Store in Dublin, to help her out.

He'd ensured she had fabrics to create the wedding dresses and given them a great deal on a machine for Aine to learn on.

Would he even remember her from June? What time did his shop open? Oh God—she was going to pass out.

"So, what next?" Tori had calmed down as she swirled the gorgeous skirt without a clue.

"I'll steam it and finish the stitching on the zipper."

And maybe scream.

"It's shocking to me that Tiffany would be so snoopy," Tori said. "I'm glad Amy fired her." She smoothed her hair in the mirror, seeming to forget that Tiffany was deceased, which was much worse than fired. "You really should do a better job of locking your studio."

"I didn't realize that it would be a problem, but you're probably right. It's just Aine and me working in here." Aine—please let Aine have an explanation. Aine had younger eyes than Rayne and could perhaps find the crystal.

"We have thumbprint recognition at the hotels," Tori suggested.

"I'll keep that in mind." Rayne helped Tori out of the gown and hung it carefully back on the dress form.

The heiress slid into her jeans and ivory sweater, exhaling loudly. "It's going to be fine. Tiffany was awful, but that's Amy's problem. Mom and Dad have taught me that you must be very careful who you trust."

That was true. Rayne knew that lesson well, thanks to Landon. "It's good you have your best friend here through it all. My best friend is in LA . . . Jenn. I miss her like crazy."

"Oh, I don't trust Amy as far as I can see her—and even then, well." Tori slipped on her shoes. Coach flats in blush leather.

"You don't?" Rayne put her fingers to her heart in surprise. Actually, considering how Tori talked to Amy, it made more sense than the besties farce.

"No." Tori rubbed her diamond on her sweater to make it shine. "This is one of those situations where you keep your friends close but your enemies closer."

Rayne reached for her coffee and sipped. Ugh. It was now cold. "I don't understand."

"Well, Amy has a thing for Jake." Tori balanced her heel to her shin like a crane, arms folded, her body ballerina graceful. "She totally made herself available to him a few weeks ago. Luckily, he turned her down. Told me right away."

Rayne put the mug down. She'd seen Amy be flirty, and it wasn't a stretch. "What did you do?"

Tori's blue eyes chilled. "I offered her a chance to be my bridesmaid on this secret getaway so I could really rub her nose in it. Jake is gorgeous, sexy, and all mine."

"Oh!" The woman with Jake wins it all?

"Don't look so shocked. You know, maybe I should let Amy know about the baby." Tori snickered. "Proof of me and Jake like rabbits would really make her jelly."

Rayne brought her hand to her forehead, at a loss for words.

"I'm starving." Tori changed the subject and glanced at her image in the mirror. "I've got to brush my hair. I mean, I appreciate the idea of a sleeper sofa, but Rayne, I won't do that another night. My father snores."

"Garda Williams should be here any time," Rayne said. "Hopefully with answers that will allow you back in the tower suites."

"All right." Tori's eyes narrowed. "You better get started on that dress."

"It's really just a matter of tightening the stitches by the zipper and steaming it. I'll work through breakfast . . ."

"No, you'd better not." Tori placed her hand on the doorknob and peered over her shoulder at Rayne. "Be prepared for Amy's questions but don't give away more than necessary."

"There is only so much time." Rayne pressed her fingers to her temple.

"You can work on it after breakfast and before that brunch thing while we are out shopping," Tori said. "You not hanging around with us yesterday is what made Tiffany so curious." She splayed her fingers over her flat stomach. "Do you think she took pictures of the gown?"

"There's no way to know for sure, until we find her phone," Rayne replied.

Tori tapped her chin. "I don't trust her. In business one must think of every situation possible to have an answering action."

"All right—worst case scenario." Rayne leaned her hip to the worktable. "Suppose Tiffany told Amy, and she took pictures of your dress, for this exposé. Everyone will know on Monday about the wedding, anyway, right?"

"Yes. The deal for people on this weekend getaway was that I would control the pictures of what was posted on social media. They signed a contract—which is probably where Amy got the idea for Tiffany."

"Tori. I hate to remind you, but Tiffany is dead."

"Yeah. And her phone is *missing*." Tori paced before the door. "Until we know where the notebook and phone are, they equal loose ends."

Rayne had an appreciation for Tori's management style and wisely kept her mouth shut.

"Monday the pictures and a news bite of our marriage will be released. Ethan is working with Jake to come up with something to prevent the studio from dropping him."

"That sounds ominous," Rayne said.

"It's for love." Tori strode to the picture window and looked out to the trees and the barn. "I think Jake's fans will forgive him for falling head over heels. We have the ability to be a power couple like no other." She glanced at Rayne. "It's not easy to find someone suitable in my age group."

"What do you mean?" Rayne asked.

"Well, other available men in my financial income bracket are usually much older and not that attractive." Tori touched the window and stared out. "When I get married, I will receive access to a trust from my Aunt Loretta." She turned and stepped toward the door. "It will be mine and unentangled with family money. Jake will be very happy that he chose me."

"I'm sure he will, Tori. He loves you."

At that, Tori shrugged. "You are a hopeless romantic, Rayne. Creating this wedding fantasy is the perfect career for you."

"Thanks?"

Tori made it to the door again and opened it. "I need breakfast. I went from not at all hungry to about to pass out."

"I'll see you there."

"Don't forget, or, well, you know there will be consequences." With that, Tori left the studio.

Rayne took another drink of her cold coffee. She had a headache and zero time for drama. She needed her phone. She needed caffeine. She had to call Nolan. First? She dropped to her hands and knees and searched every inch of the carpeted floor.

No crystal.

When Rayne left the sewing studio, she double checked to make sure it was locked.

She speed-walked down the hall—steps she wouldn't even get credit for since her phone was in her room—and passed the main staircase. She could smell herbs and spices. Sausage. Her stomach rumbled.

To the left of the staircase, five chambers down, was her room, and she ran inside, relieved to see her phone on the side table.

Two missed calls from her mother. Uh oh. Four from Tori along with a flurry of texts about Tiffany not to be trusted, which meant Amy wasn't to be trusted. The assistant was probably acting on Amy's orders.

Rayne sat on the edge of her bed, shocked that Amy had made such a play for Jake, and that as revenge Tori had invited her to be her bridesmaid.

It was a terrible way to live, never able to trust anyone.

Then again, someone had broken into her studio, moved the zipper on the bride's dress, and possibly snagged a crystal. Was it a trophy, or sabotage?

Chapter Six

Rayne looked up the business hours for Oasis Fabric in Dublin as she jogged down the hall to her studio. Once there she was relieved to see that the door was still locked.

Granted it had only been ten minutes, but Tori had seemed concerned Amy was onto her secret. It just had to be kept two more days. She imagined the uproar the news of the Montgomery–Anderson marriage would create on social media come Monday.

Would it be overshadowed by Tiffany's demise, or would the assistant's death be pushed under the carpet?

Inside, Rayne kicked the door closed with her flat boot heel and plopped on the love seat. The hours at the shop were from 9:30 AM to 9:00 PM. Dang. And there was no telling whether or not Nolan would even have the Swarovski crystal in stock as the heart shape was rare.

Dublin was ninety minutes away. There and back meant close to three hours would be squeezed from the day—yet, it would be *just* enough time before the bride would want to start dressing around three. Rayne had offered the sunroom for Tori, Amy, and Joan to get ready.

Rayne would need to be available on the fringes to oversee things. Maeve and Frances had planned the menu of Irish fare. Cormac, Dafydd, and Amos were making sure the bonfire by the gazebo tonight was set up with heating lamps so people would be comfortable, rain or shine. Ciara had hired a three-piece band to provide Celtic music.

Horse and carriage for the ride to the church. Check. A fairy-tale Irish wedding. The only things missing were shamrocks, tartans, and fairies. Rayne had laughed when learning that the Irish brides of old believed that a wedding veil protected the bride from being kidnapped by the fey. Superstition was rampant in these verdant hills.

Had Tiffany wanted to sabotage the nuptials? Or maybe, given she'd decided to do the exposé, she'd hoped to add drama or keep a souvenir.

It was too late to ask Tiff her motivation for her deeds.

How to get a replacement crystal? Rayne wondered if Maeve could spare Aine today but recalled that she was already helping Frances. She left a message at Oasis Fabric for Nolan to call her back right away.

It was a crystal emergency.

Rayne replaced the fallen scissors on her worktable and went through the items from her old shop on Rodeo Drive. She had a variety of crystals but none that matched the hearts. Her stomach clenched.

With a sigh, she grabbed her phone, double checked the lock, and hurried out to the hall. A shiver of cold air tickled her nape.

Rayne stopped and pressed her hand over the back of her neck.

She didn't have time for ghosts right now. Oh, God. What if Tiffany had joined the ranks?

Running, Rayne reached the main staircase and hurried downstairs. Where might Amos be? Maybe he could drive to Dublin for her if Nolan carried a crystal in his inventory. It wasn't fair to pull Aine when she'd be needed here. Eight-forty-five. Or Sorcha! Did the young woman mind driving?

Rayne raced outside and sucked in a breath at the crisp morning air. The rain from yesterday gave everything a fresh scent. Blarney woofed from where he'd been resting on the grass by the caution tape on twelve-inch pegs around the spot where Tiffany had landed. In his defense, there was a patch of warmth from the sun.

"Hey, boy," she said.

He didn't get up, so she went to him.

Crouching on her heels, Rayne patted his soft fur. "Did you see what happened, Blarney?"

He'd been a witness to her Uncle Nevin's murder on the lawn, according to the pet psychic her mom had contacted in Hollywood. It had been depressing for the pup, who had loved Nevin.

In the morning light, Rayne noticed the grass trampled and gravel interspersed among the blades. She blinked tears away as she imagined the assistant falling to her death and knocking pebbles free from the rooftop.

It made no sense to be afraid of being fired, especially if her severance package depended on her behavior, as Amy had said. Neither did shame for being caught writing the exposé. If that was true; they only had Amy's word for it. The starlet might be concerned for her own reputation if word reached Hollywood that she was such a cruel boss.

Rayne stood and studied the yard, walking around the tower while staying clear of the white-and-blue caution tape. The tower had been freshly whitewashed and the stones gleamed. The landscaping was done with romantic roses that were hanging onto their September blooms. They'd made an exterior staircase so that people could enter from outside, via the top floor, or inside. More caution tape crisscrossed the stairs.

She shielded her eyes from the sun and stared up at the turret, wondering what had happened. Her phone rang. Oasis Fabric. "Nolan?"

"So it is!" The man spoke with the joviality Rayne remembered. "How can I be of assistance?"

"I have a huge favor," Rayne said. "Do you carry Swarovski crystals?"

"I have a few in stock, yes indeed."

"Wonderful!" Her hopes soared.

"What are ye looking for exactly?"

"Heart-shaped?"

"Not that kind, no." And crashed again. "You'd have to order online for that."

"Oh, Nolan. There's no time." Her voice caught, and she brought her thumb to her lower lip, phone to her ear, shoulders bowed.

"What's wrong, pet?"

Why was this so blasted hard? "I need a heart-shaped crystal for a wedding gown."

"Well, you can always pay expedited shipping, though it's a fortune," Nolan advised. "When by?"

"Three today."

Nolan emitted an impressively colorful string of words.

Rayne strode toward the porch. "I'm truly stuck then. Why did I ever think I could continue my wedding business in Ireland? I feel like a fool." She had an entire village riding on her success.

Nolan exhaled. "Not as bad as all that. Never fear!"

"I'm shaking in my UGGs, Nolan." The ankle-high black boots allowed her to move quickly around the castle, but she was tempted to throw them in a Celtic rage that would get her nowhere. It was time to channel her deportment teacher, Mrs. Westinghouse, and be calm.

He chuckled. "Not wearing those for the wedding, are you?"

She and Ciara had both been invited, but Ciara had said no. Rayne was attending. "No." She liked this guy. "You have another idea?"

"We actually have two different Swarovski crystal stores in Dublin."

Two? It was a motherlode of possibilities. Her heart stopped thudding with doom, and she plopped down on a stone step next to a cedar planter of mixed autumnal blooms. Blarney joined her and butted her hand with his nose.

"I'll call them—thank you."

"You sound stressed, my sweet. Tell you what, I'll pop on over and check it out for myself. What are the dimensions?" Nolan asked.

"I'll send you a picture of what is missing—and you can't tell anyone," Rayne said, imagining the trouble she'd be in with Tori if word got out.

"I won't breathe a word."

"If you find the crystal for me, I will owe you a million. I'll, I'll . . . whatever you need, ever, I'll do." There was no way to repay such an enormous favor.

"Ha! Consider it my good deed for the day. I try to do at least one," Nolan teased.

That was very kind, and she'd think of something appropriate later. "I'll have someone drive over as soon as you give me the word that we have one."

"Deal."

"Thank you, Nolan!"

"Ta," the cheerful man said before ending the call.

Now, to find Amos. She and Blarney walked to the barn with the horses in the corral next to it. The sheepdogs were away with Dafydd and the sheep, and she hoped Amos would be inside, since the truck was parked in the gravel lot.

The truck they'd replaced in July was used, thanks to the castle budget, but it ran great. Dafydd could fix any engine, so that was a plus. Amos was the grounds manager who happened to have amazing sheep skills as well. This saved them the cost of a vet most of the time, which Ciara liked. They had Gillian for the electric and Bran for the plumbing, both working full-time hours. The castle life was hardly champagne and roses, though the hard work they'd put in certainly sold the idea of romance.

She and Blarney went into the barn. Since repairing the wall on the outside, the inside had also gotten fresh paint and boards. Rayne was surprised by how much she liked the scent of hay.

Amos's muscled back was evident in the stretch of his flannel shirt as he brushed the gray horse that was one of the pair that would be leading the carriage to the church and back. Was it wrong that she enjoyed the view for a second?

Feeling guilty, she cleared her throat. "Hey, Amos!"

Amos turned with a big smile on his handsome face. Shoulder-length waves were kept back with a brown leather tie. "Hey, yourself."

"Where's the other horse?" The open carriage was parked outside and covered under a tarp—it had been painted a glossy white with gold trim. Cormac would drive from the bench seat.

"Gillian's walking her to get any excess energy out. She'll make them lovely with the braids and all once we get the brushing done." Amos patted the gray's flank with his hand. "This one's already been out."

Rayne had a healthy respect for horses and kept her distance. She was getting better though, and her stomach didn't tighten in knots being inside the barn near one. "I'm sure it will be very pretty. I have more ostrich feathers, if Gillian needs them. Could you let her know?"

Gillian wasn't a fan of Rayne's. She'd learned the harsh lesson that not everybody would like her in elementary school and so didn't take it personally.

"I'll pass the message on." Amos straightened and tilted his head at her, his voice husky. "Anything else I can do for you?"

Oh yeah. But no. She cleared her mind. "Well, maybe . . ."

Rayne hated to get him drawn into the drama when he was needed with the horses, but she was a tiny bit desperate. There would be limited time there and back.

"You can tell me." Amos smacked the horse brush to his palm.

"I can't go into detail, but we might . . ." Rayne swallowed and looked around. They were alone except for the gray horse, a cat, and Blarney. " . . . have a problem with the dress."

Amos dropped the brush and the horse whinnied. Blarney went to the stall and put his nose through the bottom slat as if to reassure the horse everything was all right.

"What do you mean?" Amos asked with concern.

Her phone rang. Nolan. She lifted a finger. "Hang on."

Nolan said, "Rayne, lass, can you send a picture?"

She'd told him she would, but she'd wanted to see if Amos could drive first. Oh well. "Right!"

"What's the story?" Amos asked.

Rayne ended the call. "I have to go inside, but I might need some-one to drive to Dublin and back—before three this afternoon. What's your schedule like?"

Gillian entered the barn and stopped abruptly when she saw Rayne. Her hat slipped forward over her forehead and she pushed it back. Two thick auburn braids hung to her shoulders on either side of her strong face. Jeans clung to her lean figure and her riding boots came just below her knees.

"I can do it, sure," Amos said.

"Thanks! I'll let you know either way," Rayne said. "The horses look great."

Turning on her heel, Rayne nodded at Gillian. Blarney stayed with her, and they hurried back to the house. It was almost nine, and her stomach was rumbling. The apple had long ago worn off, and she wished she'd had some of the breakfast hash.

They raced inside and up to the studio, unlocked the door, where she snapped several photos of the crystals. She locked it again when she left. Aine texted, questioning where she was. Breakfast was ready and the guests were asking after her.

Coming!

As she hurried down the hall, she sent Nevin the photos of the crystals with a praying hands emoji and a heart. To Blarney she said, "And Amos probably thinks I'm ridiculous."

Gillian was attractive. Of a similar age to her and Amos, and very fit. Not afraid of horses. Single too—Rayne had asked Maeve.

Or had Maeve volunteered?

It didn't matter. What mattered was finding a crystal to match the missing one on Tori's gown. She took the stairs down two at a time, Blarney at her side.

"Out you go, boy." Since they were about to eat, she put Blarney outside. He curled up on the top step in the sunshine, content.

Hopefully she'd have time for a scone or something to fill her belly before Garda Williams arrived. It was strange that the Gardai weren't here yet. She hurried into the dining room, where the others had already started eating from the buffet.

"Morning!" Rayne called.

"There you are," Amy said. The starlet's red hair was in a waterfall of curls over her shoulder. Like yesterday, her makeup was perfect without a smudge. "I'm beginning to think you're avoiding us."

"Not true." Rayne hurried to the buffet and scanned the options. Scones, muffins, and, oh, was that quiche?

"Where were you?" Ethan stroked his goatee, his expression annoyed. "Isn't it part of your job to entertain us?"

"Rude!" Tori said. Since meeting Rayne in the studio, she'd brushed her hair and the strands shone like gold. A thin gold bracelet of Celtic knots adorned her wrist. The heiress was the picture of vibrant health.

Not even in the fine print was Rayne the entertainment. This was all so new that they were playing their roles by ear to see what worked best for the staff. "I was at the barn to check on the horses needed for the carriage ride to the church."

Ciara spluttered into her tea, knowing there was definitely more to that story.

Rayne poured herself coffee, added cream and sugar, then made a plate, choosing spinach and goat cheese quiche: fast, filling, and delicious. She sat next to her cousin. "Where's Aine?"

"Helping Frances chop veg for the medieval feast later. Why?"

"That's right." She smiled at Joan and Dylan, the Montgomerys in similar shades of blue, from Joan's dress to Dylan's casual jacket.

Josh, sitting next to Amy, winked at Rayne. Shadows colored the skin beneath his eyes from lack of sleep and too much booze. She hoped that her guests had slept well in the cottage and attributed Ethan's crankiness to Tiffany's demise.

"I don't believe you," Ciara said as she brought a bite of eggs to her mouth.

"Fair." She'd be right on the money about that.

Ciara's brow arched but she kept from blurting out what could possibly be wrong.

"Might be a teensy tiny problem," Rayne admitted in a very quiet voice. There was no way to discreetly pull her cousin to the side for a private conversation.

Lowering her tea mug, Ciara said, "To do with . . ."

"Not Tiffany." Rayne chewed the flavorful quiche. Once they had more income, she'd give Frances a raise.

"What then?"

Rayne tilted her head and brought her coffee to her mouth to whisper, "Missing crystal."

After a thoughtful expression of what Rayne might be talking about, Ciara scowled. "Off the . . . dress?"

"Yes." Rayne swallowed another drink then exchanged the mug for her fork, racing against the clock.

"What the feck."

"I know it." Rayne would never get used to feck as a non-swear swear word, but she liked it and considered it appropriate in this instance.

"What's the plan?" Ciara asked.

"Got a call to a shop in Dublin. We might need someone to pick up a replacement."

"When will you know?"

"Hopefully soon. Can we spare Amos to drive since Aine is busy?"

"Possibly. Is it a two-person job?"

Rayne showed Ciara the picture of the small crystal on her phone. "No."

"Got it. I can go," her cousin offered.

Rayne shook her head as she swallowed another bite of breakfast. "You and I have to entertain the bride and her family."

"I'd rather go to Dublin." Ciara ruffled her curls.

"I need you to help me," Rayne said. "You're very good at talking with people." She never would have believed it if she hadn't seen it with her own eyes. Joan and Ciara had especially hit it off, with Joan's mother being Irish.

"So," Joan called across the table. "What time will we need to be ready for champagne at the bakery? I'm having just a bite of fruit this morning so I can indulge myself in chocolate."

Dylan patted her hand. "We can diet on Monday. Rayne, this quiche is five star."

"Thank you. We will let our chef know. And Joan, noon, give or take," Rayne said. The dress had the potential to be a large fiasco that she needed a solution for, or she'd be tempted to hide under the covers for the rest of the day.

Rayne's phone dinged a notification.

An image of the heart crystal! She briefly closed her eyes and then sent a thumbs-up to Nolan.

"It's a go," she murmured to Ciara. Thank God! She gulped the last bite of quiche with coffee and burned the roof of her mouth.

"Slow down!" Amy said with a chuckle. "Everything okay?"

"As well as it can be," Rayne said. "There are a lot of last-minute details to make sure the day goes off without a hitch."

"That's true with any wedding," Joan said with commiseration.

"Wedding!" Ethan tossed the cloth napkin to the table and scooted his chair back to stare at Tori and Jake. "I can't believe that you are still getting married today."

"What's the problem?" Tori asked. "We've been through this last night. I hardly knew Tiffany."

"I was hoping the common-sense fairy would have visited over-night," Ethan said, "and you'd realize it's in terrible taste to have a wedding on the same weekend a friend dies."

Rayne and Ciara exchanged a glance.

Tori stood and slanted her gaze at Ethan. "You're right. If Tiffany had been my friend, it would be. I just met the woman. If you can't go with the program, then please leave. Stay in the cottage. I won't have any negative vibes today."

Jake leaned across the mound of rolls to give his assistant a warning look. "Let it go, man."

Ethan gritted his teeth. "Takes the cake that you're doing this. Or what, you're gonna fire me like Amy was going to fire Tiffany?"

Jake blew out a breath. "No! Ethan, no. I wouldn't."

Josh smirked. "Unless you're doing an exposé? I think that is def grounds for dismissal."

"Exactly!" Tori said, seemingly surprised that Josh had her back. "Amy had a reason to fire her, don't forget that. It's probably why she ju . . . well." She spun the gold bracelet around her wrist.

"Guilt can cause us to do strange things." Dylan drank his coffee.

Amy's eyes gleamed at the drama around the table. "I guess so. Tiffany was constantly writing, and I should have noticed sooner what she was doing. I didn't work her that hard, despite what you all may think."

"We get it, Ames," Jake said. "You haven't shut up about it all morning."

"Everyone owes me an apology," the starlet said.

"I am not apologizing to you for anything," Tori said. "If anything, you should apologize to me."

Amy blushed.

"What for?" Ethan asked.

"A misunderstanding," Jake interjected quickly.

Joan kept her pleasant smile pasted on her Botoxed face and changed the subject. "So. Let's go over the schedule again. I want plenty of time to get ready. When is the makeup artist going to arrive?"

Amy tilted her head with interest. "We have a makeup artist?"

"No," Rayne said. "When Tori and I had talked about the event today, she didn't mention that you needed one, just a place to get ready. I think the sunroom will be perfect."

"Well," Joan said. If she could have furrowed that brow she would have. "I have my own, but I still think we should hire someone for Tori's special day."

"Let me check around in the village," Rayne said.

"Do you lads need anything?" Ciara asked, smiling at Dylan, Jake, Josh, and Ethan in turn.

"I brought my hair product," Jake said. "Don't wear makeup unless it's for a part in the movies."

"I have my own, too," Josh said. His fauxhawk, though, was leaning a bit to the left.

"Sounds like we're good." Dylan patted his pocket and presumably his wallet.

Rayne got up. "Please, don't rush anyone. We don't have to be at the Coco Bean until noon, so you have time to shop, or hike, or whatever you'd like. The lake is lovely if you want to take a coffee and stroll."

Ciara jumped up as well. "Enjoy your morning."

She hooked her arm through Rayne's as they turned toward the exit.

"Not so hard!" Rayne whispered.

"You are not leaving without me." The cousins headed toward the door and out to the hall where Ciara said, "Now, tell me about the crystal?"

"Let's find Aine first to see if she was the one who broke into the sewing studio." But why would she?

Ciara slowed and tightened her hold on Rayne's arm. "Broke in for real? That's not good, Rayne."

"Right?" And Rayne couldn't even tell her the whole story!

They reached the kitchen. Frances and Aine were both stirring different things—Aine a sauce at the stove top, and Frances a batter for the Irish wedding cake at the kitchen table.

"Hey!" Rayne cleared her throat as she and Ciara jostled to a stop by the counter. "Aine, hon, did you happen to go into my studio last night?"

"No." Aine shook her head. "When would I have time? I fell asleep as soon we went to bed. Why?"

Rayne sighed. "I thought I'd locked it before we left last night."

"You did," Ciara assured her.

Aine glanced over from where she stirred the sauce. Scents of rosemary and oregano wafted from the pan. "I saw you do it, and I haven't been anywhere but this kitchen this morning. Why?"

"Well, someone moved the zipper on the bridal dress." Rayne rubbed her cold hands together. "Tori thinks it was Tiffany, snooping for Amy."

Perspiration dotted Frances's brow from her efforts with the batter. "What do you think?"

"But Tiffany is dead," Aine interrupted with a doubtful expression. "She was already dead when we went outside to investigate the argument."

So if not Tiffany, who? Rayne's stomach clenched at the intrusion into her sanctuary and lack of clear answers. "A Swarovski crystal is missing off the gown."

"That. Isn't. Right." Frances's words were in rhythm with her beats of the cake batter spoon to the bowl. "Loose. Thread. Or. Stolen?"

"I'm not sure. I need to find out what happened to the blasted thing." Uncertainty rattled Rayne's confidence. "My scissors were on the floor, which means that someone, I don't know who, might have removed the crystal on purpose. I was hoping Aine could check too but you're obviously busy."

"I will later." Aine twisted a knob on the stove and moved the pan to a different burner. "Those are expensive and custom-shaped."

"How much will it be to replace it?" Ciara asked.

"I didn't even ask Nolan. At the time I was making the dress, I would have bought in bulk," Rayne said. "But still."

Frances stopped beating the batter and patted her forehead dry with the interior of her wrist. Her cheeks were flushed. "Is it noticeable?"

Aine rested her hip to the stove, her single braid falling over her shoulder. "Good question. The whole thing is covered with crystals, right?"

"Yes. It's not obvious at first glance but on closer inspection there is an interruption in the pattern." Rayne raised her hand. "Nolan, my friend in Dublin, has one, and I just need for someone to pick it up, then have it back here in time." No biggie. Rayne couldn't be in three places at once. "And we need someone to do makeup for the ladies. I swear I didn't know about that until just now."

Rayne would create a spreadsheet with a checklist for future reference of every problem that arrived on this virgin wedding voyage.

"Sorcha can do makeup," Aine said. "She worked at a salon in Kilkenny for a while after high school. I'll ask her to help."

"All right." Ciara ruffled her short curls. "This is so stressful. So many details! I'm in no hurry to tie the knot." She touched the Claddagh engagement ring that Dafydd had given her.

"It will be fun when it's yours!" Rayne said. Aine nodded. Frances poured the batter into a pan lined with parchment paper. "I alerted Amos already about a possible drive to Dublin. I'll go confirm."

"I'm needed here or else I'd volunteer to go," Aine said. "Nolan is a dream. Mam is cleaning the blue parlor and will do the other rooms as soon as the Gardaí give the all-clear. Sorcha is in the laundry room."

Rayne couldn't take one more thing. She read the time on the kitchen clock. Half past nine.

Where was Garda Williams?

Chapter Seven

Without knowing it, Rayne's cousin seconded her sentiment about the missing Garda exactly. He'd said eight.

"Where is Dominic, anyway?" Ciara groused. "It's nine-thirty."

A sense of urgency filled Rayne, but she could only control so much. Sugar cookie! "I'll run to the barn to tell Amos."

"I'll go with you in case Dafydd is around," Ciara said. The shepherd didn't have a precise schedule and sheep were very unpredictable. Fluffy cute, yes, and vital to the manor, but with tiny minds of their own. "Perhaps he might drive if Amos can't get away because he and Gillian are preparing the horses."

"Sounds good." Rayne waved to Frances and Aine. "Wish us luck."

"Luck!" they said in unison.

The cousins left the manor and were greeted by Blarney. Was there anything as wonderful as the unconditional love of a pup? Rayne looked up toward the satellite antenna behind the barn just as Amos left the stone building with Gillian and walked toward them down the gravel path.

Amos was so handsome, as handsome in his way as Jake Anderson. Jeans, boots, and a fitted tee. He'd discarded his flannel shirt—no doubt too hot from his manual labor. Gillian strode at ease at his side.

Her brown khakis were suitable for outdoors, her peasant blouse stylish. She'd tucked her canvas sunhat in her back pocket and freckles graced her slim nose.

Upon seeing Rayne and Ciara, the woman immediately scowled. "I don't know what her problem is," Rayne muttered.

"Don't let it bother you," her cousin said. "I think Gillian's a wee bit upset about everything she grew up with here in Grathton being at risk. Nobody suspected that it could be lost—me included."

"Fair." Rayne let it go and focused on the path, where they met halfway in the middle of the gravel road.

Amos stretched his arm to the side to greet them. "So, lasses, do you need me to drive to Dublin?"

"Yes, please. You'll be picking up a crystal at Oasis Fabric. I'll need it back here by two-thirty," Rayne said. "Three at the latest. I'll only be able to stall the bride for so long."

"What happened?" Gillian asked.

"When Rayne and Tori were in the studio this morning, Rayne discovered a crystal missing from the bridal gown," Ciara explained. "Tori didn't notice, but she might at any time."

"Unbelievable." Gillian arched her brow at Rayne like Rayne was an idiot to lose a crystal from a dress.

Maybe so—though Rayne was willing to bet someone took it. Tori had blamed Tiffany for the break-in, but it could have been someone who didn't care for Rayne or the wedding venue. Someone like Gillian, who wanted her to fail for reasons known only to the handywoman. She was often inside the manor to assist Maeve.

"Happy to help." Amos turned to Gillian. "The horses are walked, brushed, and clipped. They just need your magic touch to make them beautiful." He shifted, his gaze landing on Rayne. "We were coming for feathers."

"Feathers?" Ciara asked.

"I have extra ostrich feathers to decorate the horse's manes, and the carriage," Rayne explained. Blarney, after sniffing everyone's shoes, loped across the grass and sprawled out like a mournful guardian next to the caution tape.

If the pup had witnessed Tiffany's demise, as he had Nevin's, Blarney might require therapy. Rayne could imagine the laugh her cousin and the other people here at the castle might give at that, but she'd ask her mom to reach out to the pet psychic.

"Mom!" Rayne brought her fingers to her temple. Two missed calls that Rayne hadn't had a chance to return. Lauren hadn't left a message.

"Huh?" Ciara asked.

"My mom called twice this morning." Rayne pulled her phone from her pocket but there weren't any other calls. "It's been so hectic." Surely, if it was important Lauren would have followed with a text.

"Well, it'll have to wait," Ciara said. "The Garda is here at last." She tossed her curls. "Lazybones. He told us eight this morning last night."

"He did," Rayne said. "Something must have happened."

Gillian looked at Ciara as if she'd cracked her head. "You think Dominic Williams is lazy?"

"And maybe he is," Ciara said. "We can't clean the tower chambers or the billiards room until he gives the okay. Our guests are being inconvenienced."

"The Gardaí station doesn't even open till nine," Gillian said.

Ciara puffed her chest like an affronted cat as Gillian began to grate on her nerves too.

Amos cleared his throat to halt the tension. "I'd better scoot," he said, "if I'm going to be back by two-thirty. Will you send me the address, Rayne?"

"On its way. Thank you," Rayne said. She pressed a button and shared the location for Oasis Fabric and Nolan's information, followed by a picture of the crystal. It would be down to the wire, time-wise.

Amos gave a two-finger salute and headed back to the barn and the manor truck they all shared. There was a small car as well, but he wouldn't fit comfortably in the two door white Fiat.

Rayne pulled her gaze from his broad back to the Hyundai as Garda Williams exited the police vehicle. He was in full uniform of blue polo shirt with a yellow crest on the arm beneath a yellow vest with a flashlight and radio attached, blue cargo pants with many pockets, and a hat with the Garda crest. Black shoes. No Garda Lee with him.

"Don't you have someplace to be?" Ciara asked Gillian when the handywoman seemed rooted to the ground.

"Don't get your knickers in a twist just because I don't agree with you that the Garda is lazy," Gillian said. "I'm here to pick up feathers from Rayne."

Garda Williams winced at the remark, having walked up in time to hear Gillian's comment.

"I've got plenty of feathers to spare," Rayne said. "Do you mind going inside and ask Aine to help you? Ciara and I need to talk with the Garda about the . . . accident."

"Accident?" Gillian snorted. "A woman jumping to her death is a tragedy."

"We understand." If Gillian hadn't been instrumental with getting the electric in the cottages up to code, then Rayne would give her two weeks' notice for bad attitude. Ciara was not so fond of Gillian at the moment either.

"If Aine is busy, then Maeve can also assist you." Rayne crossed her arms, shoulder to shoulder with her cousin.

Gillian blew out a breath, realizing neither of them would talk to the Garda with her present. "Fine. Call me when the coast is clear, would you please, Ciara?"

"Sure." As in, doubtful.

Rayne could read her cousin's body language by now and Gillian had crossed a line by throwing Ciara under the bus with Dominic.

Gillian strode toward the barn rather than go inside and talk with the Lloyds. Whatever. Rayne smiled at the Garda, hoping he wouldn't take what Gillian said personally. "Hey!"

"Morning," Garda Williams said. His green eyes were frosty so not a chance that he hadn't heard Gillian's comment. "Rayne, Ciara. I would have been here earlier, but I was waiting for test results from the coroner, who'd heard from the pathologist. Heaven forbid I arrive without anything to update you both on."

"Heya," Ciara murmured as she averted her gaze. "Sorry about that."

"It was taken out of context," Rayne said to Garda Williams. "Did you locate Tiff's phone, or those notebooks in her purse, or luggage?"

"Her handbag didn't hold anything other than her wallet and keys," the Garda said. "Lip gloss and a pen. Nothing to write on—not even tissue."

"That's very odd," Rayne said. "We both saw her carry a Moleskine with her everywhere, and her phone, right Ciara?"

"Yes, that's right." Her cousin tugged the mock turtleneck from her throat.

Garda Williams didn't look at Ciara. Pink tinged his cheekbones—a downside to being so fair skinned was that your emotions were easy to read. "I'm ready to see the tower."

"You can't go tramping around by yourself," Ciara said. "It will upset the guests, who want to get into their rooms but can't until *you* tell them it's all right."

The Garda's mouth pursed. " Are you saying I should get a warrant?"

"Oh, hey now, Garda Williams, that won't be necessary," Rayne interceded. "Can I help?"

"Yes. Come with me because I might have some questions that an owner of the manor should be able to answer," Garda Williams said tightly.

Ciara rolled her expressive gray eyes. "I'll leave you to it." Her cousin walked toward the barn rather than inside, glancing back over her shoulder.

"Gillian was rude to share what Ciara said like that. And you did say eight," Rayne explained in a casual tone. "It's been a hectic morning."

Garda Williams rocked on his boot heels, hands behind his back as he peeped toward the barn. Ciara was out of sight. "She won't forgive me for not believing her about her da right away. I understand her reasoning, but she won't give an inch toward seeing my side."

"In the end, you caught Uncle Nevin's killer, and that's what matters," Rayne said. But, the officer was also right that Ciara held a grudge. Time for a subject change. "You said you heard from the coroner?"

"The toxicology test came back." The Garda adjusted the brim of his hat. "Alcohol was high but not out of context of being at the pub and the whiskey here at the manor. Inebriated but not hammered."

Josh had made Tiffany's drinks pretty strong. "Drugs? I've known people who masked depressed emotions with recreational stuff that might do more harm than good."

"Not a thing." Williams studied Rayne with curious green eyes. "Did she seem depressed?"

"Not really. More put out with Amy than sad," Rayne said. "Ethan and Tiff had plans to chat at the cottage. When she didn't show, he went to get cigarettes, thinking she'd been delayed, but he wasn't worried. Remember that he said Tiff was afraid of heights?"

"I do. I'd like to see the turret." Garda Williams pulled out a tablet from one of his many pockets. The pants were amazing, and Rayne was tempted to buy herself a pair. There'd be room for keys, scissors, her phone, heck, she even had a mini sketchbook that would fit.

"Absolutely!" It was now quarter to ten in the morning. The sun was playing peekaboo behind a cloud but at least the rain had stopped. Blarney remained in his position by the caution tape and watched them carefully. "Would you like to go in the outer entrance, or the inner?"

After a scan of the area, possibly wondering who was around, the Garda suggested, "Let's try outside."

Rayne stepped toward the caution tape and her dog. "This way."

They went to the green lawn and a hedge of trimmed bushes. Blarney wagged his tail but didn't get up. Unusual for him to not be racing around chasing ants or butterflies or the kittens they'd gotten in June. All three tabbies stayed near the barn and kept the property rat-free.

The Garda stopped at the smoosh of green blades and dirt at the exact area he'd staked out last night where Tiffany had fallen, then leaned back to view the five-story tower. The only windows were thin arrow slits and not big enough for anyone to get out of. Tiff would have had to climb to the rooftop.

"Hey Blarney. Keeping guard?" the Garda asked.

Blarney woofed in response.

"If only he could talk," Rayne said. "I wonder if he witnessed Tiffany's fall? His howl alerted us that something was wrong."

Garda Williams didn't dismiss the idea out of hand but leaned down to scratch the dog behind the ears. "It's been quite a year. I'm glad you've kept Blarney as a pet."

The russet-colored Irish Setter had been purchased to be a bird dog and help bring fowl to the manor kitchen, but he didn't have the heart of a hunter. Dafydd claimed that the dog had been spoiled by Nevin and ruined by Rayne. Amos had been kinder, sharing that dogs had a variety of personalities, like people.

Dafydd had threatened to sell Blarney, but Rayne put her Lady of the Manor foot down, and in the end, Ciara had given Blarney to Rayne. Win–win.

"I never had a pet before," Rayne confessed. "He's the love of my life."

The Garda nodded. "I have a rescue mutt that I buy special food for because he's allergic to the regular stuff. It's a tidy sum, but he's worth it."

They shared a smile. "What's his name?"

"Bandit. Some days on the job are rougher than others, like when one discovers a dead person." The Garda gestured to the indented grass. "The pup seems to sense when I could use extra companionship."

Blarney did that for Rayne too. "Dogs are great. As a policeman, you give so much of yourself that you've got to nourish your body and mind. Heart."

"And soul." Garda Williams chuckled. "Never thought I'd have this conversation when I arrived at work today."

"We humans are multifaceted." Rayne liked the layers of Dominic Williams. He'd be a good friend to have.

Williams tipped the brim of his hat to look at Rayne with sadness. "Tiffany was thirty. Same age we are. She had her whole life ahead of her." His mouth firmed as if he was going to say more but didn't. "Let's go." He led the way around the base of the tower and stopped at the staircase, unfastening the caution tape he'd put there last night.

In the medieval past, you had to climb stairs inside to reach the turret, but they'd added these for convenience. Centuries later, the castle inhabitants didn't need to outlast a siege or fight off an army.

"The staircase still has the new wood smell," Rayne said. "Goes up five stories to the roof, where we created an outer entrance."

"I remember from when Ciara and I . . . well, ancient history, but the inside of the tower was blocked with junk." The Garda rubbed his chin.

"That it was. Nothing some elbow grease and paint couldn't fix. Also a new interior staircase! Bran and Gillian, as well as Cormac, are very talented with castle repair. Amos and Dafydd too."

The Garda's mouth tightened at the name of Ciara's fiancé. He'd been a suspect in Uncle Nevin's death, which could also explain why Ciara wouldn't let her grudge against Dominic go.

"I knew that Gillian worked here. Bran Wilson does too?"

"Yes. Gillian full-time and Bran as we need him, but he's at about forty hours a week right now since we were updating the cottages. Eventually, we'll get another three refurbished." As money came in, it would have to be parsed out to whatever needed to be fixed first.

"Allow me," Garda Williams said. He took his time, examining each wooden step.

For craftsmanship, or clues? There wasn't so much as a muddy footprint despite her guests and their luggage. The green lawn acted as a mat, she supposed.

Rayne was happy to let him take the lead. Honestly, she was surprised that he was sharing so much right now and didn't want to jinx it. "This carpentry was Dafydd, Cormac, and Gillian."

"What is Gillian's position?" Dominic reached the first landing.

"She's a handywoman with electrician skills and works both inside the manor and out. In fact, she's making the horses beautiful today for the wedding. I guess she used to ride in contests." Rayne was glad for her UGGs and that she wasn't wearing heels as she clambered up the staircase. "She's kinda prickly. Do you know her?"

"I do." Dominic reached the third level landing. "Not as well as Bran Wilson."

Just because the Garda knew Bran more than Gillian didn't mean Bran had done anything illegal. Grathton was home to only five hundred folks and the councilwoman next door had made no bones about wanting to absorb Grathton into Cotter Village. Rayne had zoned out over the politics but knew she needed to protect her family's legacy by doing all she could to keep Grathton independent.

The Garda glanced at Rayne and continued walking. "Any way that Tiffany might have accidentally fallen?"

"No. I thought so at first but . . ." Rayne placed her hand to her collarbone. "The wall is just over four feet. You'd have to climb onto it." *Jump off it.* They reached the metal gate leading to the top floor of the tower. "You'll see for yourself that the turret isn't something where she'd simply tip over. It had to be a choice."

The Garda opened the latch slowly and put up his hand. "Wait here, please. I'd like to get my bearings."

A powerful breeze *whooshed* by Rayne. The wind might have caused Tiffany to be off balance but there was no way she could just slip over the side. "No prob."

"Does it go all the way around?" Garda Williams pulled his cellphone from a pocket, opening the photo app after reading his messages.

"Yes." In the refurbishing, they'd patched any weak spots in the stone before whitewashing to make it fresh. They'd added circular benches along the way, though her favorite was the one overlooking the lake on the property. Potted plants for beauty were stuck in crevasses. Variegated ivy too.

Garda Williams snapped photos before gesturing for her to join him. "It's wide."

"Four feet high, and almost five feet across," Rayne said. "You'll notice seating along the wall so that folks can relax and enjoy the view. The lake and the gazebo are visible from the section near the front of the house."

"Where the incident happened?"

Rayne shrugged. "As you'd asked us to stay away, nobody, including me, has been up here, so I'm not sure." Peering over the edge, she saw Blarney and the caution tape a long way down. "No. The lake view is more to the front section."

"A police investigation requires not making assumptions on the manner of Tiffany's death," the Garda said. "Her body found on the ground below the tower indicates a fall. We don't know for sure that she jumped. I'm checking to see if she could have stumbled accidentally."

"I don't think so, Garda Williams." Rayne patted the stone wall that was chest-height, the turrets on the top rail tapered. "Although we have the satellite antenna, this is sometimes still the best place to get a cell signal if the weather is cloudy. What if Tiffany needed Wi-Fi to reach the states?" Rayne's pulse sped. "About the exposé?"

Williams gave a speculative hum. "The idea that Tiffany might have needed a stronger cell signal could lead to more questions in that direction—it would be helpful if we could find her mobile, or the notebook. She didn't leave a suicide note on her person."

Rayne gazed down at her dog five stories down, oblivious to her as he rested his muzzle on his paws. "Maybe there will be answers on her laptop."

"Garda Lee is checking that out this morning. Tiffany seemed to take her password security very seriously. You'd be surprised how many people put them on a slip of paper in their wallet."

Rayne raised her hand. "I do that too."

"If a thief got hold of your bag, with your phone, you're making it very easy for them to get into all of your accounts. He'd think he'd won the motherlode, Rayne." The officer shook his head and continued, "Tiffany had cash in her wallet. A receipt for the Sheep's Head. Her credit cards." He sighed. "Ethan's on the CCTV at the petrol station for buying cigarettes at the time he'd said."

Rayne followed the garda with alarm. "That's good. Uh, why were you checking out his alibi?"

"Procedure," the Garda said. "We have to confirm where everyone was. Nobody else was visible on the street camera. It's possible that Tori, Jake, and Amy were snug in the tower as they claim."

Rayne was saddened by Tiffany's death. "It might be a tougher password because she was Amy's assistant. That comes with a lot of private information about the starlet."

"And if it's true about her writing a secret exposé," the Garda said, "then Tiffany had something to hide." He glanced at her with a wry smile. "People go to great lengths to protect secrets."

"True." They continued along the rooftop, eyes on the chest-high railing as they walked, looking for where Tiffany might have climbed to the wall and leaped over.

Rayne knew a big secret and one her client feared being discovered: Tori's pregnancy.

"Tori Montgomery wants back into her suite," Rayne said. "I think it was her first time sleeping on a pullout sofa bed, and she didn't like it. You ever hear that story of the princess and the pea?"

"No." The Garda had switched from taking photos to using the video option now that they were closer to where Tiffany must have jumped.

"Well, it's basically about how a true princess is so used to luxury that she would feel a tiny pea through twenty mattresses, whereas a peasant—in this case an imposter—wouldn't notice. I think Tori proves the point." Rayne chuckled. "She doesn't want to sleep on the sleeper sofa again."

The Garda allowed himself a small smile as they rounded a curve. "Oh! What have we here?" He put his palm up in a halt gesture to keep Rayne from stepping forward.

Rayne stopped.

A piece of the stone crenellation was broken and one of Tiffany's yin-yang fingernails lay on the ground.

Scuffs from the soles of her boots marked the stonework. "I don't understand," Rayne said, staring at the scuffs. The railing. It matched the gravel pieces below on the grass.

Garda Williams gestured to the wall. "This is why I brought you with me. Was this broken prior to today?"

"Absolutely not—it was perfect for the guests, as I told you before. Could she have . . . but, no." Tiffany wouldn't have been able to drag herself to the wall and forcibly break it.

"I'm sorry, Rayne, but this is more in line with our suspicion."

Her body stilled. "Of?" She stared at the rooftop, recalling the loose sole on Tiff's boots.

The Garda took the cell phone app from video to photo again.

The scuffs were heavy, as if Tiffany had been pulled against her will and hadn't wanted to go near the wall. Rayne squinted at the evidence before her. "She was here last night, all right, and she wasn't alone."

"It doesn't look like it." The Garda straightened. "Can you think of anything, or anybody, she might have argued with?"

"Which is why you were checking Ethan out." Rayne shivered and rubbed her arms, grateful for the thick sweater.

"It's part of the investigation process, even before Dr. Rhodes ruled it as a suspicious death." Garda Williams turned to her with a grim expression.

Suspicious death. Tiffany hadn't jumped. Poor Amy! Poor Tori! "Tiff and Amy disagreed . . . Amy planned to fire Tiffany on Monday when they returned." Rayne's stomach flipped round and round. "You knew that already."

"Let's start with Amy Flores." Garda Williams pulled his tablet from one of his many pockets. "The bride's best friend, a star—up and coming but not to the level of fame of a Jake Anderson. Young. Beautiful. Not wealthy, like the Montgomery family. What can you tell me about Amy's interactions with everyone else?"

Rayne wasn't sure what she should tell, considering Tori had demanded she keep the pregnancy a secret, and her feelings about Amy in relation to Jake. "You should ask the others. I just met Amy this weekend."

"Come on, Rayne. What do you know?"

After a quick exhale, Rayne said, "Amy seems flirty, that's all. And Josh accused Amy of not letting Tiffany wear makeup or compete in the looks department." At the Garda's intense stare, she added, "and we saw that for ourselves. Tiff dressed demurely compared to the rest and did her best to be professional."

"Did her best?"

"Well, Josh liked to tease her, to make her smile." Rayne batted tears free. "Tiffany was a very lovely woman without any need for makeup."

Garda Williams kicked his heel to the wall. "And now she's dead and the altercation appears to have happened here. She might have been pushed hard enough to break the stone."

Rayne swiped her damp cheeks. Someone had physically hurt Tiffany.

"Think, Rayne," the Garda said with urgency. "Any other small details to point us in the right direction? Time is of the essence."

Didn't that seem to be the way for everything in her life right now? "Well—Aine had heard something."

"What did she hear?" The Garda lowered his arms to his sides.

"A man, Jake, arguing with someone. Loud enough that she and Ciara came to get me from the studio. That was before midnight."

"Tori?"

"No. Aine said she was sure it wasn't Tori. Tori has a higher pitched voice." It was pleasant enough but unique.

"Who?"

"I don't know! Maybe Tiffany?"

The Garda made some notes on the tablet. "Jake could have brought Tiffany up from the suite below us, correct?"

"Yes. But without Tori knowing?" The third and fourth floor were connected with an open plan. "I don't see it. Jake didn't really talk to her. I can't imagine them arguing about anything."

He tapped his pen to his lower lip. "What time did everyone split up?"

"You already asked this last night," Rayne said.

"And now I'm asking again."

Rayne rubbed her forehead. The Garda might look like the boy next door type, but he certainly had a way of getting her to spill the tea. "I was working in the studio after bringing them to the billiards room, but Tori wanted an early night so she demanded that they all go to bed at a decent hour. She said ten-thirty. Josh left for the bar, and Ethan and Tiffany planned to have drinks together. There was no rowdy bachelor or bachelorette party that might have gotten out of control."

She almost shared with the Garda about Tori being pregnant, but it was a client confidentiality thing, and she just couldn't do it.

"I appreciate your help, Rayne." After several more pictures of the scuff marks and fingernails, the Garda switched his cell phone for an evidence bag and gloves, placing the acrylic yin-yang pieces into it and then a different pocket at his calf. "I'd like to question Jake and find out who he was arguing with. If not Tiffany or Amy, who else might it have been?"

Rayne met the Garda's eyes. "Joan was at the cottage with Dylan, so, it wouldn't be either of them. Ask Aine—maybe she'll remember something else. Oh, she will be so upset. She mentioned this morning that Tiffany seemed kind of lonely."

Garda Williams nodded. "Where is everyone? I'd like to interview them all, one at a time."

"Finishing breakfast in the dining room. As you can imagine, they had a slower start this morning," Rayne said.

"Despite Ciara's remark, I was at the station by seven."

"She's just worried about the castle," Rayne said. "There is a lot at stake. How did Tori die?" The Garda had shared the toxicology report but not much else. "Broken neck?"

"No. Strangulation." The Garda pointed to the scuff marks. "It's clear she had help going over this ledge."

Strangled? Rayne rested her weight against the ledge as her knees buckled, in no danger of falling. Tiffany hadn't wanted to jump.

Someone had choked her and then pushed her over the side.

Chapter Eight

Rayne's phone dinged as she received multiple notifications, sounding like a slot machine at a casino. How could it only be ten in the morning? Aine let her know the guests were lingering over coffee. Ciara asked for an update. Amos was en route to Dublin. Amos was in touch with Nolan, and the shop owner had agreed to meet Amos on the sidewalk, so he didn't even have to park but could just grab the crystal and go. She shook her head to focus on the task at hand: get through this wedding while the Gardai found a killer.

"The wedding!" Rayne said. "Does this mean that it will need to be canceled?"

Garda Williams clenched his jaw, eyes narrowed. "Maybe not. Let me have a minute to think. I'm aware of how much this means to you and Ciara. The whole castle, and yes, the village too."

She swallowed hard and placed her hand to her stomach. "Did you realize something was wrong last night?"

"A Garda's job is to question everything. There were marks around Tiffany's throat that *might* have been caused by the fall, and it's probable that whoever did this foul deed is hoping we won't push further with the inquiry. But your comment about the broken fingernails made me suspicious, eh. If Tiffany willingly jumped, why the ruined manicure?"

"Poor Tiffany."

"Dr. Rhodes confirmed that she'd been strangled so now we'll need to question everyone again," Garda Williams said.

"Aine and Maeve haven't touched the billiards room, as you had requested." She blew out a breath. "Aine said the guests are still in the dining room with coffee. I thought they'd all split up to get some exercise in, but whatever they want is fine with me. Would you like to come in and talk with them?"

"Sure." Garda Williams sent off a text. "Just asked Garda Lee to bring in a forensics team to search the castle and grounds for evidence, then you can clean this up and have the tower back. Lee got a glimpse last night when she escorted folks to get their clothes but didn't see anything alarming. They'll be more thorough now that the cause of death is murder."

Rayne eyed the bluish gray sky and shivered. "I can't imagine Tori going through with the ceremony now that there is a killer on the prowl." No matter how desperate she was to be wed.

Rayne led the way back to the exterior staircase, the Garda behind her. "It's a sad day indeed."

She reached the gate and opened it. "It couldn't have been Amy, could it? She's so tiny, and those were scuff marks of someone pulling Tiffany and Tiffany digging her heels into the stone. Her sole was loose."

"You mustn't jump to conclusions," the Garda said. "I know that we got off on the wrong foot regarding Lord Nevin's death. I apologize. I need your cooperation, starting with asking you not to tell any of your guests about the murder."

"And how do we explain the Gardaí presence?" Rayne asked. Yes, her guests were self-absorbed but not blind.

"You can simply explain that her death is under investigation."

What was the difference? Ciara had been very hurt regarding her father's murder—when it had truly seemed an accident until Ciara had probed further, so while Rayne might forgive and forget, not so much her cousin.

Rayne loosened her clip, but it didn't stop her head from aching. "It might make things a bit easier, if they don't have details, to continue with the wedding. But I'll tell Ciara and the core staff."

"That's fine," Garda Williams said. "Shall we?"

They walked down the stairs, Rayne going first. They reached the ground and Blarney met them with a woof and a tail wag, giving up his post as if he knew that they were finally on the right track regarding Tiffany's demise.

"Blarney! Good boy," Rayne said, glancing at Garda Williams. It was nice that he had his own rescue dog. "What do you think of pet psychics?"

He laughed then stopped when he realized she was serious.

"My mom is friends with one in LA. The psychic helped Blarney with Uncle Nevin."

"Now I know you're messing with me." Williams raised his hand. "I've watched episodes of *Family Forever*, not realizing that it was your mam."

"I'll introduce you when she comes in December." They walked around the caution tape affixed by stakes in the ground.

The Garda took several more pictures from this angle, then located another broken fingernail among the rubble from the turret that matched the missing portion of stone that he placed in yet another evidence bag.

They went inside, Blarney choosing to sprawl on the top step outdoors. It was cooler for him with all of his heavy fur.

"Take me to the billiards first, would you?" Garda Williams asked.

"Sure." They had to pass the dining room to reach it on the far side to the right of the center staircase but he probably wanted to see if there were clues before he interviewed the guests, Rayne thought.

Garda Williams texted while they walked. The door to the dining room was cracked open, and they heard fragments of laughter and conversation.

It was now quarter after ten. Her guests had been in there for over an hour—but the schedule was meant to be leisurely. The bride wanted no stress on her wedding day. There were planned activities, but all designed for a relaxed pace they normally didn't have in their busy lives.

"Here we are." Rayne opened the door to the cozy space with the billiards table, the dartboard, the speakers, and the bar along the far wall. She sucked in a breath. "Oh no!"

"What?" Garda Williams stepped in so fast he clipped her boot heels.

"It's clean." Rayne's pulse fluttered with disappointment. "Aine and Maeve knew to wait."

"Tell me what was in here." The Garda entered the room. The glasses had been washed and the trash emptied. The cue sticks were lined up on a rack against the wall.

"There were lots of empty bottles and glasses. They'd gone through a bit of alcohol and sparkling water. Snacks—Josh was playing bartender." Rayne sighed. "It's not like Maeve or Aine to just forget."

The Garda studied the bar top that was clean as a whistle. "An accident . . . or possible that someone else realized that they needed to get rid of evidence."

"Like fingerprints?" Rayne asked.

The Garda shrugged. "It was worth a shot. I'd like to speak with Jake about who he was arguing with. And Amy. Could either of them have cleaned up in here?"

Rayne burst out laughing. "I highly doubt that. Too out of touch to even realize they should pick up their own mess. They are both stars."

"Got it." Garda Williams took pictures of the room, even the empty trash can.

Rayne snapped as she thought of who might have cleaned the room. "Gillian's been with the horses today, but maybe Sorcha?"

"Sorcha?"

"Sorcha Ketchum, Dr. Ruebens' granddaughter, works with us inside the castle. I bet she didn't know that we'd asked for the rooms not to be cleaned." Rayne shook her head. "Sorry, Garda Williams."

On the other hand, a part of Rayne hoped that it was Sorcha and not somebody covering their tracks. Even though Amy was the obvious choice against Tiffany, Rayne didn't dare jump to conclusions.

The Garda stepped out of the billiards room to the hall, and Rayne followed him, switching off the light. It even smelled clean rather than like the rich scent of whiskey.

"The dining room, then," the Garda said. "I'll chat with Sorcha after the guest interviews."

"This way." Rayne led them down the hall to the formal dining room. She opened the door to the chamber, which had space for twenty around the old table without needing the extension.

She had to keep Tiffany's murder from them, but wanted to alert Ciara as soon as possible, in private. "Hi all! You remember Garda Williams from last night?"

"Hello!" a chorus of folks answered. Aine was in the process of covering the food on the side table, but there was a selection of pastries and fresh fruit available, along with coffee and tea. Rayne was parched.

It was sweet that Joan and Dylan held hands. Tori and Jake didn't but sat close to each other. Tori seemed calmer, so perhaps the slow breakfast was what she needed. Ethan, Josh, Amy, and Ciara. Ciara gave her a neutral look, hopefully not upset that she hadn't answered the text. Glad her cousin had returned to the fray, Rayne hoped she'd given Gillian a warning to chill out.

Garda Williams and Rayne crossed to Aine, who was in maid mode right down to the white apron over her black shirt and black slacks. "Aine, is Sorcha here?."

"Yes, she is. Helping Mam."

"I think she cleaned the billiard room," Rayne said.

"Oops." Aine glanced at the Garda. "Sorry. I mean, I'll check to make sure, but I'd wager a pint we forgot to tell her."

"Thank you." Rayne cleared her throat and asked her guests, "Did any of you clean up after the party last night?"

"I thought you had staff," Tori said, her brow raised.

"We do. No worries," Rayne said. She smiled at the Garda, who nodded. That answered that question.

"Sorcha is here until after the wedding dinner if you need to talk with her," Aine said.

"Thank you, Aine," the Garda said. "Rayne, is there a space I could speak with the guests individually?"

"Sure. Aine, is the blue parlor cleaned?"

The maid nodded.

"If you could get that set up with a tea cart for the Garda, that would be wonderful."

Ciara stood and joined them. She'd brushed her bleached curls until they appeared springy and soft to the touch, and was wearing a hint of pink lipstick. She still wore her black mock turtleneck and slacks. Rayne hadn't had a chance to change, and it wasn't looking like she would get a moment.

"Thank you, yes," the Garda said. "I could use a cuppa."

"What's going on?" Ciara queried.

Joan scooted her chair back and joined them to hover around the hot coffee. "Is something happening that you can share with the class?"

"The Garda has some questions about last night," Rayne said. She wished she could make this easier for her guests. If they knew that Tiffany had been killed, would they cancel the wedding?

She had a sudden fear of doing the wrong thing by her client in order to make the Garda happy, but had to acknowledge that the investigation took priority.

"Officer! Did you find Tiffany's phone? Or her notebooks?" Amy asked. "She had at least a dozen."

"No, we have not," Garda Williams replied. He turned to Jake and Tori, lounging at the table. "I'd like to start my interviews with the two of you, please. Tori first, then Jake. If the rest of you could wait here? It won't take long, and I appreciate your cooperation."

"Are we all going to be interviewed?" Ethan smoothed his goatee. "I already told you everything last night."

"Me too," Amy said. "In fact, it felt a lot like oversharing."

Josh nodded. Joan glanced at Dylan. "Do we need a lawyer, darling?"

Dylan flexed his hand on the table and glanced around at everyone before settling on the Garda. Dominic Williams didn't flinch.

"Not yet, Joan, though our firm is only a phone call away," the billionaire said. "Tori, only answer what you know."

"I don't know anything," the heiress replied. Her blond hair waved mermaid-style down her shoulders. "Why do I have to go to another room?"

"Procedure," the Garda replied.

That seemed to satisfy everyone. Garda Williams had asked her to keep quiet, but she really wanted to tell Ciara. Her cousin got a fresh plate and piled strawberries on it. Joan kept them conversing in small talk about her Irish ancestors in Cork.

Tori was back in minutes rolling her blue eyes. "Waste of time. Didn't see Tiffany after we went to bed at ten-thirty. Your turn Jake, then Josh, then Amy." She looked at Ciara. "Then the maid."

Ciara nodded. "I'll go find Sorcha. Thanks for the reminder."

Rayne selected a cup of coffee and another slice of quiche as her first breakfast had worn off. Second breakfast. How very hobbity.

Jake quickly returned. "Josh, you're up dude."

Josh smoothed the sides of his fauxhawk as he left the dining room.

"How was it?" Joan looked at Jake.

"No big thing. He asked if we'd seen Tiffany after ten-thirty." Jake shrugged. "And if I'd had an argument with her, but no. Never saw her—she def wasn't in our suite."

Rayne filed that information away. That meant that Tiffany had gone up the outside tower stairs between ten-thirty when they all left and her body was found at close to midnight. Less than two hours to account for.

By the time Amy and Ethan were through, the Garda came into the dining room to see if Sorcha was available. Ciara had just beat him back.

"Sorry. She's busy in the laundry room. Frances said that Sorcha did clean the room—she didn't know better. Also," Ciara looked at Tori, "Frances wants to make sure that the medieval feast will still be going on after the wedding. Smoked pork and venison."

"I think we should have it," Dylan said.

"Me too," Tori said.

"Is it a problem?" Joan asked Ciara and Rayne.

Aine entered and topped off everyone's drinks, refreshing the pastries in the center of the table and pitchers of chilled water with lemon.

"No," Ciara assured them. "Not a problem."

"I think you should wait, Jake," Ethan said. "In addition to Tiffany's death, which is bloody tragic and completely not something I understand, I received an email from Jake's agent this morning that he's been nominated for an award for his latest action-adventure film."

Applause rounded the table.

Amy pouted slightly and seemed a teeny bit jealous, and Josh called her on it. "Bummed for my brother?"

The pout morphed to a genuine grin. "Never. I'm delighted for him! I tried out for the part opposite of Jake but didn't get it," Amy said. "Lucky you, Jakey. Still, I would have had better chemistry with you than the twit they chose."

Jake blushed. "It's a job and not a romance, by the way, Ames. Action adventure. Stuff blows up. Chase the bad guys. Catch the bad guys."

Amy fluttered her fingers as if the details were unimportant.

"Hello!" Ethan said with impatience. "I'm just saying that this wedding really needs to be on the down-low, or maybe even postponed, for your career. This award could get you superstar status."

Tori preened. "My handsome hubby."

Jake scooted his chair an inch away from her to look her in the eye and saw, as they all did, no wiggle room. Tori was not willing to wait for the wedding.

Josh snorted. "If I recall, your contract at the studio was for a long engagement. It hasn't even been a year since you popped the question."

"What do you care?" Amy said, coming to Tori's defense.

"I don't!" Josh sat back and raised his hands. "If Jake wants to tank his career, it's on him. People do strange things in the name of love, eh bro? Swept away by champagne and passion."

"A New Year's Eve proposal," Joan said dreamily. "Very romantic."

"The way I heard it, Jake barely remembered," Josh said. "No offense."

Jake punched his arm. The solid hit echoed in the room. "Shut your face, Josh."

"Hey!" Josh rubbed his arm. "You owe me a beer for that one."

Rayne winced. "Maybe two if it leaves a mark."

"Why do you put up with that, Josh?" Amy asked. "You don't have to be his punching bag."

"Family. There is nothing more important." The Anderson brothers high-fived each other.

Ethan looked at Amy. "Help me out here? You know if the studio told you to be single, you'd damn well be single."

Amy nodded and dabbed coffee from her lips with a napkin. The lipstick was so good it didn't smudge. "It's true. I wouldn't risk being blacklisted for a man."

"You're starting to get on my nerves, the three of you." Tori lightly placed her hand on her stomach. "There is no stopping this wedding."

Rayne gulped her coffee. Tori had decided to play her ace.

Josh had seen the motion and his eyes widened. "Oh, bro!"

"What?" Jake asked.

Ethan tossed his phone to the table with a loud curse.

"What?" Jake asked again. His tone filled with confusion.

"If the producer and agent are going to be pissed about you, supposed-to-be-single-yet-now-married super star, just wait until they hear about you being a daddy!"

Jake scooted back and stared at Tori, who didn't move her hand. "Babes. No, you're not."

"What?" Tori leaned back and stretched her legs, showing off her divine figure.

"You didn't!" Jake said. "We had a deal, Tori." His eyes turned darker green with anger.

Rayne was surprised to see the show of emotion. This could be the version of the superstar that Aine might have overheard arguing. If not with Tori, then who? Tiffany? Amy?

"What difference does it make?" Tori exuded sex appeal. She the goddess and he the lucky man at her feet. Only Jake wasn't used to taking the back seat.

"My career?" Jake slammed his hand to the table. "It's over before it began thanks to this fiasco."

"You signed a prenup that will leave you very wealthy," Dylan said. "You can choose your movie parts, to work or not, as you wish."

"After a year," Ethan countered, offering his two cents. It was obvious that the assistant knew the finer details of Jake's inner world.

Garda Williams typed in a note on his phone to show Rayne. *Prenup? Pregnant?*

"I am not marrying your conniving daughter," Jake said, all hint of Southern charm out the window.

With that, Dylan flew across the soda bread and punched Jake in his shoulder. He pulled his fist back and was ready to do it again.

"Not his face, Daddy!" Tori cried. "It will ruin the wedding pictures!"

Chapter Nine

Rayne snapped her mouth closed at Tori's worrying more about the wedding pictures than Jake's career, or his feelings.

"Stop it now," Garda Williams ordered. "This is very unseemly."

"Crackers," Ciara said in agreement. She glanced at Rayne with understanding dawning on her expression over why the dress really had to be altered.

Dylan reluctantly sat down. "Are you sure about this, Tori?"

Tori sniffed delicately, her knuckle to the tip of her nose. "I love him, Daddy."

"Daddy!" Josh said sarcastically. "Jake, maybe you should file assault charges? Put your new father-in-law in jail and that will def postpone the wedding."

Amy gasped. "This is not okay. Tori? Why didn't you say something? I thought we were best friends."

"The wedding will continue," the heiress declared. She gave Amy her shoulder and looked at Jake. "I love you, and I thought you loved me, Jake."

Jake squirmed. "I do, Tori. You know I do." He gazed up with angst. "We used condoms."

"That time in the hot tub?" Tori said. "Not then. Or behind the mall, in the limo? Or . . ."

"I get it!" Groaning, Jake couldn't argue.

Tension was palpable in the room, and Rayne wasn't sure what to do to ease it. This was beyond any sitcom drama she'd ever seen.

"Why don't you two go for a hike and cool off?" Joan suggested to the brothers. "Are they needed at the Coco Bean, Tori darling?"

"Yes!" Tori read the time on her phone. "But not until noon. Meet us there. All right?" She stood and put her arms around Jake, giving him a kiss to curl his toes.

Rayne averted her eyes in the event it got too X-rated. She wouldn't be surprised if steam rolled from the gorgeous couple.

Amy sank back with a shake of her head.

Josh pumped his fist and then wolf-whistled. The pair broke apart, chests heaving with passion.

"Save it for the wedding night," Dylan said in a serious tone. Rayne didn't blame him for his response.

"Why buy the cow if you get the milk for free?" Ethan asked.

Joan pointed her finger at Jake's assistant's pale face. "I don't like you, young man. You keep causing trouble. Do you get a percentage of Jake's salary or something?"

Ethan's mouth thinned. "I am offended at that insinuation. I am not going to the chocolate brunch. I will be in my cottage, trying to keep Jake's agent happy. *Maybe* I'll go to the wedding. If I don't go, I can claim not to know it happened."

"He can't know yet, Ethan," Jake said.

"I shouldn't have to work so hard on your career." Ethan headed for the exit from the dining room, raising his hand in farewell without a word.

Jake and Josh rushed after him. Jake called to Ethan's back, "Tell me again about that award, buddy." His voice trailed as the brothers left the dining room.

There was a moment of silence as Amy stared at Tori, then Joan and Dylan, hotel magnates. They would have no problem paying Jake off. Paying for whatever they wanted.

With a cunning gaze, Amy turned to the Garda. "I wonder if Tiffany found out about Tori's little secret? If it was in her notebook?"

The Garda shrugged.

"If she had, I wish she would have come to me." Dylan patted his wallet. "Most people can be paid off for cheap."

Tori patted her father's forearm. "*Dad.*"

Joan touched her gold pendant. "It's business, darling. Although it wouldn't be the first shotgun wedding, now would it? These things have a way of working out."

Ciara bit her lip as if to keep from replying. Oh, just wait until she found out the rest of the scoop!

Garda Williams read the notes from his tablet and asked, "Mr. and Mrs. Montgomery, did you know Tiffany prior to this trip?"

"No, we didn't," Joan said.

"Nope." Dylan tilted his head to look at the Garda. "Seemed quiet. Professional."

"Ha!" Amy said. "She wanted to be an actress . . . guess she played that part okay, then. She was rarely on time and being punctual is a big deal to me."

"Did she work nine to five for you?" the Garda asked.

"No. Forty hours give or take but it would depend on my acting schedule."

"It's hard to be punctual if you don't have a routine," Joan said.

Amy blushed. "I suppose." She glanced at the Garda. "Will her, er, body, be ready to go back to LA on Monday?"

The Garda tapped his pen to his tablet. "We are still searching for her next of kin. I will keep you apprised."

"She told me she was an orphan," Amy said. "No reason to lie, that I know of." She squinted across the table at Tori. "But then again, people do it all the freaking time."

Rayne conceded Amy's point with a shrug.

"I didn't want anyone to know," Tori said.

"Including Jake, obvi," Amy snapped. "You could ruin his career."

"Jake will rise above it," Tori said. "He's talented and gorgeous, and commanding top billing."

"I hope you're right," Amy said.

The Garda added another note, then looked at Rayne and Ciara. "I've got enough for now. I'd like to speak with Sorcha before I return to the station."

"It's ten-thirty," Ciara said. "Sorcha said if you were in a hurry she could chat while hanging sheets."

"Thank you." Garda Williams scanned the table, nodding at Tori, Amy, Joan, and Dylan. "I appreciate your cooperation." He read a message on his phone. "The forensics team has finished in the tower rooms, so you all may return to them. Good day."

The Garda left and Rayne placed her coffee cup on the buffet table. They had an hour and a half before they had to be at the Coco Bean Café at noon. She'd hoped to spend it with Tori's dress but had to stall until Amos returned with the missing crystal.

"Is anybody interested in a horse ride or a hike?" Ciara asked.

"No," Tori said. The others around the table concurred.

"I'd like to see the castle," Dylan said.

Rayne and Ciara exchanged a look, at Ciara's slight nod, Rayne gave up all thoughts other than being in the moment.

"A tour of the castle it is then," Rayne said in her most chipper voice. "Ciara and I would be pleased to show you how McGraths have lived since the 1700s."

Ciara's scowl was fleeting as she replaced it with a smile. They were in this together. "That we would."

"What is the dress code for the chocolate and champagne?" Joan asked. Her dress from this morning was lovely, matching Dylan's blue jacket, open to show a white and blue shirt. Diamonds in Celtic knots flashed from her lobes.

"It's casual, Joan," Ciara said. "No need to change."

Dylan and Joan stood, as did Amy, and last, Tori. The heiress said, "Let's see the castle."

"Are you both princesses?" Amy teased.

"Uncle Nevin was Lord McGrath," Rayne said.

"So, you are the ladies McGrath?" Joan asked. "How special."

"Yes," Rayne said. Ciara started to protest but pressed her lips together instead. It would be a benefit for Ciara to accept the adoption papers and become Ciara McGrath instead of Smith. Was Ciara waiting to see if they succeeded before committing to her father's name? And then when she and Dafydd got married, would she change it again to Mrs. Norman?

They gathered around the round table in the foyer. Rayne pointed to the shield with the McGrath crest.

"Ciara can tell you more about the historical facts all around us. My memories are of being a child here when I visited with my dad." Rayne missed Conor so much. "My cousin Padraig was older than me and teased me constantly that the castle was haunted."

"I knew it," Amy said. "Where is this cousin? He must be tall and handsome if he resembles you two."

"Unfortunately, Padraig passed away as a teenager. An accident on the property here." Ciara pressed her hand to her heart. "McGrath Castle, like many castles, has known its share of tragedy."

"And joy, too," Rayne said, not wanting to tank the tour before it started. "There has been a lot of love."

"How many ghosts are there?" Tori asked.

"It would be impossible to count," Ciara said. "I found a journal when we were cleaning the attic about an early McGrath ancestor who was ambushed by his enemies. A hundred or more men were killed. They fought with a shillelagh."

"What's that?" Dylan asked, intrigued.

Ciara went to the bucket by the front door and retrieved what looked like a stick with a gnarled handle. "This."

"No wonder they were slaughtered," Tori observed.

"Tori," Joan admonished.

"What? It's true—a stick against a gun?" Tori shrugged.

"They can be deadly, right cuz?" Ciara winked at Rayne.

Rayne recalled taking down her uncle's killer—not dead, but incapacitated. It was amazing what one might use to protect themselves.

"We'll tour the picture gallery," Ciara suggested. "On the second floor. You'll see the weapons for each generation."

"And the clothing styles," Rayne said. "Which is my favorite. I love fashion. But let's continue on the ground floor. It won't take long."

"To the right of the staircase are the Lloyd family's private rooms, three unique lounges, and a library. Also, the entrance to the tower." Ciara waved them on. "When we raided the third-floor attic, we discovered furniture that had been shoved to the back to make way for the next round of unwanted items. We still haven't uncovered it all."

"There could be treasure!" Amy said, clasping her hands.

"That would be handy," Rayne replied, thinking of the looming castle expenses.

"Right?" Ciara shook her head. There were only so many hours in the day. "We can put it on the list, which seems to grow longer every day."

"Home ownership at a whole other level," Dylan said.

"We were able to fit out three rooms completely. The furniture is museum quality." Rayne opened the door to the library. Wall to wall shelves with antique books.

"I love this," Joan said with appreciation.

Shrugging, Dylan said, "It's nice to look at. Old money versus new. I like my modern luxuries. Books on my e-reader take up less space."

"Nothing wrong with that," Rayne said. "Here at the manor, we've tried to offer a combination of old and new."

The next room was from the twentieth century, then the nineteenth, and the third, from the eighteenth. Not a single stick or stitch of cloth was a replica. The difference in furniture styles and fabrics was something that continually astounded Rayne.

She glanced at her phone. Eleven o'clock. Nothing from Amos. Surely, he should be halfway to Dublin!

"I prefer my floor-to-ceiling windows overlooking the ocean at home," Tori said. "This section of the castle is dark and spooky. Especially those suits of armor."

The hall ended at the tower base attached to the manor and the interior entrance.

"Let's go to the other side," Ciara said. "You're already familiar with the left part that leads to the sunroom. It's gorgeous in the summer with a view of the rose garden."

"What's behind the staircase?" Joan asked as they passed by it. The scent of lavender and lemon wafted to them.

"The laundry room and storage for cleaning supplies," Rayne said. She stepped into the long hall.

"This is our office." Ciara gestured to the left but didn't open the door. "The blue parlor, the billiards room. The kitchen and two different dining rooms are on the right of the hall. Another lounge."

"All of this furniture has been in the family for centuries?" Dylan asked. "That is impressive."

"It has," Ciara said, sounding rightfully proud of their heritage.

"The artwork too. We had a lot of talent," Rayne said. "My dad wrote poetry and painted. I sketch and sew."

"I am a worker bee," Ciara declared. "No fancy hobbies for me."

"She's a gifted horse rider," Rayne said. "Which terrifies me."

"Everyone has something they're good at," Joan said. "Tori was a dancer but didn't pursue it. I was once a model, not that I could do that now."

Dylan slung an arm around his wife's shoulders. "You could. You're beautiful to me."

They peeked into each of the rooms and last the sunroom on the corner of the manor. Even on a dreary day, the light inside lifted Rayne's mood.

Today presented blue skies without a hint of rain, just as Maeve had predicted. The roses were lush and varied in color.

"Now we're talking," Tori said. "This is where I'd stay." She plopped down on the couch. "All the time. Tea and a book."

Rayne was relieved Tori liked it as much as she'd hoped. "It's where we'll do your preparation for the wedding."

"Perfect!" Tori said. Amy sat on the opposite end of the couch while Joan and Dylan wandered around the built-in shelves filled with knickknacks.

Her phone dinged. Eleven-thirty and Amos had received the crystal from Nolan at Oasis Fabric and was back en route to the castle. She would owe both men huge favors.

"Everything all right?" Ciara asked.

Rayne patted her heart. "It's great. But we should save the upstairs gallery for tomorrow and get ready to party with Sinéad. Chocolate fountain, and champagne." She sent a thumbs-up emoji to Amos. "Can't go wrong for fun!"

"Shall we walk?" Ciara asked, eyeing everyone's footwear.

"Yes." Tori lifted her flats. "I need to stretch my legs. Nervous energy." She scanned her phone. "Jake hasn't texted me back since they left." She nibbled her bottom lip as if finally concerned about the situation.

"I'm sorry, darling," Joan said. "He'll cool down, but I agree. Let's walk."

Dylan grumbled.

"Daddy, you walk miles on the golf course. This is nothing."

Amy sighed. "Since the suites are clear, I'll run to my room and change my shoes. Be back in five."

The starlet hurried down the hall in her chunky heels. Rayne and the others followed at a slower pace. There was no opportunity for her to bring Ciara up to speed about Tiffany's true manner of death.

They went outside. The weather was beautiful, and Rayne said a quick prayer of thanks that it had stopped raining.

The group gathered on the front stoop, but Garda Williams called for Rayne, so she shut the door on the delightful breeze and waited by the bin of walking sticks and the infamous shillelagh to the hall. "Yes?"

The Garda strode toward her from the laundry room, glancing around to see that they were alone. "I just wanted to let you know that Sorcha showed me the trash she'd collected."

He reached her side and Rayne asked, "Did you find Tiffany's notebook?"

"No. Nor the phone either. The tower rooms were also clear. The hatch to the roof hadn't even been opened since you'd painted it." Garda Williams tipped the brim of his hat up an inch off his forehead. "How did the tour go?"

"It was a good use of time. I'm very grateful for Ciara's knowledge of this place. I know Uncle Nevin would have been proud too."

"Yes, I agree," the Garda said. "You make a good team."

"Thank you."

That meant a lot to hear, but she had the feeling that the Garda hoped Rayne would pass the compliment along to Ciara. She didn't get attraction vibes, but more regret from the Garda when it came to her cousin.

"I can't believe Tori sucker-punched Jake like that, with the news of her being pregnant," the Garda said. "I'm gobsmacked the wedding is still going on."

"Me too," she admitted. "But, Tori is Catholic, so I think that might have something to do with her insistence."

The Garda sighed and met her eyes. "Do you think if they knew about the suspicious circumstances that they would call the ceremony off?"

Rayne shrugged. "I honestly don't know. Tori wants what she wants, and her dad is willing to pay to make her happy."

"Not my life," Garda Willliams said with a big exhale. "Thank God."

"I feel the same." Rayne hooked her thumb toward the door. "We have an appointment with Sinéad at the Coco Bean Café at noon. Do you think somebody in the wedding party argued with Tiffany and killed her? Is anyone else in danger? Should I be worried?"

"Be aware, that's all. I'll have an extra Garda around the castle grounds and one at the church for the ceremony. Garda Lee went to the pub and talked with Beetle. Beetle said Tiffany and Bran Wilson were kissing Thursday night."

"The first night they were in!" Rayne shook her head. "I thought they'd all gone to bed and stayed there."

The front door opened, and Tori arched her brow. "Hey! Where the heck is Amy?"

Just then the soles of sneakers racing down the hall squeaked. "Don't leave without me!" Amy called.

The starlet arrived with pink Nikes on her feet, her purse, a glittery pink cap on her head, and another in her hand.

"What took so long?" Tori asked in a snarky tone.

It hadn't, though. Rayne understood Tori was upset with Amy for what she might view as siding with Ethan about Jake's career.

"I hurried." Amy offered Tori a pink glittery cap that read BRIDE along the side. "For you!"

Tori burst into tears and placed it on her head. "Thank you! I'm sorry about all of this . . ." she said, allowing the sentence to trail.

"It's okay!" Amy pulled another one from her purse. "MOTHER OF THE BRIDE."

"Cute!" Tori declared. "Mom will love it. Let's show her."

The Garda tapped his hat to Rayne. "I think I've got all the pictures I need. But if you don't mind me walking around a bit?"

"Not at all," Rayne said. She knew he'd be as discreet as possible.

The two guests went outside. Blarney peered in the front door, which was open a crack, as if wondering what was keeping her.

"Rayne!" Aine peeked from the kitchen and waved for Rayne.

"Why don't you go on out, Garda Williams? I'll be just a second," Rayne said. The Garda nodded, noticed Aine, and went outside with a bemused smile. It was a lot of chaos.

Rayne hurried to the maid. "What is it?"

"Dafydd was going to smoke a whole hog, but the smoker thing went out, and he didn't notice, and it won't be done in time for tonight's meal."

Rayne blew out a breath. The suckling pig with the apple in the mouth was the centerpiece of the medieval feast. "Sugar cookies," she said.

"Right? It's feckin' awful," Aine whispered. "Frances is cooking a leg of lamb, the venison roast, and we will triple the side dishes. It's not like they eat a lot anyway. But, it's the experience, eh?"

"Exactly." Rayne clasped the maid's fingers. "I approve of the changes—whatever you need to do so we can bring this off. Did you talk to Sorcha about the makeup?"

"Sorcha will bring her makeup kit at three, but she said a lot of ladies have their own. Did you hear from Amos?"

"He's on his way from Dublin with the crystal." Rayne's pulse sped with apprehension. "He'll be here by two, which is when the chocolate and champagne celebration should be over, and we should be heading back to the castle." Sweat gathered on Rayne's forehead. "We've got this."

Aine scowled. "Did you know Tori was preggers?"

"I can't say."

"That's a yes. I'm not sure, but I think I feel sorry for Jake Anderson." Aine ducked back into the kitchen.

Rayne hurried outside. Blarney raced from Ciara to Garda Williams to Rayne. Her dog loved to chase butterflies and often went on walks with her across the manor grounds.

"Stay here," she told Blarney so he didn't follow her to the café.

"He only listens to you," Ciara said.

"Sometimes." Rayne palmed her cell phone. Amos was working with Rayne and Blarney so he would be a good pet—Irish Setters were sweet and loyal but had a willful streak.

Rayne and Ciara took the rear of the group walking down the path. Trees grew thick and provided shade over the road. It was a half mile to the main street. It wasn't a big village, with less than five hundred people in it, but it was theirs—hers and Ciara's. It was their joint responsibility to protect it for the future.

How could Ciara do that if she wouldn't use her dad's name?

Rayne sensed that she might be able to use this argument to prompt her cousin into action.

"This is simply lovely," Joan said. "The weather. The landscape. I can feel my mother's Irish energy here. I can't wait to tell my friends that we were at an actual castle."

"Well, we'd be sure to make them welcome if they wanted a stay," Rayne assured the hotel magnate.

"Do you think a discount might be in order?" Joan asked slyly.

This was why rich people stayed rich.

Ciara glanced over her shoulder at Rayne. Rayne nodded. "I'm sure that something could be arranged," Ciara said.

"Wonderful." Joan clasped Dylan's hand.

They reached the main road. To the left was the café, gas station, and pubs; to the right was the doctor's office, pharmacy, the town hall, and some small businesses, including the vintage shop where Rayne had found her favorite sweater. The church was a few blocks away.

Two cars zipped by and then Ciara led the way across. "It's a Saturday and our farmer's market is very busy. Organic fruit and veg."

"I don't care about that," Amy said. "I like my food to just magically appear before me ready to eat. I am not about the chef lifestyle. I played a part once where my character dated a chef. Moody."

"It wasn't real though," Tori pointed out. The brim of her pink cap sparkled. Joan carried hers, perhaps not wanting to mess up her hair.

"I learned enough to know that cooking isn't for me," Amy stated.

From the way they'd left the billiards room, neither was cleaning. Good thing Amy would be famous and have enough money to pay for staff. This might be the lesson needed to treat them better.

"I don't like to cook either," Joan confessed.

Dylan smiled. "We hire the best chefs for our hotels. Why bother?"

Rayne agreed with Dylan's point. Until she'd arrived at the castle food had been fuel carefully monitored for caloric value with taste secondary.

Her views had changed since being here. Not that she was ready to tackle the stove, but she certainly enjoyed flavorful bites.

A man whizzed by on his moped—Bran Wilson—and went to the pub. Bran had been kissing Tiffany on Thursday! The girl had been in town for what, two hours, and making out with a stranger at a pub?

It was Saturday, and Bran's day off from the manor. It was no business of hers that it was just noon and early to begin pounding pints.

She shook her head and reminded herself that pubs in Ireland were a lifestyle of food and community and not necessarily drinking. And wasn't she having champagne?

Bran, instead of getting off his moped, circled in the lot and came back, zipping inches away from Rayne.

"Hey!" Rayne and her guests were mere feet from the blue door of the café. A bench and some planters decorated the space between the shop and sidewalk, then the main road.

Bran stopped with a shriek of rubber to gravel and stared at Tori, then Amy, then Tori again. "Blondie. You the bride?"

Tori stepped back. "Did the hat give it away?"

Bran winked. "Saw your fiancé earlier."

"Where?"

"The pub, where else?" Bran revved the engine by twisting the handlebar.

"So? It's his wedding day," Tori stated. "He's allowed to celebrate."

"Didn't seem none too happy gettin' hitched," Bran chortled.

"Knock it off," Rayne said. She held eye contact and spoke softly, "Or we won't hire you again."

"For what?" Bran demanded. "Having a conversation?"

"Please go," Rayne said. How hadn't she noticed his bad attitude before now? Did he and Gillian have something personal against her or the castle?

"This is my day off." Bran shook his head at Amy, then the Montgomerys. "We don't need your feckin' money."

Ciara shoved Bran's shoulder. "Shut your gob. You are drunk and obnoxious, Bran Wilson. Go home."

Chapter Ten

To Rayne's surprise, Bran wobbled off on his moped. Unfortunately, he didn't go home, but returned to the pub. Was he right, and Jake and Josh were drinking there as well, complaining about the upcoming wedding?

Jake had been given the news of his fatherhood in a pretty awful way, so Rayne couldn't blame him for drowning his sorrows.

"Rude!" Amy declared.

Sinéad opened the door to her café, the sweet scent of chocolate escaping. "Come in! Oh, geez, so sorry if Bran was hassling you."

"What did he mean about not needing the money?" Tori asked.

Joan, thank heaven, supplied an answer, and Rayne didn't have to come up with one. "Your dad flashes his wallet around sometimes, and he may have done that yesterday at the pub."

Dylan blushed. "I thought it was a nice thing to do, buying rounds."

"It was," Rayne said. It wouldn't be good for the Montgomerys to discover that Rayne and Ciara had an entire village on the line and that the hotel billionaire's money was definitely needed.

Bran was an idiot for being so vocally against the castle bringing in revenue to save the village, of which he was a member.

"It really was kind," Ciara seconded. "Ignore him."

"You didn't see him say no to a pint, did ye?" Sinéad asked in exaggerated disbelief. "That didn't happen, on my life."

"No," Dylan said with a chuckle.

"Welcome," Sinéad said. "The café is just us so you can relax and not worry about anybody botherin' you."

"This is adorbs," Amy stated. The white, glass, and chrome décor was modern compared to the rest of the village. Sinéad had warmed the café with bright tablecloths and shelves full of succulent plants along the walls. The stove, display case, and register were to the left, and the ten tables in an L shape on the right with a window at the front.

"Thank ye," Sinéad said. "My husband, Liam, will be back soon. He just had to run out for . . . a sec."

Sinéad motioned to the tables she'd covered in white cloths with gold and silver glitter shaped like horseshoes and shamrocks. At the back of the small shop was a round table where a large silver bucket was filled with champagne that Rayne had special ordered, splurging on a decent label.

It was important to show that they had the means to cater to an heiress for her wedding. Would Tori even have a glass now that she was pregnant?

Sinéad waggled her brows at Rayne. Had Sinéad heard about Tiffany's death? Rayne couldn't answer any questions and hadn't even had a chance to talk with Ciara about Garda Williams' awful news.

Focus on the now.

Rayne could have done with fewer than two cases of champagne for today—but she'd store the extra for the next wedding in November. She imagined Tori telling all her friends and social media immediately following the secret wedding would set her up with that waiting list Amy had mentioned.

Arranged around the silver champagne bucket were five table-sized chocolate fountains with three flowing cocoa ribbons: white, milk, and dark chocolate. Each fountain was chocolate shaped in an

Irish symbol. The Irish harp, a shamrock, a Celtic cross, a beer stein, and a pony.

"Chocolate!" Dylan said. "My Achilles heel."

"It's true," Joan laughed. "It's my secret weapon when I want my way."

"TMI!" Tori said with a raised palm.

Rayne liked the older couple together and hoped that they'd be a good example for Tori and Jake, despite the rocky start.

"This is for dessert," Sinéad said. "And lunch is a variety of meats and cheeses, along with fresh baked bread. Everything here is locally sourced."

"Charcuterie style?" Tori questioned, seeing the sausage sliced on a board on top of the tall display case. Her skin turned a bit green.

"Is everything all right?" Sinéad asked with alarm. "I should have asked if there were any food allergies! Oh no, you're not a *vegetarian*?"

Rayne would have laughed at the horrified expression on Sinéad's face, but it wasn't at all funny.

"Worse!" Amy laughed and smacked her hands together. "Our bride is knocked up. Feeling queasy, Tor?"

"Amy!" Tori said. "You have a big mouth." She removed the pink cap and crushed the brim.

Amy winced. "It's true though, and you're the one who let the cat out of the bag this morning, so it's on you to own it." The starlet pouted. "I'm supposed to be your best friend and I didn't know."

Tori backtracked. "It's not for sure," she said. "I haven't been checked out by a doctor. I'm just late. Could be a false alarm."

"Maybe that's what you shoulda told Jake," Amy said with disappointment. "He might not have run off with Josh. Or Ethan could have been brought around."

Sinéad snapped her mouth closed at this insanely personal conversation.

Ciara focused on the floor, shoulders shaking. Rayne would wager her cousin was trying not to laugh.

"When I was carrying you, Tori, I craved chocolate." Joan patted her daughter's arm.

"That's true," Dylan said with a laugh. "It was wonderful to spoil you, Joan, because you're so strict with your diet."

"I gained thirty pounds," Joan said, scandalized.

"Thirty pounds?" Tori shook her head. "I can't gain that much weight."

"We'll get you a personal trainer to take it off," Joan assured her. "Every woman should have the chance to indulge like that, and motherhood is the best reason."

"Where is the rest of your party?" Sinéad asked, then blushed. "The men. I, well, we heard that there was an accident at the castle. Is everyone all right?"

"There was," Dylan confirmed. "The police have come and gone."

"What happened? If you don't mind my asking," Sinéad said.

"Garda Williams is looking into things." Ciara gave an uninformative answer. "Now, how about we all take a seat. Sinéad, should I bring everyone waters?"

"Thank you!" Sinéad had filled two pitchers, still or bubbling, of water with sliced lemon and strawberry.

Ciara made sure everyone had a tumbler, leaving the flutes for the champagne. "Here we are."

"I'm about to shoot my husband," Sinéad said. "Liam promised to hurry back. Rayne, can I have a word in my office?"

"Certainly."

Ciara went around to Amy, Tori, Joan, and Dylan, pouring their water of choice. Rayne glanced over her shoulder, but Ciara was focused on their guests.

"What is it, Sinéad?" Rayne closed the office door.

"Oh, Rayne, I'm so sorry about what happened to that poor woman," Sinéad said.

Garda Williams' imploring eyes came to mind asking her to keep things under wraps. "What do you mean?"

"Bran is telling everyone that a woman jumped to her death from the tower. The tower that was just on fire. He's saying that the tower is cursed and that the ghosts of McGraths past don't want anything to do with the new wedding venue."

"Bran has to shut his mouth." Rayne pinched the bridge of her nose and briefly closed her eyes.

"Is it true?" Sinéad sank back against the desk and crossed her arms in disbelief.

"I can't comment."

"But, dead?"

"There has been a death, but the tower is not cursed." Rayne drew in a calming breath.

Sinéad's expression fell at the confirmation. "I warned Bran to get out of here—he wanted to drop off some postcards about the wedding this afternoon to sabotage it."

"What?" That was it, he was not going to be employed by the castle any longer. "Why postcards?"

"I'll show you." Sinéad reached into the drawer of her desk and handed the postcard from Bran. A photo of the castle with an X through it. Below it in block letters: MCGRATH WEDDINGS BAD FOR BUSINESS.

"This is unreal," Rayne said. "We are taking Bran off the payroll starting now, I don't care how good of a plumber he is. You don't bite the hand that feeds you!"

"I don't understand his actions," Sinéad said. "Then again, he lives at home with his mam and doesn't have a lot of expenses. I'm sure Nancy is hoping he'll get married, and some other woman will take him off her hands."

"What?" Rayne shook her head. "That can't be a viable strategy!"

"Oh yes," Sinéad said. "Bran's tolerable-looking, has all his teeth, and the local lasses don't seem to mind his lack of career aspirations."

"Tiffany and Bran were hooking up," Rayne confirmed. "I don't see it."

"He'll get his mam's place after she dies, so he has an inheritance, so to speak," Sinéad said. "Some sheep and land."

"Which he could lose if the village fails." Rayne was at a further loss as it seemed Bran had something at stake.

Sinéad turned beet-red.

"What?"

"Well, the folks in the rural areas might not be as loyal to the McGraths, especially if they are closer to the Cotter side of the village." Sinéad continued at her open mouth. "They might get more services if Grathton and Cotter combined."

Rayne snapped it closed. Back to politics again. "I need to under-stand the local government better," she said.

"Come to a meeting," Sinéad suggested. "Every four months at the town services building. We need to elect a new council member, anyway. November."

"Why's that?"

"Nevin's seat will need to be filled," Sinéad said in a quiet voice.

Rayne backed up a step. "Not by me!"

"It is traditional," Sinéad countered.

"I'll speak with Ciara—she can do it." Rayne couldn't handle one more thing on her overfilled plate. "Are there a lot of people who are ambivalent about the fate of the village?"

"I can't say, as in, I don't know." Sinéad stood and brushed her hands together. "What is taking my husband so bloody long to find out what is happening at Beetle's?"

"Maybe he's with the groom and best man." Rayne shook her head. "You might have guessed that things are not rainbows and roses."

"I'm worried about you guys at the castle. What if . . . what if the tower is cursed, like Bran says?"

"It's not cursed, Sinéad—please don't spread that around. Your business will grow with tourist dollars."

"I know," Sinéad said. "And I am team McGrath. I just wanted to fill you in with what was happening behind the scenes."

"Thank you. Maybe I'll have Ciara talk with him about his intentions." She considered this then said, "Even better, we can sit him down in Uncle Nevin's office, all official. Get Bran to see our side."

"I like that," Sinéad said.

Rayne and Sinéad stood. Rayne's phone rattled with notifications. From Amos.

"I have to make a call," Rayne said.

"Stay in here if you like. I'll try to find something to feed the bride that won't make her queasy. I feel awful about the meat situation," Sinéad said.

"We just found out yesterday." Rayne squeezed the café owner's shoulder in commiseration and shut the door as Sinéad went to nourish her guests.

She dialed Amos.

"Rayne," Amos said. His voice boomed through the speaker on her phone.

"Hey! What's up?" Last time he'd checked in he was going to arrive around two. She'd have just enough time to run to the castle, sew the crystal on the dress, and meet in the sunroom for makeup at three.

"Rayne, I just want to warn you I might be a little delayed due to road construction. It's putting me in Grathton at two-twenty."

Her head swam. "Okay. Okay." It had to be okay, and he sounded worried for her. "It's all right. That's fine."

"I'm sorry, lass."

"For what?" Rayne asked. He was flying there and back and couldn't be faulted for trucks on the road.

"For not being faster."

"Amos, you have been my *hero* today. Just drive safe so you arrive in one piece, all right?"

"All right."

"Thank you and see you soon."

"Ta." He ended the call.

Rayne braced her shoulders and left the office—just as Jake and Josh arrived, with Sinéad's husband, Liam Walsh. He towered over his wife in height, well over six foot, with broad shoulders and muscled biceps. Brown hair, bearded chin, and round-framed glasses perched on his strong nose.

"Look who I found!" Liam said. He ushered the Anderson brothers before him through the front door of the café.

Jake and Josh were grinning ear to ear.

"Right on time, right, babes?" Jake said.

Tori smiled at Jake, who was irresistible. "Close enough, hon." She reached out her hand and tugged him to her.

Josh went for the champagne bucket and the corked bottle on ice, stumbling a bit.

"Let's wait a sec on that," Dylan suggested. "Get some food in ya before you start on the next round. Can't have you passing out during your best man duties."

Amy shook her head. "Good plan."

"And ruin the buzz I've spent all morning creating?" Josh huffed but sat at the table with Amy, accepting a glass of water from Ciara. "Thanks."

"Welcome." Ciara nodded after watching him drain the tumbler, refilling it for him.

Rayne hoped that they could all settle down and learn about the art of chocolate after a nice lunch.

Tori's nausea passed with a sip of the sparkling water, and she was able to enjoy the meal, though she stayed away from the selection of sausages.

Liam made the sausage from scratch, and he told them how he did it, without going too far into detail and focusing on the herbs and spices rather than the ground meat.

"What was going on at the pub?" Sinéad murmured to her husband while everyone was eating.

"Bran. That man is a menace," Liam said. He didn't elaborate but Rayne could imagine after reading the postcard he'd handed out. Did all the businesses get them?

Rayne should show it to Garda Williams and ask if he could put a stop to the mailers . . . she glanced at Ciara, wanting to share what she knew, but Joan was conversing with her. The two really had hit it off.

At last, it was Sinéad's turn to shine and showcase her skills as a chocolatier. "Sinéad went to culinary school and specialized in chocolate," Liam said. "We've been here for ten years now and hope to grow our online pastry sales. The sausage has a steady following already."

Her husband cleared the plates and put them in the sink, inviting everyone to wash up as he popped two bottles of champagne before he filled the flutes.

Everyone took one.

"A lover's treat," Sinéad said. "Champagne and chocolate. I've made up a basket for your room tonight after the ceremony, Tori and Jake. I wish I'd thought to include sparkling water."

"Thank you!" Jake said with drunken enthusiasm.

"It's fine," Tori said. "It's a special occasion. A glass or two won't hurt, will it, Mom?"

Amy's brow hiked in judgment.

Joan patted Tori's hand. " "Perhaps you should stick to the sparkling water. I didn't know I was pregnant with you until my third month, but it's better to be on the safe side."

"Good idea, Mom."

* * *

"Now, for the chocolate, we need a low heat." Sinéad had placed a sculpted chocolate fountain for two on each table. Amy paired with Josh and the shamrock, Joan and Dylan with the Irish harp, then Tori and Jake with the Celtic cross.

"I thought there would be eight, so Ciara and Rayne please share one," Sinéad said. "Take the Connemara pony. I don't want it to go to waste."

"The what?" Amy asked.

"The Connemara pony is unique to Ireland. They come from the west and are raised in a harsh landscape of bogs and craggy hills. They've become a symbol of trust and strength," Sinéad said. "They can be show horses, but also hardworking."

"Style and function," Rayne said. "Perfect mix." She perched on the edge of her chair, able to see the others. Here if needed, but not in charge.

"I won't say no," Ciara said, sitting down.

"You can start with the dark chocolate, white, or milk chocolate," Sinéad said. "There is enough fruit and biscuits to try all three flavors and go back for more."

"What are the differences in the chocolate?" Joan asked.

Sinéad rubbed her hands together. "I'm so glad you asked!"

"It's her favorite question," Liam teased his wife.

Sinéad swiped dark chocolate on Liam's mouth, and he just grinned before he licked it off. "Ignore him—I'll be brief. The main thing in common is that all three have sugar and cocoa butter. Milk chocolate has . . . what?"

"Milk!" Josh guessed.

"You got it, and white chocolate does not have the cocoa powder," Sinéad said. "You can vary the amount of cocoa butter and cocoa powder to adjust flavor and color. I prefer a strong dark chocolate. What about you?"

"I like it all," Dylan said.

Joan chuckled. "The white is really buttery so it's my favorite."

"Milk," Jake said. Josh agreed.

"Dark for me," Rayne said.

"I'm with Dylan—I like it all." Ciara smacked her lips.

"Why choose?" Liam asked.

"A word to the wise—a serving of dark chocolate has about the same amount of antioxidants as a serving of blueberries," Sinéad said.

"Give me the dark chocolate!" Amy said with a laugh. She swooped a pineapple triangle through the glossy stream. "It's the prettiest."

"And the easiest to melt because of the fat content." Sinéad shrugged. "It's a winner in my book."

"How fun!" Rayne said. The strawberries were bright red and plump, triangles of golden pineapple, dark red cherries, and firm raspberries. And there were thin cookies that smelled of ginger, or chocolate crisps.

Jake and Tori fed each other chocolate-coated fruit. Josh tried to feed Amy a piece, but she poked him with the tiny fruit prongs.

"Back off, Josh." Amy wasn't messing around with the man.

Josh raised his hand. "Sorry. Too bad your buddy Ethan isn't here."

"He's not my anything," Amy said.

Ciara swirled a pineapple chunk in the dark chocolate. "I can see sharing this with Dafydd as a romantic feast. You could sell a chocolate date night for two, Sinéad."

Sinéad smiled with pleasure. "You think so?"

Rayne nodded. "Hey, I'm single, and it still tastes great," she said.

Amy spluttered and laughed, sipping her champagne. "Amen, Rayne!"

Rayne didn't miss Landon, her ex, at all. But when she thought of chocolate and kisses, she imagined Amos across the table from her, nibbling chocolate from her fingers.

Her phone dinged a notification, and she wiped her hands, reading the text from none other than her sexy Viking.

ETA 2:30. Sorry!

Shoot. How on earth could she stall the wedding party?

Second thought was a fervent prayer that Amos wasn't too late for her to fix the dress completely. Well, she could dig through her cubic zirconia shapes as a last measure though it wouldn't fool anyone looking closely.

"You all right?" Ciara whispered. "You're as pale as this white chocolate here."

"Amos won't be here until two-thirty," she murmured back. "Construction is causing delays. And he'd been making such good time!"

Ciara's gray eyes darkened with concern.

Her mom called again. Third time but no message?

It had to be important. Lauren was very aware of all today's wedding signified, being the first in hopefully a long line of happy couples in the future.

"I've got to take this." Rayne stood and surveyed the group of very contented chocolate lovers enjoying the decadent treat.

It had been a good idea, something Rayne suggested to Sinéad while in for a cappuccino last month after seeing Sinéad's chocolatier certification on the wall. Maybe they could play up the chocolatier to the castle angle for promotions moving forward . . .

She scooted out the front door, her phone to her ear. "Lauren! Are you okay?"

That seemed to be her question of the day.

"I'm fine! Forgive me for interrupting today but you've got to be forewarned."

Rayne's stomach clenched with nerves at the cautious words combined with the Mom tone. "What is it?"

"Landon escaped from jail."

Chapter Eleven

"Escaped?" Rayne's fingers shook so hard that she dropped her phone to the cement sidewalk outside of the café. She hoped the screen hadn't cracked; the way her luck had been going, she wouldn't doubt needing a replacement.

After examining the device—no breaks, thank heaven—Rayne prayed she'd heard wrong. "I dropped my phone. Say that again?"

"Snickle fritz!" Lauren exclaimed harshly. "Landon Short escaped from jail—they had him in low security, the fools—and he hasn't been caught. Yet."

"How long ago?" Rayne didn't consider Landon to be a dangerous man. Sly, cunning as a weasel, but not dangerous. He was average height, and she was tall. She hadn't realized he liked wearing the gowns she made. No, she wasn't shaking in her UGGs about facing down her ex.

"That nice Officer Peters let me know this morning, on the down low," her mom said. "She asked me to warn you to be careful."

Rayne didn't understand the need for caution. He was in California, and she was in Ireland; across the ocean. "Why?"

Her mother exhaled before sharing, "It seems that inside Landon's cell, he'd carved your name over and over with a sharpened toothbrush. We had an episode of *Family Forever* where the con escaped after carving a key from a block of soap. That was in the old days though and not the point. He's obsessed."

Rayne shivered.

"And, it's possible he wants to find you for who knows what reason," Lauren continued. "It can't be a good one!"

"How does he know where I am?" Rayne hadn't told anyone, though maybe her mother had shared with friends. Hardly newsworthy.

"It was a big deal when Landon was captured," her mom said. "The local stations blasted how you'd inherited a castle and didn't need a cross-dressing thief for Prince Charming."

Oh. Rayne processed her mom's words. Guess it had made the news. She'd paid zero attention to the newspapers back home, too invested in saving Grathton Village one handbag at a time.

She got the feeling she was being watched and goose bumps dotted her skin. Scanning the area, she didn't see anybody. Not even Bran the backstabber.

"So, you must be on guard, darling, until Landon's caught. I asked the officer to let you know when she could, but they are very understaffed at the police station. They've got a security alert at the airport as well as the Mexican border. He is conniving and I don't trust him."

"I'll add it to the drama of the day," Rayne said. She quickly updated her mother about the murder, the missing Swarovski crystal, and Amos's mad dash to Dublin.

"And they're still getting married?" Her mother's shock was evident in the rising tone of her words.

"Tori's pregnant and feels like Jake will come around. Dylan mentioned a healthy prenup that works in Jake's favor. They don't know about the murder part of Tiffany's death as Garda Williams wants to use that to his advantage. He told me that Bran Wilson, currently doing freelance work at the castle, was making out with Tiffany on Thursday night. This same Bran is passing out postcards to the local businesses saying that supporting the wedding venue will be a detriment to the village."

"What on earth?" Lauren said. "That's a lot you just unloaded there, honey. I'm not sure what I'm more stunned about. I think Bran not wanting the village to succeed. . ."

"Not the murder?" Then again, her mother hadn't witnessed poor Tiffany but was hearing about it secondhand. Rayne would never forget the tragic sight for as long as she lived.

"Remember the motives are usually passion or money," Lauren said, pulling on her twenty-plus years of experience in Hollywood studying characterization. "Bran's motivation for failure is a mystery. What does he want?"

"I'll find out," Rayne said, putting it closer to the top of her to-do list. "How's the holiday shoot going?"

Her mother sighed. "All right. Paul's being really sweet to everyone, making sure we have anything we could want on set, so it feels like a real Christmas."

"Is it working?" Rayne eyed the blue sky. In LA the sky would be even bluer, as paradise should have nothing less.

"No," her mom muttered. "All of us realize it could be the last time we are together as the Carter family. Which makes me miss you, my only real family, all the more! I hope to be in Ireland for Christmas."

"Yes!" Her mother was overcoming her fear of flying to be with Rayne, and Rayne couldn't be happier. "With Jenn?"

"We are looking at our schedules," Lauren confirmed. "But no matter what, I will be there, Rayne."

"Stay for as long as you want, all right? Maybe buy a one-way ticket?"

"I saw how that worked for you." Her mother laughed. "You never came home. I need to go, but please, please, please be careful."

They ended the call, and Rayne went inside after another quick glance around to make sure nobody was spying on her.

Freaking Landon.

"Everything all right?" Sinéad asked.

Rayne swallowed as she thought of and discarded shareable reasons for an emergency phone call from her mother. The door closed at her back.

"It was very important actually." Rayne grinned. "Lauren McGrath will be done with filming the holiday bonus episode of *Family Forever* in time to be here for Christmas."

"Brilliant!" Ciara said.

Joan clapped her hands together. "I adore that show."

"Me, too," Amy said. "Your mom is an incredible actress—and what a dream job to be in such a long running sitcom."

"I learned my work ethic from her dedication," Rayne said.

Amy leaned toward Sinéad. "Doing that cameo for the Faith episode is where I learned about Modern Lace Bridal Boutique and Rayne."

"I'm so glad you did," Tori said. "My dress is gorgeous, and this venue, well . . . it couldn't have come together like it did without Rayne and Ciara." The heiress raised her glass of sparkling water to the cousins. "My thanks."

"It's our pleasure," Ciara said.

"You're so welcome." Rayne drank from her flute, loving the fizzy bubbles. There was so much work to do yet before now and the ceremony at four-thirty, but it was a crime to rush such scrumptious champagne.

Bran out to get her and Landon escaped from jail. Rayne switched her flute for water to ease her suddenly dry throat and resumed her seat across from Ciara. Focus on the moment and entertaining the bridal party. "You said that the dark chocolate was more meltable than the milk chocolate? I would have guessed the other way around, Sinéad."

"It's all about that delicious fat content," Sinéad said. "Who wants more?"

"Even I am full, and chocolate is my favorite," Dylan said. "It's been a treat."

They were still talking at two, when Bran returned and dismounted off his moped, pounding on the glass window of the Coco Bean. "Two murders is no way to begin a business!"

Rayne's eyes widened in alarm. Luckily because he'd been drinking, his brogue was too thick and slurred to be understood clearly, as she saw from the confusion on the guests' faces.

Liam strode outside and grabbed Bran by the shirt front, biceps flexing rather impressively. "Sleep it off, Bran. Don't come back here again talking trash."

Red-faced, Bran muttered that he would not be treated in such a way. "I know what's going on at the castle," he said.

"A wedding, mate," Liam said.

"Murder. It won't be the last," Bran decreed. He pulled free, hopped on his moped and weaved toward the street. A passing car nearly hit him. He flipped them off, two fingers rather than the American single middle digit, and kept going.

"Local charm," Ciara said with an exaggerated eyeroll.

The comment broke the tension. Joan tapped her ear. "What was he saying? I couldn't really understand."

"Who knows with that one?" Sinéad shook her head.

"Shall we go back to the house?" Rayne suggested. It would be quarter past two by the time they got there, and then she could pace the foyer until Amos arrived. Not at all suspicious, she chided herself. Maybe she'd wait in the kitchen, or better yet, keep Blarney company by the rose garden. Flowers for the bouquet! Was that handled?

If not, there were lovely fresh blooms that would need to be tossed together in a flippin' hurry. That question would be added to the checklist moving forward.

"Let's go back," Tori said in a mellow mood. She hooked her arm through Jake's. "Honey, I love you, and I'm sorry about the chaos. Maybe we can find Ethan and set up a special interview for your agent to assure him that you take your career seriously. We were just swept away by romance."

"Good idea!" Dylan said. "Already working on compromise."

Jake shrugged, not seemingly a hundred percent sold. "It's in the fine print that Ethan showed me earlier today that I would be 'available' in the public's eye."

Tori sighed as if Jake was the one putting her out rather than the other way around.

Josh winked at Amy. "Want to get more drinks, babe?"

"No," the starlet replied sharply. "I really don't. And I think you've had enough."

After goodbyes and thank-yous to Sinéad and her hubby, the group gathered before the blue door of the café. No sign of Bran or his moped, thank goodness.

The Sheep's Head pub was hopping, and there was an increase in traffic on this Saturday afternoon. Rayne looked down the road, hoping to see Amos in the truck but no. He was still a good twenty minutes away.

Blarney woofed and waited for them across the street.

She'd feared for his safety but so far, the dog seemed to have an innate sense of how to avoid traffic.

"So, what's the plan, then?" Amy asked.

Josh raised his phone. "Ethan's coming to the Sheep's Head."

"I really want to talk career with him," Jake said to Tori. "I promise not to drink too much. Okay?"

Tori appeared ready to argue but relented. "All right." She turned to Amy. "How about a stroll along the shops here?"

"Sure, bestie," Amy said, adjusting her bridesmaid cap. She gave Tori the smooshed bride hat. "Whatever you want to do."

"Can we tag along, girls?" Joan asked. She clasped Dylan's hand.

"Of course!" Tori said. "We should buy a few souvenirs to remember the trip by."

Ciara and Rayne looked at one another. At last, they'd have a second to catch up.

"We will see you at three sharp in the sunroom for makeup," Rayne said. Inwardly she was jumping with joy. If only Amos were here! "There's a quaint vintage shop beyond the church."

"Sounds wonderful to me. I haven't bought a single memento," Amy said. "I do love me some cute shops."

"Same here," Joan seconded.

Rayne figured that was a good thing for the ladies to bond over, though Joan still refused to wear the MOTHER OF THE BRIDE cap Amy had brought for her. The champagne and chocolate had mellowed the group.

"See you soon!" Rayne said. She and Ciara waited for the traffic to clear and crossed the road.

Blarney wagged his tail, his golden-brown eyes gleaming. She'd read research online claiming dogs had an intelligence level of your average human toddler. Her dog was much smarter than that, and with empathy besides. She scratched his head and straightened.

"So, what's the story with your mam?" Ciara asked once they were a few steps down the road toward the manor. She'd removed the lightweight denim jacket and slung it over her arm. The black mock turtleneck had short sleeves.

"That's the truth—she's coming for Christmas." Rayne glanced at her cousin. "You'll love her, I know it."

"I'm sure I will. But, what else? I've noticed when you're nervous you tend to touch your collarbone."

"I do?" Rayne dropped her hand from the place a necklace would sit. "Oh, you're right." She wouldn't go into the benefits of tapping therapy right now. With a quick glance to make sure they were all alone, she said, "Well, my ex . . . Landon?"

"Yes," Ciara said. "Landon Short, crook."

"He's escaped from jail, and it seems he carved my name all over his jail cell. Mom and the police are worried that he is after me."

Blarney stopped from where he'd been patrolling ahead, sniffing gravel, to look at Rayne.

"That's awful!" Ciara grabbed Rayne's elbow. "Are you scared?"

Rayne did a gut check and answered honestly. "No, I just think it's strange."

Blarney woofed, darted to Rayne, and then chased a dragonfly.

"We've got to alert Dominic," Ciara said.

"It's not a big deal," Rayne said. "We can, but we have bigger fish to fry."

Ciara's brow lifted. "We must tell the others—not the guests, but the Lloyds. Maybe even the rest of the staff."

Rayne nodded. "They can be on guard for a shaggy blond with good taste in clothes. What was I thinking to be conned by Landon?"

"The key word, cousin, is conned." Ciara glanced at her as they walked. "I don't understand why you're not scared. He broke out of jail and targeted you."

Rayne tilted her head and quickly banished the image of a bedazzled jail cell. "My concern has to take a back seat until Monday when our guests are gone; the wedding over and the money in our bank, with glowing reviews."

Ciara switched arms for her jacket. "The money will be a boon to the bank account. At the rate the visit is going, the positive reviews aren't a sure thing."

Tension rose and Rayne gave a small exhale. "Don't say that! I hope the social media boost from the Montgomery–Anderson wedding will have us booked every weekend through the first of the year." It would take the pressure off the manor regarding the number of sheep born, needing to be sold. Rayne considered the sheep gig a risky business.

Ciara scowled and tugged at her turtleneck. "You think? We'd need to hire on more folks than Sorcha, Bran, and Gillian."

"True." Expansion sometimes had an upfront cost they'd had no choice but to incur. "Maybe villagers who like me can be a criteria?"

"Don't be daft." Ciara shook her head. "You don't need friends— we need able bodies willing to put in a hard day's graft. Gillian will do anything from electric to horses to dusting."

Now it was Rayne's turn to frown. "With an attitude. You weren't immune from it this morning either."

Ciara's scowl deepened at the memory of Gillian throwing her under the bus for her comment about Garda Williams being lazy. "Could be she's waiting to see if we can pull it off and then she'll come around."

Not a team player, then. "Did she say so?"

"No. I asked Dafydd about it. It's not just Gillian; several of the villagers are afraid to get their hopes up in case we fail."

Rayne stopped, her stomach tight at the lack of support. Blarney, not paying attention, walked into her calves.

Ciara pulled Rayne forward to keep walking. "It was a blow to my ego to hear that, since I wasn't raised here, they don't think I understand the true extent of what it means to be a McGrath."

"Baloney."

"And you, Rayne, they consider an outsider—a McGrath, aye, but ruined by American heritage."

"Is there anything we can do about it?" Rayne blinked quickly, blaming dust on the road for the sting in her eyes. It would take a miracle to get them on their side.

"Nothing more than what we are doing for the ungrateful sods." Ciara raised her hands and wiggled her slender fingers. "We are already working our fingers to the bone."

"Is that all?" Rayne kicked at a loose pebble on the road. "Ciara, we need to let Bran go, right away. He's inciting trouble. Sinéad showed me postcards he's handing around town to the businesses." Rayne explained about the image and how Sinéad had also shared that Bran was fine with being absorbed into Cotter Village. "Also someone needs to step into your dad's shoes as the new council member. It should be you."

"No! I won't!" Ciara exclaimed. "I don't do politics."

They rounded the corner and the view of McGrath Castle loomed before them. Blue skies, lush trees, and the turret, stone crenellations visible in the distance. Roses and lavender.

Blarney trotted at her side, tongue lolling.

"You have to, Ciara. As you just mentioned, the villagers aren't sure about me. They trust you a lot more."

"But not by much." Ciara peered at Rayne before focusing on the road. "Dafydd thinks that it will matter if I accept the adoption paperwork and Da's last name, so . . ."

Joy filled her heart at this news from her unsuspecting ally. "He does?"

"Yes." Ciara's hair bounced with each stride. She tossed her jacket over her shoulder.

And then doubt again. "Will he expect you to change it to Norman when you're married?"

"No. In fact," Ciara glanced at Rayne, "I was wondering how you'd feel if he took the McGrath name?"

It was progressive, and Rayne didn't mind a bit. "Why is that?"

"If we were blessed with weans then they would carry on Da's last name." Ciara's nose turned red with emotion.

"I think that is beautiful." Rayne hadn't really considered children, having concentrated on her career.

"Well, he might not go for it, so," Ciara shrugged.

"You asked me first?" Rayne smiled at her cousin. "Sweet."

"We are family. We share a village. It seemed right."

Rayne burst out laughing. "No sentiment, got it."

Still, they'd come a long since their first prickly meeting in June.

"I thought I was going to die when Bran announced that there'd been two murders at the castle and the wedding business was doomed," Ciara said.

Rayne's stomach had risen to her throat in sheer panic until she'd realized none of their guests could understand what he said. "His brogue was hard to decipher, thank heaven. Talk about awkward!"

"He's an eejit."

Rayne agreed with that sentiment. "I want to find a different handyman with plumbing experience. Actually, now that the two best cottages are done, we aren't in a rush for a plumber anyway. We should fire him on Monday."

Ciara waved her hand. "Good riddance to Bran."

"I mean, if the village is incorporated with Freda's, that isn't good for anyone, is it?" Blarney brought her a stick. She threw it forward, and he raced after it—forgetting halfway what he was doing as a squirrel chittered from a treetop.

"Some folks think merging Grathton and Cotter is better than our village dying out completely." Ciara shrugged. "I was talking with Father Patrick about it. Irish folks can be a wee bit fatalistic in their approach to daily life."

Rayne had noticed that for herself. Nothing certain in this life but death.

Her phone dinged a notification. "Amos is ten minutes out!" Two-twenty ETA—he must have had the pedal to the metal. "He's amazing. Oh, please be careful. He doesn't have time for a speeding ticket."

"Can you do it without alerting Tori?" Ciara tucked a wayward curl behind her ear.

"It's a single crystal strategically taken to be noticed but I'll get it done." Rayne had the needle and thread at the worktable ready to go. The zipper too.

"Do you think that Tiffany took it out of vengeance?" Ciara asked.

"I don't see how. I guess we could ask the Garda if it was in her possessions. It wasn't on the floor in the studio," Rayne said. "Tori can't have more enemies, can she?"

Ciara tapped her chin. "What if it wasn't against Tori, but the wedding?"

"What do you mean?" Rayne was open to any possibility that would provide motive, as her mother had pointed out regarding Bran.

"What if the bridal gown shenanigans are against Jake, or to simply stop the wedding from going forward," Ciara suggested.

Rayne considered this, seeing a Garda wandering the property, not Lee or Williams as she remembered the tragic details regarding

Tiffany's death. "Ciara, Garda Williams asked us not to say anything." She grabbed Ciara's wrist to keep her cousin close. "Tiffany was murdered, and it was made to look like she jumped."

"What?" Ciara raised her hands in surprise. Her jacket dropped to the road. "And you're just now telling me?"

"When have we had time?" Rayne looked at her watch. "In the seven minutes since we left the Coco Bean there hasn't been a single lull in the conversation."

"Fair." Ciara picked up her jacket, brushing dirt from the black denim. "Tell me everything."

Rayne reported the Garda's findings, the extra security from the Gardaí, and ended with, "Dominic found out from Beetle that Bran and Tiffany were making out in the Sheep's Head Thursday night."

"That was fast," Ciara said. "I thought she'd gone to bed. I didn't get that impression of Tiffany at all."

"True." She'd been putting on an act. Who was the real Tiffany Quick? "The more important thing is that Bran doesn't like me, or our business. He's vocal about it to the point of sabotage with the postcards. Could he have killed Tiffany, in a fit of rage, or a drunken interlude that got out of control?"

"No," Ciara said. "He's a jerk, eh, but not a killer."

Her cousin didn't sound so sure.

"Someone convinced Tiffany to meet at the top of the turret even though she was afraid of heights. Aine heard an argument," Rayne said. "Before Tiffany, and possibly Bran, went up?"

"Not Bran," Ciara repeated.

They arrived at the porch. Rayne put her foot on the bottom step to go inside, but Blarney barked and raced around the area to where the caution tape remained. When he barked a second time, Rayne joined him. "What is it?"

Blarney scooted under the tape and started to dig.

"No!" Rayne reached for him, knowing this was one of the frowned upon puppy behaviors, especially in Maeve's garden. Though this wasn't the rose bed, the digging activity was discouraged. "Bad, bad, puppy. No digging!"

Ciara clucked her tongue to her teeth, shaking her head. "I understand what you mean about Blarney's selective hearing."

Blarney returned with a wadded-up piece of paper dangling from his slobbery jaw.

Rayne unfolded it, dripping wet. "Ew."

Ciara stopped shaking her head, her expression alarmed as she studied the damp page. "Is that from Tiffany's Moleskine?"

It was impossible to read any of the handwriting because the page was wet. "I don't know. I can't tell." She lifted it, thinking the size was the same as Tiff's notebook on the dining room table.

Ciara's gray eyes widened with concern. "Oh, I really hope that Blarney isn't the Moleskine thief. That won't go over well with Dominic."

Blarney wagged his tail, not at all upset by his prize. Rayne didn't dare let go of the page in case her pup decided to play with it some more. She tucked it between her body and elbow, and gave a quick glance around for the Garda on patrol, out of sight of course.

Rayne pulled out her phone. "I'll call the Garda and see what he wants to do."

Oh, Blarney. It rang and rang. Drat.

"No answer," Rayne said. She was forced to leave a message.

Chapter Twelve

Rayne was halfway through with the recording when Garda Williams called her back.

"Hey! Blarney found a piece of paper that might be from Tiffany's journal," she said. "It's been soaked. so it's impossible to read, but the size is right."

"I'm at the petrol station and can be there in five minutes. Will you stay outside and wait for me? Maeve isn't pleased that I've been tromping mud through the house." His tone was irritated. "I've been knocking my shoes on the porch as best as I can."

"Sure." Rayne ended the call and chuckled as she met Ciara's gaze. "I don't think our housekeeper ever got over being a suspect in your da's death and holds a grudge just against Garda Williams—none of the other Gardai." Would Ciara admit to feeling the same?

"I don't blame her. She's known Dominic since he was a boy." Ciara changed the subject and nodded at the paper under Rayne's arm. "If that page was there all along then why didn't the Garda find it earlier when they were searching? Where is the rest of the notebook?"

"Good questions." Rayne patted Blarney for bringing it to them and hoped that he hadn't absconded with the entire Moleskine and phone in the first place. He'd once stolen a Jimmy Choo that had been ruined by the time he'd finished burying it around the property. She peered into his golden-brown eyes. Was he innocent now?

Hard to give the dog the benefit of the doubt, considering his track record.

Any discussion on Blarney's behavior was interrupted by a car but instead of the white Hyundai and Garda Williams, it was the manor truck with Amos behind the wheel, coming around the corner toward them at a fast clip.

Two-seventeen. Rayne's heart raced with anticipation. At last, something was going her way!

"I've got to get upstairs. I have forty minutes before the Montgomerys come back for makeup."

"They could return anytime," Ciara said, unknowingly adding to her anxiety. She'd learned from one of the LA gurus that anxiety could be channeled into creativity, making nerves a positive experience rather than something to dread. Once she could get upstairs, she'd channel away.

Amos drove by her and Ciara waiting on the lawn by the porch to park at the barn. "Hey!" she called to his taillights.

"I'll be back," Amos replied out the open window.

But then another car was heard, and of course, it was Garda Williams.

Blarney, having followed Amos's truck, now raced toward the Garda in welcome. Surely this man was a friend, since he kept visiting.

"Hi, boyo," the Garda said, patting the pup after he'd exited the police vehicle. He looked at Ciara and Rayne with a cautious expression. "Hello again. It seems I was just here," he joked.

"You were," Ciara remarked. "Rayne told me about the *murder*."

"We're keeping it quiet, though." Garda Williams tapped the brim of his hat.

Rayne offered the wet paper to the officer once he'd reached them. "Here. Blarney dug it up."

"Where?" He placed it in an evidence bag.

"Same place Tiffany fell," Ciara said. "I'll show you. Now, don't be mad at Blarney. The dog is wee bit of a kleptomaniac."

"I'm not mad at the dog, Ciara," Garda Williams said in a manner that suggested she was way off the mark.

"What's that tone?" Ciara asked.

Rayne glanced down the road to the barn as Amos took large strides toward them. He wasn't carrying anything. Oh, no. Where was the shopping bag with the crystals?

She gulped. Please, please, let nothing else be wrong.

"No tone," the Garda said, backtracking.

"Could be the pup buried the whole notebook. Blarney has no regard for caution tape," Ciara said to Garda Williams. "Why should he?"

"I see that." The Garda knelt down and used his baton to poke at the loose ground to see if there were any more papers—or even better, the notebook.

Blarney nuzzled the Garda's arm.

"Nice work, pup." The Garda stood, his lips pursed. No other papers.

"What is it?" Rayne asked, sensing his agitation.

"Where is everyone?" Garda Willliams asked.

"Shopping after a champagne brunch at the Coco Bean," Rayne said.

"And the ceremony is at four-thirty," the Garda stated.

"On the dot," Ciara confirmed.

"Well, I wish them a happy life even if it did get off to a bad start." Garda Williams wiped the mud off the baton and retracted it to place on his belt. On his vest was a radio that crackled. "The Coco Bean offers champagne?"

Rayne thought the Garda to be a kind man. "We supplied it for brunch, though the chocolate was amazing. I have a complaint regarding Bran Wilson. Nothing to do with kissing Tiffany, but because he's handing out postcards with the castle Xed out in red marker saying that the wedding business is bad for the village."

"He is?" The Garda shook his head. "Well, there isn't anything I can do about that. He has a right to his opinion."

"It's wrong, though! Sinéad explained a little about the villagers and how some folks might not mind us combining with Cotter Village." Rayne crossed her arms, not understanding that at all.

"I'll keep my eye on anything untoward," the Garda said. "So far, it's not against the law."

"Tell him about your ex," Ciara said, raising her brows.

"Your ex?" Amos repeated as he'd just reached them within earshot. "The cross-dressing gown thief?"

The Garda tilted his head and sucked in a smile. "Yes, please do share."

Embarrassed, Rayne said, "Well, Landon Short was put in jail for stealing my wedding dresses and a lot of money. Money I really wish I could get back." Officer Peters had basically told her not to hold her breath about that.

"Cash is difficult to recover in a crime," the Garda said. "So?"

"Landon escaped from jail."

"What?" Amos asked, alarm evident in his tone.

"No!" the Garda said. "I imagined American prisons to be grand and impossible to escape from."

"It was a low-risk lock-up because the nature of his crimes wasn't violent," Rayne said. The heat in her cheeks began to fade.

"I hope they catch him," the Garda said.

"Are you in danger, Rayne?" Amos demanded.

Rayne scrunched her nose. She didn't think so, but her mom had warned her to take care. "They discovered my name carved everywhere in his jail cell."

"That's no good, if he blames you for his arrest," the Garda said, patting his baton.

Amos stepped closer to her side. "You need to be protected."

"All right, guys, back up a bit." Sweet, but Rayne had a wedding to get through. "I doubt he can get on a plane without being caught, all right? Let's concentrate on getting this wedding finished, which will be money in the bank."

"Will the Montgomerys pay up if the wedding doesn't go as planned?" Garda Williams asked.

"It's not our fault that somebody pushed Tiffany over the edge," Ciara said.

"They did?" Amos asked in alarm. "Poor lass! I thought she'd jumped?"

That's right, he wasn't here when Rayne had discovered the truth. She nodded at the Garda to explain. Amos was a trusted member of the staff.

"Someone strangled Tiffany and pushed her over the edge of the turret." Garda Williams tucked his thumb into his cargo pants pocket.

"And Bran Wilson is handing out postcards to local businesses saying the wedding venue isn't good for the village. He's also spreading rumors that the tower is cursed," Rayne said. "Maybe we should hire a medium to cleanse the place, just in case."

"That would be silly," the Garda said.

"If it gets the villagers who are not on board to support us, then I'm happy to find someone to do it. We need their cooperation, and Bran is actively against us," Rayne said.

Amos scowled.

"A medium isn't going to stop the gossip . . ." The Garda stammered beneath Ciara's glare.

"You aren't in charge of how we run our business." Ciara crossed her arms. "If Rayne wants to waste money on hocus pocus so be it. How about you just concentrate on Bran Wilson. He was with Tiffany at the Sheep's Head. He'd best not be a killer."

Hocus pocus!

"What's the story with Bran?" Amos drew attention from the Garda, to get him out of the heat of her cousin's ire.

"Bran was pished and pounded on the window of the café while we were eating brunch, saying that two murders had happened in the village, and it wasn't safe to be here." Ciara jutted her chin.

"And the postcard with McGrath Castle and an X," the Garda said as he tapped his temple, suggesting he'd heard and would act if Bran did something illegal.

"How long can you keep Tiffany's murder a secret, Domi . . . Garda Williams?" Ciara asked.

"I hope until I can check everyone's alibis. Bran's too." Williams sighed.

"So, the wedding guests don't know it was murder, and Bran was with Tiffany on Thursday night," Amos summarized. "Could he be your one?"

"Bran was born in his mam's house in Grathton," the Garda said. "But I will question him, no matter. He will explain why he's sabotaging the wedding business. It's possible a conversation might make things right."

"That was my plan—a conversation, but to fire him," Rayne said.

"I agree," Ciara said. "We don't need to have the enemy on the payroll, even if they do have a gift with pipes and fittings."

"Sometimes it's worth it to pay a wee bit extra," Amos said. He pointed to Blarney and the fresh dirt beyond the white tape. "What happened there?"

"Blarney found a sheet of paper—or buried a sheet of paper," Rayne said. "But it was too wet to make out."

"The writing is all gone," Ciara said.

"Was it from Tiffany's notebook?" Amos asked. "That everyone was looking for yesterday?"

"We don't know," the Garda said, raising his hand to put a stop to any further speculation.

"Amos, do you have something for me?" Rayne asked, eager to get upstairs and finish the last tweak to Tori's bridal gown.

"I do." He reached into his jeans pocket and passed her a tiny Ziploc packet with two, count them two, heart-shaped Swarovski crystals.

"Thank you!" Rayne stepped toward the porch.

Blarney barked and raced by her to greet two figures walking quickly their direction from the barn and the cottages. Gillian and . . . Ethan? He was supposed to be at the pub with Jake and Josh to talk about Jake's career.

"Rayne, that Nolan guy is brilliant," Amos said. "He sends his regards."

"He is a doll. Oh, did you get a receipt? I'll pay you back right away."

"It's no bother," Amos said. "They were just three euro each. How many were on the dress?"

"A thousand."

Garda Williams, Ciara, and Amos collectively gasped at the amount—three thousand dollars in crystals. "But," she jiggled the baggie, "I got a discount for buying in bulk."

"And you had to spend that much time sewing each one on?" the Garda asked.

"Yes." Rayne flexed her fingers. "By hand."

"No wonder those gowns are to be cherished," the Garda said.

Garda Williams surprised her. They'd gotten off on the wrong foot and there was more to him than met the eye.

"It's a fifteen-thousand-dollar work of art," Ciara said.

"And heavy," Amos said. "I remember that from when they arrived and how low the boot was sitting to the ground."

Rayne curled her arm and tapped her biceps. "I'm strong."

"Seamstress strong," Amos joked.

"Aine told me about a dress with crystals that was twenty-thousand euro," Ciara said. "I suppose it's not a big deal to spend so much for some ladies. When it's time, my gown won't need to be so fancy."

Rayne beamed, floating on air as they realized the value of her creations. Her phone rang with an alarm she'd set to keep her on track. Two-thirty! "Gotta run. Please remind Sorcha for three o'clock makeup in the sunroom. Thank you everyone for all you're doing."

"Do you miss life in a village?" Gillian asked Ethan as they approached.

"Not a bit," Ethan exclaimed. "Grandpa's place in East Sussex was more rural than this, from sheep to fowl. I escaped to London, then Hollywood. Thought of being a star but preferred the business aspects behind the scene."

"And did you know Tiffany well?" Gillian asked.

"Not really," the assistant said. "Unlike me, Tiffany still wanted to be a star."

Ethan stood next to Gillian. He smiled politely at Rayne and Ciara, not so much at the Garda.

"Tiffany wanted to be a star?" the Garda repeated.

"Yeah." Ethan shrugged. "As cruel as Amy can be she nailed it about Tiffany's lack of whatever it is that makes the camera love you."

Williams nodded. "You're sure you and Tiffany weren't an item? Traveling together with the family?"

"No!" Ethan's left eye twitched. "This is the first time that we've all been in the same spot like this. Tori and Jake's relationship happened quick."

"True love," Gillian suggested.

"Passion flares bright but then dies," Ethan said, popping the romance bubble. "Rayne, how well do you know Tori Montgomery?"

Rayne stepped back at his attacking tone. "Why?"

"I think it's strange that this happened so fast, that's all." Ethan lowered his voice when he realized how he must have sounded. "This place is gorgeous and perfect for the fairy tale wedding. You must be booked."

Rayne smiled at Ethan as he echoed Amy's sentiment. "We are new, actually. Ciara and I inherited the property recently."

"Very," Gillian seconded.

"I see." Ethan looked around again and noticed the dirt dug up. "What happened there?"

"Blarney is a digger," Rayne said. "He's a puppy still and being trained for appropriate behaviors. Do you have a dog?"

"No," Ethan said. "With my schedule I have no time."

"Is Jake your only client?" the Garda asked.

Ethan winced. "Do I need a lawyer present for this conversation?"

Rayne raised her brow. What was Ethan's problem?

"Only if you want one." Garda Williams smiled.

"Yes, Jake is my only client. Being a movie star takes a team of support that I manage, when he's honest with me." Ethan smoothed his goatee. "When he's not, well, I'm tempted to move on."

"We thought you were at the pub," Ciara said. "Talking strategy with Jake and Josh over a pint."

"No. I didn't go." Ethan checked the time on his phone. "We are out of coffee in the cottage kitchen, so I thought I'd get some more."

"I offered to bring it to him," Gillian said. "And we just ended up chatting the whole way. I can't fathom leaving Ireland."

"Opportunity for a smoke anyway," Ethan said. "There is life outside this country, Gillian. You might like spreading your wings."

Rayne's phone alarm sounded again.

"What's that for?" Gillian asked.

"I really must go," Rayne said, not answering Gillian. "But Ethan, we'd be happy to stock your kitchen. Is there anything else you need?"

"No. Just with everyone staying over at the cottage there was a lot of caffeine consumed this morning. I imagine they won't be staying out of the tower for their honeymoon?"

"They're free to return to the chambers," the Garda said.

Ciara nodded. "I'll go inside and get it, Gillian. Are you and Amos done with the carriage to take the bride and groom to church?"

"Nope," Gillian said. "Amos deserted the ship, but now that he's back we can get to it. It's a two-person job."

"Right." Amos hid a smile at the woman's verbal poke. "Let's go, Gillian. Rayne and Ciara, should we let you know when we are done?"

"Tell me," Ciara said. "Rayne is doing the gown and then makeup in the sunroom with Sorcha. She needs to concentrate on those things."

"Do I need to be someplace at a certain time?" Ethan pulled a pack of cigarettes from his pocket.

Guess he decided to attend the wedding after all. "We're going to follow the carriage from the barn to the church on foot so please join us here at four," Rayne said. "The ceremony is scheduled for four-thirty. All right?"

"Sure." Ethan put a cigarette to his lips.

Rayne stepped again toward the long porch of the manor. After sniffing the crystals in her palm, Blarney followed Amos and Gillian. The dog had a thing for her shiny stuff. Maybe Blarney liked bling and that's just who he was inside. She could make him a shiny collar to celebrate his uniqueness.

"I can wait here and enjoy my smoke, if you want to get the coffee," Ethan told Ciara. "I have to walk back anyway."

"All right," Ciara agreed.

Up another step. She heard laughter coming from the road. Amy and Tori? The Montgomerys.

"I've got to go!" In a rush, Rayne waved goodbye to everyone and darted up the stairs and inside before anyone else could stop her.

Ciara, to her surprise, was right on her heels as they slid into the house and the foyer.

"That was close," Ciara said. "With the time. You can do it, right?"

"Yes. Also, can't talk to you right now unless you want to run upstairs with me." Rayne was already halfway across the stone foyer.

"That's fine," Ciara said. "But what about Jake's lie?"

Rayne stopped and turned toward her cousin. "What do you mean?"

"Jake and Josh are supposedly with Ethan at the pub to discuss Jake's career, remember?"

"Right. It could have been a misunderstanding." Rayne shrugged.

Ciara shooed her up the stairs. "Hurry! I'll drop in after I take the coffee to Ethan."

"Thank you," Rayne said.

She reached the second floor and hustled to the right and down the long hall. There were family photos and suits of armor. Paintings of battles and statues that her cousin Padraig had terrified her with.

As she passed the more recent pictures, she worried that she might not be able to save their heritage.

"Not with that kind of stinking thinking," Rayne chided herself aloud.

She reached her sewing studio and unlocked the door, rushing inside. The bridal gown was on the dress form where she'd left it last, the tall windows allowing the September sun to strike the crystals and create rainbows throughout the room.

Had she left the curtains open?

Or the door to the vanity and large closet that was her Aunt Amalie's pride and joy? Goose bumps dotted her skin, and she could smell her aunt's perfume.

Rayne rubbed her arms. "If you're here, you better be friendly," she said more to chase away the spooky feeling than expecting her warning to make a difference.

She quickly set the crystals on the worktable, grateful that Nolan had scored her two just in case.

Like the professional she was, she got to work, sewing in the zipper, and creating beauty with her needle and thread.

Chapter Thirteen

Rayne secured the heart-shaped crystal, one of a thousand, and had just snipped the silken thread when the door to the studio swung open.

She gasped and fell backward in alarm. Please don't be Tori!

Aine strode toward the large window, glancing at Rayne, still kneeling on the floor by the gown hanging on the dress form.

"What are ye doing?" Aine asked, stopping at the window to peer outside. The top of the barn and the satellite antenna were visible from this second-floor chamber.

"Fastening the crystal. Come see—does it match? My eyes are crossing this close."

Aine held up her hand and continued looking out the window. "Hang on. Yep! I knew it." The young redhead squinted and scowled when she was normally of a very cheery disposition.

"What?" Rayne asked.

Aine exhaled. "Bran Wilson. He's skulking around on the property, and I don't like it. I asked Mam and Da, and they said he wasn't working today and has no reason to be here."

"Yes, well, your instincts about him are right on the money. He's been handing out postcards to the businesses in the village saying that our wedding business will hurt Grathton. Can you believe it?"

"That chancer!" Aine said.

"We told Garda Williams already. Bran's been drinking, a lot, and interrupted the champagne and chocolate brunch." Rayne closed her eyes in panic.

"I warned him to behave. He makes us look bad to our guests, eh?" Aine left the window and joined Rayne.

"Well?" Rayne knelt and smoothed her finger over the crystal.

"Yer a miracle worker, no doubt," Aine declared. "This is stunning and there is no evidence that it's different than the other crystals."

Rayne blinked tears from her eyes. "Thank God." She exhaled. "This is hard enough without an employee turning on us like a rabid dog."

Aine scooped Rayne's elbow and helped her to stand. "Now what?"

"I have to get the ostrich wrap feathers fluffed. Check the shoes. Tori's got her own jewelry that she will bring to the sunroom. Oh, flowers! I need to see about the flowers."

The door slammed open. Rayne winced at the force of the knob hitting the wall.

"Sorry!" Amy cried. Her cheeks were splotchy, and she'd ditched the pink BRIDESMAID cap. Her hair was in a messy ponytail.

"What's wrong?" Rayne's immediate thought was that Tori and Jake were calling things off. That they'd found out that Tiffany had been murdered. That they'd blacklist the wedding venue at Grathton Village.

"Come with me. Hurry!" Amy grabbed Rayne's hand and pulled her from the studio. Her pink Nikes allowed the starlet to hustle.

Aine shut the door and made sure it was locked before coming with them.

"Is everyone okay?" Rayne asked.

Amy's lips pursed. "What?" She shook her head, practically at a jog. "It's not a person that was hurt. I think my chamber is haunted."

Rayne pulled and slowed so she wasn't sprinting. "I don't understand."

"Tiffany did it," Amy said. "Her mean and nasty spirit. Or maybe she did it before she kicked the bucket. Just wait till you see. Un-freaking-believable."

Amy hurried down the main staircase and went right toward the tower entrance.

"I thought the tower chambers were off limits at that time?" Aine said in a puff. "If there was a mess, we would have cleaned it for you."

"Not the problem." Amy tossed a glance over her shoulder as if to make sure they were alone. "The room was clean already. It's only been two days. One night in the castle room, one night at the cottage, and tonight here in the tower again." She shivered. "Maybe. I might get drunk and bunk with Ethan."

Amy had left the interior door unlocked to the tower.

"Where is everyone else?" Rayne asked.

"Tori went to her parents' bungalow with them to get some Irish lace from her grandmother. Haven't seen Jake or Josh. Not Ethan either, come to think of it." Amy smoothed a loose strand of hair over her ear.

"You're the only one here?" Aine asked.

"Yep." Amy unlocked the chamber on the second floor with a flourish.

Rayne's eyes adjusted to the dim interior. Bed unmade, suitcase open and partially unpacked. Wardrobe door ajar. Bathroom door closed.

Amy flicked the switch. "I just don't know how anybody would have gotten in. This place is loaded with ghosties. I'm sensitive that way. My mom can do it too; sense spirits around us."

Rayne bit back a retort.

"Really?" Aine said. "My friend Sorcha has the gift. The one who is doing your makeup at three."

"Gift?" Amy said.

"She's a medium," Aine said.

"I didn't know that," Rayne said. Sorcha would totally understand about the pet psychic. Maybe for a bit of extra cash, she could spiritually cleanse the tower.

"That's good," Amy said. "Have her clear this room. I know I could have treated Tiffany better, but I don't want her ruining my shit. Banish that be-yotch to the light, right?"

Rayne crossed her arms, not sure that was the correct attitude. "Something is ruined?"

"Tori is going to freak the hell out," Amy declared. She crossed the room, widened the wooden wardrobe door, and removed her bridesmaid's dress.

The original colors for the Christmas wedding had been crimson, charcoal, and huntergreen with diamonds to accent. The dress Amy showed them was crimson—but had been shredded from bodice to hem.

"Oh no," Rayne said. It was destroyed. Now what? Her knees buckled, and she stumbled back into the wall.

"Tiffany did it. A ghost is the only one who could have gotten in here like that. She's the only one who might have had a grudge against me." Amy's face was pale with fear. "Let's get that Sorcha here and do a cleansing, or I'm not staying tonight."

Aine and Rayne exchanged a look.

Rayne had been training Aine in the design portion of her job as Aine wanted to be a designer as well someday.

Rayne lifted a brow. She did not have time to tackle another gown without being late to makeup in the sunroom. "Is this fixable?"

Aine took the gown and laid it on the bed. She put her fingers to her chin and studied the wide slashes. She gave a tiny head shake.

Sugar cookies. "Is this the gown that Tori approved?" Rayne asked. Maybe she could find something similar.

Amy waved her fingers. "Since the change of venue was last minute, she wasn't particular. It had to be nice, obvi. Please tell me you have a solution, Rayne. This wedding is so important to Tori, and I can't let her down. I never should have brought Tiffany. I thought I was being efficient. I've got to nail my part in this next movie, and she's—was—great with advice on my scripts."

Rayne was fairly certain she had gown samples that might work on Amy's small frame. "Let me think."

"We've got to tell Tori," Amy said. "And I don't want to."

"Do we?" Rayne frowned. "Tori really doesn't need any more stress right now, with the baby and everything." Amy shouldn't have fired Tiffany before they'd gone home, but it was a moot point at the moment.

Could Tiffany's ghost be taking revenge on Amy for killing her?

Amy scrunched her nose, clearly wanting to be in the center of drama despite her words to the contrary.

Could she have done this to her dress herself, as a way to protest the wedding? Did she have an ulterior motive when it came to Jake, who she thought should be her leading man?

Rayne shook her head to clear the images of Amy as a seductress getting her comeuppance from a ghost.

"What are the accent colors for the groom and best man?" Aine asked.

"Crimson and charcoal, unless it changed . . ." Rayne replied.

Amy shook her head. "I realize you are an amazing seamstress but there is no way this can be fixed." She lifted a shred of fabric and let it fall. "Period. Even if you didn't have, oh," she looked at her phone, "an hour until the carriage ride to the church."

Rayne blinked as her vision swam before her eyes. This was beyond normal wedding stressful. "Aine is my intern, and she's very fast, but I agree that we need to scratch the notion of a fix and go to Aunt Amalie's closet."

"Yes! Amalie and Amy were the same height at least," Aine agreed. "Her closet might have something."

"I can't miss this wedding," Amy said. "I will show up in tatters. Or, well, a different color if necessary. You're bound to have something. A black sheath will do. Mourning the loss of the sexiest man alive."

They headed for the door, Rayne grabbing the destroyed gown for any possible ideas. While Amalie was the same height as Amy, the starlet was much thinner than her aunt had been.

Aine made sure the door was locked as they left, and they raced down the stairs, across the hall, up the staircase to the second hall past the pictures, to Rayne's studio.

Out of breath, the ladies went inside.

Placing the ruined gown on Aine's worktable, the only clear space, Rayne eyed the silky crimson fabric. There was no way to rescue even a portion of it. Whoever had destroyed it had meant every slash.

Rayne moved away from the gown, and handed out bottles of water, uncapping hers and taking a big drink.

Amy collapsed on a love seat and sipped from the bottle. "This is so crazy. What do you think did that? Claws? Maybe Tiffany turned into a demon. Wouldn't be surprised."

Aine shook her head and caressed the cuts. "Scissors or a knife. It's a clean cut with no jagged edges."

"A knife?" Amy straightened.

"Or scissors," Aine said, not allowing Amy to get too far out of control.

"We've got to tell Tori and let her decide if she wants to go through with this. I mean, come on." Amy gave a little pout. "My assistant is dead. My dress is ruined."

Rayne studied Amy. The starlet could have gotten scissors from anywhere and destroyed her dress to try and stop the wedding. "How close are you and Jake?"

Amy flushed red. "Why?"

"You said that you thought you would be his perfect leading lady on screen." Rayne shrugged. "You said just now that you were mourning the loss of the sexiest man alive. Do you care for one another?"

"No." Amy downed the rest of the water.

"Does he love you?" Rayne persisted. She wasn't going to bother Tori if Amy was the one to ruin the dress. She would tell Tori later, like, Monday on the way out of town, but not yet.

"No." Amy stared at Rayne, the vein at her neck pulsing.

"Do you love him?"

Amy quieted.

Uh oh. Did Tori realize this?

"Subject change," Amy declared. "Show me my dress options."

Amy would have had access to the tower since she was staying in one of the rooms. Maybe not direct access from the fourth floor, but what if she'd been sneaky?

It wasn't hard to imagine her being underhanded in the slightest.

Rayne cleared her throat and opened the closet door to showcase her aunt's quality clothing. Many of the shifts were classic in design, which meant that they could be timeless.

"Here's the motherlode! And color coordinated?" Amy sounded impressed as she moved the hangers around.

Aine had a sour expression, as if she wanted to pull Amy from the closet but didn't dare. The starlet wasn't winning popularity points with Aine at all. Rayne stepped between them and urged Amy backward, next to Aine, on the love seat.

"I'll bring out some of my top picks." It was now two thirty-five. Rayne's phone dinged a notification.

Tori.

"What?" Aine asked. Her tone warbled with nerves.

Rayne read the text with relief. "Tori's running behind." She exhaled.

"Thank God," Aine said.

"What she said," Amy seconded. "You got anything to drink in here?"

"Let's wait on that." Rayne brought out three calf-length crimson gowns probably meant for the holidays but they were subdued in trim.

Her phone rang and she hung the dresses on the door, pressing the button with no small amount of trepidation, "Hello?"

"Rayne, we have a problem!" Ciara said.

Rayne held the cell phone to her ear and paced to the window. How had her cousin found out about the destroyed dress? "I know, but we are working on finding Amy a substitute gown instead."

"Not that!" Ciara exclaimed. "Dear Lord, I'm afraid to ask what you are talking about."

Ciara had been checking on Amos and Gillian after getting Ethan coffee. "Is the cart all right?"

"I think so, but that's not the issue." Ciara drew in a breath. "The church. You have got to hurry—and come alone. Father Patrick found something odd, and he wants you to see it."

With that, her cousin ended the call.

Aine started to ask a question, but Rayne gave a slight negating motion of her head and chose the first of three dresses. "I think this one would be very pretty on you, Amy."

Amy nodded as Rayne held the gown to the starlet's figure. "Uh, I guess. But the boobs. I don't have the rack your aunt had."

Aine raised her hand. "I can pin you into it—but I will need to help you get out of it too. When are we supposed to meet for makeup?"

"Three-twenty," Rayne said.

"That gives us forty minutes." Aine expelled a breath. "We can do it."

"I really don't like this one after all," Amy said. "It's kind of old."

"These gowns are classics," Rayne said. What was Amy's deal? Beggars could not be choosers.

"Let me see the other two." As if oblivious to the tension, Amy perched back on the sofa and crossed her ankles.

"All right." Rayne handed a second one, then a third, and Amy pursed her mouth at them all. Time was a ticking.

"I'm not digging the red," Amy said.

Rayne ducked back into the closet where her eye snagged something in gray. "Hang on," she said. "What color are the guy's suits?"

"Charcoal," Amy said snidely. "You should know that."

"I just wanted to be sure. Here." Rayne offered a stunning silk chiffon piece to the love seat.

"Oh, now we're talking," Amy said.

"It's brilliant," Aine said with approval.

Amy stripped from her clothes—again, without a thought to modesty.

Aine and Rayne helped her into the lovely dress.

"No zipper," Aine said, "so I can make this fit the bosom like a dream."

"Yay!" Amy said. "I want to look pretty. Not as pretty as the bride, obvi." She frowned at Aine. "You're sure you can handle this? Maybe Rayne should do it."

"I have something else to check on," Rayne said, "but I will meet you two in the sunroom."

"What about shoes?" Amy asked. "I'm a seven."

"Aunt Amalie was as well, so maybe you can find something," Rayne said. "What did you bring?"

"Nude."

"That might work just fine," Rayne said. "Jewelry?"

"I have crimson hoops and a necklace," Amy said.

"That might be just enough so that you match the guys a little." Rayne went to the crimson gown that had been destroyed.

"What are you thinking?" Aine asked. "I see the wheels turning."

"I wonder if we can use some fabric here to make crimson accessories. Like, little rosettes?"

"I am on it!" Aine promised.

"Thank you so much." Rayne looked from Aine to Amy. If she left Amy with Aine, she knew her intern would have her hands full.

But could Aine be in danger?

"I have my phone here, as you've heard." Rayne tried to judge by Aine's expression how she felt about Rayne leaving her.

"Okay," Aine said. "I have mine too. Go, Rayne. We'll be fine."

"The flowers!" Rayne said again. "Amy, do you know if Tori had made arrangements for bouquets?"

"No," Amy said. "Maybe you could whip something up?"

Did these people think that things just appeared with no prior planning whatsoever? Rayne would need to find out.

She sent Tori a question about a bouquet.

An answering text came.

No. Can you help? Red roses would be lovely.

Rayne's head pounded.

I will see what I can do. Something very very simple maybe.

Thanks!

"Let's meet at three-twenty in the sunroom—bring your makeup and jewelry." Rayne couldn't very well run to the church without getting sweaty, and she hadn't even had time to change. She sent a message to Ciara for a ride. She was walking down now.

"What about Tori's dress?" Aine asked. "Should I bring it?"

"I'll do it." Rayne walked to the dress. Had Amy been the one to take the crystal? Would she give herself away?

For the first time since they were in the room the starlet's gaze landed on the bride's dress. "Wow. This is something else." Amy didn't glance at the place where the crystal had been taken, so not guilty. Probably.

"Thank you," Rayne said.

"I will definitely spread the word about your bridal gown skills," Amy said. "You are an artist."

Her compliments made Rayne glad she hadn't accused Amy of sleeping with Jake or murdering Tiffany.

Chapter Fourteen

Rayne was outside the manor in five minutes, after a quick stop into the kitchen to leave a message with Frances for Maeve about the blasted bridal bouquet. She was getting her cardio today, no problem.

Blarney met her on the porch with his tail wagging. "Good boy." He'd probably found a clue if only they could decipher it. Unless he was the thief, in which case, she would work on his penchant for stealing.

To her delight, Amos was waiting for her in the truck, the window rolled down. "Ciara said you needed a lift to the church?"

"Oh, yes, yes, I do. Do you believe in curses, Amos?" Rayne opened the door to the passenger side and climbed in.

"No, lass, I sure don't." Amos tugged at his smooth chin, eyes glinting. "It's been that sort of day, though, it has . . . is the crystal attached?"

"Yes. Do you know what Father Patrick found at the church?"

"No. Ciara only said you would need a ride." Amos pointed to the clock on the dash. "It's three on the nose. Cutting it a little bit close for further disasters."

"Right?" She made room for Blarney next to her in the front seat, then pulled the door closed. "Let's go. No disasters. We don't have time. Ceremony is supposed to be at four-thirty. We are meeting at the barn at four. Is the cart ready?"

"It is. Covered in ostrich feathers, gray ribbon, and red roses. Very festive," Amos said. "We tied a bunch of horseshoes to the back of the carriage."

"Thank you for all you're doing." Rayne exhaled loudly as they arrived at the main road.

"Are weddings normally this much trouble?" Amos asked.

"No. Maybe? I don't know, honestly." Rayne's mind was spinning. "I'm the designer and that is what I knew how to handle. I wasn't the wedding planner before. A castle with ghosts . . ."

"What are you saying?" Amos signaled to turn right, toward the church. It was across the street and down a few blocks. Traffic seemed to be heavier than normal.

"Amy's dress was slashed to ribbons while the tower was locked up and nobody was there," Rayne said, glancing at Amos as she petted behind Blarney's ears. "She thinks that Tiffany's ghost did it."

"She's an actress, and perhaps one for theatrics," Amos said. "Does she have an extra gown to wear?"

"No." Amy was an actress, and Rayne had to remember that. Jake was an actor, and a good one. If the pair were having an affair, it was possible Tori would never know.

"What will she do then?" Amos asked. "No offense, but Tori doesn't seem the kind of bride to be okay with things not being just so."

"It's fine," Rayne said. But it wasn't. Blarney rested his head on her knee, and she patted his smooth russet fur.

"How so?" Amos crossed the street and turned down the road to the church. It was several blocks but all within walking distance. The carriage ride would be something magical that the castle provided. It would bring success to everyone. Why couldn't the villagers see that and be supportive?

"Aine is sewing her into one of Aunt Amalie's dresses. Charcoal chiffon—classic choice. We aren't telling the bride, so, uh, maybe don't mention it." Rayne scrunched her nose at Amos.

"Won't say a word." Amos parked at the church. "I've got your back, Lady McGrath."

"Ha!" Rayne knew he was teasing her and smiled. She could really use a friend.

They hopped out, even Blarney, to sniff around the Fiat Ciara had driven. Father Patrick waited with her cousin outside. The parking lot had several cars from parishioners who had volunteered to help with the wedding mass and decorations.

"Rayne, lass, howareyetheday?" Father Patrick O'Murphy greeted her. "It's a splendid afternoon despite the lashing rain yesterday. I said a few prayers about it." The priest pointed heavenward to the blue sky.

"I appreciate that." Rayne shook the priest's hand. He wore street clothes of black slacks and a black shirt with a clerical collar, not having donned his vestments yet. Dark hair with silver at the temples and thin brows hovered above compassionate blue eyes.

Though Rayne wasn't religious, she went to church every Sunday, having taken her mom's advice to pray how she liked while satisfying the expectations of the villagers. Grathton as a whole was bigger than she was.

She didn't take the sacrament as she wasn't baptized. Father Patrick often hinted that it was never too late to find our Lord. She'd found her version and believed in a Higher Power—she was content to leave things as they were.

Father Patrick sensed that she had her line and didn't push too hard.

Ciara had been baptized at birth, her mom Catholic already, so it was no issue for her to take part in the religious ceremonial bits.

"I'm sorry to be a bother on such a busy day," the priest said, "but we found several cameras installed around the entrance and inside the foyer."

Cameras? "Oh no! The Montgomerys were very clear about no filming or paparazzi." Rayne's brow furrowed. "Did you remove them?"

"We did so." The priest handed over three cameras. "Here you are. I don't know what the world is coming to."

"Thanks so much, Father. I hope that was all of them. I never would have thought to search the church," Rayne said. "Do you have security cameras, to see who might have done this?"

"No," the priest said with a chuckle. "Nothing like that. This is God's house, and I trust Him to protect it."

Rayne's phone alarm went off.

Ciara raised a brow.

"Three o'clock," Rayne said on an exhale. This day couldn't race by any faster.

"You're late," her cousin said, concern in her gaze. "I don't know why you aren't tearing your hair out by now. It's been one catastrophe after another, and your head's still on tight!"

"Deportment classes," Rayne said with a shrug. "I'm seriously a mess on the inside. Also, Tori is behind, so I have a whole twenty minutes. I haven't even changed yet! And Aine is literally sewing Amy into a new dress."

"Amy?" Ciara asked. "Why?"

"She claims that Tiffany's ghost slashed the fabric of her gown and ruined it as payback for Amy firing her."

Father Patrick's eyes widened, and his brows rose accordingly. "Oh dear!"

"It was shredded with scissors." Rayne kept the knife option to herself. It wouldn't make any difference but only add to the fear factor.

"A ghost wouldn't do that," Ciara said. "That sounds like an angry human being."

"I agree." She kept to herself her suspicion of Amy doing it herself to somehow stop the wedding.

"That seems like vandalism," Father Patrick seconded. "Could it be related to the cameras?"

"I don't know how," Ciara said. "Garda Williams will need an update about all this, including the ruined dress."

"I suppose you're right." Rayne exhaled. "Is there anything else that you might have noticed out of place here, Father Patrick?"

"Well, I wasn't going to mention it, but there were several loosened boards on the porch here. It could be time, or it could be on purpose. I don't like to think that we can be so cruel to one another." Father tapped the wood with the toe of his loafer. "Especially on a day such as this."

Amos studied the long boards. There were five stairs to the top of the porch but no hand railings. "Should I fix it, so nobody trips later?" Amos asked.

"Lucas already did," Father Patrick said. "Had him take a gander around the place to make sure it was tip-top for the sacred sacrament here this afternoon, which is how we discovered the cameras."

"Lucas?" Rayne asked.

"A parishioner with incredible carpentry skills," Father Patrick explained. "He was an altar boy many years ago and is familiar with the quirks of this old building. He takes excellent care of the place."

"I'd wondered how you found the cameras," Ciara said. "You did the right thing to call us."

"Thank you, Father Patrick," Rayne said with all sincerity. Tick, tock, tick, tock. "But, I have to go. Amos?"

"Let's go, lass. See you at the manor, Ciara!"

"*Slan!*" Father Patrick said.

"Good-bye!" Rayne got into the truck, Blarney too, the windows rolled down.

Amos had just pulled out onto the road and had to pause for a sheep break. There was no hurrying the wooly beasts.

Rayne patted Blarney as the pup stared out the window at the sheep. "Have you seen Bran around the property today, Amos?"

"No."

"Aine has, and she's not happy about it. Thinks he's up to no good, which after seeing the postcards at the Coco Bean, I happen to agree with." Rayne dug her fingers into Blarney's soft fur. "Are you friends with Bran?"

"Not really, no." After another sheep joined the first, and then another, Amos put the truck in park to let it idle as if they had all the time in the world. "We're polite and all, but we don't have so much in common. He's a racetrack fan."

"What does that mean?"

"Likes to gamble on the horses, is all." Amos tapped the steering wheel. "I prefer to keep my money."

"Are he and Richard friends then?" She was trying to figure out a reason for Bran to be on McGrath property when he wasn't working, and now would not work there again. Richard had a cottage though. "Maybe Bran was visiting Richard?"

"Maybe, maybe not. Richard left this morning for London on holiday with one of his mates," Amos said. "But yeah, they are friends."

"What about Gillian?"

Amos's brow rose in query. "Am I friends with Gillian, or is Gillian friends with Bran?"

"Funny." Rayne arched her brow right back at him.

"Actually, yes to both," Amos said. "I am friends with Gillian, and Gillian is friends with Bran. They might have been an item back in the day, like secondary school."

Rayne scrunched her nose. She didn't see the appeal of Bran, though he obviously had something that attracted the ladies. "Could Bran be visiting Gillian, then?"

"Gillian lives a few miles north of here, so he wouldn't have a reason to visit her while she was at work," Amos said. "I didn't see her and Bran talking today."

Rayne stroked Blarney's soft fur. "Could Bran have put the cameras in the church?"

"He has the ability, sure, but why?" Amos asked.

"To stop the wedding, or to destroy the new business before it gets off the ground by filming when the Montgomerys don't want it public knowledge yet?"

"Ah, that," Amos said. "I'd like to have a chat with him myself. Find out what's going on in that brain of his."

"What about Gillian?" Her cheeks burned to suggest a friend of his might be at fault. "Could she have done it?"

"She's got the skills, sure." Amos glanced at Rayne. "I think Gillian's an asset to the manor and the property without any reason to hide cameras where they don't belong. She attends Sunday services, so it would be natural for her to be at church. It is possible but not likely in my humble opinion."

"Who then? This wedding is supposed to be very private—no leak of it on social media until afterward." Rayne bowed her head and prayed for Monday to hurry up already. The last sheep crossed, and Amos began to drive again.

They passed by the pub. Blarney barked from the open window as Jake and Josh stumbled out of the dim bar to the bright sunshine.

Jake blinked and tripped over his own feet; Josh helped him up. The brothers were both handsome, but Jake was just that extra bit more.

"Pull over, Amos," Rayne said. "Let's have them get in the back."

Tori would no doubt appreciate her groom being sober and clean. All Rayne could offer at this point was to suggest a cold shower to the Andersons. There wasn't even time for a twenty-minute catnap.

Amos slowed to a stop before them, and Josh grinned. "Hey!"

"Want a lift?" Amos asked.

"You're the besht," Josh slurred.

The guys fumbled with the back tailgate, so Rayne got out and opened it for them. They smelled like pub and not in a good way: beer, smoke, fish and chips.

"You better shower and sober up," Rayne said to Jake, then looked at Josh. "You help him get ready, all right? You're his best man."

They climbed in. Jake gave her a bashful wink. "Am I in trouble?"

"Not with me, but you might be with Tori if you show up smelling like the Saturday night haddock special."

Josh laughed.

Rayne shut the gate to the truck.

She climbed back in and closed the door. Blarney gave her hand a lick as if trying to see if she'd had the fish or a pint.

Amos's shoulders rumbled as he tried very hard not to laugh.

"This has to be worth it," Rayne muttered. "The wedding. The new business. I have a list a mile long of things that need improvement by November."

"It's a lot." Amos put the truck in drive. "I so regret any thoughts I may have had about you being a princess. You are an incredibly hard worker, Rayne."

"Thank you." She wasn't offended as she hadn't arrived in Grathton making the best impression. "Considering we live on a working castle with sheep, that is something."

Amos passed under the canopy of trees to the porch. "Should I let you off here?"

"Yes." Rayne glanced behind her to the Anderson brothers in the bed of the truck. They were singing off key. "I'll get the guys too."

Gillian waited on the bottom step of the porch. Her hat was in her hand, she had ostrich feathers in her braids, and a scowl on her face.

"Now what could be wrong!" Rayne asked.

"Uh oh," Amos said as he parked. Rayne and Blarney climbed out.

Jake and Josh jumped from the bed, falling into one another as their shoes slid on the gravel. "Dude!" Josh said, slinging an arm around Jake's shoulders.

"Go shower," Rayne instructed in a firm voice. "Meet at the barn at four. You have," she looked at her watch. Three-ten, dear God, "fifty minutes, got it? Do not be late."

"Yeah," Jake said. "I hear you, Mom." The mega star squinted his green eyes as if trying to focus on Rayne. "I just can't see you."

Ugh. "Josh, you make sure you have the rings and whatever else you need to help your brother," Rayne said. "Showers, now. Suits. And brush your dang teeth."

"Kay," Jake said.

With that, the brothers went around toward the outer stairs, and she hoped they didn't fall and break their foolish necks. They stopped laughing at the caution tape, their mood somber by the reminder of Tiffany's death.

"Idiots," Gillian said as they disappeared out of sight.

"Yep," Rayne agreed. "What happened to your hair?" She waved her fingers. "You have ostrich feathers everywhere."

"The wheel was loose on the cart." Gillian plucked a feather free.

"Oh no!"

"I was able to tighten it, fine." Gillian gritted her teeth. "The tape for the ostrich feathers wasn't sticking so I tried glue and now both are in my hair."

Rayne brought her fingers to her forehead. Things literally could not be more out of control. "I'm sorry!"

Gillian pointed at Amos. "He was supposed to help me."

"I was just gone for ten minutes, lass," Amos said. His tone was calm.

"I needed *you* to be there." Gillian shook, her body trembling with outrage.

Rayne was suddenly very clear on why Gillian didn't like her. The woman was in love with Amos.

Amos mustn't know. Unless he did? She had more sympathy for Gillian, now understanding the reason for her awful behavior.

"Let me help you now, Gillian," Amos said.

Gillian's chin raised as if she was brewing for a fight.

"Um, okay, I'm going." Rayne passed by Gillian on the step. "Did you talk with Bran today by any chance?"

"No," Gillian said, not meeting her eye.

Whatever. "I will meet you at the barn at four."

"Sure," Amos said.

Gillian ignored her.

182

Did she see Rayne as a threat?

Rayne wasn't in any position to have a relationship. She thought Amos was attractive, of course she did, she wasn't blind, and her stomach had been known to do the occasional twirl when she caught sight of his broad shoulders and wavy hair, but that didn't mean anything.

Her last choice had been a man who had duped her, stolen her dresses, stolen her money, stolen her confidence.

That man was currently on the lam, as they said in the movies.

Yes, single was best for now.

"Bye!" Rayne hurried up the stairs with Blarney, not understanding the reason her eyes were misty with emotion. She blamed the lack of sleep and the obstacles coming at her from every single direction.

At the top of the staircase, she and Blarney raced left to her bedroom, and she quickly changed into her chosen outfit for the wedding ceremony.

Tori had asked her to be a guest at the wedding—a witness on hand to assist if needed. Ciara and the rest of the crew would be here to prepare for the medieval feast. She sank to the edge of her mattress and sorted thoughts in her mind.

Flowers. Gown. Romantic carriage to the church, with the horses in braids and feathers, to make a beautiful entrance.

Only once Tori said "I do," would Rayne breathe a sigh of relief.

Chapter Fifteen

Rayne refreshed her makeup and spritzed a light waft of perfume. Her goal was to be stylish yet comfortable in the event she had to hustle.

So, understated light gray skirt with gray leather boots and a white and silvery gray blouse with muted polka dots. Hair up in a loose bun out of the way for the walk to the church.

It was only half a mile, and everyone had agreed to it beforehand.

Blarney sprawled on the bed and wagged his tail in approval when she dipped her head and said, "Good enough?"

Her skirt had deep pockets, perfect for her phone and keys, so she didn't need a purse. It was twenty past three, and it was a miracle she wasn't late.

"Let's go!"

Locking her room, Rayne headed to the main staircase and listened for voices. The chambers were fairly noiseproof because of the dense stone walls. It was quiet as they descended the stairs. Blarney loped before her and went for the front door, so she let him out with a warning to behave.

He gave no promises. Was that a wink?

She shut the door and headed to the sunroom at the very end of the manor opposite the side with the tower. It was one of her very favorite spaces because of the windows, lush, cozy furniture, shelves of books and knickknacks, and the view of the roses.

Irish rain created an amazing garden.

Who knew what century the owners had added on a space for beauty as well as function? Cormac didn't think it was an original part of the manor, but still a hundred and fifty years old—it was "new" compared to the rest.

Her Aunt Amalie had reupholstered the couches and armchairs in a soft taupe corduroy made to last. Color was brought in with seasonal pillows. Summer blue for now, but Maeve had showed her a closet of slipcases in a rainbow of hues.

The sunroom door was open, and she heard low laughter—Joan and Ciara. The pair had hit it off so well she wondered if they would remain friendly after this was over.

A hotel billionaire was not a bad ally, in any case, but her cousin didn't care about those things, which was something Rayne appreciated.

Ciara wasn't the least bit fake. Growing up in Hollywood, that was a quality Rayne had encountered all too often; she'd had to learn to separate a real friend from one who wanted to know her because her mom was famous.

Jenn, her bestie since middle school, had her back, just as Rayne would do anything for her, no questions asked. Jenn's parents were also famous, though Jenn had decided to be an accountant rather than follow in their footsteps. She'd had several child-acting gigs, some commercials, but her heart was in finance.

"There you are," Ciara said.

"Sorry to be two minutes late, but I had to change clothes for the wedding, and this was my only chance."

"Smart of you," her cousin said.

"I would love for Ciara to join us for the ceremony," Joan said. Her raised brow at Rayne brooked no room for argument.

"It's fine with me," Rayne said. "Up to you, cuz."

"I don't have anything that would be proper," Ciara said. "I am no fashionista, like Rayne."

"You are both the same size," Joan noted. "I'm sure Rayne has something you can borrow."

"You are welcome to my closet any time, Ciara, you know that." Rayne was laughing hysterically inside, but merely allowed her lips a small twitch.

Sorcha arrived with Aine, carrying two big bags of accoutrement that she placed on a high table by the window where Tori was already seated.

Amy followed Aine, carrying her shoes by the straps—she'd gone with nude, a wise choice with the dress.

Aine had done a superb job of making the gown fit—her intern had mad skills! And it was a natural talent. Rayne would help Aine in any way.

Maeve came into the room next with a trolley carrying champagne and a variety of water from still to sparkling, tea, and delicate finger snacks.

"I can't eat a bite," Tori said. "Rayne, where is my dress?"

"We thought you might change upstairs after your makeup, so that we could come down the staircase to make a grand entrance for photos." That had been Ciara's idea.

"Whatever you think," Tori said. Her skin was flushed with good health.

Maeve uncorked the champagne, and Aine passed out flutes to everyone. Sorcha didn't take one, as she was busy with the makeup, and Tori stuck with sparkling water.

Rayne, Ciara, Amy, Joan, and Aine stepped back to watch. Rayne sipped the cool bubbly and sighed. "Delicious."

Joan was dressed in a stunning dark periwinkle calf-length gown fitted to her figure. Her blond hair was in a twist, and her diamond earrings were so large they made her lobes sag just a bit. Her shoes matched the dress exactly, and her makeup was already done.

"Go change, Ciara dear. I insist."

Ciara downed the rest of her champagne in a single gulp. "Truly? This is really out of my comfort zone." She glared at Rayne. "I don't suppose you have fancy slacks?"

"You know I do," Rayne said. Her love for clothes meant that she had many outfits. She scanned the group for issues, but everyone seemed to be in a decent mood. "We'll be right back, if everyone's okay?"

Tori sipped her sparkling water as Sorcha set her hair in an elaborate style with rolls and cubic zirconia pins. "Hurry though. Can't be late for my own wedding."

"I'll go after you, right, Tori?" Amy asked. She swirled the chiffon of her skirt.

"Yes. You know that already." Tori's tone was very cool.

Had the ladies had another disagreement?

"You won't be late," Rayne promised.

If the cart was broken, then they'd offer to lead the couple on horseback—whatever it took to reach the finish line of the Montgomery–Anderson nuptials.

Rayne and Ciara went to the studio that was above the sunroom. After unlocking the door, Rayne led Ciara to the section of her Aunt Amalie's walk-in closet where Aine had stored Rayne's clothes.

"I'm not wearing anything poofy," Ciara declared.

"I wouldn't suggest that in the first place." Rayne tapped her chin and studied Ciara. Her cousin had a bone deep beauty, gray eyes, dark lashes and brows, short, bleached curls.

They were the same height and close to the same weight—close enough that Ciara would fit into anything of Rayne's.

"I know just the outfit."

She'd fallen in love with an haute couture designer at a fashion show where she'd purchased a two-piece pantsuit in maroon with light gray pearls on the sleeves and ankles. Gray flats for her feet would allow her cousin to walk with no worries.

"What is that on the arms?" Ciara asked with suspicion.

"Pearls."

"I don't know," Ciara said.

Rayne's phone dinged. She read it, thinking it would be Tori telling her to hurry, but it was a text message from her mom that Landon had been seen at the airport. LAX? What happened to the police surveillance?

"This is so ridiculous," Rayne said, completely taken aback. "Landon's out of his mind."

"What is it?" Ciara asked.

She showed her cousin the message.

"No!" Ciara said. "Like, he's on his way to Dublin?"

"Good question." Rayne gently nudged her cousin into the closet. "I'll ask, you change. The gray flats too."

Ciara grumbled but closed the door. The inside of the closet had lighting and mirrors galore.

She called her mother, who picked up immediately. "Lauren?"

"Rayne, you have got to be careful!"

"I thought the police were watching the airport?"

"Well, Landon flew out of San Diego rather than LAX. To Dublin. I'm so worried for you, honey. Just, sugar snaps!"

"I'll be fine," Rayne said. "They'll catch Landon when he lands." This wasn't something she had time for. She'd remind Garda Williams about it, to be safe. They had nine hours at least before he'd be anywhere close to McGrath Castle.

"Darling, I'm trying to tell you that Landon is already in Dublin."

"What? How do you know this?"

"I've been on the phone with Officer Peters. She insisted there were patrols at LAX though Landon is not considered a dangerous criminal. She went through the flight information, and when Landon wasn't on it, drove to San Diego airport on her own."

Death at an Irish Wedding

Rayne brought her palm to her suddenly racing heart. "Holy smokes!" San Diego wasn't far from Los Angeles and wily Landon had correctly assumed the heat would be around LAX.

"The other policemen told Officer Peters she was wasting time and department resources since they have killers on the loose, and Landon is a white-collar criminal. You were not his first victim, I'm sorry to say. Officer Peters figures Landon probably has several different stashes of cash, clothes, and ID for a quick getaway. He's not considered a threat, but I think differently, and so does Officer Peters."

Rayne was shocked but had to compartmentalize. Wedding first, then Landon.

Ciara exited Aunt Amalie's closet with an exaggerated flourish. Her cousin was so beautiful, and she could see Uncle Nevin in her direct charcoal gaze, a trait they shared.

"You must take this seriously, Rayne."

"I will, Mom. Let's talk later!" Rayne buried thoughts of Landon to the back of her mind and ended the call. "You look amazing, Ciara. Freaking gorgeous."

Ciara blushed and walked stiffly to the center of the room. "The shoes pinch."

"They go perfectly." Rayne tilted her head, scanning Ciara from head to toe. Her cousin could be a runway model, with her dramatic dark eyes, slender figure, and against-the-rules bleached hair.

"What did your mam say?"

"Oh, well." Rayne sighed and brushed an imaginary piece of lint from Ciara's shoulder. "Landon's in Dublin."

Ciara rocked the fitted pants but didn't seem to care. "Rayne. We have to call the Gardaí."

Rayne shrugged. "Garda Williams already knows. We must concentrate on the wedding—this is what we've all worked so hard to accomplish—and get that money in the bank. I can worry about Landon later. Let's stick to the plan." She wouldn't allow Landon to ruin their big day. And truthfully, Landon was third or fourth in line for priority with Tiffany's murderer still not caught and Bran Wilson sabotaging the business.

Ciara crossed her arms and arched a brow, uncertainty stamped on her expression. "He already ruined your life, Rayne. What else does he want?"

"Don't know," Rayne said. "Just trust me—he's a wimp, honestly, and doesn't deserve our attention."

Ciara scowled.

Her phone dinged again, this time Tori wondering what the holdup was. "We gotta go."

"I don't like it," Ciara stated as she shut the closet door. "I'll update Dominic about the situation. It's scary that Landon sneaked his way into Ireland after escaping jail to find you."

"The police at home don't consider him to be all that dangerous. He's a thief, not a killer," Rayne said. She kept Officer Peters' opinion on the matter to herself as it wouldn't ease Ciara's concerns. "I agree that we should alert the Gardai, but let's focus on the wedding. Also, consider that outfit a gift. I've never worn it, and you look amazing."

Rayne locked the studio, and the cousins went down the back-stairs that was a servant's shortcut in the old days—they arrived at the sunroom in less than a minute.

"There you are!" Tori said. Her makeup and hair were flawless. Golden tresses in an updo with Irish lace peeking at the nape, crimson lipstick, and a flawless porcelain complexion. Sorcha had a gift for maximum coverage without it seeming too heavy.

"Well done, Sorcha," Rayne said. "Yep. Here I am with," she glanced at her phone, "twenty minutes to go." Her stomach tightened. They'd be down to the wire.

"Thank you," Sorcha said. "Amy, are you ready?"

The starlet giggled and sat in Tori's vacated seat.

Tori, in passing, commented on Amy's charcoal chiffon dress. "Where did you get that?"

Her cheeks flushed with champagne and guilt . . . guilt?

Tori stopped completely. Joan, who'd been complimenting Ciara on the pantsuit, turned as well to listen to her daughter's question.

"This old thing?" Amy said. It was lovely, as was the redheaded starlet.

"I thought you were wearing crimson," Tori said.

Amy glanced at Rayne and fluttered her lashes. It was clear that she wanted to tell Tori about the dress but also, that it would be unsettling to know that the original dress had been slashed to ribbons.

"There was a . . . tear . . . in the dress that she'd brought," Aine said, jumping into the drawn-out moment with an explanation that wasn't a lie.

"And since you'd already changed the venue from Christmas, we thought perhaps light gray would match with the guys' suits rather than the crimson gown. It seemed more appropriate for evening, and this is better for afternoon. I hope you don't mind?" Rayne crossed her fingers in her pocket.

"You did say that you didn't care about which dress," Amy said with small pout.

"That's true, but why didn't you tell me?" Tori asked. "I don't like you being so sneaky."

Amy paled.

"Oh, it's not her fault. That was my suggestion," Rayne said. "We didn't want to upset you on your big day. There's already so much going on."

Tori nodded and topped off her sparkling water. "Fine. I guess it doesn't matter."

Amy's smile faltered.

"Time is ticking, girls," Joan said. "Tori, hon, can I come with you to help with the dress?" She fussed with the delicate Irish lace at her daughter's nape. "I wish my mom could see you now."

Tori gave her mother a hug. "Grandma's here with us . . . I promise to cherish this lace from her veil, but I want it to be a surprise when I come down the staircase at five to four. I can't wait to see your face! I'm kinda regretting not having a professional photographer."

Joan braced her shoulders. "Of course, dear. Whatever you think best."

"I have a camera as well as my phone," Ciara offered. "I'd be happy to take some pictures."

"Great." Tori's lipstick, crimson, was perfect. With her skin tone, Tori needed a deeper red rather than a lighter one. Sorcha's training at the makeup counter hadn't been wasted today.

Amy, uneasy, perched on the chair. "Tor?"

"Let's go," Tori said. She walked past Joan and Ciara to Rayne. "This day is speeding yet dragging at the same time."

"I've never been married, but I imagine that it would be a mix of excitement and anxiety," Rayne said.

"You were engaged, weren't you?" Amy called across the room. "Your business partner, Landon Short—he robbed you and went to jail."

"He did." And just why had Amy tossed Rayne to the wolves so dramatically just now?

"Is that relevant?" Joan asked coolly.

Tori nodded at her mother. "It's not. That is old news, Amy. Did Tiffany share that snarky gossip from her snooping around?"

Amy sipped her champagne, shooting daggers at Tori from her seat. "Tiffany collected secrets about *everybody*," she said.

"While unfortunate, what happened wasn't a secret," Rayne said. "We were business partners but never engaged." She calmly relayed the humiliation of her thirtieth birthday in June in a smooth tone, but it still stung. She'd thought power lunch, power couple, and Landon had taken her money, her designer dresses, and her confidence.

Rayne opened the door and Tori stepped out. "I apologize for Amy. She sometimes gets excitable. I forget how young she is," the heiress said loud enough for the rest to hear.

"It's fine." Rayne closed the door of the sunroom. "Want to see a secret passageway? It will save us five minutes."

"Yes, please." Tori tightened her hold on the crystal flute. "How fun."

They walked up the narrow stairs to which Rayne had added battery operated sconces. The walls were stone, the steps wooden.

"This is creepy," Tori said. "I love it."

"It's growing on me. I was here as a kid with my dad," Rayne explained. "I told you, my cousin Padraig used to tease me with ghost stories." They stepped from the dim staircase to the hallway outside Uncle Nevin's room, and what had been her Aunt Amalie's pink parlor.

They'd decided to keep her uncle's room as it was for now—Ciara was content in her small chamber even though if she moved into her da's it would have an en suite bathroom.

"This is so great, Rayne." Tori rubbed her arms as if chilled. "And a tiny bit spooky."

"Do you believe in ghosts?" Rayne asked.

"No. Not really. I'm too practical to believe in the supernatural." They crossed the hall to the studio. "Do you?" Tori asked.

Rayne smiled at the heiress. "Maybe."

Tori laughed. "Maybe . . . I like that. Not definitive but a possibility."

"Sometimes I smell my aunt's perfume. Or, I would swear that I've closed a door that is open, that kind of thing." Rayne unlocked and opened the studio door. The sunlight on Tori's bridal gown was magical as each crystal created a prism of color on the walls.

"Oh!" Tori gasped. "It's wonderful." Tori nudged the door closed behind them with her hip, not spilling her sparkling water. Once it was closed, she faced Rayne. "Now, cut the crap. Tell me the truth about Amy's dress. That girl looked so guilty that I know something is going on."

"That was the truth!" Rayne said. "The crimson gown had been . . . damaged. What we weren't telling you is that it must have been . . . on purpose."

Tori cradled her flute and tilted her head. "How?"

"Funny story," Rayne said. Not so much now that she understood Tori's stance on the paranormal. "Amy thinks that maybe Tiffany's ghost did it."

"A ghost?" Tori drawled.

"Aine—"

"The maid?"

"She's also my intern as a seamstress," Rayne explained. "Anyway, Aine examined the fabric." She walked to the dress form, focusing on Tori's gown. Time was of the essence. "It wasn't jagged, but clean slashes."

"And a ghost isn't going to be that precise?" Tori's brow arched. "Come on, Rayne. You don't believe that nonsense, do you?"

Rayne shook her head. "No, I don't think it was an evil spirit, but sharp scissors wielded by a human hand."

"Whew. I was starting to worry about your state of mind," Tori said. "Amy's a loon anyway."

"Do you think so?" There was no love lost between the supposed best friends.

Tori wandered to the dress form and her stunning dress with the heart-shaped crystals and ostrich feathers around the tiered hem. The heiress had no idea about the missing Swarovski and that was exactly how Rayne wanted it.

"My money is on Amy doing the dirty work and blaming a dead woman. It's just like her," Tori said.

Tori drained her glass and set the empty flute down on Aine's worktable. A scrap of crimson fabric from Amy's old dress remained behind that Aine must have missed from when she'd cleaned up.

The gown itself was on the sofa, and Rayne wished she could hide it—out of sight, out of mind.

Amy doing the slashing herself certainly fit with Rayne's hypothesis. Her only question was *why* . . .

Chapter Sixteen

Rayne sucked back a comment to nod with empathy all while reeling that Tori had brought Amy with her as her bridesmaid. Was the heiress trying to trick Jake into making a mistake with Amy?

Her hopes that Tori wouldn't notice the crimson gown vanished as Tori zeroed in on it, lifting it up to the natural light. "Amy wants to be the center of attention, all the time, and it's exhausting."

"Let's get you into your gown," Rayne said, attempting to keep things positive.

White heels, the wrap of ostrich feathers, the jewelry—everything was prepared. All that was left was to dress the bride.

Tori dropped the crimson gown as if it was toxic and blinked back tears.

Did Rayne dare offer compassion? Time was running out! She couldn't help it even though if Tori cried, the makeup Sorcha had put on would run.

"Are you okay, Tori?"

"No." The heiress shook her head and answered honestly.

Dang it.

Tori waved her fingers. "But, that is normal. Ish. Am I making a mistake, marrying Jake Anderson?"

Rayne fluffed the ostrich feather wrap and draped it over the sofa. "Only you can answer that." She watched Tori for cues as to what she needed from Rayne. Sometimes people just wanted to talk.

"My answer is, so what? All he has to do is stay married to me for a year and then he will get a very large settlement. He'll still be in his prime to woo the fans of his next action-adventure movie. Damn, he's a gorgeous man." Tori touched her engagement ring. "Talented too."

Rayne nodded. It seemed her client just needed to vent, so Rayne would listen.

Tori kicked off her shoes, then her pants and shirt. The bridal gown would be worn without a bra and over a skimpy lacy thong.

"He loves you," Rayne said. "You love him." She didn't dare offer that as a question as the heiress already had her exit strategy in place.

"I thought he did," Tori said. "It broke my heart to hear that he and Amy had a thing, before me, but it makes you wonder, you know?"

Amy had made a play that Jake had told Tori about—what about the ones he hadn't mentioned? Rayne removed the gown from the dress form and held it out for Tori to step into. "Here you go."

Rayne slowly raised it up, zipping the gown closed. It was tight, but it was done.

"Thank God." Tori stepped into the white heels with crystals and stared at Rayne with wide eyes. "I was worried—it's okay to admit that you were too, now that it's on."

Rayne nodded. "All right. I was. There was no more room to budge."

"I will one hundred percent recommend you and your business to everyone. I'm sorry that your ex was such a jerk." Tori looked over her shoulder at Rayne. "It's stories like yours that make me not so trusting."

"I appreciate the word of mouth," Rayne said, not commenting on her personal life though Tori had left the space open. "It's important for a new business."

"Are you dating again?"

"No."

"You loved Landon." Tori stated this as if it might be a reason for Rayne to stay single.

"I loved who he claimed to be, but that was a lie." Rayne scrunched her nose. "How about happy thoughts, huh? This is your special day."

"Happy, happy, happy. My therapist says I can choose." Tori shrugged. "Some days are easier than others."

"I agree with that. An attitude of gratitude," Rayne said.

"Blessed." Tori snorted. "Are we seeing the same therapist?"

Rayne laughed hard at that. "But if it works . . ."

Tori's eyes narrowed as her gaze landed next to the flute on Rayne's table. She noted, of course she did, the extra Swarovski crystal in the plastic bag.

"Are you always so prepared?" Tori asked.

"I try." Rayne smoothed several ostrich feathers.

"Was I missing some crystals?"

If only she felt comfortable lying but she didn't, and it didn't matter now. The gown was fixed. Rayne said, "Just one."

"Where?" Tori studied the front of her dress, and then the back. Her brow rose in question.

Rayne showed her the spot. "You can't tell."

"Was it loose?" Tori asked. "I hadn't taken it from the garment bag once since our last fitting in LA."

Rayne bit her lip. "I don't think so."

Tori whirled from Rayne, her face immobile. "Someone took it . . . why? To ruin my day? To keep a token?"

That reminded her of the church. Bran. And Gillian, too. They wanted the wedding venue closed down. Gillian, and Bran, would have access to the tower rooms.

Could this be their way to protest progress? And maybe Tiffany had caught them and they argued . . . she shook her head.

"I don't know. And just a word to the wise—Father Patrick found some video cameras in the church this morning." Rayne couldn't risk telling Tori, her client, about the opposition from the villagers regarding the wedding venue.

"What?" Tori exclaimed.

"It seems that someone wants to commemorate your special day," Rayne said. "With or without your permission."

Tori paled beneath her bronzer. "I promised Jake on my life there would be no paparazzi."

"Father Patrick and his groundskeeper, Lucas, searched everywhere on the church property and discovered three." Rayne winced as she moved on her knees, fluffing the hem.

"Shit." Tori stared down at Rayne. "Who would do such a thing?"

Other than Bran or Gillian? Rayne cleared her throat. "Could it have been Tiffany, maybe, trying to get information for that exposé she was writing?"

Tori tilted her head. Around her neck was a gorgeous platinum and diamond choker that had been her mother's. "Something old, something new, something borrowed, something blue," she whispered. "Grandma's Irish lace, my dress, my mom's necklace, and my eyes."

"You've got all the avenues covered," Rayne said.

"I can't afford a mistake." Tori tapped her necklace. "Tiffany worked for Amy. Jake hooked up with Amy. All roads lead back to Amy. If Jake and I don't get married today, it's not like he will marry *her*."

Yep. Jealousy, competition, love: Rayne could name three reasons off the top of her head for Amy to sabotage Tori's wedding. Using her mother's reminders to look for *why*, that meant Jake remained the number one motivation.

Rayne decided to change the subject before they both broke down in despair. "You look beautiful, Tori."

"I feel beautiful. Can you believe I'm going to be a mommy?" Tori's blue eyes glistened. "I can't wait. I only plan on having one. No nanny. Well, maybe. I just want my little one to know that I love them with all my heart. Silly, huh?"

"You will have a lucky baby." And Rayne would bet that after the first sleepless month, the nanny would be more hands-on.

"Yeah." A smile faltered on her face. "Jake will come around."

"Did he want children?" Rayne asked. The pure white ostrich feathers added luxury to the crystals and silk.

"Sure. But later on down the road," Tori said. "He'll be a great dad."

"Family seems to be very important to him." Rayne rose and her skirt settled around her calves. "You ready?"

Tori grabbed Rayne's hand, her fingers chilled. "Yes. I am."

Rayne handed Tori the wrap of white ostrich feathers and the heiress donned it like a movie star. She could see Tori next to Jake on the red carpet with ease.

"Glamorous!" Rayne said. She locked the door behind them, and they walked down the main hall, past the gallery of McGrath ancestors.

No matter what, she and Ciara had done their part for this Irish wedding, despite many, many obstacles.

"I'm so happy for you," Rayne said when they reached the staircase. At the bottom were Amy, Ciara, Joan, Sorcha, Maeve, and Aine.

Amy and Joan clapped enthusiastically.

Rayne inched back from Tori to let her have the spotlight, accidentally bumping into a suit of armor, making it clang. The things were sturdy, thank goodness.

Ciara snapped photos with a camera on a strap around her neck, as well as her cell phone.

Amy also took plenty of pictures with her phone too.

Joan just watched her daughter with maternal pride and love in her eyes. "You are so beautiful, Tori Montgomery."

"Thanks, Mom."

Tori slowly descended each stair, letting the wrap drop stylistically as she went. Amy started forward to grab it, but Joan stopped her.

"This is Tori's moment, darling." Joan's tone conveyed dislike for the starlet.

Could Amy have slashed her own dress? It was possible, and Tori believed so too.

At four o'clock, Rayne's alarm went off, a system to keep her on track and she couldn't imagine not having it in place with all of the freaking distractions.

Tori reached the round table in the manor's foyer and the others applauded. "Just gorgeous!" Joan said. "Ciara, make sure to send me those, will you?"

"That I will!" Ciara said.

Rayne hurried down the stairs. "It's time to go to the barn and give you a fairy tale carriage ride to the church, Tori." She swooped up the lightweight ostrich feather wrap.

Excitement filled the air and Aine opened the door. "Good luck to you! Blessings!" the maid/intern said.

Maeve and Sorcha echoed the sentiments. "Oh! The bouquets." Maeve returned from the kitchen with a bridal bouquet of red roses, green ivy, and white Queen Anne's lace from the gardens. She'd wrapped the stems in white ribbon and a blue Mary Magdalene pendant. "Here you are, love."

"Thank you! It's classic and simple." Tori smelled the heady rose fragrance.

"And Amy," Maeve gave the bridesmaid a smaller bouquet of roses, the ribbon a soft dove gray.

"Thank you!" Amy said.

"I didn't do boutonnieres for the men, but I did have Sorcha deliver some red roses to the church so the flowers will match." Maeve clasped her hands with a question on her expressive face.

"It's perfect, thank you, Maeve," Rayne said.

The group went outside. Rayne searched the area for Blarney, who liked to sleep on the top step of the porch, but the dog wasn't there.

She squinted toward the barn. Drat. No sunglasses. Oh well. She heard a bark behind the closed barn doors—maybe Amos had put the pup in there to be out of the way of the bridal party and excitement.

Her gaze next went to the white carriage and the gray horses attached to it. Cormac held the reins from his driver's bench seat. His black suit had been elevated to fancy with the addition of a top hat.

Gillian and Amos stood on either side of the horses. Gillian had turned them into magical beasts with ribbons, roses, and ostrich feathers.

"That looks incredible," Ciara whispered to Rayne.

"It does." Rayne blew out a small happy breath. Surely the Montgomerys, and the Andersons, would tout the castle wedding venue.

Rayne looked to the left by the rose garden and noticed Garda Lee, in civilian clothes, but with a Garda-like pose, her hands behind her back, waiting for the event to begin.

Where was Garda Williams?

Before she could ask any questions, Tori started to walk down the manor stairs, reaching the grass, and followed the gravel path to the cart. The gown showcased the heiress's figure, crystals shimmered with each step, her toes playing peekaboo from the feathered hem.

They all went with her toward the barn, a court of admirers around the queen.

"Where's Jake?" Tori asked, studying the folks near the carriage.

Rayne saw Josh, Ethan, and Dylan. No Jake.

"He's probably primping. This is his big day too," Amy suggested.

"Or sleeping off his beer," Joan murmured. "The boy shouldn't have been drinking so much."

"Mom!" Tori said, her tone sharp.

"Sorry." Joan didn't sound the least bit apologetic.

Ciara glanced at Rayne with a bitten back smile.

Joan was a straight shooter and maybe that was what Ciara and Joan liked about each other's personalities.

They continued down the path and arrived at the carriage. The gray horses whinnied in welcome, and Rayne gulped, edging back.

"Baby girl, you look stunning," Dylan said, pride and love in his eyes too.

"Thanks, Dad. Josh. Ethan." Tori nodded at them all, displeased that Jake wasn't there. Rayne didn't blame her.

The guys all wore charcoal gray with crimson accents. Dylan had a periwinkle tie that matched Joan's dress.

Rayne carried Tori's wrap. "Josh, when did you last talk with Jake?"

"I shoved him in the shower like you said, Rayne." Josh tugged at his bow tie. "I grabbed a nap."

"Ethan?" Tori asked. The red roses in her hand trembled. "Have you heard from Jake?"

"Last I saw he was returning to the tower to get ready for his wedding," Ethan said. His cologne was pine, his near-black goatee and hair shining. As a guest of the couple, he'd chosen a black suit with a soft gray button up shirt, the collar loose without a tie.

They all turned to face the manor house and specifically the tower. Rayne could make out the caution tape from here. It was hard to believe but Garda Williams had managed to keep Tiffany's murder a secret.

Tori punched Josh's arm with the hand not wearing the diamond. "Call him. You're his best man. Make sure he's here, for heaven's sake. You can do that one job, can't you?"

"Ow!" Josh pulled his phone from his pocket and shot off a text. At Tori's glare, he called. In the end, he left a message. "Bro, your chariot awaits."

"Clever," Tori snapped. She turned her back to Josh.

Josh rolled his eyes. "Maybe he fell asleep in the shower."

Ethan sighed and brushed his lapels. "Should I go check?" he asked, since Josh wasn't volunteering. "Someone should make sure he's okay."

"Daddy, will you go?" Tori asked. "What if Jake is hurt or something?"

Rayne shivered. Tiffany was dead, murdered, but they didn't know that. She was now worried too.

"Hurt?" Josh quipped. "Hardly. Drowning in regret, possibly."

Dylan puffed out his chest. "Sure, honey."

"Want me to come with you?" Ethan offered.

Jake's assistant seemed more even-keeled after his time in the cottage, away from the rest of the group. Amy watched Ethan with warm eyes.

"That's all right," Dylan said. "Gives me a chance for some one-on-one with my new son-in-law. Why don't you guys drive the cart up to the porch?"

"All right," Joan said. "Tori, sweetie, do you want to get in?"

"I'll wait for Jake." Tori's chin firmed.

"How unusual," Josh declared. "You're not the waiting kind."

"Shut it, Josh," Tori said. "Our relationship is none of your business."

"Sure it is, *sis*." Josh winked. "We're about to become family. Back in the hood, family matters more than anything else."

"The hood? Puhlease," Tori said. "Hilton Head doesn't have a hood."

"You know what I mean!" Josh countered. His fauxhawk gleamed like a blade.

Amy chuckled and stood closer to Ethan. Of the two available men, she was staking her claim on Jake's assistant.

Dylan reached the tower and went around out of sight. Rayne smiled at Amos and nodded toward the carriage. "This looks wonderful. Well done."

"Thanks. Gillian did most of the creative stuff," Amos said. "I am no good with the delicate twists. My fingers get in the way."

Gillian blushed and adjusted her straw hat, uneasy at the compliment from Amos. She'd combed the ostrich feathers from her hair.

"Thank you," Rayne told her.

"Welcome," Gillian said.

Rayne heard Blarney bark from inside the barn. "So, that's what you did with him." Understandable.

"Had to," Gillian said defensively.

"Thanks for thinking of it," Rayne said, taking a step away from the bristling woman. She had bad vibes. Could she be a murderess?

Amos smirked. "Dog's a Houdini, so we'll see how long he stays locked up."

"I added a lead," Gillian said to Amos. "Just to be safe."

Rayne checked her watch. It was now ten past four. They were supposed to be at the church at four-thirty.

Tori shuffled her feet in her white heels, getting angrier by the second.

What was taking so long? Rayne hoped everything was okay. They still didn't know what had happened to Tiffany—who had choked her and pushed her from the turret, or why.

What if Jake was the next target of a crazed person? Gillian was here. "Like Bran," she murmured, recalling how he'd hopped off his moped to pound his fists against the glass of the Coco Bean Café. That took passion.

Ciara glanced at Rayne. "Bran?"

"Did you know that Garda Lee was here?" Rayne answered a question with a question.

"Yep. And another two Gardaí are here too. Dominic said he would have extra security, to help," Ciara said. "Garda Lee is also here for you."

"Me?"

"Because of Landon," Ciara said in a low voice. "I told you I was going to let them know that Landon was in Ireland."

Rayne didn't think it would be a big deal. Annoying, yes, because of the timing of his arrival in Dublin. In a fair fight, she could probably take Landon down. Still, it was thoughtful of Ciara. "Thank you."

Their attention was taken from Blarney's barks demanding freedom to the tower, where Dylan strong-armed a very reluctant Jake Anderson toward the carriage.

The handsome actor was as pale as Ciara's bleached curls, his heels creating divots in the gravel.

Rayne wasn't sure what to do about Jake's father-in-law literally dragging him to be married. The scuff marks reminded her of the marks Tiffany had made on the turret. Resistance for her had also been futile.

Chapter Seventeen

"What the hell?" Josh asked as he pushed by Rayne toward Dylan and Jake struggling. Joan stepped in front of him. His fauxhawk listed to the side.

"He can't do that!" Ethan protested. "Tori, your dad mustn't drag Jake to the altar. It's outrageous. Archaic!"

"He can." Tori's eyes narrowed. "Daddy can do anything."

Jake's dark hair, soft and flowing, fell into place as he stopped fighting and stood still. Dylan had his hand on Jake's upper arm. The charcoal suit was tailored to perfection.

If acting, then Jake was channeling the part of a terrified groom. Rayne didn't think he was putting on a show, but truly dreaded the upcoming nuptials.

Dylan's words carried on the wind toward them. "A hundred grand in your account Monday morning."

Rayne knew a bribe when she heard one. Ciara's mouth gaped before she closed it with a snap.

The amount was enough for Jake to nod and shake off Dylan's grip.

"Not another word from you, or it's off," Dylan said.

Jake's shoulders shook.

"Your oath?"

"Fine," Jake said. "I swear."

When the handsome actor turned around to face them, he seemed like the Jake Anderson Rayne was familiar with from the screen.

Sexy and brooding, yet approachable. Happy to be there.

Tori's body relaxed slightly. That was a close call, and the heiress knew it.

Why the rush to wed? To please her parents because she was already pregnant? To please the church? It certainly didn't please Jake and could ruin his career. It was selfish.

Jake and Dylan walked in sync to the horses and the open carriage. Originally, the couple was to have ridden in it alone, but now Dylan helped Tori, then his wife, and then made sure that Jake entered before clambering up after them.

"It's illegal," Josh said to Dylan. "To coerce someone into marriage."

"Were you coerced?" Dylan asked Jake, slamming his hand on the younger man's leg.

"No." Jake's chin jutted.

"Daddy?" Tori said, on the verge of tears.

This had to be a nightmare for the heiress.

"It's fine, sugar." Dylan smiled at his only daughter.

"Just fine," Jake seconded. His crimson bowtie was askew, and he straightened it. "*Sugar.*"

Amy snorted, and Ethan elbowed her.

"Sorry!" Amy muttered.

"This isn't right," Ethan declared. "Jake, do you want me to intervene? I can call someone, the cops for starters."

"No, I don't." Jake smoothed his hands over his knees, the charcoal suit pants a slim fit to show his physique.

Jake wanted that hundred grand. Stay married for a year and then get more money with a small risk of dinging his career. People made comebacks all the time.

It probably wouldn't hurt him, though, Rayne acknowledged. He was a beautiful man and women (movie viewers) would forgive a lot, if Ethan and Jake's agent spun it right.

Amy and Ethan walked on one side of the carriage, while Josh, Rayne, and Ciara were on the other. The horseshoes behind clanged musically.

Amos and Gillian waved them off as the carriage rolled under the shady trees toward the main road. It was lovely and worth several photos. She sent Amos a text to snap some of the carriage that Rayne could use for the castle's website.

Done! Amos replied.

Rayne watched her guests in the carriage. They had no choice but to touch hips and legs on the snug benches. Tori held her flowers, the ostrich feather wrap around her shoulders. Her face was frozen.

When the couple had arrived on Thursday in Grathton, Jake would have put his arm around Tori, but not now. Now, he was playing a part, and affection was too much to ask.

Joan patted Tori's hand, the one with the diamond.

Rayne wished they would call it off—but then remembered the money that would be deposited in her account for the castle. Was she as bad as the Montgomerys, wanting something so much despite the emotional cost?

Everyone knew what they were getting into. Sad, yet this was a fair playing field. She was selling a place to wed but couldn't guarantee true love.

Ethan was texting madly—to whom? Jake's agent, wondering how to avoid destroying his only client?

Ethan and Tiffany . . . the pair hadn't seemed at odds, but what did she know of their relationship?

Tiffany didn't wear makeup or draw attention to herself in a way that might detract from her employer, the starlet Amy Flores.

Amy was so young yet was on track to be as famous, she hoped, as Jake. If Amy had ruined her own dress to stop the wedding, it hadn't worked.

They reached the road. Three more blocks to go. The shade had prevented them from getting too hot on this lovely September afternoon.

Villagers, aware of the private ceremony, were lined up on the opposite side of the road and down the blocks leading all the way to the church. As if it were a parade! The spectators had cell phones out, snapping pictures and taking video.

"No photos," Jake growled. The movie star glared at Tori, but then turned to his assistant on the ground beside the carriage. "Ethan?"

"I can't stop anybody from using their phones, Jake," Ethan said. His tone shared what he thought of the request at this late stage in the game. Everything had been a whirlwind, and he'd been out of the loop.

Ethan had warned the movie star, who hadn't listened to a thing he'd suggested. Long engagement for starters and downhill from there.

What did they know about Ethan? Rayne channeled her mother and asked the "why" question. Would he have a reason to consider Tiffany a rival or a threat?

Though slim in build, Ethan was muscular. Tiffany would have met him on the roof—maybe for a cigarette? Gossip? No, they shared a cottage and didn't need extreme measures to meet up in private.

Jake turned to Rayne with a scowl. She averted her gaze and pretended not to notice his displeasure.

"Smile, darling," Joan prompted her daughter. "You look like a princess. Can't appear miserable for the public."

Tori did as her mother directed. She was lovely as she put on a bright smile guaranteed to fool anybody not peering too closely at her damp eyes.

The ladies along the road all whistled at Jake, recognizing the superstar. Amy waved as well, but nobody called her name as they did Jake's. She waved a little harder, her bridesmaid bouquet a red blur.

It was almost over, Rayne assured herself. She heard a boo from the sidelines and scanned the crowd for the naysayer who would dare such a thing.

There was Sinéad and her hubby, Liam. Beetle. One of the waitresses at the pub, with a giant picture of Jake. Freda Bevin, the councilwoman from the village over. Rayne squinted.

Yep, Freda waved from the side of the street, standing next to some young ladies who hollered Jake's name. The middle-aged woman considered herself a fashionista and wore a canary yellow blouse over plaid capris. Her lipstick was hot pink.

"We love you, Jake Anderson!" one of the young women with her shouted.

Ethan exhaled and bristled.

"Is that Freda?" Ciara asked Rayne in a low murmur.

"Yes." Rayne and Freda hadn't been friendly after Rayne had accused her of wanting to kill Uncle Nevin.

"What is she doing here?" Ciara asked. Her tone was very suspicious, and Rayne agreed that her presence was highly questionable. Nobody was supposed to know the names of their high-profile guests.

Yet, Tori had requested the carriage ride from the castle to the church. Perhaps she'd hoped that Jake would come around before now.

"I don't know. How did she find out the identity of our guests?" Rayne countered. She was answered by Bran coming up to Freda and the other ladies, talking to them in whispers.

Freda handed an envelope to Bran that he tucked in his jeans pocket.

"Bran told her!" Rayne said. He'd been dropping off postcards about the castle, and probably alerting everyone while he did so. "That, that . . . ugh!" He was going to ruin everything, on purpose.

"That moron." Ciara balled her fist.

"Is Bran a problem?" Ethan's eyes narrowed. "We should have security. I am not happy with this whole arrangement."

"I'm sorry that you're upset," Rayne said automatically moving into control-mode for the event. "That man is a local. He's fine." But was he? *Fired, fired, fired.*

Ethan focused on Bran. "That's the guy at the pub Tiffany hit it off with. I know they exchanged phone numbers."

Rayne slowed her steps. This correlated with what Garda Williams had discovered about Tiffany and Bran locked at the lips.

"That drunk dude from the café and Tiffany knew each other?" Amy asked, her brow raised.

"They had a pint, yeah. Maybe two. Not a big deal," Ethan said. He kept his distance from Amy, no matter how many times she wanted to be arm in arm.

"Right. That was Thursday night. Are you saying that Friday night, Tiffany was having a drink with Bran at the pub?" Rayne smiled encouragingly at Ethan. They'd all split up at ten-thirty, and Ethan had gone for smokes at midnight. What had Tiff been up to for that time? Hanging out with Bran?

"I wasn't sure that she did it—he invited her, but Amy had her running around like a crazy woman, spying on everyone. Tiffany never confirmed."

Amy whirled on Ethan. "I did not!"

Josh nudged Amy. "Yeah, you did. We all know it."

Amy fumed. "Lies."

"You're the liar," Josh said. "Wouldn't be surprised if you'd told Tiff to gather information on everyone for that exposé done by *you*, and she beat you to it."

"Josh Anderson, you are . . . despicable." Amy's eyes welled.

Was that regret underneath her sassy exterior?

The knowledge of who had stolen the crystal heart, or taken Tiffany's phone, and the notebooks, could lead to Tiffany's killer.

In fact, Tiffany's phone might prove whether or not she and Bran had met together for a drink Friday. The Gardaí searching the grounds couldn't move any faster.

Ethan fell back from the group walking toward the church and snapped his fingers. "I'll catch up." He didn't wait for permission but left, dashing across the street toward the manor.

The spire of the church was visible and only a block away. Cameras flashed and folks called Jake's name.

Tori's too, but mostly Jake—he was the megastar marrying the hotel heiress.

Dylan and Joan had happy expressions on their faces—probably fake—but in the event the wedding made the paper or the internet, it wouldn't look like they were all reluctant to get this over with.

Josh was using his phone to video the spectators and the carriage as they neared the church parking lot.

A man with a giant camera, like from an actual newspaper, snapped photo after photo. "Jake Anderson!" he called, the flash clicking when Jake turned his direction.

Jake cursed. "Tori, you promised. And you lied."

It would be difficult for damage control. Had Bran announced the wedding on the radio or gone house to house like the freaking town crier?

Cormac, driving the carriage like a pro, halted the horses before the church door. "Here we are!"

Applause from Jake's fans and the villagers rang out. "Jake, Jake, Jake, Jake!"

Rayne winced as Tori's bravado faltered but she covered by burying her nose in the roses of her bouquet. She had to focus on Tori, her bride-client, and push the rest away.

"Jake Anderson," the man with the large camera called, "what do you think your fans will say about this secret wedding?"

"Not so secret," Dylan muttered. He stood and helped Joan out of the carriage and jumped down himself.

He held out a hand for Tori and there was an audible intake of breath as the folks saw her gown and the ostrich wrap.

Rayne knew that dress was a hit and felt a shimmer of pride at how Tori showed it to perfection.

Jake, going with the momentum of fan adoration, stood next to Tori and the couple radiated wealth, success, and beauty.

Love was missing from the scene, Rayne thought.

Jake climbed down, then placed his hands around Tori's waist to swing her around. Tori landed on her feet and Rayne was there to catch the featherlight wrap.

Amy took it from Rayne. "I'll do that! I am her best friend and bridesmaid," she said, speaking loudly to be heard by those closest to them.

Dylan went inside with Joan. Tori with Amy and Josh. Cormac moved the horses and the carriage to the side in the shade, the hooves clomping.

Ciara, Rayne, and Jake were the last to enter. Jake's green eyes were filled with misery. The wheels of the carriage groaned to a stop and almost drowned out a *thwack* followed by a thud above the door of the church. Rock chips scattered to the ground. The horses neighed.

Rayne whirled. Where had that come from?

She scanned the crowd of villagers who hadn't been invited inside for the private ceremony. Behind them was the street and across the road were trees, hills, and, naturally, a flock of sheep.

"What was that?" Rayne called out.

"Go home!" a voice shouted. Another person echoed the sentiment.

Were they protesting, like Bran had wanted? And where was he, not brave enough to show his face?

Throwing mudpies or stones was childish. She studied the throng. The villagers had to support this process or Grathton Village would be no more.

Ciara waited for her, toeing the rock pieces with her boot. "What happened?"

Josh pulled Jake into the lobby. "People throwing rocks?" Josh asked. "Rude. Boo yourselves," he called, raising his fist.

Father Patrick frowned and peered out but then gathered the wedding party inside toward the front of the church.

Ciara and Rayne stepped in at the back of the group. Cormac stayed with the carriage and the horses, which was probably a good idea since the villagers were restless. She gave a last look for Ethan, but he hadn't returned so she shut the door. She wondered if he was putting out feelers for a different client, maybe one who listened to his advice.

213

The stone church had been around since the mid-nineteenth century. Thick timber joists were visible in the ceiling. Wooden pews that sat a hundred folks were mostly empty as the Montgomerys and Andersons had wanted privacy.

Father Patrick stood by the altar and welcomed everyone, with a reminder that this was a day of peace and joy. That one had to embrace the new or risk losing the old.

In other words, throwers of rocks in protest, behave.

Red roses with white and gray silk ribbon adorned the front—the subtle scent was better than perfume. Maeve had created beautiful bouquets, given the last-minute conditions.

The Catholic ceremony took a good forty minutes before the actual nuptials.

Tori and Jake sat next to one another. Josh and Amy behind them. Joan and Dylan were opposite the aisle. Rayne and Ciara sat in the center row.

Rayne believed in a higher power but didn't take the sacrament. It seemed the brothers had forgotten their Catholic school days, as Tori had to prompt them. About a dozen brave parishioners had filed in as if unaware they were not welcome but stayed in the back two rows, although it had been posted a private event in the church newsletter and on the corkboard.

Father Patrick at last was ready to say the wedding vows. Tori handed Amy her bridal bouquet. Josh sent a pleading glance to Jake.

It was sad that Jake had to be bribed. How could this union lead to lasting happiness? Rayne had so many questions, but there was no answer for most of them.

Ethan hadn't returned. Did he have a reason to harm Tiffany? Or could it be Bran, in league with Freda, who wanted to absorb Grathton Village into hers?

Was Bran correct that if Grathton and Cotter Villages merged, he would be better off somehow? Rayne would need to learn the local politics, quick.

What could Rayne and Ciara do to personally assure the villagers, so they'd rally around McGrath Castle? So that when Bran spouted his nonsense, they would know Grathton Village was safe.

She tried to picture Tiffany and Bran on the turret, perhaps arguing over something to do with the castle. Had Tiffany been strangled out of passion, or had it been calculated to stop the McGraths from being successful, within the timeline allotted by her uncle in his will?

Like Amy possibly destroying the dress to prevent the wedding, had Bran killed Tiffany to stop the cousins' new business?

The wedding had gone on, as would the bridal business—mere obstacles that hadn't stopped forward movement at all.

Tori and Jake promised eternal love, the bride appearing tragically lovely. Ciara and Rayne exchanged sad glances.

Rayne doubted they'd make it a full year, no matter how much money Dylan plied Jake with.

Chapter Eighteen

"I pronounce you husband and wife," Father Patrick said in a firm, clear voice that echoed to the rafters and around the stone walls. "Mr. Anderson, you may kiss your bride."

Jake was green around the gills.

Tori arched a brow, her gaze icy.

All of the whiskey the Andersons had been swilling to get through the day seemed to seep from Jake's pores. He swayed.

Josh gave him a shove to keep him in place. He rolled his eyes at his brother as if not believing that he'd gotten himself into such a mess.

Amy leaned toward Tori, holding both bouquets, studying the heiress and Jake as if she wanted to memorize each second.

"No kiss, Jakey?" Tori taunted. She pursed her perfect lips.

"Already had more than that," Josh murmured.

Father Patrick cleared his throat.

Jake gamely cupped his hand behind Tori's nape and kissed her in a manner meant to make any female viewer envious, but it did nothing for Rayne.

Applause burst from the back pews. Flashes from cameras flickered like candlelight. Rayne glanced behind and didn't see Ethan. Was he being passive aggressive toward Jake for his boss not listening to his advice?

"Em, well, that's a kiss," Ciara said, fanning her face.

Jake and Tori, arm in arm, strode down the aisle, followed by Amy and Josh, then Dylan and Joan.

And though they hadn't asked for witnesses from the village, that didn't stop several Jake Anderson fans from showering the newlyweds with rice in an old Celtic tradition as they left the church. Rayne and Ciara were the last to leave, other than Father Patrick.

Cormac hopped down from the bench seat where he'd been waiting and ushered the couple into the carriage.

"Congratulations!" Rayne called. "Mr. and Mrs. Anderson."

Tori flashed her large diamond—so large it made the Swarovski crystals on her gown appear insignificant, now with a platinum band.

Amy beamed up at the couple, glancing at Josh as if looking for someone to pair up with herself as Ethan remained MIA.

"Where's Ethan?" Jake asked.

"He didn't come back," Rayne said.

"Too much whiskey," Josh said.

"Not everybody is an alcoholic like you," Amy snapped.

"Down kitten," Josh said. "Feeling lonely? Not in the spotlight?"

Amy smacked her bouquet against his arm.

"Hey!" Josh said. He shook his head at her. "Don't hit me again."

"Do you children need to be separated?" Tori called from her perch inside the carriage.

Now that the deed was done, Dylan was happy to walk along with Joan, hand in hand, outside the carriage. Jake and Tori sat opposite each other. The horses neighed and stomped their feet, braided manes and tails swishing. The sound of horseshoes clanged against the pavement to scare away the fairies. It was amazing how many traditions were meant to keep them away from a beautiful bride.

"We are fine!" Amy called with a big grin. "Just playing."

"All right, then," Tori said. She smiled down at her supposed best friend rather smugly.

"Now what?" Jake asked.

"Back to the manor for a medieval feast," Cormac said as he resumed his seat on the driving bench. He picked up the reins for the horses.

"I'm starved," Josh declared.

Rayne nodded at Cormac, and he headed the horses toward the road, out of the parking lot. Most of the villagers had dispersed now that the ceremony was over.

No sign of Bran or Freda. A woman Gillian's height strode ahead of the party. Rayne recognized the straw hat. It wouldn't be amiss if she'd come to see what she could after helping decorate the carriage and the horses, but why not join them?

It seemed odd.

Joan, Amy, Dylan, and Josh all walked together, talking about the beauty of the wedding. Nobody commented, or seemed to care, about the cost to make it happen, or that Jake had been paid to show up and stand there.

"We'll just be a second," Rayne said to Tori, grabbing Ciara's elbow so that her cousin didn't follow along with her new friend Joan.

"Champagne in the blue parlor, right?" Joan asked.

"Yes," Rayne said. Just a little reception before dinner in the dining room at seven. The wedding cake. Then, Celtic dancers and a bonfire in the gazebo by the lake, then, only one more day to get through before they went home on Monday.

"See you there," Ciara promised. She turned to Rayne. "What is it?"

"Ethan never came back. We should talk to Garda Williams," Rayne said. "About Bran and Freda, and the note. What if she gave him money to sabotage us?"

"Dominic lives in the same village as Freda, and he won't take her interfering seriously. He didn't last time," Ciara said.

"I remember." Rayne shielded her eyes to study the side of the church building for anything out of place. The surface was pebbled, making any new marks hard to find.

"What is it?" Ciara asked.

"We need to borrow a ladder." Rayne could just make out a shadow that might be a hole. "To see if there is a divot in the stone."

"Why?"

"I don't think throwing mud or a rock would fragment the wall." Rayne arched her brows. What if it was something stronger?

Ciara's eyes rounded with understanding. "A gun? I know Father Patrick has a ladder. He'd put it in the closet after getting the cameras down."

She'd forgotten about the cameras. Who had been the target of the attack? Had it been a warning? Bran and Tiffany. Bran and Freda. Bran with a grudge against Rayne and progress for the village. Gillian speedwalking away from the church—and who knew why?

Ciara went into the church foyer. Rayne waited outside, standing guard as she searched the trees and fields for anything unusual. Sheep, lots of them. Hills. The cemetery attached to the church went back hundreds of years; the trees and headstones offered places to hide.

Moments later, Ciara returned with the ladder and Father Patrick too. "Ciara thinks there is a hole in the stone?" Father Patrick sounded incredibly dubious. "These walls are thick."

"We're just checking, Father," Rayne said. "It could be a mud pie. Either way, it was kinda rude to chuck things, don't you think?"

"That I do." Father Patrick exhaled loudly. "About half of the village isn't sure it's worth the effort to grow and change. They don't realize what will be lost by giving up Grathton."

"Thank you, Father, for understanding," Ciara said.

"That was a lovely wedding, and Dylan Montgomery gave me a tidy check for the church coffers. I say it's a good thing to grow. Those same people who will need help during the winter will have more that I can offer because of it." The priest gave a sad sigh.

Rayne squeezed his hand.

Ciara unfolded the ladder and placed it against the wall. "Here?"

"No." Rayne moved it a few inches. "I'll do it."

"Look at you!" Ciara said with a chuckle. "Climbing ladders in your heels."

"These boots are nothing at all. Not much I can't do in them," Rayne said. "Practice." Her smile faltered as she stood on her tiptoes.

Ciara held the ladder still.

"Careful, lass," Father Patrick said.

"I am." She glanced down at them. "I see something shiny."

"A rock?" Father Patrick asked.

"I don't think so." Rayne's stomach clenched. "Like metal."

"A bullet," Ciara said. She pulled her phone from the pocket in her stylish pantsuit. "I'll call Dominic."

Rayne snapped a photo of the possible bullet buried in the stone. While in the States, guns and shooting weren't uncommon, it wasn't so in Ireland. Not even the police carried weapons unless they were a special task force.

"He's on his way," Ciara said when Rayne climbed down.

"I can't believe this." A gun. Her skin chilled with goose bumps.

"He was at the Coco Bean, so a few minutes is all." Ciara held the phone.

"Why was he there?" Rayne asked.

"He was talking to Sinéad about Bran's postcard and grabbing a coffee. Garda Lee walked to the manor," Ciara said. "By the time she realized that we weren't coming back with the carriage, it was too late to leave the others without being obvious."

"I've heard rumors of trouble," Father Patrick said. "A mysterious death."

"Tiffany Quick was killed, though you can't mention it, Father, and the murderer hasn't been found yet," Rayne said.

The priest bowed his head and murmured a prayer. "You don't know why?"

"No." Rayne sighed. She started to close the ladder but realized the Garda would need to use it too.

"Could this be about Jake rather than Tiffany?" Father Patrick suggested. "Since Jake was the one shot at."

Ciara made a humming noise as she considered this idea. "Perhaps you're onto something."

Any further thought was cut off as Garda Williams' patrol car arrived in the church lot, minus sirens, where he parked near the front entrance.

"Hey," the Garda said once he got out of the car. His uniform had a damp spot on the knee that smelled like coffee. Definitely in a hurry to join them.

"Hi!" Father Patrick said. "What is the world coming to, Dominic, when a man is shot at coming into church?"

"I don't know," the Garda said.

"Use this to climb up." Rayne rested her hand on the ladder.

"What made you think to look for a hole?" Garda Williams asked.

"Well, the sound, for one—like a muffled thwack when it hit the stone wall. And it's a hard surface and yet pieces of stone crumbled," Rayne said. "Doesn't suggest rocks or mud pies to me."

"You have a good eye for detail, Rayne. Where was Garda Lee when this happened?"

"Inside the church already," Rayne said.

The officer climbed to the top of the ladder and took several photos with his phone.

"Well?" Ciara peered up at him.

"It does look like a bullet," the Garda confirmed. "I'll have the team come in to remove it, but I'll wager it's from a hunting rifle."

Those were everywhere. Rayne knew of several under lock and key in the gun cabinet in the barn as well as the manor.

The Garda jumped to the ground. "Tell me everything that's happened since we last spoke."

The three of them filled him in on the ceremony, the photographers, the villagers being against the wedding venue, and those who were for it.

"Sinéad at the Coco Bean shared her views on the dilemma. She's for the castle and the village," Garda Williams said.

"Yes. She's smart, Sinéad." Ciara nodded.

"Good lass, always was," Father Patrick agreed.

"What about Bran, Father?" Rayne asked. "Is he good? 'Cause I think he's trouble. And he was hooking up with Tiffany, maybe, Friday night too."

"I don't know about *that*," Father Patrick said.

Garda Williams made a note in his tablet and then stepped away to say into his phone, "Garda Lee? We'll need a team to get a bullet out of the stone in the church."

"Bran drinks too much and was seen with Freda today—she gave him money," Ciara said.

"Rayne said an envelope," the Garda corrected as he ended the call with Garda Lee and turned his attention back to them. "You don't know what was inside."

Rayne conceded that he had a point. "Fair. But it looked shady. What if Bran was paid to kill Tiffany so that our wedding venue fails, and Freda scoops up our village and adds it to hers?"

"I'll ask Ms. Bevan," the Garda said. "Have you seen Landon? Garda Lee isn't happy you gave her the slip or that she missed the shot at the church. What if you are the target, Rayne, and it was Landon?"

"I didn't do that on purpose," Rayne said. "Besides, Landon is deranged and lost his mind but he's not a killer."

"You don't know that," Ciara said. "You are the target of his craziness. He could have changed while in jail."

Rayne, nervous now, scanned the trees and surrounding hills but there was no sign of his shaggy blond head. "I don't think he's here."

"He's cunning, right?" the Garda persisted. "Could he be the shooter?"

She sucked in a breath. In all of the activities they'd shared, Landon's prowess with a gun hadn't come up. Why would anyone want to harm her? Two different reasons sprung to mind: maybe Bran thought she'd go back to LA if he scared her bad enough—hadn't someone shouted to go home? Or Landon, for a motive unknown.

"We can't let down our guard," Ciara said.

"Ah, you sound like you care," Rayne teased. She was nervous despite her light tone. She'd never been a target of any crime before Landon.

"I can't do this save-the-village thing without you," Ciara declared. "So—stay healthy, and let's get through the year."

Not warm and fuzzy, but there was time. So long as Landon didn't get to her. Or Bran. Rayne shivered. "It will be fine."

"Bran," the Garda said. "He's been making a nuisance of himself. Drinking too much and harassing folks."

"He was with Freda and accepted the envelope. I wouldn't put it past him to try and shoot at Jake—maybe just to scare him off?" Ciara suggested.

"The shot was very high," Father Patrick noted.

"Bad aim, or excellent aim?" the Garda smoothed his chin. He faced the fields and the trees across the street.

"Plenty of places to hide and take a sneaky shot," Rayne said.

"Bran is high energy, but I don't think he's a killer," the priest said. "He needs guidance is all."

"If he's behind this," Williams said, "there will be consequences. Bran can't shoot at people to make a point."

"Agreed!" Rayne said.

"What about Ethan?" Ciara suggested.

"What about him?" the Garda asked.

"He left after Jake was upset with him for folks taking pictures and never came back, though he said he would."

"I'll have a talk with him right now," the Garda said.

Proof of Tiffany and Bran's hooking up might just be on her phone. Rayne sighed. "Have you found Tiffany's phone, or the notebooks?"

"Not yet," the Garda said.

Rayne tipped her head. Was that a howl? She hoped Blarney stayed out of trouble. The carriage and horses were probably back at the barn by now.

"And Amy . . . she is very jealous of Tori, and her relationship with Jake," Rayne said.

"She tried to blame the ghost of Tiffany for shredding her dress," Ciara said with a snicker.

"What?" Garda Williams removed his cap and wiped his forehead with the back of his hand.

"Yeah, it's true," Rayne said. "Anyway, we found another dress for Amy—Tori doesn't trust Amy at all."

"Everything has worked out," Ciara said. "By the skin of our teeth. Right down to the missing crystal off the bride's dress."

"Loose thread?" the Garda asked.

"I don't think so. I think somebody took it." Rayne shrugged and explained about the scissors on the floor.

"Let's go back to the castle," Garda Williams said. "I've got to let everyone know they are not allowed to leave due to Tiffany's *murder*. That this might have been a murder attempt on Jake." He looked at Rayne. "Or you."

Father Patrick shook his head at the brutal assessment. "In the house of the Lord!"

"I'm sorry, Father," the Garda said. "We will find out who is responsible. It's my promise to ye."

Ciara seemed impressed by the statement. Heck, even Rayne was moved.

Chapter Nineteen

Rayne and Ciara rode in the back of the Garda's patrol car to the manor. It was 6:00 PM, and they had a feast to host at seven followed by dancing in the gazebo by the lake.

"This has been the longest day," Ciara murmured, her manner quiet as they rode beneath the canopy of trees.

"Right?"

"We'll need a break to recoup when the guests all go home on Monday morning. At least I hope they're able to leave," Ciara said.

Just as Rayne was going to ask Garda Williams about how much longer the guests needed to stay because of Tiffany's murder, her phone dinged, and she read the message from Aine. "Aine has everyone in the blue parlor with drinks and appetizers. She's an angel."

"That she is. How's the mood?" Ciara asked.

Rayne texted Aine, who replied with a thumbs-up emoji.

"All good." Rayne pocketed her cell.

The Garda parked the Hyundai to the side of the manor, and all three exited the police vehicle.

"What's the plan?" Ciara asked.

"I'll speak to everyone about the incident," Garda Williams said, "find out where Ethan was at, and then return to the station. One of the Gardaí has discovered information from Tiffany's laptop."

225

"That sounds hopeful," Rayne said. "I'm glad you're going to tell them that Tiffany was killed. It's hard to keep such a secret."

"Perhaps," the Garda hedged. "I'll read the room. There are many clues to be discerned from conversation."

The trio climbed the stairs and as they reached the top step, Cormac, minus his top hat, opened the door for them. Before she went inside, she was greeted by Blarney butting her leg. The leather leash had been chewed apart, which explained his freedom.

She removed the leash and the pup darted past her to the foyer, his russet hair flowing. He disappeared, possibly to find Frances in the kitchen for a meaty treat. It smelled heavenly and Rayne was suddenly starving.

"The guests are in the blue parlor," Cormac said. "Are you lasses all right?"

"Fine," Ciara said.

Rayne nodded.

Garda Williams blew out a breath as if he disagreed with that assessment, but he didn't argue the point as they followed Cormac down the hall to the blue parlor.

Rayne was ready for a whiskey, but she didn't dare. She'd celebrate the end of this long day later with a double.

Cormac widened the door and announced, "Your hostesses are here," before he urged them into the room, coming with them and shutting the door. He stood before it, hands at his sides.

The Montgomerys, the Andersons, Ethan, and Amy looked toward them, pausing in their conversations. Tori literally sparkled in her gown, and Amy's choice of the charcoal dress melded much better than the original crimson with Joan's periwinkle.

Where had Ethan come from? His attendance would make it easier for Garda Williams to question him. The mood of the wedding party was lighter now. For better or worse, the ceremony was over, and the couple could begin the next step in their married journey.

"Hi!" Rayne said.

Ciara lifted her palm. "Heya."

Garda Williams, between them, cleared his throat and crossed his arms behind his back, the brim of his police cap shining.

"Do you have news, Officer?" Amy asked. "About Tiffany?"

What other reason would he have to be here? Rayne could read on their faces the expectation that things would be wrapped up and they could go home.

"None that I can share as of yet." The Garda withdrew his tablet. "Congratulations on your wedding," he said first, with a smile at Tori and Jake.

"Thank you," Tori said.

Jake nodded. "Thanks, man."

Garda Williams must have decided to try the shock method for questioning and announced, "Do any of you have enemies who might feel compelled to shoot at the church?"

Josh paled. "Did you say shoot, as in a bullet?" He glared at Rayne. "Not rocks?"

"What?" Dylan exploded.

Tori trembled and Jake put his arm around her slender shoulders. "When? I didn't hear a thing," the heiress said.

"You'd just gone inside," Josh explained, again tossing a glare at Rayne and Ciara. "You said it was someone with a rock."

Rayne bit her tongue.

"What are you saying, Officer Williams?" Joan demanded. "Is my family in danger here?"

"Why would anybody want to shoot at me?" Jake asked. "I have fans!"

"I thought you didn't let anybody have guns in this backward country," Amy declared.

"There are rifles to hunt deer or ducks with," Aine explained as she brought a bottle of champagne around to top off flutes. Her nose scrunched in confusion. "Who was shot?"

"Nobody," Ciara said. "Nobody was hurt."

"You're not making sense, dear," Joan said.

"A bullet hit the church just as Jake was going inside." The Garda gestured to Jake, then the cousins. "He, Ciara, and Rayne were the last to go in."

Cormac frowned. "I didn't hear anything, and I was right there."

"You had moved the horses and carriage around to the side," Rayne said to the butler who'd acted as their carriage driver. "The sound was more of a thwack and was muffled by the carriage wheels and horses clomping."

"Could have been a silencer used," Josh said. "That happens, right Jake? You use that while on location sometimes."

"I guess. I mean, it makes the weapon quieter, but you can still hear—more of a pop." Jake gave a shrug. "I suppose it could be covered up. Be straight with us now, Garda Williams. Someone shot at me?"

"First, Tiffany, and now Jake?" Amy said, her fingers to her heart. The starlet whirled to Rayne, her accusatory gaze similar to Josh's. "What if Tiffany's death was no accident? What if we are being targeted? It's the cruel price of being rich and famous."

The noise level in the room exploded as everyone had an opinion and wanted it heard. Rayne glanced at Garda Williams, who watched the group with intent interest.

The way that Amy had presented the situation made Rayne fear that the castle would never recover from an accusation, or conviction, of murder of a guest by a villager.

"I don't like this, Jake," Tori said. "What if you were hurt?"

"We didn't see anything out of the ordinary," Dylan said. "But there are a lot of trees a shooter could hide in. Rolling hills."

"What if Tori had been hit?" Joan said. The crystal champagne flute in her hand quaked.

"I'm fine, Mom." Tori studied the Garda, then Rayne. "How did it happen? You were closest. Surely you should have said something."

More accusations.

Rayne wondered how she could spin this to her benefit without alerting their guests that the village was divided, to simplify, on modernization. After exchanging a glance with her cousin, she opted to share some of the truth in hopes it might ease the pressure of expectation off her and Ciara.

"It's a little tricky," Rayne said. "When Ciara and I inherited the castle, we were tasked with bringing the village into the modern era, with Wi-Fi and all."

"I noticed the satellite antenna," Ethan said.

"Of course, you did," Amy quipped. She sipped her champagne.

"We painted it in camouflage so it wouldn't be an eyesore," Ciara said. "I was against it myself, so I understand where some of the villagers are coming from."

Rayne nodded. "It was important to my uncle, so we are taking small steps forward. You remember Bran, the man on the moped at the Coco Bean?"

The guests who'd been there murmured in the affirmative.

"He has very strong opinions," Ciara shared. "Doesn't want to modernize."

"I like what you're doing here," Tori said. She was more business-minded than Jake or Amy, who tended to be reactionary. "Rustic but not too. It's important to have internet."

"We are doing our best to retain what's working with the old while switching to the new. Like mattresses and sheets," Rayne said.

Dylan chuckled. "I approve. And I liked that Sinéad—she's a real go-getter. I could see putting those Guinness chocolate cakes into our hotels."

Joan and Tori nodded. Evidently, they'd discussed this among themselves already.

"We even asked Sinéad if she'd be willing to move to New York, but she said, no," Joan said. "I can't blame her. Grathton Village is lovely when compared with the hustle and bustle of the city."

Garda Willliams' brow rose. Seemed he hadn't known about the job offer.

"I've never been shot at in New York." Jake shook his head. "What does this have to do with why you didn't raise the alarm when there was an attempt on my life?"

Rayne flushed. "Well, I didn't realize it was a bullet—as Josh can attest to; I thought it was a rock."

Josh scoffed. He pointed his tumbler of whiskey at her. "You're just trying to cover your own ass."

"Hey!" Ciara protested. "Watch that tone."

Rayne inwardly smiled at her fierce cousin while shrugging at Josh. "As Cormac can tell you, it wasn't a loud sound. I noticed the stone from the wall on the ground, and assumed it was Bran, possibly throwing something."

"Like a rock," Amy repeated with layers of doubt.

"Yes," Rayne said. "To protest our moving into the twenty-first century."

"To stop modernization." Joan shrugged. "You can't live in the past. Peaceful protest is one way to handle things."

"A rock isn't peaceful. A rifle is also not peaceful," Amy said.

Dylan scoffed. "Money. Show them the money, and they'll come around," the billionaire advised.

"I want to leave," Jake said. "No offense Rayne, but if someone is willing to kill me over modernization, I don't want to be here."

Well, that had backfired on her. "We've got extra security with the Gardaí," Rayne said.

"And it might not be you that was the target, Jake," Ciara said.

Rayne blushed. She really didn't want to explain how her ex had broken out of prison to come to Dublin. She'd never get another bridal wear client or the wedding venue off the ground.

Garda Williams stepped in to save her. "We don't know for certain who the bullet was intended for," he turned to Jake's assistant. "Ethan, Rayne said you didn't make it to the ceremony?"

Ethan drank from his tumbler. "Sick stomach. Sorry guys."

"No worries," Jake said.

Josh laughed. "Unless you shot at Jake. Is that what the Garda dude here wants to know?"

Garda Williams didn't look away from the assistant.

"Of course not!" Ethan declared. He glared at Josh. "Did *you*?"

"Idiot!" Josh said. "I was in the church the whole time."

"Well, I was . . . indisposed." Ethan ruffled his hair. "Fresh from the shower, my hair is still damp."

Garda Williams glanced at Rayne. It would explain Ethan's haste in leaving the crowd heading for the church.

She nodded.

"In any event," the Garda put his hand in his pocket, "I'd prefer none of you leave just yet."

"We're going home on Monday," Dylan stated. His demeanor left no room for argument.

Her guests all nodded. "We all traveled together on the Montgomery plane," Ethan said.

"Our pilot will be waiting for us at noon," Joan said.

Of course, the Montgomerys had their own plane. It was a different kind of rich.

"We shall see," Garda Williams said. "If you think of any detail you may have forgotten, no matter how small, please let me know."

"About Tiffany?" Amy asked. "Or who might have taken a shot at Jakey?"

"Either," the Garda replied.

"And what about Tiffany's . . . body?" Ethan asked. "How will it get back to Hollywood? Does she have anyone to claim it?"

"We have a call in to her roommate for more answers," the Garda said. "We won't rest until we uncover every stone to find out what happened."

Tori pushed away from Jake to confront the Garda. "What do you mean by that? By *what happened*? I thought it was clear that Tiffany jumped. She was depressed about being fired."

"Her death is under inquiry," Garda Williams said. "I can't tell you more than that. We ask you not to depart for the states until we've received conclusive evidence that we expect any time. I hope it won't interfere with your travel schedule."

Amy rocked unsteadily on her heels into Jake, who placed a familiar hand on the small of her back. She stepped forward as if his hand was on fire.

"I have several Gardaí patrolling the grounds for added security." Garda Williams tipped his cap.

Rayne had to help find Tiffany's killer, to ensure that her guests were comfortable so they'd share their rave reviews over social media about the wedding venue. Having one of the wedding party murdered was a difficult hurdle to overcome, but she would do her best. She prayed that it wasn't Bran behind the passionate push over the edge. Or Gillian, who had been sneakily walking away from the church earlier.

Cormac escorted Garda Williams out of the blue parlor.

"He's cute," Amy said, twirling a strand of red hair around her finger. "Boy next door kinda cute. Is he single? I should get his number and see what he's doing later after the bonfire."

Ciara bristled.

Aine offered to fill champagne flutes and whiskey tumblers, her shoulders shaking at Amy's blatant appreciation.

"Garda Dominic Williams is single," Ciara said coldly. "You should have his card from when you were questioned about your assistant's death."

Amy rolled her eyes. "Right."

"Ames, you are a ho," Josh declared.

"Am not," Amy said, releasing the curl with a bat of her lashes.

"That's enough," Dylan said. "Uncalled for, Josh."

Amy brightened at this unexpected champion.

"Bro, come on," Jake chided. "Behave yourself in a way that would make our mother proud."

"Sorry," Josh said.

Ethan smirked and mumbled something about a shoe fitting.

Rayne cleared her throat. "We take your safety very seriously. If you see Bran Wilson on the property, please let us know right away, or alert the Gardai if you are in danger."

"Of course, dear," Joan said. "I for one don't hold either of you responsible for a crazy man. How could you have known?"

Ciara placed her hand to her heart in gratitude.

Rayne nodded her thanks. "Ethan, you'd mentioned that Tiffany might have slipped away from the manor on Friday night, to meet with Bran. The Garda knows that she was at the Sheep's Head on Thursday, but I'd love for confirmation of Friday as well."

"Check her phone," Josh said. "Oh, that's right. It's missing."

"I don't think she went," Amy said. "I asked her to stick around here in case I needed her. Sometimes she helps me practice reading through my scripts."

"That is so like you," Tori said. "You should have cut her some slack and given her the night off."

"Easy to say now," Amy said.

"It's true," Ethan agreed.

"What is?" Jake asked. "Tiffany left to meet up with this local dude, or that Amy should have cut her some slack?"

Ethan smoothed his goatee. "Amy had high expectations for Tiffany, but I was referring to Tiff meeting Bran at the pub."

"She wouldn't have left Friday night," Amy repeated.

"I think she may have," Ethan said. "Behind your back. And if so, what if this Bran guy killed her, and then shot at Jake today?"

That sounded very possible. Rayne's fingers itched to pour herself a whiskey. This was not good for the village if one of their own was killing people.

Guests of McGrath Castle in particular!

Amy began to cry. "Poor Tiffany!"

Rayne smoothed the front of her blouse, nervous but needing to be the leader. "We asked Father Patrick about Bran today, and he doesn't believe that Bran is the type to do such a thing. Big mouth after drinking, but not violent."

"Father Patrick was very wonderful," Joan said. "Reminded me of my family priest as a child. He said that Bran wasn't violent?"

Being a Catholic, that might hold some weight with Joan, who Rayne would bet, held some sway with her husband's opinion. "Yes."

"Obnoxious, eh, that's true enough" Ciara said. "But we are taking Bran's actions very seriously. Garda Williams is having an officer check out whether or not he has access to a rifle on the homestead he shares with his mother."

"That's good," Tori said. "I don't want to be a widow and not married twenty-four hours yet."

"We aren't certain Jake was the target—the shot was high," Ciara said. "A warning, maybe? We need more answers."

"Do you have guns here?" Josh asked.

"We do, under lock and key in the gun cabinet," Rayne said. There were two actually. One in the house, the other in the barn but they didn't need to know that.

"Have any of you gone hunting before?" Ciara asked. "My da was a duck hunter."

"No," Amy and Tori said.

Joan sipped her wine. "Skeet shooting, for fun, when I was young."

"Yep, on safari in Africa," Dylan said. "There is nothing like man against beast to feel so insignificant."

Jake and Josh shook their heads. "I mean, not in real life," Jake clarified. "For a part sure. I do action-adventure films so I know how in theory."

"Right." Rayne studied the group of wealthy guests. Jake was very captivating on film with his adventure movies. The trouble with actors was you couldn't be sure if they were telling the truth or not.

Amy, for example, could be shining them all on and might be a bullseye target shooter or something. But, like Josh, the starlet had been in the church the whole time and couldn't have been the shooter.

Rayne looked at Ethan, recalling the conversation he'd had with Gillian. "You lived in East Sussex?"

"Aye. My brothers and I were expected to hunt," Ethan said. "Fresh meat supplemented the family larder. We didn't have much money growing up."

So, at least three folks here had experience with a rifle. Rayne turned toward the door as she heard a scratching sound.

Blarney?

She had a sudden urge to check on her dog. And while outside, she'd track down Gillian, and ask her if she'd been to the church earlier.

It was only half past six. If she hurried, Rayne could get info on Amy before their meal. "Since you're all set for drinks, Ciara and I will go see how dinner's coming. Aine will escort you in at seven. You'll have plenty of time to change into warmer clothes after our feast for the bonfire and Irish dancing."

"Thank you," Joan said.

"Yes, Rayne and Ciara, thank you." Tori turned to Jake and nuzzled his ear. "It will be a wedding to remember."

Rayne and Ciara exited the blue parlor, and Rayne pulled her phone from her skirt pocket. She texted her mother about Amy Flores the starlet and what she thought of her from the episode she'd been in for *Family Forever*.

"Whatchya doing?" Ciara whispered as they let the door close behind them. The hallway was well lit.

Rayne sighed. No sign of Blarney. Maybe there was another ghost running loose around McGrath's stone halls. "Texting my mom about Amy. To see what she thought of her."

"You think she's lying about Tiffany?" Ciara brought her hands up as if squeezing something. "Could she have, well, strangled her assistant?"

Amy and Tiffany were of a similar size. The scuffmarks on the fifth floor rooftop had showed someone very strong and bigger than

Tiff. And to choke someone? "I just don't know—it's a room full of actors."

"Good point." Ciara paused by the round table in the foyer. "But Amy couldn't be the shooter. Are we really checking with Frances about dinner?"

"You know me too well." Rayne sighed. "I have something I want to try but you have to promise not to laugh."

"Okay." Up went Ciara's brow.

"I want to ask Blarney if he knows where more of the notebook is."

Laughter exploded from her cousin's mouth and she actually doubled over. "A, we don't know that it is Tiffany's notebook. B . . . you've lost your mind, cuz."

Chapter Twenty

Rayne and Ciara went outside, and Rayne whistled for Blarney. She didn't catch a hint of his gorgeous fur. The dog had ways of entering and exiting that she hadn't quite figured out, but believed one of them was through the cellar somehow.

"Did your pet psychic tell you to ask Blarney?" Ciara said. The idea of it cracked her cousin up and she smacked her hand to her knee.

"I haven't talked with her about it yet, but I might," Rayne warned. "That notebook is bound to hold answers. Who took it? Why? It's got to lead to who killed Tiffany."

Rayne's phone dinged repeatedly as her mother answered her questions and finally the dots stopped moving and the device rang in her palm.

"My mom," she told Ciara as she answered, "Lauren! Ciara and I are outside. We've got twenty minutes until dinner. Wedding's over but someone shot at the church while Ciara, Jake, and I were on the porch."

"Landon?" her mom asked.

Rayne switched the phone to speaker mode. "You're on speaker, Mom. No, I don't think Landon is around—I haven't seen one strand of his shaggy blond hair. I think maybe Bran, the unhappy villager. We saw him with Freda."

"The councilwoman?" Lauren had a memory like a steel trap.

"Yes. She gave Bran an envelope as she and some others waited on the sidelines of the procession from the manor to the church, yelling out their love for Jake Anderson."

"I thought the event was supposed to be private?"

"We think Bran told everyone, and possibly even contacted the media. There was someone with a giant camera." Rayne sighed. "Wouldn't be surprised if it's already hit the news or social media."

"Oh no!"

"It's done—they're married despite all of the obstacles," Rayne said.

"Can't stop true love," her mom said.

Ciara snorted. "I would put a wee wager that the marriage won't last a year."

"That long?" Rayne scoffed. "This wedding has all the hallmarks of a true telenovela drama. Amy, the bridesmaid, slept with Jake before Tori and Jake got together. Josh, the best man, is protective of his brother no matter what, Ethan, the groom's assistant, didn't even show up to the wedding. He said intestinal distress, but I bet he's looking for a new client."

"Oh, girls," Lauren said, laughter in her tone. "I can't wait to be there. I am counting down the days."

"I'm looking forward to meeting you, Lauren," Ciara said.

"Mom, what did you think of Amy?"

"She was a sweetheart on the screen but a real diva behind the scenes. Young, beautiful, and hungry."

"Like a cute little raptor," Ciara said. "With red hair."

Lauren chuckled.

"How's filming?" Rayne asked.

"It's sad because it's the last thing we're doing together," her mother said. "And I admit, I'm worried about what's going on there. You're sure you haven't seen Landon?"

"Positive," Rayne said. "The Gardaí even added extra officers to patrol the property—not only for me, but for the guests too." All the same, it hadn't stopped someone from shooting at the church.

Blarney raced toward them from the barn. The carriage was still decorated in ostrich feathers and horseshoes, but Gillian and Amos were taking the braids from the horses' manes.

"I worry for you, sweetie," Lauren said.

"No need." Rayne smiled at Ciara. "If all goes well, we will have permission to blast the wedding on Monday afternoon and McGrath Castle will be on the map for an intimate wedding venue."

"And money in the bank account," Ciara said. "To get us through until November. It's stressful running a place this size. I wish I'd learned it from Da rather than have him shoulder the entire burden alone."

"Many hands make light work, as they say," Lauren said.

"Thank goodness!" Rayne petted Blarney, who had an ostrich feather above his ear.

"I've got to run—but I'll text if I hear anything about Landon," her mom said. "You do the same."

"Bye!" Ciara and Rayne said in unison.

Rayne knelt before her dog and looked into his eyes—they were intelligent and warm, caring. "Blarney . . . do you know where Tiffany's notebook is? Or more paper that you found?"

Blarney wagged his tail and went to the hole he'd dug in the place where Tiffany had landed.

Ciara's jaw gaped.

"That would be too easy," Rayne said. She followed him and the dog dug in the loose dirt, retrieving another wadded up piece of paper the same size as before, only this time there was a legible scrawl barely possible to read. She thought she could make out the word Tori. Maybe. They knew the Garda had checked there, which meant Blarney had put another page there to be found.

"Good boy. Is there more?"

Blarney barked and loped off across the lawn.

"I think he wants us to follow him."

"You're crazy," Ciara said. She glanced at her watch. "We don't have time for you to chase all over the property after Blarney. Dinner is in fifteen minutes."

Rayne did a heart and gut check. Going with Blarney felt like the right thing to do.

Blarney had stopped and barked at her, darting toward the path leading to the bungalows and the lake, the gazebo, and the firepit for the bonfires.

"I'll hurry."

Ciara rolled her eyes. "I can't stall them, and I am not leading the dinner so if you aren't here, they aren't eating. Don't do it, Rayne!"

Her cousin was playing hardball.

Rayne had to protect her guests and this new business.

Blarney barked again.

"I swear I'll hurry!"

"I'm calling Dominic!" Ciara stomped toward the manor and Rayne raced after Blarney, twisting her ankle in her haste.

"Sugar cookies!" Rayne took off her boots with the two-inch heels and continued after her dog. Limping, she batted tears from her eyes.

Suddenly, Amos was at her side, and he swooped her up before him on the gray horse. No saddle, hard thighs, and a muscular chest. She was so shocked she didn't have time to be afraid.

"What are you doing, lass?"

"Chasing Blarney."

"I saw you twist your ankle."

"Yes." Amos's grip on her was strong and assuring. Could she be faulted for melting back just a tiny bit?

"And remove your shoes. Where to?"

"Follow Blarney please!" The horse galloped up the hill.

"It's six-forty-five, and dinner is at seven?"

She nodded, fighting tears. What a day.

"It must be important."

"It is." Amos was so accepting of her despite her quirks.

Blarney waited on the ridge leading down to the gazebo and the bonfire that would be lit later tonight. He barked several times.

"I think Blarney found another page of Tiffany's journal."

"And what did it say?"

Rayne pulled it from her pocket. "Maybe Tori. I can't tell for sure. Most of it's wet." The paper was smudged with mud and the letters smeared. "He'd buried it where Tiffany died."

"And you just asked him to show you where the rest is hidden away?" Amos queried. The horse galloped down the hill. Rayne could see swans swimming in the lake and a tent over the broken smoker they'd planned to prepare a whole hog in.

"I did, actually," Rayne said. "He's a smart dog. Unless he stole it in the first place, and then, well, we will need to work on not being a thief."

Blarney raced ahead and back and then around the bonfire.

They arrived at the gazebo. Amos slowed and assisted Rayne to slip down off the gray beast. Her fear of horses was abated while in Amos's arms. The pretty braids and ostrich feathers helped too.

Now that she was down? They were huge with big teeth and large eyes. Rayne scooted nervously out of the way.

Amos jumped to the ground and wiped his hands.

Blarney was digging by the post of the gazebo. The pup returned with a burned Moleskine notebook. It fell open and a woman's scrawl was clear enough to detect. Rayne read, *Tori's vows changed.* "Good boy!" She remembered the first night they'd arrived, and Amy had said that she and Tiffany had been working on tweaking Tori's vows.

In the chaos of the actual ceremony neither Tori nor Jake had gone off the script.

"Wonder what happened?" Amos asked.

"I think whoever stole it, and possibly who killed Tiffany, tried to burn this in the fire but didn't do it properly, and Blarney was able to rescue a portion of it."

Blarney woofed and wagged his tail.

"I can't believe Tiffany was killed," Amos said sadly.

Rayne examined the notebook. "We need to make sure we don't add our prints to the notebook just in case the Gardaí are able to get some off of it."

She didn't have a scarf or even shoes as she'd lost her heels along the way.

Amos removed his hat and offered it to Rayne to use as a bucket.

"My hero," she said, peering up at him with gratitude. He'd helped her a lot today.

"Anytime." His eyes flashed briefly with humor before his gaze darkened with confusion.

The horse whinnied. Rayne shivered and studied the notebook as she used a stick and some leaves to scoop it inside the hat. "What is so important in here? Tiffany was supposedly writing an exposé about the group. Garda Williams will have to find out if this is the notebook Tiffany wrote her secrets in."

"Secrets are rarely good things," Amos said.

Rayne patted Blarney as the dog wagged his tail. "Tori suggested that Amy had tasked Tiffany to collect secrets and give them to Amy."

Amos's hair, no longer confined by his hat, lifted in the breeze. "Why? For blackmail purposes?"

"I really don't know. My mom worked on the set with Amy, which is how Amy found out about Modern Lace Bridal Boutique for Tori's wedding dress. Mom said Amy was a hard worker but a diva behind the scenes."

"Tell me again how we came to provide the venue."

"Tori was overwhelmed by having a large Christmas wedding. She'd planned on four hundred people." Rayne knew there'd be no way to hide a pregnancy that far along. Probably a major factor.

"That's almost as many as live in our wee village," Amos said. "It's perfect that you were able to offer her this instead."

"Yes. It's beautiful, but then, it hasn't turned out to be magical." She pulled her gaze from the forlorn wooden smoker. "Not with Tiffany dead and someone shooting at Jake."

"What did you just say?" Amos asked.

Oops. "Everyone but me, Ciara, and Jake had just gone inside the church when someone shot at the building—a rifle, Garda Williams said."

Amos jammed his fingers into his hair in alarm. "Just slow down and repeat that."

"This afternoon, before the wedding, Ciara and I were standing with Jake on the little porch thingy."

Amos withdrew his fingers to clamp his hand over Rayne's shoulder. "Could it be Landon, and you were the target?"

It couldn't have been Landon. "I didn't see him, so I really doubt it. You know who I saw? Gillian."

Amos clenched his jaw. "Where?"

"Walking away from the church."

"That's no crime," Amos said.

"She's trusted around the house and the grounds," Rayne said.

"Because she's a hard worker. I wouldn't have recommended her, otherwise," Amos said.

She couldn't blame him for his defensive tone, but she wasn't willing to let it go. "Aine heard Jake arguing with a woman, not Tori. Would Gillian have any reason to chat with Jake? She's certainly chummy with Ethan."

"Gillian goes home to care for her sick mam, so I don't think she'd be hanging around here at night," Amos cautioned.

Rayne averted her gaze. It figured that Gillian would be a saint. She noted that ten minutes had passed with concern. "Amos, I'm really worried that Bran might have killed Tiffany."

"What?" Amos shook his head. "Lass, you gotta stop or we won't have employees left to accuse."

Rayne flinched. "Hear me out. We saw Bran get an envelope from Freda today—Freda knew about the wedding that was supposed to be secret. There were pictures, professional photographers with flash cameras and everything."

"And the movie star wanted privacy." Amos shrugged. "Bran's a weasel and not a killer."

Amos had been at the property the whole time. "Did you see Ethan come back early from the ceremony? He didn't feel good and returned to the bungalow."

"I saw him, yes, but it was afterward."

Rayne considered this. "He and Tiffany had a friendship of some sort that I don't understand. He says not romantic."

"Do you believe him?" Amos asked.

"Ethan has no reason to lie about it. He was at the gas station when we found Tiffany so not even here. He couldn't be responsible for her death."

"Could Tiffany have something in there on Bran?" Amos gestured at his hat with the notebook she held.

"I don't know. We can't forget that Bran and Tiffany might have hooked up that night. Ethan saw them Thursday, and knew Bran was interested to see her on Friday." Rayne exhaled, glad to have found the Moleskine but they needed more definitive answers. "Where is her phone?"

"I dunno, lass." Amos nodded at her and then Blarney. "Try asking him. We have her notebook, thanks to you and the pup."

"I have to call Garda Williams." Rayne pulled out her phone.

No signal.

Panic spread through her at an alarming rate, and she could feel perspiration dampen her nape. "I have five minutes to get to dinner."

"My lady." Amos mounted his horse and placed her on his lap, racing toward the manor, Blarney barking with excitement.

Amos reached down like a rodeo performer to swoop up her heeled boots where she'd dropped them while they were riding along. They reached the manor steps at one minute until seven.

Once in range of a cell signal, she texted Garda Williams that a notebook had been found, and she had it in her possession.

"Here we are!" Amos said. He helped her slide carefully from the horse.

"Thank you, Amos."

He pulled a twig from her hair and steadied her so she could jam her shoes back on her feet. She winced at the twisted ankle she'd forgotten about.

"Can I keep your hat?" She'd give the whole thing to the Garda.

"Sure," Amos said. "I know where you live to get it back."

"Thank you."

The front door opened, and a furious Ciara stuck her head out. "There you are! Get in here. I've stalled for as long as I can."

Waves of frenetic energy spilled from Ciara to Rayne, but she didn't take it personally. Ciara had more than stepped up to participate in this venture.

"I'm here, I'm here. Thank you, cuz."

"What's that?" Ciara pointed at Amos's hat that Rayne cradled, afraid to lose it.

Perhaps Rayne was a tiny bit smug as she replied, "The notebook."

"No!" Ciara clapped her hand to her mouth, gray eyes wide.

"Yes." She couldn't stop a grin.

"Blarney found it," Amos said. "Rayne asked him to take her to it, and he did. It's amazing."

"I don't believe it," Ciara declared, giving Blarney the side eye. "I'd rather believe in ghosts than a telepathic dog."

"Well, believe or not, he did it when I asked." Rayne ruffled her dog's ears. "Extra treats tonight." Her fears that he'd stolen it had dissipated, as her dog had no thumbs to light a fire.

Ciara pulled at Rayne's hand. "Come on! I can't talk to these people, other than Joan, I just don't get them."

Rayne squeezed her cousin's fingers, so Ciara was forced to stop. Looking into her similar shade of gray eyes, she said, "You are Ciara Leah Smith of McGrath Castle; yes, you can."

Amos chuckled. "Rayne, do you want me to give this to the Garda for you?"

Just then, the white Hyundai pulled through the canopy of trees with a familiar officer behind the wheel.

"There he is!" Rayne glanced at Amos. "But thank you. I was totally going to take you up on it."

"Dominic called me back," Ciara said. "There's news from the station. Seems that Garda Lee was able to read some of the page from her notebook after all." She blew out a breath. "It is absolutely Tiffany Quick's handwriting."

"What did it say?" Rayne asked.

"As if the Garda would tell me that!" Ciara pursed her lips. The maroon of her pantsuit made her lipstick pop.

It was true, Garda Williams might want to keep what he'd learned to himself. Or he could be one step closer to finding out who killed Tiffany. He was going to freak that they'd found the entire notebook.

And Rayne recognized some of the words, which proved it was also Tiffany's handiwork.

Who would spill their news first?

Chapter
Twenty-One

"Officer, we have got to stop meeting like this," Rayne quipped. Blarney raced between Dominic and Rayne, Ciara, Amos, and the horse. He loved to play and was obviously excited to have shown her the notebook he'd found.

"There are Gardaí patrolling the grounds, so tell me how it happened that you are the one to find the notebook?" Garda Williams clasped his hands before him, not responding to her jest.

"She asked the dog to find the notebook, and Blarney did," Ciara said. "Woo-woo. He and Rayne are perfect for each other."

"Is that supposed to be an insult?" Rayne patted his soft head. "We're besties, aren't we, Blarney?"

"Why did you pick it up and not leave it there for me and my officers to recover?" the Garda asked in a clipped tone.

"Sorry!" Rayne heard the censure and knew he wasn't pleased despite their find. The fair-faced Garda tugged his smooth chin, eyes narrowed, before he gave a single nod.

Rayne handed the officer the hat with the Moleskine, or what was left of it. "Here you are. We didn't touch it but used a stick and leaves. I mean, there might be Blarney drool . . . he didn't kill Tiffany so you could cross his DNA off. And, we didn't see any of the other Gardaí, or I would have had them collect it."

Garda Williams accepted the hat and studied the contents. During the ride the burned cover of the notebook had fallen closed again.

"I hope it's not too destroyed. I deciphered a few words on the pages but it wasn't easy," Rayne said. "Your officers must have mad skills to figure out Tiffany's handwriting. That page was practically blank. Remember disappearing ink? I loved playing with that as a kid." Nerves made her babble like the village idiot. "Magic."

Jaw clenched, the Garda said, "We were able to confirm the handwriting belonged to Tiffany Quick by using *technology*."

Ciara snickered at Rayne's expression.

Rayne smoothed her hair off her forehead. "You'd mentioned finding something on her laptop?"

"Yes. We located her roommate in Hollywood," the Garda said. "She confirmed that Tiffany wanted to be a star and viewed her job with Amy as a necessary evil. According to the roommate, Tiffany was quiet, kept to herself, and wrote all the time."

"That fits with how she was here," Rayne said. "No family?"

"An orphan," the Garda said. "Amy was correct."

"It's so sad that there is nobody to mourn Tiffany's death," Amos said. "What will happen to her body then?"

"A pauper's grave," the Garda said.

"Surely we can have Father Patrick say a few words?" Ciara shivered. "We can cover the costs of a cremation and marker."

"Let's discuss it with Amy and the guests," Rayne suggested. "They might pick up the ball and bring her back to LA."

Ciara arched her brow. "Maybe Joan, but I don't know about the others. Speaking of—we need to get into that dinner." She cursed as she saw the time on her watch. "Ten after!"

"You can't go now. I need to see where the notebook was found," Garda Williams said.

Torn and unable to be in two places at once, Rayne looked at Amos. "Do you mind showing him?"

"Not at all." Amos dismounted from the gray horse. "But I won't be carrying the Garda pillion."

An expression of distaste briefly crossed Garda Williams' face. "We can walk."

Chuckling, Rayne said to the Garda, "Please let me know what we can tell the others, before you leave?"

"I'll be in afterward. I have some questions about Tiffany and her secrets for this supposed exposé—somebody has got to know more about her," Garda Williams said. "Nobody leaves that small of a social footprint these days."

"It seems that she and Bran were plenty social," Rayne said.

"Bran's MIA but definitely a person of interest." Garda Williams clutched Amos's hat as a strong wind lifted it. "I've left a message with his mam to call me."

"And what about Freda Bevan?" Ciara asked, her hand on the doorknob.

"Ms. Bevan says she gave Bran a wee bit of cash for information here at the castle," the Garda said. "To keep tabs of what was going on. Her friends were Jake Anderson fans, so they came along to see the star."

"Why does she want to keep tabs on us?" Rayne asked. What a pain in the backside.

Garda Williams only sighed.

The councilwoman was nosy, all right, and wanted Rayne and Ciara to fail. Paying Bran wasn't illegal, but it was . . . rude.

Cormac opened the front door. Ciara released the handle in surprise, then tugged Rayne inside. Rayne limped along with her cousin behind the butler as he said, "They are asking for their hostesses. We are not prepared for such a rowdy group. So here you are." The butler widened the door to the formal dining room and gently shoved them inside.

"Hey!" Rayne grinned at their guests, compartmentalizing what had just happened until she could spend some time sorting through her feelings. That was not today. "Sorry to keep you waiting, but we had some final details regarding the bonfire later."

Since the smoked whole pig with an apple in his mouth had been scrapped when the embers had gone out, Frances had substituted a large venison roast with stag horns as a central focal point on the long table, and candles in deep silver sconces. Chalices for ale or mead. Jeweled goblets that they'd discovered in the attic while cleaning. The Irish wedding cake would be brought out afterward. It was very medieval.

"Splendid," Ciara murmured to Rayne. "I can see Da and Uncle Conor living here or McGrath ancestors from hundreds of years ago."

The guests hadn't started to eat yet as they milled around and snapped photos for their social media later.

They just had to get through Sunday, as the wedding party left early Monday morning. Rayne and Ciara would be able to breathe a smidge easier with the buffer of cash in the castle account. Hopefully Garda Williams could clear the guests once he read through Tiffany's notebook. She feared Tiffany's finger would point to Bran.

Almost done.

Aine, Maeve, and Sorcha all wore crisp black uniforms and circulated with whatever a guest might want, from sparkling water to whiskey.

"This is pure luxury," Jake said to Rayne and Ciara. "I feel like a king." He raised the gold goblet with sapphires, rubies, pearls, and emeralds. "Is this real?"

Before they could answer, Tori interjected, "It's been quite something." She raised her chin, the glistening diamond at her throat shining. "I could easily imagine myself as royalty."

"You are, darling," Joan said with a wink, "hotel royalty."

"This reminds me of a time travel rom com I did once," Amy said, twirling her red hair. Her charcoal chiffon gown floated around like a gossamer cloud. None of the guests had changed clothes. The scene deserved their finery.

"I've never done something medieval like this, but I might be open to it," Jake said, raising his goblet to Ethan. "What do you think?"

Ethan drank and shook his head. "It wouldn't help your career."

"Why not?" Josh asked, coming to his brother's defense. "Jake can play any part and rock it."

With a put-upon sigh, Ethan explained, "The consumers want to see a sexy single leading man saving the world on screen. Car chases, gun fights, and shirtless men. That's what they expect when they see a Jake Anderson film. If you don't give the viewers that, you will lose them. It's not rocket science."

Jake scowled, realizing his assistant was probably right. "Buzz kill."

"Ignore him, Jake," Josh said. "You're the star and can do what you want."

"At your peril," Ethan warned. "It's already going to be tough to explain to the studio how you went away for the weekend sexy and single, as promised, and returned married."

"To an heiress," Joan said, flicking her fingers as if money solved all problems.

Maybe it did in the Montgomery world.

"I've had it with that excuse, Joan," Ethan said. "Jake whisked off the market isn't going to sell movie tickets when that isn't the viewers' expectation. What would your hotel patrons think if you suddenly cheaped out on the sheets?"

Tori hefted her chin. "I'm not going to apologize to you, Ethan. Jake and I are in love, we got married, and that's the end of the discussion."

"There was no discussion!" Ethan said. "There was a 'hey meet at the airport on my family's private plane to see Ireland' group text. Hardly a talk."

"Is that why you're upset, man?" Jake asked. "Because I didn't ask your permission to live my life?" The affable actor sounded legitimately upset.

"Jealous," Amy suggested. "Ethan is jealous of Josh, because of how close you brothers are, and now Tori. They are both more important to you than he is, plain and simple."

Ethan's cheeks turned ruddy. "Shut up, Amy."

The starlet dangled her goblet between two fingers. "Why should I?"

"You have no room to talk when it comes to being jealous," Ethan said.

"Oh?" Tori prompted.

"Amy is pea-green with envy over you, Tori," Ethan said. "You have money, beauty, and now you even have Jake."

Tori studied Amy as if this revelation couldn't matter less. "More old news, isn't it?"

Ethan stepped toward Tori with a finger pointed at her. "I'll give you something new. Tiffany was on a mission to bring you down, paid for by Amy."

"Liar!" Amy said. Her face paled, which made Rayne wonder if Ethan had hit on the truth. Paid her salary or was there a bonus in it depending on what Tiffany discovered?

Perhaps the truth would be found in the Moleskine someone had been careless in their attempt to burn.

Ethan had a lighter, because he smoked. Could Ethan have been the one to argue with Tiffany? To kill her? Perhaps Aine hadn't heard Jake at all.

Except, he wasn't at the manor—he was at the gas station, buying cigarettes. Out of all of them, he had an alibi on CCTV.

"Would you care for something to drink?" Aine asked Rayne and then Ciara.

"I could go for a whiskey," Ciara said. "I'll get it. You did a grand job with the display of food. Brilliant."

"Thanks." Aine smiled and offered Rayne a drink from her tray. "Champagne in the flute, wine in the goblet, ale in the stein."

"Wine, please." She'd wait for something heavier until the evening was over, at the bonfire. They just had to make it to the bonfire.

At quarter past seven, Cormac announced for them all to be seated.

"Dylan, here, then Joan." Cormac held Joan's chair as she sat down. Jake did the same for Tori. The rest managed their own chairs.

Frances left the kitchen with a second platter of pork she'd cooked in the oven and placed it next to the leg of lamb.

"Our chef, Frances," Ciara said.

The guests applauded and her face went crimson.

"It's been my pleasure to cook for you," the crochety chef said. She brandished the butcher knife over the venison. "Who wants pork, and who wants venison?"

"I'd like some of each," Dylan said.

"All right," Frances replied. "Is it safe to say everyone would like to try all three meats?"

"Yes please!" Jake said, followed by a chorus of agreement.

Frances dished out the meats with her customary lack of chit chat. Once done, she gestured to the bowls and platters in the center, and Cormac and Sorcha began offering the side dishes.

Roasted vegetables, mashed potatoes, fresh greens, pureed carrots, and heavenly soda bread rounded out the meal. Perhaps it was in response to the deliciousness of the fare that there was no conversation for a good ten minutes.

The feast was interrupted by Cormac bringing in Garda Williams, who crossed his hands behind his back. "Should I add a plate?" Cormac murmured to Rayne and Ciara.

"Oh, no, no," the Garda said, his expression abashed at the possible faux pas. "I just have a few questions."

"It's all right." Rayne smiled up at him, her tummy pleasantly full. No matter how grouchy Frances might be, she'd remember her culinary greatness.

"What is it?" Ciara set down her fork and knife.

"Why are you here again, mate?" Josh asked. "Can't you see we're having a wedding dinner for Jake and Tori?"

"I apologize for interrupting. It will be just a second." Garda Williams removed his cap. Rayne got the idea that he was putting on a show. "I can ask here, or the Gardai station if that is more convenient?"

"Here is fine," Tori said, waving her cloth napkin in surrender. "I can hardly move, I'm so full."

Amy sipped her wine. "Please tell me you've found out who killed my assistant and tossed them in jail."

Garda Williams' eyes narrowed. "It could be that we are getting closer."

Rayne's stomach clenched.

"Yes?" Amy prodded. She plopped her goblet to the table, visibly annoyed at the officer's way of drawing out the tension.

The Garda patted the pocket of his cargo pants. "Did Rayne tell you our Gardaí were able to decipher some of the words in Tiffany's notebook, from the page Blarney found yesterday?"

Tori glanced at Rayne with frost in her blue gaze. "No. Our hostess neglected to mention that."

"I didn't know if I was allowed to share, and it's not like I knew what the words said," Rayne replied. She was growing tired of being the target for the heiress's sharp comments.

"That's true." Garda Williams shifted, again patting his pocket. Where was the notebook she'd given him in Amos's hat? "It's been a hectic few days. Police inquiries take time, despite what you may see in the movies, and yet this case seems to be flying at hyperspeed."

"Like the movies," Amy drawled. "Maybe I can play the part of myself if it were to make it to prime time."

That remark made Rayne wonder if Amy had been behind the exposé as Ethan had suggested, blaming Tiffany after Tiffany was dead.

"What did it say?" Jake sounded nervous.

Odd.

"Yeah?" Josh seconded. "What did the budding novelist have to say? It has to be taken with a grain of salt, considering."

"Did you know Tiffany Quick was an orphan?" the Garda asked, not answering the question.

"I told you so," Amy replied. "She'd mentioned not having anybody to rely on for help. Tiffany only had herself to count on."

"Eh, the poor lass has no family. Parents died when she was a babe, and she was in the foster system, escaping with movies. She only wanted to be a star." Garda Williams kept his gaze on the redheaded starlet.

"Poor dear," Joan said, with genuine remorse.

Amy rolled her hand as if to tell the Garda to get on with it. "And?"

"We found her phone by the lake," the Garda said, switching gears.

"You did?" Rayne replied. She hadn't known that—it must have been near where Blarney had buried the Moleskine.

"Aye. Garda Montrose has taken it to the station. Won't be long until we unlock it and discover who she was talking with on Friday evening."

Rayne watched the guests around the table. All seemed alert.

They'd be concerned for sure. There was no clear motive for her death—other than Bran or Gillian trying to stop the wedding business. She feared what the Gardaí would find. How could they recover with a guest murdered?

"Do any of you know the password for her phone?" the Garda asked.

"No," Amy said. "Ethan?"

"No," Jake's assistant said. "I had no reason to ever have her phone." Rayne heard the ring of truth.

"What did the notebook page say?" Jake asked again. "I hope it was informative."

"Oh, yes. It was very interesting," Garda Williams said.

"Lame!" Josh replied, scowling at the Garda. Rayne realized that Garda Williams's method was actually quite effective as tension grew around the table.

"Garda Montrose has already taken the phone back to the station?" Ciara asked.

"She has . . .I have Gardai checking the cottages right now," Garda Williams continued.

Joan and Dylan exchanged a glance and a nod.

Ethan, however, protested. His mouth thinned, and he dropped his fork down by his plate. "That's private!"

Jake peered at his assistant as if wondering at the vehement tone.

"Shouldn't you have asked permission first?" Rayne asked. Privacy for a guest seemed paramount of importance.

"They already gave it, the night Tiffany was killed," Garda Williams said.

"For that night only," Ethan replied. "It wasn't meant to be a swinging door for the officers to come in and out."

"My assistant has a point," Jake said. "Is it a problem, though, Ethan?"

Ethan averted his gaze from Jake's questioning one.

"What do we care?" Josh said. "Got nothing to hide. I give you permission to go into my tower room. Knock yourself out."

Rented spaces meant a lack of privacy, which was implied. Rayne wondered if this was another item to add to the list for the next guests.

"Does anybody have a light?" the Garda asked.

"Sure." Ethan pulled his lighter from his pocket.

Garda Williams nodded. "If you could place that on the table?"

Ethan broke out into a sweat but did as the Garda requested. "Why?"

Garda Williams donned plastic gloves and took the damaged Moleskine notebook from his side pocket. It had been stashed in a plastic bag large enough to turn the pages.

"Sir, can you explain how this was burned?"

Ethan paled. "I have no idea what you're talking about. I didn't do that."

"You say that you don't recognize this notebook?" The Garda's tone held disbelief.

Amy squinted at the charred object. Though in plastic, it was clearly a black Moleskine. "That belongs to Tiffany!"

The Garda stepped around the table next to Ethan. "Ethan Cruz. Did you kill Tiffany Quick?"

Chapter
Twenty-Two

"I did not kill Tiffany!" Ethan shouted. "And I didn't burn her notebook. Why would I do such a thing? I wasn't under her microscope for secrets."

Garda Williams continued as if he didn't believe Ethan, and Rayne wondered if the Garda was correct. His actions pointed to his guilt. "I would like to get your fingerprints. I'll have an associate bring in the kit so it will be nice and simple."

Rayne stared at Ethan. The guy looked sick. The petrol station was five minutes or less by car so he could have been there and back with time to kill Tiffany and provide himself an alibi by buying cigarettes.

Her mom's voice whispered in her mind about the all-important *why*.

"Dude, you got some explaining to do," Josh chuckled at Ethan's discomfort.

Gloves on, the Garda withdrew the charred Moleskine notebook from the evidence bag and tilted the pages from side to side. Rayne could see writing on it, as it hadn't been completely consumed by flame. This was a different page than the one she'd seen, and closer to the end of the book.

"I can make out something about J . . . Anderson." Garda Williams allowed his brow to pucker. "CHI . . . not HH . . . she uses several exclamation points."

"Don't know what it means," Ethan said, his jaw set.

"Let me see!" Tori said.

"In a moment," the Garda countered. He continued to peruse the page as if it was the morning paper and not a possible clue.

Cormac entered with Gillian, red-faced and angry. A normal expression to Rayne anyway. The shocker was Garda Lee behind Gillian wearing gloves and carrying a hunting rifle.

"What is *that*?" Jake demanded.

Rayne's stomach rolled and she pressed her hand to it. Was that the weapon responsible for the shot at the church earlier? She homed her gaze on Gillian, who oozed guilt, fury, and maybe a hint of embarrassment. The woman wouldn't look at Rayne but stared at the floor.

"A hunting rifle," Garda Lee said. "A match for the bullet in the church stone. Found it in the barn tucked under some straw."

The barn. Rayne had seen Gillian walking away from the church and thought it had reeked of sneaky vibes.

"Gillian?" Ciara said. Her tone was filled with betrayal. "What do you know about this?"

Gillian didn't answer, so Rayne addressed Cormac. "What's going on?" She knew the woman didn't like her, but had assumed it was due to Gillian's feelings for Amos. Not because she wanted Rayne dead. "Were you shooting at me?"

Jake's body relaxed. "I wasn't the target, then." He regarded Rayne with confusion. "Maybe you should take a how-to-win friends course . . ."

Cormac spread his hands to the sides. "I'm so sorry, milady. I never thought to be suspicious of our own staff."

"Did Gillian ask for the gun?" Rayne asked their miserable butler.

"No. I'd dropped the keys, and she returned them . . . or so I thought. I'm one key shy on the ring," Cormac said, bringing it out to show them.

"Do you have the key, Gillian? Why?" Rayne stood. "Why were you trying to shoot me?"

"Not you," Gillian spat. "I didn't kill anyone."

She put her hand in her pocket, and Rayne froze in fear. Blarney nosed open the door and slid into the dining room, growling at Gillian.

"Hush, pup," Gillian said. "It's just the key." But when she pulled the key free to give to Cormac, a Swarovski crystal fell to the floor.

"You took it?" Rayne shook her head in disbelief.

"She stole a crystal from my dress?" Tori said. "You are seriously delusional, lady."

Rayne exchanged a look with Amy. "I thought Tiffany did it."

Amy scowled at Gillian. "Did you slash my dress?"

"That I did." Gillian still wasn't making eye contact. Garda Williams was listening closely to the exchange. Had he hoped to get answers with his attack on Ethan even though he'd been previously satisfied with the alibi?

There was one answer Rayne wanted, and she knew she'd be adding her mother's advice to her internal list for decision making. "Why?"

"I have exquisite aim," Gillian said, at last meeting Rayne's eyes. "If I'd wanted to shoot you, you'd be shot. I wanted to stop the wedding, but with this group nothing affected them."

Ciara stood in a rush and put her hand to her heart. "Is that why you killed Tiffany, but it didn't work?"

"I did not touch a hair on Tiffany Quick's head," Gillian said. "When I heard about Landon Short escaping jail, I thought I could make Rayne nervous. Shut off the smoker. Share ghost stories with the guests. Make her stop the wedding to save her clients from her mad ex, but she didn't care about them, only herself."

"That makes no sense." Ciara sat down. "You're fired, effective immediately."

"Since she'll be at the Garda station," Garda Lee said, "that works out fine, doesn't it, Gillian?"

She had the grace to look ashamed before being hauled out by the arm by Garda Lee, along with the gun.

"I apologize profusely," the butler said, speaking to the officers as well as the company in the dining room.

"If someone wants to be sneaky, they will," Garda Williams assured him.

The three left the dining room.

"I can't believe it," Dylan said. "What was she talking about, Rayne, with your ex? He was in jail?"

"It's a long story," Rayne said.

She could see they wouldn't be dissuaded so for those that were not familiar she gave them a quick recap, "And now he is on the lam."

"There is more drama this weekend than a movie set," Amy declared.

"And," Garda Williams cleared his throat, "I don't think we're done yet." He tapped the Moleskine with his gloved finger.

"Can I see it?" Tori repeated. "Or maybe Amy would be familiar with her assistant's penmanship."

"One at a time," the Garda said. "Amy first."

Amy stood and walked toward the Garda. Her nose scrunched as she peered at the open page. "Between the damp and the scorch marks, and her messy handwriting, it's impossible to make out."

The starlet returned to her seat.

Stunned by Gillian's actions, Rayne got up next to take a turn. She knew she had to help in some way or else risk losing any respect from her guests.

CHI, that was often short for Chicago. J Anderson could be Josh or Jake . . . but if Tiffany was uncovering secrets that required many exclamation points, well, that probably meant the secret must be about Jake, the famous brother.

Made her feel just a tiny bit sorry for Josh, to always be second best.

"Does Chicago mean anything to you guys?" Rayne asked.

Jake shook his head, his smile smooth.

Josh fidgeted and drained his tumbler.

The younger Anderson brother was lying.

Rayne said, "What could HH mean?"

"Hilton Head," Tori said.

Ethan sputtered. "Can I get anybody more to eat?" The assistant stood and carved another slice from the side of the roast pork.

"I'll take some," Dylan said. "Thanks."

Ethan passed a portion to Dylan.

Rayne sounded out what looked like a third H, or an N. No . . . t. "*Not* H H." She swallowed hard as she put the pieces together. "Oh!" She hovered the tip of her finger below the sentences. "J Anderson from CHI, Chicago, not H H, Hilton Head, if Tori's guess is correct."

The Garda nodded and studied the guests as voices erupted around the table at the possible new fact.

"Is that true, Jakey?" Amy asked.

"It better not be," Tori said.

Ethan ran around the table to grab the Moleskine. "Give me that."

Garda Williams glared at Ethan, and the assistant stopped cold when faced with the law. "Sit. Down."

Ethan did, sweat glistening on his forehead.

"What's going on, Ethan?" the Garda asked. "Spill, or I will charge you with murder."

"Ethan, dude," Josh warned softly.

"I didn't kill Tiffany! All right? Yes, it's true that the brothers are from Chicago. I tried to keep it quiet." Ethan bowed his head toward the table. "But Amy said Tiffany wanted to do an exposé. I reacted quickly, burning the Moleskine and tossing the phone in the lake. Not far enough, since it was found."

Tori touched the diamond at her throat, staring at Jake. "I don't understand. Why the big secret about coming from Chicago?"

Jake shrugged.

"Is that the only secret Tiffany had on you, Jake?" Tori drummed her fingers to the table, her wedding ring brilliant in the candlelight. Rayne couldn't help but watch the heiress to see if she was truly surprised.

"It's nothing." Jake shrugged and downed the whiskey. "Top me off, Josh."

"You got it," Josh said.

"Industry standards," Ethan said. "The studio decides the background for an actor that might be more, appealing, than the actual birthplace. No big deal."

"How did Tiffany find out that you two are from Chicago and not Hilton Head?" Amy demanded, glee in her eyes.

"Who cares?" Joan said. "We knew Jake didn't come from money."

"It's not worth killing over," Tori agreed. "It makes sense, but what I don't like is the dishonesty. You should have told me before the wedding."

Jake's brow arched. "You really want to play that game, Mama?"

Tori bit her lower lip and didn't pursue it further.

"I don't buy that," Garda Williams said to Ethan.

Ethan squirmed. "I had to protect Jake. The studio had devised a story, and Josh, the blabbermouth, was flirting with Tiffany and let it slip."

Josh had been drinking heavily this whole trip. "When was this?" Rayne asked.

"Drinks with Bran that first night at the pub." Ethan glowered. "Thursday."

Jake leaned forward, "Is that what happened, Josh? Dude, you are supposed to have my back."

"I was wasted, bro." Josh yanked at the spikes on his fauxhawk.

"It's a problem, drinking too much," Tori said. "We know a nice rehab in Colorado. In the mountains, for some time away."

"Not now," Jake countered, cutting his wife off.

Her brow arched in surprise at his tone. "Excuse me?"

"You heard him," Josh said. "Butt out. It's family business."

"I won't let you talk to my daughter like that." Dylan stood and towered over the Anderson brothers.

"The alibis don't mean anything if everyone's lying about where they were," Rayne said. "Tiffany and Bran, Josh and Ethan . . . but you were at the gas station."

"I didn't harm Tiffany," Ethan repeated. "I left Josh and Bran at the pub Friday night and was waiting for Tiffany at the bungalow."

The Garda tapped the next page in the charred notebook, as if barely listening, but Rayne could tell that this conversation was very helpful. Who to prod next?

Would Josh spill the beans about Bran? Had he seen Bran arguing with Tiffany, perhaps? Maybe she'd broken off their date and he got angry. Lost his temper, shouted, and strangled her. Only Bran sounded nothing like Jake, from the tonal quality to the accent, especially after he was drunk.

Rayne studied Josh. Who else might sound like Jake, but his sibling? It was Josh Aine must have heard! "What were you arguing about with Tiffany that night, Josh?"

Garda Williams alerted at her question. This was someone he must not have considered.

Josh flipped his hand in dismissal. "No argument."

"Our maid heard you arguing—she thought it was Jake. Even though you don't resemble one another, the audio is the same. Right, Aine?" Rayne hated to be cruel, but her family business and reputation was on the line.

Aine, who had been waiting by the back tables to clear before serving the Irish wedding cake, nodded. "They do sound exactly alike. I was noticing that tonight at dinner."

"It was nothing." Josh glared at Aine. Maeve stood between the young man and her daughter, seeming to grow in size.

Josh looked away. Josh and Tiffany had been flirty, with chemistry even. *Why, why, why.* Would he have been jealous of Bran taking his conquest for the wedding weekend?

"Rayne, can you make this out?" Garda Williams showed her the next to last page.

J A maned. No, mare. Maed. Marred. Her stomach clenched, and she squinted to be sure.

Josh Anderson *married.*

That wouldn't be a big scoop.

But, if Jake Anderson was already married?

Holy sugar snaps. Rayne's knees buckled, and she leaned against the table to balance herself. "I think I can . . ." She glanced at the Garda and then her wedding finger.

"Well?" the Garda asked. He didn't understand the reference.

"What did you find, Rayne?" Tori asked. Her voice quivered, and Rayne worried for her client. It would be a new item for the checklist: Make sure that wedding guests aren't already married.

Would that be anything that Father Patrick would get in trouble for?

Poor Tori—considering the money at stake, she was surprised that it hadn't come up in a background check by the Montgomerys.

"What?" Garda Williams asked again.

Rayne tapped the word and said, "What if Tiffany discovered that *Jake* Anderson is already married?"

The Garda rocked back. Ciara sucked in a breath.

"Now, that's a secret worth killing someone over," Amy replied, eyes wide with shock.

Chapter
Twenty-Three

Rayne's heart broke for Tori as she placed her hand over her stomach, the crystals of the gown catching the candlelight from the center of the dining table.

"Jake, is this true?" Tori's big blue eyes shimmered with tears, her voice low and wounded, somehow. "How could you do that to me?"

"Don't give me that shit!" Jake crashed his goblet onto the table so hard the dishes shook. "I've been trying to avoid this marriage all damn day."

That was true—and now Rayne knew the real reason why.

"You could have told me, us," Tori said, gesturing to her speechless parents, "the truth."

"And what? Have it splashed all over the news that I already have a wife?" Jake leaned back in his chair, then looked at Tori. "I've been trying to get a divorce for years from my first wife, but she refuses to grant me one."

Ethan slumped over his plate, his nose slipping in the carrot puree. Josh patted him on the back.

"I take it you didn't know?" Amy quipped to Ethan. "Not quite in the inner circle?" The starlet drained her champagne—seemingly put out that she wasn't one of the cool kids either. "So, that's why you killed Tiffany?"

"I did not kill anybody!" Jake said. His hair was wild, his eyes too.

Josh would have known about the marriage and the cover up. He would protect his brother at all costs, Rayne knew that.

"You're a liar, Jakey. Who killed my assistant, if it wasn't you?" Amy exhaled, her voice shaking. "Where is this Bran guy Tiff was hooking up with?"

Rayne wondered about Bran, too, but something was connecting in her mind about that night. Josh and Tiffany. Sharing passion. Maybe she'd flirted her way into Josh lowering his guard, and he got mad. Erupted in a temper. "Josh, we know you argued with Tiffany that night. Were you mad because she was just using you to get closer to Jake, the megastar?"

Josh pursed his lips at Rayne. "Another bitch that just won't let things go."

Garda Williams placed the notebook on the table, his hand at the baton on his waist.

With a heavy sigh, Josh said to Jake, "I didn't tell Tiffany about your marriage, bro, I swear."

"How did she find out?" Jake asked. His jaw was clenched tight as he stared at his brother. Just the two of them.

"I let it slip about growing up in Chicago that first night. Thursday, at the pub. She was flirting with that Bran dude. Maybe I had way too much to drink, anyway, she must have researched us in Chicago, and not Hilton Head, and found the marriage records," Josh said with a helpless shrug. "I'm sorry."

"What did you do?" Jake pulled at his hair, far from perfection now.

"I tried to help you, I swear," Josh said. Josh bowed his head, his fauxhawk giving him a roostery look. "I begged her to not say anything, offered to pay her. She was wicked, man, saying that I'd made her fortune and that she'd play Amy in the movie when the exposé sold. This was her ticket to fame. I did it for you, bro."

Eerily similar to what Amy had said earlier in the evening.

"You freaking killed Tiffany, Josh?" Amy pushed back from the table, shouting the words Rayne was merely thinking.

Tori bent her head to the side as if she was going to be sick, and Joan crooned and rubbed her daughter's back, soothing and protective.

"Killing Tiffany," Jake said, dazed. "Dude."

Josh broke down in gut-wrenching sobs. "She laughed at me. Laughed, said I would never be as good as you. I lost it, bro."

"That's no excuse to kill someone," Tori said. Her lips were pale, her skin the color of the Irish lace in her hair.

"I, I," Josh stuttered, "Tiffany was out to get you, Jake, and I couldn't let her do it."

Blarney had snuck beneath the table to lie across Rayne's feet—offering comfort with his presence.

Tori scooted forcefully back from the table as the truth seemed to settle in her mind. Married to the hottest man in America—who was already married. "Hold the presses for a damn minute!"

Everyone looked at the gorgeous bride as she pounded her fist to the table, her tears drying.

"Yes, dear?" Joan said quietly.

"This means that Jake Anderson is a bigamist!"

"I'll call our lawyers," Dylan said. "Don't worry, pumpkin." He jabbed Jake in the chest. "You made a big mistake."

"Everyone stay in their seats." Garda Williams stepped near Josh. "Josh Anderson, are you confessing to the murder of Tiffany Quick?"

"Don't say anything, Josh," Jake said. "I'll get a lawyer. It was self-defense or an act of passion—something. We'll figure it out."

Ethan shook his head. "Unbelievable. Jake, you can't do that."

"You need to help me fix this, Ethan," Jake demanded. "Make today disappear."

"Did you not love me at all?" Tori asked in disbelief.

"Sure, I did!" Jake said, his back to her as he stared from Josh to Ethan. "It was complicated."

Rayne briefly closed her eyes.

"You know what's not complicated?" Tori asked, her body seething.

"What, babes?" Jake asked.

"This baby's daddy is my yoga instructor," Tori said, her eyes shining with malice that took Rayne by surprise. "*Babes.* Daddy, can you talk to the priest and get an annulment?"

"Yes, I will," Dylan promised. "First thing in the morning."

"You sl—" Josh said to Tori.

Dylan slugged Josh in the chin, and the younger man rocked backwards on his heels. Garda Williams caught him and yanked his hands behind his back.

After reading him the caution, Garda Williams put handcuffs on Josh. "We can talk about this at the station," the Garda said in a low voice to Josh. "The more you struggle, the worse it will be."

"I want to press charges against that old man," Josh said, yanking at the restraints despite the Garda's words of warning.

"Josh, just chill out. I'll be there as soon as I can get a cab or an Uber." Jake splayed his hands on the table. "Unbelievable."

"You can get one from Kilkenny," Rayne said.

"I want to leave," Joan said to Garda Williams. "Take my daughter out of this place. Oh, sweetie. What a nightmare for you." She kept her arm around Tori.

The Garda nodded. "I have your contact information."

"We'll be at the Marriott penthouse in Dublin," Dylan said.

"All right. I'll be in touch." The Garda looked at the others: Amy, Ethan, and Jake. "For the next day or two, remain here on the castle grounds in case we have questions, if it's okay with Rayne and Ciara."

After a nod from her cousin, Rayne said, "Of course."

This was not how she'd wanted the weekend to go.

And, she hated to be rude, but she wanted to get paid before they all disappeared on her.

"We have to pack," Joan said. "Tori, darling, maybe Amy can help you? We'll be back shortly."

And like that, Dylan and Joan Montgomery left the medieval feast, heads high.

Tori sneered at Jake and then Amy. "I don't want anything to do with Amy. I can't believe you invited that viper to my wedding. Rayne, will you help me please? I don't want either of these two snakes around."

"Certainly."

Aine elbowed Sorcha, who had been watching with her mouth agape. "Shall we get this cleaned up?"

Rayne shrugged. "That's fine with me."

"I'll help," Ciara said, rolling up her pearled sleeves.

Garda Williams ushered a protesting Josh from the dining room.

"What am I supposed to do?" Amy asked petulantly. "I didn't do anything wrong, Tori, so there is no reason to be mean to me."

"You flirted with Jake constantly," Tori said. "I'm pretty sure you did more than that, but I don't want to know. Stay out of my way until I'm packed."

Amy bowed her head.

Rayne recalled how Tori had told her at the start that Amy was someone to be kept close—an enemy, not a friend.

"It didn't mean anything," Jake piped up. His voice was cruel. "A quickie here and there, right, Ames?"

Guess the Montgomery–Anderson relationship was truly not something that could be revived.

Ethan tugged his goatee. "You should probably just shut it, Jake. You're in enough trouble. Let's head back to the cottage and try to fix this—or else my career as your assistant is also up in flames. Married?"

"I'm coming too," Amy said, following the men.

The starlet didn't meet Rayne's gaze as she slipped out of the dining room after them.

"Wow," Aine said, forgetting herself.

"I think you had a close call, Tori," Rayne said.

"Can you imagine the scandal of me, a Montogomery Hotel Billionaire, marrying a bigamist?" Tori shook her head.

"I think Jake's ratings would definitely plummet if word got out," Rayne said.

"Agreed!" Ciara clapped and raised her hand. "Should someone anonymously alert the media?"

"Everyone signed a confidentiality agreement," Tori said. "Daddy would have sued Tiffany so fast that her documentary or movie would have been squashed in the making."

It would be empowering to have so much money at one's disposal.

Rayne glanced at her watch when the alarm on her phone went off. "Nine PM. Time for the bonfire and the Celtic music. We should let Amos know to cancel the band," she said. "About Gillian, too, if he isn't already aware."

"I'll update him with the latest," Sorcha offered. "I think Gillian really liked Amos, which is why she wanted the wedding venue to fail."

Aine scrunched her nose. "As if. Can't believe she stole Da's key to swipe a rifle to shoot at the church. And the missing crystal, and the slashed dress. The smoker!"

"Gotta say, Rayne, I'm glad I'm not the only one who brought crazy to the party," Tori quipped.

Rayne gave a sad chuckle. "I am so sorry about everything."

Tori shrugged. "Let's go get my things. I'm sure Mom will be here soon. She knows how to pack in a hurry. Life skills to emulate."

"Why is that?" Ciara asked.

"Oh, Mom and Dad traveled a lot until they had me. She wasn't born to money but met Dad while she was a flight attendant."

"No!" Ciara said. "I assumed she was born with a silver spoon."

"Yep, that's where it all began. She was in first class though," Tori said.

"I like your parents," Ciara said.

"Me too," Tori said. "They have the kind of marriage that I want to have . . . and now, I'll get a second chance to do it."

"With the yoga instructor?" Aine asked.

"No." Tori put her hand to her stomach. "I think this baby is going to be fine without any additional drama. I'll take this as a sign to wait for true love."

On that cheerful note, Rayne, Tori, and Blarney left the dining room and walked down the hall to the entrance to the tower.

They went up the stairs, Blarney at their heels.

"He's a wonderful dog," Tori said. "Irish Setter?"

"Yes. Do you have pets?"

"No," Tori said, "I never replaced my little Sheba when she died. She was a toy Pomeranian. Same breeder as Paris Hilton bought hers from, back in the day. We grew up together, being in the hotel business."

"Both beautiful," Rayne said. "Did you model too?"

"I'm too short for that," Tori said. "I loved dancing, but I wasn't good enough to be professional. I excel at business so I'm on the board for the hotels. Did you go to college?"

"Yes. I always knew that I wanted to design dresses," Rayne shared. As they conversed about life, Rayne acknowledged that this was the Tori she could imagine being friends with. Sincere and warm with no hidden agenda.

Sometimes not getting married was the right choice.

They entered the suite from the third floor.

Rayne helped Tori out of the gown when they were inside. The silk stitches had held for the zipper, the heart-shaped crystal remained, and the bride had looked stunning.

"I can't believe all of the work you had to do to make this seem so effortless," Tori said as she stepped free from the gown.

"It's what I do," Rayne said.

"Well, it's appreciated."

"Would you like me to put the dress in the garment bag?"

"No." Tori brushed her hair from her cheek. "I don't want it anymore."

Rayne's stomach clenched. "You don't?" Well, how could she blame the heiress considering the awful memories it would carry?

"Maybe you can sell it?" Tori suggested.

"But it was custom made for you," Rayne said. All the work for nothing and the bride didn't even want to keep it. "It's fine."

"I will definitely order my next wedding dress from you." Tori slipped on designer jeans, Coach sneakers, and an ivory cashmere sweater.

Rayne packed Tori's things, wondering what she could do with the dress. Would the heiress want the money back? It would be a disaster. If she had to sell her Hermes handbag, they'd be down to zero backup for the castle.

She closed the suitcase, a gold Chanel with a matching vanity case that Tori was zipping up.

The heiress grabbed her Dolce and Gabbana handbag, opened it, and withdrew a checkbook. She wrote it out and handed it to Rayne.

It was $50,000 instead of $32,500.

"For the trouble," Tori said. "It was a lot to ask."

It had been so much work. Rayne smiled. "I'll share it with the staff."

"You're a kind person, Rayne," Tori said. "And I know that we talked about using the photos for your website . . ."

"It will be a big plug for the wedding venue."

"Well . . ." Tori shouldered her purse.

"Yes?"

"I'm sure you understand why we can't mention anything. Not a peep about the weekend."

"But!" They'd agreed. That, however, was before the entire event had blown up into disaster.

"It would be a fiasco, especially since I'm sure Daddy will talk to the priest and make sure that this wedding doesn't count. I won't be guilty of bigamy when I do get married for real."

"But what about the paparazzi?"

"That was my mom's doing," Tori said with a wink. "To make sure we had something to hold over Jake if needed."

"That's . . ." Rayne bit her lip.

Tori burst out laughing.

"It's life as a billionaire," Tori said. "I'll let people know about you and this magical place on the down-low, but, no wedding happened, okay?" She removed the special Irish lace from her hair and placed it in her handbag.

"What about Amy?"

"She signed that agreement like everyone else, but just to be sure, I swiped her phone clear of all photos earlier while having drinks in the blue parlor."

"Oh!"

Tori's chin raised. "I saw ones of her and Jake in bed, so don't feel bad for little Amy Flores. Cats always land on their feet."

Rayne's mind spun with all of the additional drama.

Tori grabbed Rayne in a hug. "Thank you for all that you've done, and I will absolutely use you for my next bridal gown, though probably not the venue. I'm thinking one of our hotels in Italy or Greece might be nice."

"Both places are beautiful, and I understand."

Rayne and Tori left the tower, followed by Blarney. Joan and Dylan's voices were heard in the foyer, echoing down the hall. Ciara's voice too. Dylan boomed a goodbye and compliments, while Joan was quieter but no less effusive in her praise.

Joan kissed Rayne's cheek. "You girls ever come to LA, stay with us. We'll put you up at one of the hotels downtown with a rooftop pool." Ciara and Joan hugged.

Dylan pressed cash into Rayne's hand.

"Oh, no," Rayne said. "It's been taken care of."

Tori laughed and nudged her shoulder. "Just say thank you."

With that, the Montgomerys were gone.

Rayne counted the cash. Five grand! She would split it with everyone for all of the extra work that they'd done.

"And, Tori paid in full, also with a little extra," Rayne said.

"Finally good news!" Ciara said.

They walked to the front porch and sat down on the top step.

Rayne tried to give Ciara the cash.

"You dole it out, tomorrow, with everyone getting equal shares," Ciara said.

"All right." Rayne blew out a breath. Blarney collapsed by her side.

"Family is a complicated thing, eh?" Ciara said into the night.

"It is." Rayne flung her arm around her cousin's shoulders. "Josh was trying to fix his mistake, which could have ruined Jake's career if Tiffany had shared it with the press."

"Ultimately Jake's also at fault for getting engaged while already married," Ciara stated. "Eejit."

"I agree with you." Star qualities without integrity were a bust for Rayne and she wouldn't pay a dime to see the next Jake Anderson movie.

"What happens now?" Ciara asked.

Rayne tucked the cash into her pocket. "We are safe through the winter. The November weddings should get us through March. When do sheep start doing the baby thing?"

"Lambing happens in the spring." Ciara slowly expelled a breath. "Is being in the black enough to satisfy Da's will? Or do we have to get the support of the villagers? That will be an equally hard task. Father Patrick has an idea about how to get the villagers on our side."

They hadn't found a new solicitor. And as her mother had pointed out, the terms had been shady, and who would contest it?

"Success is making sure we take care of the village and the inhabitants of this manor," Rayne said. "We are out of the red, and for today, that's good enough."

Ciara elbowed her. "You just don't want to part with that fancy pink handbag."

"I really don't," Rayne said with a laugh. "Let's keep Hermes for a rainy day."

"That's not saying much," Ciara said. "It always rains."

Acknowledgments

A story requires many people to make it into a book—I'd like to thank the very patient Dublin Coroner's office with the many emails back and forth. Any mistakes made are my own. Thanks to my editor Tara Gavin, and the team at Crooked Lane. I love everything from the editorial process to the brilliant covers. And none of this would be possible without Evan Marshall, best agent ever. I am grateful every day that this is what I get to do.